It's in the Cards

Lisa Hogan

Published by Lisa Hogan, 2018.

To the best
Librarian in
the land.

Lisa Hogan

This is a work of fiction. Similarities to real people, places, or events are entirely coincidental.

IT'S IN THE CARDS

First edition. October 16, 2018.

To my supportive husband Dan

and all my children

Chapter One

"Futz!" I curse. A sledgehammer is having its way with my brain, or at least, it surely feels like it. My ears ring so loudly, I can't hear my own thoughts. Slowly, I open my eyes; things are a bit blurry.

Okay, they're a lot blurry.

My name is Dr. Zelda Harcrow. It is extremely important to note that certain spells, including those to bind certain elements, must be performed during the proper lunar phases of the moons. *And how!*

I shake free of the ringing in my ears and the blurriness of my vision and survey the damage to my laboratory. Putrid cadmium, green smoke, small fires, and bits of broken glass litter every surface.

Well, it could be worse.

"We should get the broken bottles cleaned up immediately, before their contents mix. I don't want another explosion."

"What about the fires?" my assistant asks, but my attention has already moved on.

"It didn't break in the explosion." Warmth spreads through my hand from the amber reagent bottle that I've snagged from the debris. I hold it up to the light to examine it and pull a magnifying glass from my lab coat pocket to get a closer look. There don't appear to be any etchings or striations. "I think we just hit on something."

"Doctor, could we, just once, discover something without blowing up the lab first?" Brittle fragments of silicate crunch beneath my assistance's shoes as she heads over to the utility closet to gather the cleaning supplies and a fire extinguisher.

I am a doctor of, well, pretty much everything, as well as a bit of an overachiever. My mother thinks I need a husband. My father,

Titus Harcrow, president of Harcrow Alchemy Inc., thinks I am the very link between the imaginable and the unbelievable. Of course, he is my father, so he might be a bit biased.

I currently have three projects I'm assigned to. The one that just went a little kablooey is to create a formula for glass that can withstand high thermal heat energy and shock. The glass is needed for a manned capsule that will be sent off-world to explore Gaia's smaller moon, Biota. So, I not only have an impeccable fashion sense but also get to be part of shaping the future of our planet, Gaia, and putting the country of Tesla on the map.

"Huh. All the apothecary bottles and jars either shattered or melted." I pace back and forth, tapping my finger against my temple. "If I can just find the last element to add to the formula, I think I'll finally achieve the glass strength I require."

Clover cocks her head. "What about the solar protection?"

Clover Bode has been my assistant for almost three rotations now. She has been the longest-lasting assistant I have ever had. The other goofs who have called themselves my assistants in the past all quit after only a few minor explosions. Clover though has stuck it out. She's such a good egg. Father promised that a job would be waiting for her after university if she finished out her three-rotation internship with me. If Titus Harcrow promises someone a job, then she has surely got the goods. In working with Clover over these past few rotations, I must say, I certainly think so.

"I will form just the right tint on the glass to diminish the damaging light rays yet achieve full visibility. And Professor Ferrum's designing the blast shield, so no need to worry that the glass might break during liftoff."

Professor Ferrum, the occupant of one of the labs down the hall, is actually an immigrant to Tesla from the country of Baekeland. Gaia is made up of several large land masses, most of which are their own countries. Besides Tesla and Baekeland, there is Elione, Presper, and Hyde. The final, smallest land mass acts as a trade port for the rest of the countries.

"Clover, get a wiggle on, and let's mop up this disaster."

"Are you all right, my dear?" asks a funny figure of a man from the doorway of my lab. He's short in stature and has white hair and a matching goatee.

"She's fine, as always, Father," pipes up my brother, Ephron, from behind him

Ephron also works for Harcrow Alchemy Inc. as a chairman of the board. He secures contracts from different councils and independent companies for an array of projects. He is my big brother and my boss, and he never lets me forget that I'm the reason he keeps a bottle of whiskey in his office.

"Zelda!" Ephron snaps. "The Tesla Space Exploratory Council is due here at any moment for a meeting you are supposed to attend, with your latest report. Just look at you! You're a mess!"

I bite my lower lip and brush my hair behind one ear. "About that report . . . can I give it orally?"

"You were to have a written report. They expect a written report!"

"Well . . ." I crinkle my nose against the smell of rotten eggs and burned hair still hanging heavily in the air. "It kind of went up in smoke."

"Attagirl, Zelda! See, Ephron my boy, everything is just berries!" Titus's eyes widen merrily. "Was it a good explosion? I love a good explosion. I'm sorry I missed it. You should tell me the next time you're having one."

"Father, her report exploding is not a good thing," my brother bites out, a bit exasperated with the old man.

Ah, my father, the great Titus Harcrow. Titus comes from a lengthy line of paratechnologists, alchemists, chemists, and physicists—oh, and inventors too. Titus Harcrow is a quiet man who loves his family—four of us and my mother—to a fault. He is a bit scattered in the brain, but aren't all geniuses?

"In my defense," I speak up, "had I not blown up my laboratory, I would not have stumbled upon a possible answer." I want to stick my tongue out at him and claim "Nana nana na na," but I think better of it.

Ephron combs his short golden hair back with his fingers and answers a call coming through on his wireless communicator. "Yes. I see. Show them into the conference room."

"Whoopee!" Father claps his hands and rubs them together. "They're here! Come on, Ephron. Let's go slay them."

"You're all balled up. 'Slay' means to make them laugh," Ephron corrects him.

"Dear son, don't try to make them laugh. You don't have any sense of humor."

My brother shakes his head. As he leaves, he calls back to me, "*Do not* be late. And do something with your hair."

"What's wrong with my hair?"

The swish of broom bristles and the scraping of glass against the floor don't mask Clover's next comment. "Well, you might want to consider bangs."

I run into the private lavatory attached to my laboratory and office. I take one look in the mirror. "Jeepers creepers!" My normally chin-length golden hair, which I colored pink to complement my outfit this turn, is singed in the front.

I blow a raspberry as I grab a pair of scissors. "Thbpt! Bangs it is, then." The scissors snip-snip, and singed hair floats to the floor.

By now, I'm completely late for the meeting. There's no time for me to change out of my soot-covered lab coat and clothes, rinse the smell of burned silica out my hair, wash my face, or replace my cosmetics. There's only one way to get out of the mess I've made, and it's frowned upon by the Time-Space Council. I'm going to have to bend a little time.

Bending time only affects the conjurer. Basically, the conjurer moves through space at a faster speed than the events occurring around them. Everything around their space keeps moving at a normal speed and time, whereas the conjurer moves quickly within their space.

I generally recommend doing such a spell in private. Firstly, the spell needs absolute concentration. Secondly, to those around the conjurer, it will appear they have vanished. That would give the average Joe the heebie-jeebies.

Closing my eyes, I take a deep breath and focus on the slowing of time and my ability to move through it in a flash. Opening my eyes, I let my stare burn into the gears of the timepiece on the wall of the lavatory.

"Turn, turn the hand of time slowly; time stand still, I order you. No time shall pass 'til I complete my task. Time stand still, I order you." I close my eyes and suck in a deep breath. When I open my eyes, the clock has stopped.

Not everyone can bend time. Only a few can, and it isn't all that safe for the mind of the one bending time within space. The Time-Space Council, whose job is to prevent time travel, has been around for over one hundred rotations. Beyond the obvious ramifications of traveling back through time, traveling throughout time-space can, after a while, destroy the conjurer's mind and drive them mad. Our benefactor, for whom our country was named, found us using this form of travel. By his last visit, it is written that he had become a bit delusional. It is also written that he could talk to birds, especially a particular species found on his planet called a pigeon. I have an aversion to running around talking to birds, so bending a little time-space is as far as I plan to ever go.

Time bending takes a moment to conjure, but the ability to have complete and instant focus is paramount. Any distraction could be disastrous. I once heard a story about some Joe who was late picking up his girl. He thought he could make up the time. Unfortunately, he lived with his mother and lost focus when his mother—who had been a bit corked—started banging on his bedroom door, breaking the dope's concentration. Things went a bit backward from there. He showed up three months later for his date, still expecting his sweetheart to step out with him. Things didn't work out so well: she had already moved on with his best bud, and his mother had rented out his room. Lesson learned.

With time stopped, I trim the front of my hair into bangs that flow down into a point in the middle of my brow. A quick rinse in the sink then removes the remaining pink. Opening one of the lavatory cabinets as I dry my hair, I eye the extra outfits I keep on hand. I choose dark-amethyst trousers, a white blouse, and a long duster that matches the trousers.

Once dressed, I look into the mirror and smile. The color of the outfit brings out the purple flecks in my yellow eyes, which I proceed to line with charcoal cosmetics. I also brush my eyelashes with charcoal to match. After I smooth on some lip rouge, I decide to add a thick white-and-amethyst headband scarf.

I look swell!

All done and put back together, I end the spell and reenter the laboratory. "Ta-da!"

Clover gives me a thumbs-up. "Real spiffy, Doctor!" Raising an eyebrow, she adds, "Pretty fast too."

I give her a wink. "Make sure you finish putting down the neutralizer before you try to sweep up the chemicals and crystal powders. Be careful."

"Ab-so-lute-ly!" She gives me a salute.

I head down the long narrow hall past two other laboratories: one belongs to Professor Ferrum, and the other belongs to Dr. Olga Ravenscroft, a real middle-aged prude. I hit the stairs and gallop down to the ground level and into the hall that leads to one of the large conference rooms.

Pairs of marble columns mark the transition from the large, oval hall and staircase to the front lobby, where the security team checks in all visitors and employees. The ceiling of the large, oval hall towers over the full four stories of the building and features domed glass tubes that light the space of white walls and gleaming metals. Off this hall are offices and conference rooms, each with their own frosted glass and silver-colored double doors.

It's into one of these conference rooms that I enter. I am greeted by Ephron, my father, and five other individuals, whom I figure make up the newly formed Tesla Space Exploratory Council.

"Now that everyone has arrived, please be seated and we will begin." Ephron starts the meeting. Father pulls up to the carved wooden table, rests his chin in his hand, and stares off into space, feigning attention.

"As you well know, Harcrow Alchemy Inc. has been part of Tesla for over one hundred rotations. We have proudly served and worked for the benefit of our country and our planet since the company's founding by my grandfather, the great alchemist Tobias Harcrow. My father, Dr. Titus Harcrow, and I welcome the opportunity to continue serving our fine country of Tesla in the development of the sciences. We are especially honored to be chosen to assist in exploration and possible growth offworld, as well."

Ephron drones on for a bit more. Father's eyes are beginning to close when the meeting turns to me and the advances I have made in the projects placed in my "talent for blowing things up" hands.

Standing up next to Ephron, I rub the back of my neck and take a deep breath. "Council members, I thank you for this time to update you on the current status of my projects. I realize you were looking for a more formal report. However, with the sensitivity and constant advancement of both projects, I felt an oral report would be more appropriate." My father lets out a giggle and Ephron smiles at my quick thinking.

"I have made great strides in the shock-proof thermal glass. In fact, we made a significant breakthrough just today. We are maybe sixteen turns—a fortnight, you might say—away from completion on this particular project." I continue with a more detailed description, without giving away too much.

Next, I move on to the second project assigned to me by the council—the discovery of a lightweight, continuous fuel source that can be used to sustain the chemical reaction of the Tesla Space Capsule's fuel cells. Now, this project I have been having a bit of difficulty with, so I kind of bull my way through.

"I have been experimenting with hydrogen and some hydrocarbons, though I have not yet found either to be efficient or renewable forms of energy at this time." I further explain my findings, where I'm headed in my experiments, and that I feel I am close to a solution. "It's just a matter of time before the answer is clear."

As those last words leave my lips, a sonic boom and vibration rocks the building.

Chapter Two

Ephron takes one look at me, and we both feel it—both know it. The explosion came from my laboratory! Ephron grabs my hand and sweeps me out of the conference room. Alarms sound off, obscuring panicked footsteps looking for a safe retreat. Laboratories are automatically being sealed off to prevent further loss, and the security team is now busy evacuating the building, including our council guests.

"Clover!" I scream. "Clover! Clover!" I have no idea if she was in the lab when it exploded. Ephron and I push and struggle up the stairs against the stream of those evacuating. We finally find our way up to the third floor, but we're halted by the company security team. I can't see Clover, and without notice, tears burst forth from me alongside the guilt.

"Jep," Ephron says, speaking to one of the security personnel. "What's the status? Any sign of Clover?"

"No sign of Clover yet, sir. The explosion was contained to Dr. Harcrow's lab and the hall outside. The automatic emergency containment doors did their job. There's still quite a bit of smoke in the hall, but once the exhaust fans clear it, we should be able to locate her. The other labs are secure, so she could be in one of them."

"Have you contacted the Safety Council?"

"The Fire Brigade is on its way to assist with any investigation and cleanup, sir." The Fire Brigade, like all community services, works under the Safety Council.

"When can we begin an investigation into this untimely explosion?" inquired Ephron.

"This is unbelievable." I use my sleeve to wipe the runny mascara from my cheeks.

Ephron pats my back. "We don't know anything yet, Zelda. Stay calm."

"The ceiling extinguishers put out the fire," Jep reported in a firm, deep voice, "and the containment doors closed almost immediately after the explosion itself. Other than a little blowback into the corridor outside, everything was contained in the lab and private office."

I find my voice again. "How bad?"

"We don't know for certain yet, but it doesn't look too keen, Doctor."

The smoke slowly clears from the hall. The exhaust fans pull the smoke-and-chemical-filled air out of the building and into a stack fitted with air filters and scrubbers, which empties cleaned air out into the atmosphere.

Suddenly, I catch my breath. Slumped against the wall across from my laboratory's entry is a body. I battle past security and my brother and hurry over to the little, crumpled figure.

With Ephron on my tail, I reach the very still Clover. "Clover!" I yell over the drumming of the exhaust fan. "Are you all right? Clover, can you hear me?" Her skin is cold and clammy as I feel for a pulse. It's weak, but by glory, it's there! "Clover, can you hear me?"

By now, my brother is kneeling beside me. "Zelda, let the medics take her down to the infirmary. You can go with her."

Hugging my waist, I watch as the medics gently check her vitals and quickly scan her body for any injuries. I keep a bit of distance until she's safely on the gurney. We travel to the lift at the other end of the corridor, which has been unaffected by the blast.

"Don't you worry," I tell her, not caring if she can't hear me. "We'll have you right as rain on the Weather Council's day off in no time."

We arrive at ground level, where the infirmary and the entrance for the garage and tinker offices are. Once inside the infirmary, I have no choice but to step aside and let the nurses, medical physicians, and medical intuitives do their bit.

I begin to pace. Nothing in my laboratory should have caused anything like this. If anything happens to Clover—

No, I have to be positive. Nothing good has ever come from negativity.

"Healer Vaidya," I call out to the head of the infirmary.

"Zelda, my dear." The soft-spoken physician takes my hands in her gentle ones. "I cannot tell you much right now. We are still doing the scans on her body."

"Has she regained consciousness yet?"

"No, not yet. She received quite a blow to her head; it may take a while yet. But she will, I am sure."

Just as the healer returns to her patient, Ephron appears next to me. "What's the scoop? Any news on our girl?"

I look down; my hands are shaking. "The body scans aren't complete, and she's still unconscious. Ephron, I don't understand what happened; I'm all balled up about this. I can't fathom how this large of an explosion was even possible. And to take out my private office as well? What do our boys and the Fire Brigade have to say about what happened?"

Ephron put a brotherly arm around me. "Attagirl, Zelda. Clover will be just fine. You just keep your chin up."

I clench my jaw. "And what of my lab?"

"We don't have any answers yet. Tomorrow, I'll have the tinkers and security begin working on a new space for you to continue your work. It'll be a few turns, but I'll have you up and concocting, experimenting, and discovering in no time."

"When will we know what caused this?"

"If we're fortunate, I should know by morning. Zelda, this isn't your fault. You couldn't have predicted this."

I shrug away his arm and elbow him in the ribs. "I should have sensed it. I should have predicted it. I know what is in my lab; I saw nothing that would—" My voice cracks. "Nothing, Ephron. Nothing in my laboratory should have caused this much damage."

I cross my arms, and we stand silent for a moment. "I need to know, Ephron. I need to know what caused this. I need to know if I caused this."

It's not like I read tea leaves or something. Or even read weather patterns to forecast the future—which, by the way, is a lost art since the Weather Council chooses if it rains or shines. I can't get behind stolisomancy; putting a shirt on inside out or a dress on backward, in my experience, usually just means you're bent, blind, blotto, or hungover. I don't even read crystals or tarot like my lovely well-meaning mother, Ave.

I don't do anything fancy or of exact certainty. I just feel. And now I'm not sure what I'm feeling.

Ephron is still rubbing his side from my not-so-boney-but-still-sharp elbow when Healer Vaidya approaches us with one of her medical nurses in tow.

"I have completed the THR scan, and two of my medical intuitives have completed their psychic scans as well. I have concluded there's no internal bleeding. However, Clover has several broken ribs, one of which punctured a lung, which we have successfully reinflated. She is also suffering from a concussion to the head. The scans have not revealed any major swelling in her brain."

I brush my hair behind my ear. "Is she awake yet?"

"She is starting to come around. Remember, the blast appeared to have knocked her back against the wall. She hit her head pretty good. It may take time for her to be fully aware. She needs rest, Zelda."

"Can we see her?"

"Yes, but only for a few moments." She leads us over to the examination room.

"Clover girl, can you hear us?" I whisper.

Ephron leans over as Clover flutters her eyes open. "Hey there. How you feeling?"

"I'm sorry." Her words are barely audible. "I think I goofed up, sir."

"You did no such thing!" I interject.

I look at Ephron, though my words are for Clover. "It's unknown what caused the explosion. You are the darb of assistants, and that on the up and up."

"You got that right," Ephron adds. "Clover is the best of interns, and that on the level."

Clover gives a meager smile. She's clearly in quite a bit of pain.

"Attagirl! Feel better and just rest. I'll check on you in the ante meridiem," I tell her. "No worries."

Ephron and I leave Clover to rest in the infirmary. We head through the main lobby and up to his office to talk.

Chapter Three

I stop and check in with the old man on my way to the garage, where I keep my fully restored steam-powered Zenith motorcycle.

"Dear girl, all will be well. I talked to your mother for you and assured her you were fine and in no danger."

"She worries too much about me." I hug him and place my head on his shoulder, just as I did when I was younger. "I'm a bit tired; I'm going to head home."

"Zelda, why don't you stay with us?" Titus insists. "I'll call my driver and have him take you to the house."

I kiss my father on the forehead and shake my head. Leaving his office, I continue on to the garage and my independence.

I have two modes of transportation: my bright-yellow solar-electric roadster and my beloved Zenith cycle. The Zenith uses a cyclone engine that is both solar electric and steam powered. They just don't make them like this anymore. It took an entire painstaking rotation of Gaia around our sun star to fully restore this baby, and she is one fine iron. My girl is pure chrome and steel—black and silver, with clean, flowing lines.

As I come out on ground level, I pass by the infirmary. Knowing that my assistant lies there damaged by what could possibly be my fault, I shake a little.

On my other side are the tinker offices. Tinkers are some of the most ingenious people when it comes to machinery. More than once, I employed the tinkers here for their assistance when I was restoring the Zenith.

"There's my baby," I say, talking to my ride. "I am so looking forward to putting you between my legs and riding you all the way home. It has been a rough turn."

A chuckle comes from behind me. "I'm ready when you are."

I laugh and glance over my shoulder. "Sorry, Tick. Bank's closed."

Tick Croft, Head Tinker, is almost as old as my father. I've known him for most of my life, and I can always count on him to bring a smile to my face. He's a bit short and pudgy, smells of grease and acetone, and is the best tinker in Tesla.

Tick's blue eyes sparkle as he grins. "Rats. Well, I guess I'll have to settle for a smile."

I give Tick that smile as I move toward the Zenith. I reach to get my riding gear out of the saddlebags when a sudden cramp hits my midsection. Something isn't right with my cycle. I can't put my finger on it, though.

"Tick, has anyone been looking over my cycle?"

Tick shakes his head. "Not that I'm aware of. Why? What are you sensing?"

"I'm not sure, but it's off somehow."

"A tinker reveal spell might do the trick," Tick suggests. "With the enclosed bodywork this cycle has, it's the best way to see what may be up with her."

"Okay, I'll give it a go." I close my eyes to center myself. Opening them, I put my full concentration on my cycle. "Reveal, reveal, let no deception conceal." I say the words three times, close my eyes, and re-open them.

My spells are generally pretty accurate. I come from an extensive line of Teslans gifted with the ability of instant manifestation of intention, or what some may call magic.

"There's a glow near the cyclone engine, Zelda." We kneel next to the bike. Tick pulls a wrench from his tool belt.

"Tick, can you take off the engine cover?"

Tick removes the chrome cover that houses the cyclone engine. A cyclone engine basically works by heating and cooling water in a closed system. Electricity is what heats the water to create the steam by which the engine is powered. At first, neither one of us can see anything amiss.

"Repeat the spell," Tick says. "Whatever is going on is being hidden from us."

I repeat the spell three more times: "Reveal, reveal, let no deception conceal."

A small glow twinkles in the water containment coils.

"It seems there's a puncture in one or more of the coils." Tick grabs a magnifier from his tool belt.

"How could that happen?" I ask the experienced tinker.

"It didn't just happen, my dear. Someone sabotaged your cycle. A rapscallion has put that deadly hole there."

"Deadly?" That's a bit overdramatic. I mean, really, I know my lab is in shambles—okay, my lab is destroyed. But holes in my engine, deadly? That's a bit much.

"Halfway home, and the pressure from the heated water and steam would have caused the engine to blow. At high speeds, you would surely have caused a very inconvenient accident—most likely leading to a very inconvenient death."

"Death would be a bit inconvenient." I have too many projects going on to die. Plus, I have a lunch planned for tomorrow with my best friend, Mae, which I keep putting off. There's no time for death. "You're sure this was deliberate?"

"As sure as a tinker's magic." Tick scurries to his office to find materials and a tinker spell for a patch. The patch will get me home, but the cycle will have to be brought back here to be repaired.

I've gone from a very unhappy girl to an extremely unhappy girl.

With the patch complete, I'm on my way. My pants are tucked into my laced-up knee-high boots, my blazer is changed out for a recycled-leather duster, and my scarf is traded for my leather skull cap and goggles—fashionable yet sensible.

"High ho, and away I go," I say and give Tick a wave. As I drive away, I wonder why someone would sabotage my bike.

It's dusk now, and the light is fading fast. I look forward to a quiet evening at home. I drive along the feeder road to the underpass that will put me on the thoroughfare.

The thoroughfare is one of three that lead from Industria Island, where Harcrow Alchemy Inc. sits in the middle of Fyrest River, into Fulcrum City. When the thoroughfare hits the outskirts of the central city, it splits. A feeder route circles the city, while the main thoroughfare enters the heart of Fulcrum.

As soon as I enter the thoroughfare, a shiver runs up and down my back.

It's the only warning I get before my tire is bumped.

Chapter Four

"Hey! What the fuck?"

The color falls from my face as the Zenith jerks forward. A forceful breath bursts from me with a scream. The sound is quickly lost in the rush of wind beating against my face as I speed up.

I'm bumped again. The chrome-and-steel beauty beneath me shakes and begins to swerve out of control.

"You twit!"

I quickly right my black-and-silver sweetheart. I'm too angry to be frightened now. The Zenith is my baby, and this scum is hurting her. And I plan on staying vertical.

Shifting gears, I can it and pull away from the offending vehicle. Peering into the mirrors that sit on the Zenith's chrome handlebars, I try to identify the tin can that hit me. The many red vertical stalks that line the thoroughfare, topped with round, glowing disks fed by solar energy collected throughout the turn, look like finger-painted streaks against the horizon. The thoroughfare lights, though many, are dim, which makes it easy to see the stars and comfortable enough to see the road, but it's difficult to identify the hoods trying to do me in or their piece of tin.

Traffic is never too heavy due to the fact that the majority of Fulcrum City's over 260,000 inhabitants use train and transit systems. Still, things slow down a bit at this juncture, and I'm hammering down on it fast with someone of not-so-good intentions on my tail. "Crud!" I slow my clean-lined, elegant machine, noting the malevolent vehicle coming up fast behind me.

At the river junction, the marginal feeder route would take me to Rivulet Allotment, where I, and about thirty thousand others, reside. Tonight, I'm going to either lose these thugs or end up horizontal. Going home, it seems, is not an option. I'm a bit nervous and a whole lot pissed.

The thoroughfare is a four-laner. Two lanes keep heading into Fulcrum, where speeds slowly decline and exits lead into the center circle of the city. I decide to take the city route, versus the familiar two lanes that circle the city margin and feed into the different residential allotments. If I can keep these creepers off my tail, maybe I can lead them to the main constabulary, be safe, not eat asphalt, and get a good look at the vehicle.

Since I had to slow the Zenith, I've lost my advantage of speed as a getaway. I now need to use my brain cells and my cycle skills to keep myself intact.

I can hear the tin can's engine coming up behind me, and I'm arriving fast on the motors in front of me. All four lanes are covered side to side with metal. There's no lane open for me to zip through.

The evil is coming up next to me this time. The tin is black as night, its windows tinted as dark as their intentions. The darkness swerves into me, and I countersteer the Zenith to avoid metal on metal.

I hit the brake—illuminating the word *STOP* on the lens of my taillight. Without fully halting, I maneuver the steel and chrome up to the driver side of my new-found enemy.

I thought if I could hit the berm of the thoroughfare and can it past the upcoming traffic, I might have a chance. But nothing is that easy.

Countering my obvious move, the black menace turns directly into me.

I scream.

Tires screech.

We're gaining on the slowing traffic now.

I lean in.

I put on the steam.

With determination, I hammer down and drive straight in between two side by side roadsters, just missing being laid out on the pavement.

I think I make out a few choice words from the occupants as I fly by.

But it isn't over. The threat knocks one of the cursing roadsters into one of the many dully lit light posts to make room as it stampedes toward me.

I receive a jolt from behind.

My head cracks the Zenith's windshield. "Crap! Fuck! Ow!" Tears sting my eyes. It's back on my tail now, and there are more machines carrying folks, and I'm barreling straight toward them.

Another jolt.

And another.

The black chrome valance mudguard is being dented against the back tire; I can hear the chafing of rubber against metal. I have to get out of this.

My assailant and I barrel down on the innocent commuters, carving in and out of traffic. I squeaked by, while the dark horse scrapes and bumps pretty much every motor as it tries its damnedest to mow me down.

Serpentining around vehicles, I attempt to keep up my speed. I head for the city center and the Constabulary Council building. My head is pounding full of thoughts as my anger melts away and fear replaces it. Vehicles are beginning to move out of the way of the onslaught of the tin wrecker and me, its victim.

One would think the Transportation Council would have gotten wind of the mess being made on their precious pavement by now. I need help. However, it doesn't appear that any is coming. I'm on my own.

My shadowy nemesis, whom I'm trying to evade—not very successfully for a while now, I might add—is gaining on me. I keep changing gears smoothly, countersteering, and leaning in, all to prevent capture and to escape from surfing the pavement.

I come upon large delivery movers, no doubt transporting supplies to the many restaurants, clubs, and businesses that call the fast-moving city of Fulcrum their home. I hit the berm and speed along the rail beside one of the trucks. I cut the big truck off, forcing a little brake action on the driver, which allows me to hop in between the commuters and slow down my unknown assailant.

The Zenith is keen on speed and handling—a real dream—and I zip past the on and off ramps along the spiraled city streets toward my destination. The motors slow as the commuters navigate their exits. Lane splitting now, I'm free and clear, leaving the bulldozer behind delivery vehicles too large for it to bully.

I'm free!

I exit off onto the feeder road leading to the C-shaped avenue that makes up the center of Fulcrum. The building I head for is made of steel and glass, with large brass lettering on the face of the roof line: *Fulcrum Legere Legalis Headquarters*. Long, centered stairs at the front of the ten-storied building lead up to its entrance. Rails running up the middle and flanking each end of the marble steps lead to tall brightly polished nickel-plated, glass-framed doors.

I pull my slightly battered and tired Zenith to the curb of the brick walkway that fronts all the council buildings. I pop down the cycle's kickstand and dismount, standing still for a moment to catch my breath and slow my two pounding hearts. Once I'm a bit calmer, I slide my goggles to the top of my head and watch for the hoods and their black ride. I survey the surrounding area in search of any sign of the threat. Nothing. Not a mark of them around. Breathing a sigh of relief, I eye my baby for the damages resulting from the chase.

The usually even, smooth rocker covers that taper down toward the rear axle show stress from the constant barrage. The rear mudguard is dented in, as I suspected, and now touches the black silverspoked tire.

I sigh. "Definitely needs a bit of bodywork."

I turn my attention to the building behind me. Littering the front walk and the steps are all manner of beings: coppers, fly boys, some high hats, and a few other eggs. The bailed-out hoods and dolls with fellas beat it quickly, not wanting to stick around the joint.

I start up the marble steps, not sure anymore what I'm even doing here.

"Problem, sweetheart?" asks a deep voice.

A deep voice belonging to a tall, broad-shouldered hunk of handsome.

Chapter Five

I hate being called sweetheart.

He stands near one of the outside handrails, a young well-dressed man standing next to him.

"You lookin' for some help, sweetheart? You look a bit confused. Lost, maybe?" He smirks.

"And you are?" I ask with as much attitude as I can muster.

"Inspector Chance Greyson at your service, sweetheart."

With a tilt of my head and a raised eyebrow, I study the inspector. He's certainly a looker: tall with a chiseled jaw. His hair, topped by a fedora, is short but shaggy, in need of a cut, and the color of dirt scattered with strands of gold. Eyes the color of pure blue celestite seem just as capable of chasing away nightmares as the magical crystals themselves. His build seems muscular under his slightly wrinkled three-piece suit and overcoat.

What am I going to say? Some unknown person possibly sabotaged my bike and, when that didn't work, tried to run me down? And if I am the target, is it because of my work? I'm unable to divulge the nature of my experiments to anyone outside of my father or brother.

"This is Deputy Second Inspector Flynn," the inspector introduces. The younger man stands not quite as tall as the inspector, and his hair, the color of gritty sand, is tipped a deep mazarine blue that matches his eyes perfectly. He tips his gray felt fedora and smiles at me, revealing some very white teeth and dimples that complement his roseate complexion.

I nod my head in acknowledgment of the young DSI.

"What can we do you for?" the inspector asks.

A stupid grin covers my face as I change my mind. I turn and head back down the steps toward the Zenith.

"Hey!" the inspector calls after me.

I wave and hop on the Zenith. I slip the goggles back down over my eyes and start the cycle up. The inspector has followed me down the stairs, leaving his DSI. I have no time for questions I can't answer. I smile and can it, leaving the inspector in a little of my dust, standing on the walkway with a very sour face.

I head out of the city center and back onto the thoroughfare, keeping my goggled eyes peeled for my attackers as I drive back out of Fulcrum and onto the junction that will lead me home. So far, so good; no sign of trouble. I travel along River Junction from Fulcrum toward Rivulet Allotment, which is filled with single-family homes, doubles, and four-unit apartment buildings. On one side of the junction between Fulcrum and Rivulet is the Rivulet Mall of Shops. On the other side of the junction is a large green with a park, a lake, and a waterfall that generates power.

I live in one of the four-unit apartment buildings along the riverside. I have a coveted view of the Fyrest River from my second-floor unit. Rivulet Allotment is an upper-class allotment directly across the river from the exclusive Seaside Village, in which I grew up and in which my parents still live.

I pull the Zenith into the ground-floor garage of my building and enter the main lobby from there. The front lobby, decorated formally with rich shades of ruby and bright, ornate steel, contains a tall counter that faces the front entry doors and is staffed by a doorman.

I greet the doorman as I enter the building through the double doors leading from the parking garage on the first floor. "Good evening, Carston."

"Evening, Dr. Harcrow," replies the doorman. "And it's Carlton. Hope you had a good turn."

"Any correspondences arrive for me today, Carpton?"

"Carlton," he mumbles before checking behind the counter with a frown. "And no, ma'am. Not today."

"Thank you and have a good night, Carlton."

"Thank you, ma'am! And you have a nice evening as well." Oddly, he sounds quite chipper after I thank him.

I head up the curved staircase from the lobby to my suite. I reside in the top left apartment of the building, a large one-bedroom unit. I adore it, especially the view. I have not only a view of the river from the bay window of my breakfast nook but also a large balcony off my boudoir that faces the river as well. The apartment also includes a front tiered terrace and a shared rooftop garden that I rarely use.

I don't require a key to my place. One of my many talents is the ability of telekinesis. Telekinesis is a very misunderstood gift. A person cannot go around moving and lifting things all willy-nilly. It takes diligent practice, knowledge of the subject, patience, and tons of time. When I unlock my door, I am moving a physical system of tumblers and mechanisms. I literally had to take the lock apart to study it and learn how it functioned, as well as practice moving the mechanisms, to be able to lock and unlock the door. It took time to master my door lock. However, now I can lock and unlock my door with a wave of my hand.

I'm happy to be home. Grabbing the goggles and skullcap off my head, I pick up my wireless and make the connection.

"Ephron?" I ask.

"Zelda, what's up? Are you okay?"

"We've gotta talk," I say without answering the question.

"Tick told me about the Zenith. I gather it got you home okay."

"Yeah, I made it home. Barely." I fill him in on the details of my exciting yet life-threatening ride home. "I left the Legere without spilling. I figured I'd best talk to you first."

"Thank the stars you're not pavement meat, Zelda. I'm still at the office; I'll talk to Father." I can hear the worry in his voice.

"Is there any more news on the explosion in my lab?"

Ephron clears his throat. "Have you finished the specs on imitation silk?"

I cross my eyes and stick my tongue out every third word as I answer him. "I assure you that the completed project is with Father for review and not lost with my demolished lab."

"This could be a boon for the economy. A manufactured imitation silk would be more affordable than the natural spider silk produced and spun by Abalone spiders in Elione. And stop it; I know you're sticking your tongue out at me."

"Can you have Tick send someone to pick up the Zenith for some engine and bodywork?"

"I'll let him know."

"Thanks."

"Are you sure you're going to be okay?" he adds.

"Ephron, I have a doorman, a wireless, and the anger over my Zenith. Believe me; no one is going to bother me tonight."

He surrenders. "I'm just uncomfortable with you being there alone."

"I love you too."

I disconnect with Ephron and head for a long soak in the bath.

Chapter Six

My apartment is very simple and a bit sparse. I spend so much time in my lab that I'm almost never home. The main living area's furniture sits on a snow-white substantially plush round area rug covering the stained hardwood floors. The curved stark-white sofa, matching curved armless chair, and curved partial-backed lounger sit around a dusty crackled-glass cocktail table. My walls are adorned with modern pieces of art created by local Tesla artists.

I need a stiff drink. I drag myself over to the cocktail cabinet. Opening the inlayed wood front cabinet panel reveals bottles of a variety of fermented and aged liquors on a mirrored shelf and crystal glasses in holders on the shelf below. My drink of choice is a sweet fermented flower-and-fruit drink called ruby vinum.

I sip on a glass as I walk through the arch into my kitchen. I don't cook: I never have time. Plus things have a way of exploding in my lab, so it is a smart idea not to even put forth the effort in the kitchen. My mother, Ave, read my cards once and was convinced I would starve to death, so she has her house chef put together meals for me that I can heat up later. I'm not going to argue about having gourmet food brought to my doorstep. The food will warm while I soak in the tub.

My bathing room is located between the kitchen and my boudoir. The room is narrow but more than spacious enough for the necessities. One such necessity is my inclined high-back white porcelain tub that sits next to a large window overlooking the river. I open the silver spigot to allow the steamy clear water to fill up the tub. I peel off the rest of my clothing as I enter the boudoir through a second door connecting the two.

I finish the last gulp of my vinum and set the glass down on one of the mirrored nightstands flanking my comfy bed. Gazing out the boudoir balcony window, I reflect for a moment on my turn. I run my hands through my hair, shaking myself back to the present and head in for my bath. My robe drops to the floor, and I step into the overly warm bath, which I have filled with perfumed oils of geranium, lavender, and bergamot to help me relax and destress me. A little aromatherapy is in order after the turn I have had.

The star that holds Gaia in orbit has just finished setting beneath the horizon. The shadows that have been cast over the river melt into the darkness of night. I sit in the bath, peering out the large one-way window into the blackness. I can't help but think of what has happened.

I imagine I should find out how and why my lab blew up and with me not in it. Was the object to kill me or just to damage the lab? Why sabotage the Zenith? Was the damage done to my Zenith before or after the explosion?

I squint and speak aloud. "What about that road business? Were they trying to scare me or kill me?" I splash the water with a slap of my hand. "It's all dark, just like the sky." I close my eyes and sink beneath the water in defeat.

I look at my pruney hand and notice that the water has cooled down quite a bit. I've lost all track of time. I emerge from the water and wrap my tired muscles in a fluffy body towel. A waft of burning animal flesh hits my nostrils then, and I rush into my boudoir to slip on my lounging pajamas. Jumping up and down as if I were on a pogo stick, I pull up my bottoms and hustle to the oven. I successfully retrieved my dinner with minimal burning of food or fingers.

Against the far wall of my living room sits a thin crystal screen—a Visual Entertainment Receiver. It stands upright on a tripod and receives transmissions of news, weather, educational programs, music, visual plays, human interest stories, and council updates. After turning the dials this way and that, I find a music channel streaming with sweet, soothing tunes. The music fills the apartment with blues notes, improvisation, polyrhythms, and syncopation, soothing my frayed nerves. The next song has vocals, and I find I'm feeling more settled now. The singer has a deep raspy alto voice, and the way she sings is so melodic and melancholy.

Lazing back on the sofa, I begin eating my stew. I must remember to thank the chef the next time I'm over at my parents'. Unfortunately, the ruby vinum is not a great complement to this dish; a dryer and more delicate vinum would have been more appropriate.

"Hmm . . ."

I jolt upright at the intrusion of a constant buzz.

Striding over to the intercom on the wall, I pick up the handset. "Yes, Carpon?"

"This is Carlton." He doesn't sound as happy as he did earlier. "Sorry to disturb you, Doctor, but there are two gentlemen here to see you."

I'm not expecting anyone. "Carol, tell the gentlemen that the hour is late and not appropriate for callers." Being a modern girl, I really don't care what time a man comes or goes; I'm just too tired to see anyone right now.

"Ma'am, they're from the Legalis." Then he adds, "And it's Carlton."

"Yes, I recognize your voice, Carston, but I'm not dressed for callers. Can they come by tomorrow?" I have no idea if my brother sent them or if they came on their own, and I frankly don't care. I'm done for the turn and not up for it.

"Carlton," the doorman whined before disconnecting.

A very forceful knock on my door made me jump.

"Maybe they'll just go away," I mumble.

The knocking gets a little harder and louder. "Zelda Harcrow, this is Inspector Greyson and DSI Flynn. We need a word."

I wonder briefly why Crapton the doorman would have let them up.

The knocking becomes thunderous.

My shoulders slump, and I sigh long and hard before opening the door with a jolt. My smile freezes as my callers are revealed. "How can I help you, Inspector?"

His eyebrows rise. "You." He looks me over.

"Me," I reply, stating the obvious. I haven't bothered putting on a robe. I greet him in my lounging pajamas. The corners of his mouth rise a little, and now I wish I had put on a robe.

"May I come in?" he inquires in a way that makes it seem like there isn't any appropriate answer other than yes.

I blow out another sigh. "Do I really have a choice, Inspector?"

"We all have a choice, sweetheart." He sweeps past me into the apartment.

"Do come in," I mutter meaninglessly. Leaning out into the hall, I add, "What about you DSI?"

DSI Flynn averts his eyes. "I'll wait out here, ma'am." He tips his hat and goes back down the stairs.

I shut the door and turn slowly toward the inspector. "Why are you here?"

"Aren't you going to offer me a seat, sweetheart?" he asks.

I extend my arm toward the sofa, where once upon a time I was eating, relaxing, and listening to music. Now my food is getting cold, the VER is silent, and I'm no longer calm. "Do have a seat, and please call me Dr. Harcrow."

He studies me like a jigsaw puzzle. I can see the wheels turning in his head. "Thank you, Doctor." He takes off his hat and finds a place on the sofa.

I move his hat, sit down right next to him, and lean in a little. He wants to make me feel as uncomfortable in my own home as he possibly can, but I'm not going to let that happen.

He fires back at my forwardness with his own. He holds the collar of my top between his thumb and finger as if to feel the fabric. "Soft," he whispers.

Ha! If he thinks I will pull away and act all demure, he has another think coming. "Yes," I whisper. "Very soft."

His Adam apple jumps. "Beautiful color," he says without even looking at the outfit.

I'm getting a little steamed up. "I'm sure your wife would enjoy a set."

Without missing a beat, he replies, "I'm not married."

"Girlfriend, then?"

He smiles at me. "Not yet." His smile gets wider. "Did your fiancé get these for you?"

I swallow hard. The word *fiancé* is difficult for me to hear. "No, no fiancé. And before you ask"—I narrow my eyes and lean in—"no boyfriend, either—"

"Not yet," he finishes for me.

"Drink, Inspector?" I offer, changing the subject. I lean back against the sofa, not so much for effect as to cool off a little. He's a looker and has sex appeal a kilometer long.

"Maybe another time. I like an amber grain alcohol, smoky and smooth. Not something you would have, sweetheart." He smirks.

I lean back in and glare at him. "You'd be surprised—baby."

He snickers and smiles slightly. Then his mouth hardens quickly. "I do, however, need to ask you about an incident that occurred today."

"And which one would that be?" I smartly answer.

He raises an eyebrow. "Is there more than one?"

"It depends on what incident and if I was even there for it."

"Listen, sweetheart, I really need you to be straight with me."

I know he said sweetheart again to get under my skin, so I'm not done playing. I gently sweep a lock of his hair from his forehead and reply seductively, "It's Dr. Harcrow."

He grabs my wrist. I can see he's getting a bit perturbed. "Doc, the incident I'm talking about is the game playing on the thoroughfare. Did you think we wouldn't notice?"

He called me Doc. My cheeks flush, and I avert my eyes from his. "So you think I was playing a game?" I break free from his grasp and stand up. "Give me a ticket, then, or whatever you do. And please feel free to ticket the other driver as well."

I decide to fish around for some information about the other driver. "Or did you already fine the other driver?"

"No," he says bluntly. He stands to face me. The top of my head just barely reaches his nose. I have to look up at him, which is when I realize how close to me he stands. "I thought I would come here first."

I turn, walk toward the accordion terrace doors, and cling to the sheer pearly drapes. "Well, why don't you go bother the other driver? I've had a long turn and can't be bothered with such things now." I pull back the drapes a fraction and look out past the terrace into the night sky. The smaller moon, Biota, is almost full while the larger is barely visible.

The inspector comes up behind me. He stands so close to me that I can feel the heat and vibrations coming off his body, and I know his mind isn't just on my driving. He smells of whiskey and musk. I lean slightly into him, my body betraying me. Attempting to compose myself, I ask, "Well?"

"Tell me where I can reach this other driver, and I will happily bother them." His breath is hot on my ear.

I close my eyes. It hits me then that he has no idea who was in that auto, either. He and his puppy came here on a fishing trip. I turn into the inspector, our bodies almost, but not quite, touching.

"I think it's time for me to go to bed."

"Swee—" He stops himself. He places his hands on my shoulders. I shiver a bit under his touch.

"You need to leave."

"Doc, you obviously need help. I'm here; I can help." His voice has lost its edge as he pleads with me softly.

I look up into his protective blue eyes; I can see he's concerned. "I'm sorry you wasted your time, Inspector. If there's a fine or something, please feel free to send it." I shrug his hands off.

He returns to being pushy. "We may have to impound that beautiful cycle of yours."

"That won't be necessary. It isn't drivable at the moment and will be heading in for repairs."

"Local repair shop?"

"Harcrow Alchemy. The tinkers will take good care of her."

"Dr. Harcrow . . . Harcrow Alchemy . . . I see." The *ah-ha* is all over his face. He gazes across the room for a moment. "Do you have another vehicle to get around in?"

"Yes, a yellow roadster. Why?"

"Be careful driving, Doc, that's all." He releases me and walks over to the sofa to retrieve his hat. "Goodnight, Doc. We'll be seeing each other again soon."

I walk over to the door and open it for his departure. "Inspector?"

He gazes at me for a long moment before answering. "Yes?"

"Thank you for stopping by." There's no more I can say. No more I want to say, really. This is something that needs to be handled by the company and my brother.

The inspector nods, puts his hat on, and exits the apartment to join his colleague down in the lobby. I shut the door and close my eyes for a moment to recenter myself. I open my eyes and take in a deep breath. Nothing more can this turn bring but a decent night's sleep and telling dreams. I dump what's left of my dinner into the trash and head off, still hungry, to my boudoir and to my bed.

Chapter Seven

As always, the sun star comes up whether or not I'm ready for it. I forgot to pull the drapes closed last night, so now the bright morning light assaults me in my bed. My sleep was restless and filled with dark dreams. There were no answers to be had in sleep, so I will have to find them in the waking hours.

Mae, my best friend, calls early to confirm our luncheon for this afternoon. "Darling, I thought we would dine at the Facere Tearoom. They're going to be showing some the new season's fashions, and I really need a wardrobe update."

"Mae, you have more clothes than you or the entire population of Fulcrum could ever wear."

"Pshaw! No such thing," she says.

"What time? Shall we meet? Or—"

"I'll come by and pick you up. I just bought a new motor. Just wait 'til you see it, darling! It is the darb!"

"Mae, what happened to your other auto?"

"Well, there was this small incident with this very small man, several liters of paint, and a tall building in Fulcrum," she rambles. "So, I bought a new car. Where should I pick you up?"

"What?" I spit out at the receiver. "Oh, Mae, what were you doing?"

"Well, I decided to open a small exterior decorating business."

"And . . . ?" I ask, encouraging her to give me a little detail.

She becomes very matter of fact. "And now the business is closed. It really wasn't my cup of tea. I need a more creative outlet."

"More creative than . . . what did you call it? Exterior decorating?" I hold back the giggle that is sure to escape me.

"Steel, white, gray, brass, blah, blah, blah. Blech!" She moans. "Boring, boring, and more boring. Buildings are dull, Zelda dear. I have to be around much more excitement."

"And it had nothing to do with the little man and a lot of paint?" I wait for her to respond, but I'm met with silence. I swear I can actually hear her annoyance with me.

Growing up in Seaside Village as well, Mae Griffin has been my best friend since our minders brought us out to the park to play when we were toddlers. Mae is a bit eccentric; she changes careers like one changes clothes. She never has to worry about funds. Her family is very well off and connected to councils and businesses here in Tesla and abroad. Once, Mae decided to be an aerial photographer. Oh boy. She thought that piloting and taking pictures at the same time was an innovative idea. That didn't work out well at all. She let go of the yoke to take several exposures, and ironically, the plane and Mae ended up in the top floor of the Fulcrum City Safety Council building. Another career ended as soon as it started. Kooky as she can be, she's the most loyal, loving, and kind person I know, and I am blessed to have her as my best friend.

"Well," I say. "You'll have to fill me in when we have lunch, then."

She clears her throat. "Zelda, I think it is you, darling, who needs to fill me in."

"Why?" I ask, panic creeping into my voice. "What have you heard?"

"Well, Poppy said," she begins. Poppy is what Mae likes to call her father—something to do with when she was little and Poppy was traveling a lot. "There was quite the explosion at Harcrow yesterturn and Clover was injured . . . and it wasn't an accident."

"How come I get the feeling you know more than I do?"

"I don't quite know what you mean, darling," she quips.

"Fine, don't tell me," I say. "But I promise you I'll wriggle it out of you later."

"We'll see about that. Now go get ready, and I'll pick you up at HA later." After a brief pause, she added, "Do be careful, Zelda darling."

"I promise I will."

I make a quick cup of ginseng and ginger green tea to rev me up. I open a small salty-smelling seaweed salad—definitely a meal to give me long-lasting energy for my morning. After a few stretches, I'm ready to take on the turn. Still feeling a little scattered, I choose a more calming, comfy outfit for today: a lined, wide-legged, crème-colored lacy pair of pants with a patterned, green-and-blue-hued spider-silk blouse. The blouse's low neckline and gathered bodice flatter my full chest. I choose to do my hair a light blue to match my mood and outfit, as well as a crème cloche hat with light-blue and green feathers at the band. I take one last gander in the mirror, and with a wink I'm out the door.

Tick has already sent a couple of tinkers to take my Zenith back to HA—as everybody likes to call Harcrow Alchemy Inc.—and so I'm left with my pretty yellow convertible roadster. With my hat secured with a ruby hatpin and my sun goggles on, I start the engine and off I go.

The skies are a deep blue dotted with small fluffy clouds. The Weather Council has announced that the temperature will be mildly warm with light winds for the next few turns, so I drive with the roadster's top down. Wind blowing past my face, I inhale the fresh fragrance of the water as I drive over the bridge connecting the island to the mainland.

Once parked in the HA garage, I skip over to the tinker lab and Tick's office to check on my Zenith.

"In here," Tick calls out from one of the laboratories.

I follow the sound of his gravelly voice and find him exiting one of the smaller labs, which contains pieces of mangled metal gears, glass, and copper wires. "What's all that?"

The latch clicks as the door closes behind him. "Well, I'm not sure if I should be discussing it with you."

"Tick, what do you mean? It can't be for my project. That's a mishmash of burned up . . ." My voice trails off as I realize what I'd seen. "Those are pieces of a bomb, aren't they?" My throat tightens, making it feel like I'm trying to breathe through a straw.

Tick rubs my back as though that would ease my panic. "Zelda dear, you know I can't discuss my findings with you."

"Looks like more than just bomb parts, Tick. Wait! Findings?" I narrow my eyes and stare at him.

"That's all I'm going to say, my dear. If you want more, talk to Ephron and Titus."

"Fine," I curtly respond with a frown. "What about my cycle?" I cross my arms and let the subject change.

"It came in this morning. I'm waiting on some parts, so it'll be a few strings before it's ready."

"I thought maybe a couple of turns, not strings!" I whine. "That long, really?" Jeepers, there are eight turns in a string. A couple of strings means a load more time than a turn or two of Gaia. The thought of being without the Zenith that long is highly depressing.

"That long," he says. He's a softy, though, so he soon adds, "Oh, all right. I'll see what I can do."

Finally, something to be happy about! I jump up next to him and plant a big wet kiss on his chubby cheek. "Attaboy! You're the best!"

He blushes.

I cross the hall to the infirmary. As I enter the sterile area, the scents of rubbing alcohol and burned sage accost my nose. Immediately, I catch a glimpse of a good-looking young boy visiting with Clover. I didn't realize Clover had a beau. It hits me then like a load of bricks: I really have no clue about Clover's personal life. I've always been so wrapped up in work, I've never thought to ask. I decide not to interrupt; instead I seek out Healer Vaidya to ask about Clover's progress.

"Healer Vaidya, how is my assistant coming along?"

She shakes my hand. "Dr. Harcrow, it's nice to see you again."

"Oh, nice to see you again as well." I've never been all that good at pleasantries.

"Yes, indeed." With the pleasantries over, Healer Vaidya is all business. "Clover is making remarkable progress. I'd like to keep her another turn or two to make sure the concussion is healed and the lung is repaired."

I smile. "Sounds promising."

"Clover will still need rest for a string or two," the healer adds. "She will not be able to head back to work any time soon."

"I understand." I look over at Clover's room. Her visitor is gone, so I decide to check in with her.

"How is the finest assistant around fairing today?" I keep my tone upbeat as I enter her room.

"Much better, Doctor, thank you," Clover mumbles through a yawn. Her fair complexion seems even lighter than usual. The sickly pale emphasizes her freckles and frizzy reddish-gold bobbed hair.

"Attagirl," I say, understanding that she's putting on a brave face.

"I should be ready to go back to work in no time." Her voice sounds like it's softened by pain.

"When Healer Vaidya says you're okeydokey, then you can come back to the lab." *Not that we have a lab to go back to just yet.*

Clover closes her eyes. "Yes, ma'am."

I gently pat her hand. "You're tired. I shall stop by later for a better visit."

"Mm . . . Hmm . . ." Clover drifts off. She must be on some good drugs.

"Attagirl," I say again as I tiptoe out. I didn't get a chance to ask about her gentleman caller; I'll have to remember to ask later.

I head upstairs to the executive offices on the main floor. It's time to meet with Ephron and Father and get the scoop on the explosion in my lab.

Chapter Eight

I enter the double glass-and-steel doors that lead to the executive offices. The reception area houses comfortable sofas for those guests who have to wait for a long time and long curved desks where the executive assistants sit, keeping guard for their remarkably talented bosses.

Ephron's assistant of the string waves me over.

"Ooh . . . you must be the beautiful Dr. Zelda Harcrow!" the elderly assistant squeals. "I have heard so much about you. The elder Dr. Harcrow and Mr. Ephron are waiting for you in Mr. Ephron's office."

I smile at the overly rouged and perfumed older lady. "Thank you for the compliment. Are you enjoying working here at HA?"

The assistant peers at me from behind her very thick eyeglasses. "Who are you?"

"Excuse me?" I look around the room. Didn't she just call me over? "I'm Zelda Harcrow, remember?"

"Ooh . . . you must be the beautiful Dr. Zelda Harcrow!" the apparently senile assistant began again. "I've heard so much about you. Mr. Harcrow is waiting for you in his office."

I do a double take. "Ah . . . thank you?"

The assistant looks down at her desk again and then looks back up. "Do you have an appointment?"

"Yes?" I look sideways at the crazy lady behind the desk. "They're expecting me?"

She blinks, her eyes huge and magnified. "Are they expecting you?"

I let out a long whistle, scoot by her soon-to-be-vacated desk, and enter Ephron's office. I close the large sculpted wooden door behind me. "Okay, who is the nutty bird?"

"Isn't she a hoot?" Father comes over and gives me a hug and kiss. "You look very casual today. Are you going somewhere?"

"Mae and I are headed out for a luncheon and tea later."

He strokes his goatee. "I like tea, but do be careful, dear."

"You will have to excuse my soon-to-be-departed assistant." Ephron smiles as he comes out from behind his ornately carved wooden desk to give me a hug and kiss as well. "She was another complete mistake the Employment Council sent over. She is an improvement, though, over the one they sent last string."

"What was wrong with the one last string?" The leather cushion lets out a whoosh of air as I plop into one of the two matching chairs in his office.

"Oh, let me tell her, Son." My father then starts laughing so hard that his face turns the color of ruby vinum.

I look at my father, cockeyed. "What's so funny?"

"Never mind, Ephron; you tell her." Father can barely get the words out, he's laughing so hard.

"He refused to touch anything," Ephron says, "even to sit down." He throws his hands up. "He was afraid that he might contract a disease from touching or sitting on furniture that others had used."

"Okay . . . so how did he work?" It's a silly question, but I still have to ask.

"He didn't—"

"He just stood there." With tears running down his face, my father tries to finish the story. "Just stood there all turn"—he dabs his cheeks with a white handkerchief he pulled from his pocket—"with a mask over his mouth and nose so as not to breathe in germs. And the gloves—oh my, gloves too!"

I hold back a giggle. "So . . . you fired him after the first turn, right?"

"He tried—" Father has to sit down to catch his breath, settling into the other deep leather chair in front of Ephron's desk.

"He wouldn't leave," Ephron says, taking up the story. He slides our father a look. "He just came back turn after turn and just stood there."

"How did you get rid of him?"

"Well, I sent out a memo—just to him, mind you—that a deadly pathogen had been reported missing from one of the labs and was deadly only to males fitting his description." Ephron smiles. "Needless to say, he quit."

"He fell for that?" I can't believe it. "Where was I while all this was going on?"

"A paranoid person will believe just about anything, Sister dear," Ephron says, and my father, the great Titus Harcrow, nods in agreement. "And where were you? No doubt with your head buried in a test tube, as usual."

"Really, Ephron, you must find a decent assistant. It's a new one every string." I shake my head and take a breath before changing the subject. "Now, what about my lab."

Immediately, my jovial father stops laughing and remains very quiet. The corners of his mouth droop.

I take another deep breath, close my eyes, and exhale. "Tell me."

Ephron's demeanor changes as he leans back against the front of his desk, his arms crossed. "We have part of Tick's report and the full reports from our security and the Safety Council on the explosion in your lab."

"Well, don't keep me in suspense."

"Tell her," Father directs him.

"Tell me what?"

"After the dust cleared, so to speak, the Fire Brigade found a point of origin for the explosion in your private lavatory."

That's perplexing. "My lavatory?"

"Our security team then investigated and found remnants of an explosive device."

My mouth goes dry. "A bomb? It's confirmed, then; what I heard is true."

"Let your brother finish, my dear."

"I'm unsure what you heard or from whom—we'll talk about protocol later—but yes, a bomb had been planted in your lavatory." Ephron puts his hand up to hush me so he can continue. "Jep and his security team, alongside the tinkers, sifted through the debris and have pieced together what happened."

"I'm listening." Well, I'm listening as much as I can over my very loudly pounding hearts.

"It seems, somehow," my brother explains softly, "that someone placed an explosive device inside the wall clock in your lavatory. It was scheduled to go off at a time when you and Clover would assuredly have still been in your lab. Fortunately, the clock's timing mechanism was wrong, and the bomb went off later than it should have."

I drop my head into my hands. "The time-bending spell."

My father's ears perk up. "What say you?"

Ephron stands upright.

I take a deep breath and tuck a bit of hair behind my ear. "I was a mess and I needed to get ready for the meeting, so I performed a time-bending spell. I must have forgotten to manually reset the wall clock."

The color drains from my father's face as he slumps back in his chair. "Dear me, Ephron my boy, do you know what this means?"

"With the thoroughfare incident too—it appears it may be more than just sabotage," Ephron notes.

My voice rises. "What are you two going on about? Was it sabotage or not?"

My father nods to Ephron. "We're unsure if it is simple sabotage or if it was an assassination attempt. The time bending throws our investigation in a new direction."

I rub my brow. I can feel a headache creeping on. "All righty then. Now what? Mae is going to be here soon to pick me up for shopping and lunch."

Father's voice goes up an octave as he stands up and places his hands on my shoulders. "Now, you have a fine turn with Mae; that is what you do. We'll meet again here—let's say, after lunch?—to discuss this new development. What say you, Ephron?"

"Sounds like a plan, sir." Ephron straightens his tie. "Did you say Mae is coming here?"

"Yes sirree," I reply. "She bought a new sporty motor and wants to show it off."

Ephron begins, "What happened—"

"Don't ask, dahling!" Mae swings open the office door and struts in, dropping her r's and hitting her t's hard. She really knows how to make an entrance; she fills up every corner of the room with her presence.

"How did you get past granny?" I ask, greeting her with a hug.

"You mean that old lady sleeping at her desk?"

Ephron raises his eyebrows. "Sleeping?"

Father opens his arms for an embrace. "Mae, my dove! How is the most interesting gal in all of Tesla?"

Mae reciprocates with a well-planted red-lipstick kiss on the old bird's cheek. "Titus, you old dapper egg, you look marvelous!"

Ephron steps forward. "Hello, Mae."

There have been times when I've thought my bother has a thing for my best friend. I don't think anything could ever come from it; Mae is a free spirit, and I can't see her sticking to one man or woman.

My friendship is the closest I think she'll ever get to a long-term, stable relationship.

"My, my, my, Ephron. I think you get handsomer every time I see you," Mae croons. "I am just befuddled on how some pretty little thing hasn't captured your hearts yet."

I laugh. "Jeepers, Mae, spreading it on a little thick, don't you think?"

Ephron's face is turning red.

"Pshaw, Zelda darling, your brother is quite dreamy," she coos as she pats his reddened cheek.

"Thank you, Mae." My brother shoots me a look and then his expression changes very quickly to one of confusion.

"What's wrong?" I ask.

Ephron's eyes widen. "Mae, what did you mean, my assistant was sleeping?"

"Well, darling, she was sort of just sitting there peacefully, slumped in her chair with her eyes closed." Mae closes her eyes and slouches to mimic the old woman.

I turn to Ephron. "You don't think the old lady—"

As all brothers do, he finishes my sentence. "Kicked the bucket?"

My father squints and then begins to howl. "Ephron my boy, this one didn't even last a full string! And you won't have to fire her!"

Ephron shakes his head and beats it out of the office to find out if granny has ceased to be or is just taking a nap.

"I think we better call somebody," he yells in from the reception area. "And I think I need a new assistant."

"Well, it looks like your brother's assistant has retired—permanently." Mae shivers.

"Let's ankle," I say. "This is giving me the heebie-jeebies."

"I'm keen for that."

We hotfoot it out of Ephron's office, holding our breath as we pass the small crowd that has developed around the now-deceased senile assistant.

"Definitely gives new meaning to the phrase *temporary assistant*."

"Tell me about it," Mae whispers back.

"Where you parked?"

"Out front."

Mae's new motor sits right along HA's front walkway. The small sporty garnet-red Jasper is a two-seater coupe with a sliding glass roof and a mosaic-design interior. And it's surprisingly comfy.

"Snazzy tin can you have there, Mae."

Mae pats the hood. "A beaut, isn't she?"

We slide into the coach, Mae starts up her new toy, and away we go. Mae's both driving and talking fast. "Zelda darling, we must put our heads together and find this torpedo of yours. With you being my best friend, we mustn't have assassins running around all willy-nilly trying to do you in." Mae makes everything sound high-hat, dramatic, and all about her. "I overheard Poppy dear talking to Titus. It seems a bomb was planted to destroy your lab and private office."

"This I know, Mae. Spill on something I don't."

"Titus told Poppy his head tinker had informed him your cycle had been purposely sabotaged." The tires screech as she recklessly drives around another tin.

"Still nothing new, Mae." I'm losing my patience, and if she keeps driving like this, I'm going to lose my breakfast too.

"Well, there's more; don't get your panties in a bunch, darling. Poppy and Titus also discussed your adventures on the thoroughfare. They're convinced some forces are trying to sabotage your work with HA and that it should be considered an issue of national security." She guns the engine, lays on her horn, and passes a driver.

I grit my teeth, hold onto the strap handle with one hand, and brace myself with the other on the dashboard. "I still don't understand where you're going with this."

"I believe there's something more." Mae swerves around another fellow speeder. "You need to investigate before the torpedo hits his bull's-eye."

"I'm the bull's-eye, I'm guessing?" I squeeze my eyes shut in anticipation of a crash.

"Yes, darling Zelda, you are the bull's-eye." She nods and hammers down on the pedal.

I hang onto the door for dear life. "What do you suggest I do? Where do I start? Also, why can't the National Security Council just handle this?"

"Last first and first last," Mae babbles.

"Last first . . . what?" I'm confused, the fear of crashing at high speeds making it hard to focus.

Mae looks at me sideways. "Last first-ski, darling."

"What-ski?" I shoot back.

"Here is something you don't know, abercrombie. If the National Security Council takes over, they will pull all council projects from HA, and I mean all. Titus, your family, and the company will all take a big hit. Once private companies hear that there's a security issue, they'll start canceling contracts. That's not something Titus can recover from, not even with Ephron at the helm."

I wince as she takes a corner fast. "Oh."

"Next, where to start? The auto—we find the auto. Finding the tin will take us to whatever our next step is. And first, last, I suggest you stop hiding in a lab, get out there, and save your family's company and, in the process, your own skin."

"Mae, does it really look like I hide?"

"I love you, darling; you are my best friend. But the answer is yes. You are so oblivious to anything other than what happens to be in a test tube or under a microscope." I wince. She doesn't mince words.

"I'm sorry." The traffic melts into one changing multicolored line at this speed.

"It has taken me over four strings to get you to go out to lunch with me. You have canceled on me so many times, I've lost count."

"Mae, I'm so sorry. Please forgive me."

Mae laughs. "You are forgiven, darling, because I know why you do it. Now, let us get back on track and figure out how to find the vehicle." She hits the accelerator again.

Chapter Nine

Mae drives like a madwoman along the thoroughfare, weaving in and out of traffic. I just hold onto the Jasper's door with one hand and with the other, my hat.

"Mae, slow down!" I yell. "I won't have to worry about an assassin; you're going to kill me first!"

She laughs. "Oh, don't be silly."

She takes a turn hard and almost drives several other vehicles off the road. The horns are honking, and Mae is yammering on about something or other.

"Zelda! Zelda!" Mae yells at me. "Are you listening?"

"Yes! No! I mean—oh goodness, Mae, watch where you're going!" I scream, and Mae puts on the brakes, almost plowing into the truck in front of us.

Mae lays on the horn and screams at the driver of the slow truck—*no, the truck isn't slow; she's just going too fast.* The trucker makes a rude hand gesture at Mae, and she does the same as she speeds around the truck and cuts him off.

Mae turns to me. "Where should we start looking?"

"Look?" I scream. "How about the road? Look at the road!"

Mae waves her hand and acts as though her driving like a maniac is inconsequential. "Oh, do relax, darling. You are just wound too tight. That's another reason you need to solve this sabotage problem."

"Mae, exit off the thoroughfare before you kill someone!" I request very loudly. "Like me!"

Mae takes the first off-ramp, which leads around the outskirts of Fulcrum. The buildings in this area are restricted to one side of the street. The opposite side, facing the river, is all green space too unstable to support any type of building, including small ones like those on the other side. Keeping the frontage buildings short and small offers a river view to the high-rises that circle behind the outer marginal road. Mae takes the marginal road and pulls to the curb.

"Where to?"

"For?" I pry my hand from the dashboard; it's paralyzed with fear like the rest of my body.

"The car, darling, the car. How shall we track down the car?" She leans back and lights a gasper.

"Well, let me think." I sit there in quiet meditation for a few moments. Mae takes out her compact, checks the powder on her face, and refreshes her lip rouge. I think about the chase on the thoroughfare and how the onslaught of the dark vehicle damaged the Zenith. Then I smile. "Mae, I believe there's a motor repair or body shop somewhere up here on the way to the river."

Mae snuffs out the butt and puts the Jasper in gear. She drives, this time at a more reasonable speed, along the marginal road. "Why are we going to a repair shop?"

"Well, I was remembering how the motor plowed through traffic and sideswiped several vehicles. I thought if we visited repair shops, we might find out information about the car that hit them. I know it's a long shot . . ."

Mae pulls into Riverside Body Shoppe. "But it might work."

Mae parks the car, and we get out and ankle on over to the pedestrian entrance of the shop. The Riverside Body Shoppe is a fairly large operation. There are eight bays for vehicles, which are all filled, and several other motors line up outside, waiting their turns inside a vehicle bay. Inside each bay are at least three tinker mechanics working on an individual vehicle.

The scents of burned rubber, dirty oil, and the cloves of the gaspers hanging out of the mechanics' mouths spill out of the bays and attack us as we approach the building. Attached to the garage bays are offices and a reception and customer waiting area. We enter the reception area, and Mae heads right toward the desk and the young pimply-faced boy behind it. I follow closely behind Mae, wondering how we're going to get this kid to spill any information he might have.

"Well, hello there, fella," Mae says flirtatiously. "I so hope you can help me."

The young man smiles at Mae. "Ah, yes, ma'am."

Ooh . . . ma'am! Not a good start. Mae's face is turning red, and I can see her blood pressure rising. It's a bad idea to call Mae *ma'am*. She feels that unless a woman is unquestionably old or married, it's not right to utter the word *ma'am*. *Miss* is always a better idea to call a young, single—by choice or not—woman. Of course, there are worse things to be called.

Before things can get out of hand, I push Mae. She stumbles sideways slightly and scowls at me.

"Yes," I say to the boy, ignoring Mae, "my car was in a bit of a fender bender on the thoroughfare last night. My fiancé brought the car in for repairs, but I don't remember which shop it was. Could you check to see if he brought it in here? It's a roadster—a red Vanvooren, fully electric."

The young man looks through the ledger for anything coming in that fit the description. "Uh, what was the name? We got quite a few tins and trucks in that evening. I heard there was some kinda trouble going on. Of course, you know that."

"What do you mean?" I ask nervously.

"Your car, silly." Mae's face is no longer red.

I'm happy to see Mae's composure has returned. "Yes, of course—uh . . . It. Was. Terrifying. So, do you have my motor here?"

"Nope, sorry. Doesn't appear so." He looks up from the ledger.

"It was such a terrible experience for her. Did they catch the hood that smashed up the thoroughfare?"

"Actually, I heard there were two chasing around," the young man says without answering the question.

Mae's face begins to redden again.

"I just remember the one," I say. "A black vehicle. You hear anything about that?"

"Not really," Pimple Face says. "I don't think they've found the driver yet."

"Thanks." I sigh. Dead end.

Mae motions to me with her hand. "Let's go, Zelda. It has to be somewhere; the tin couldn't have just disappeared."

The pimple-faced kid behind the counter no doubt thinks she's referring to the red roadster I asked about. "You know, Rivulet Mall Body Shoppe might be where your car is."

"Oh?" I raise my eyebrows.

"Yeah, they're known for their work on roadsters. High-end stuff they do there."

"That's ducky! You're a doll." I grab Mae's hand and head out the door. Once back in her Jasper, we head back down the marginal road, which feeds right into the rear of the Rivulet Mall and Rivulet Mall Body Shoppe.

Rivulet Mall is like a small town in and of itself. The mall is open and filled with shops, cafés, theaters, markets, and restaurants lining cobblestone streets. No motor vehicles are allowed inside the streets of the mall; a trolley runs up and down the streets, taking customers to their destinations. The stores are all fronted with flat sidewalks for pedestrians and outdoor seating areas for the cafés and bistros. For those who drive to the mall—rather than take a train or street car—there are several valeted parking areas for the customers. In the case of the body shop, there's a rear entrance for the motors and customers, as well as a front entrance that allows the customers to easily shop or eat while they waited for the tinkers and mechanics to finish with their vehicles.

We decide to bypass the rear entrance and drive around the outside of the mall to the valet parking. Our luncheon reservation is at Facere Tearoom, which is located inside the city-like mall. It makes sense to park once and take the trolley down to the body shop and then over to the tearoom.

Mae pulls up to the valet station, which is manned by a young lady with bright-pink curly hair and a clashing chartreuse valet uniform. "Good thing I have on my shades, darling. I may go blind looking at our valet."

"I don't think she has a choice on what get-up she wears, dear," I respond.

"Maybe not, but she can choose her hair color!" Mae retorts as she exits the motor.

The brightly color-clashing gal comes over, smiles, and gives Mae a numbered ticket for retrieving her car later after our excursion through the mall. "Here's yous are, Miss. Please keep yours ticket safe. Enjoy your shoppin', Miss."

Mae smiles back, slips her a little kale to encourage her to take care of the shiny new tin, and sashays across the street to wait for the next trolley with me. We only have to wait a moment; the trolleys here run every five minutes to encourage shoppers to spend moola by making it easy and convenient to traverse the massive mall.

"I've got it!" squeals Mae.

"What? The car?" I clap my hands together. "You know how to find the car?"

Mae looks at me like I'm a dumb Dora. "Don't be a sap. Of course not."

"For crying out loud," I say a bit too loudly. "What are you going on about, then?"

"Pipe down, Zelda. I figured out my next career move."

"Good grief."

"I could design uniforms."

I think for a moment about what she's said. "Uniforms? Why?"

"Well, uniforms should be comfortable yet shouldn't clash with one's own features, darling," Mae explains, obviously thinking of our poor valet girl. "If uniforms are going to clash with the people wearing them, then the people need either new lines of work or new uniforms. And since some people unfortunately need to work, I think uniforms should be made to be a bit more appealing."

"Mae, that actually kind of makes sense." I'm shocked that Mae has for once had an idea that doesn't sound crazy.

"Yes, I think I could design an attractive uniform. A classy rag design, of course, maybe with stripes. Yes, stripes—ones that go vertical, of course. Horizontal stripes make people look so wide and squishy. Black and white . . . yes, I am thinking neutral . . . ." Mae goes on and on.

I shake my head. Nope, the crazy is back. I can see it now: every uniform in the city consisting of black and white vertical stripes. I'm getting dizzy and nauseated just thinking about it.

"Mae, let's put the uniform idea on the back burner for now and focus on finding the tin." I love my friend, but she can be a bit screwy.

She sticks her tongue out at me. "Dry up."

I sigh, look at her, and laugh. "Our stop is coming up."

Mae and I pop off the trolley at the corner across the street from the body shop.

Mae straightens her hat, looking around. "What's the plan?"

The body shop is across the cobbled street from where we stand. We stare at the building, trying to formulate an idea for how to get the information we need.

The Rivulet Mall Body Shoppe's mall entrance is stylish and inviting and fits in with the rest of the quaint shops, restaurants, and buildings along the street. The bright-white stucco one-story garage has one main entrance of glass-and-steel double doors and a horizontal-step-style roof with a vertical cylinder tower that has large neon orange letters reading *GARAGE*. The shop has two showrooms featuring new and vintage vehicles on either side of the main entrance, with large picture windows facing the street. Behind the showrooms are the bays, where the body shop's tinkers work.

With no plan in mind yet, we cross the street and walk in through the main entrance of the garage. The décor is minimalistic—white walls and ceilings—and the empty lobby is small enough to encourage customers to explore the mall and spend at the other stores. The lobby contains black leather club chairs that line the walls on each side and end at a counter that seats two employees. One employee is in the midst of helping a frustrated customer, and the other is a plain middle-aged woman who smiles a big bright-white smile at Mae as we approach.

"You take on Sunshine behind the counter there," I tell Mae, "and I'll go through one of the showrooms and sneak back to talk to the mechanics. They employ tinkers here—I saw it on a plaque on the window outside—and who better to talk to tinkers than me?"

"Another tinker?" Mae replies sarcastically.

"Ha ha."

Mae and I split up—she to gab with the customer service lady with bright-white teeth and me to wheedle some info from some fellow magically inclined Janes and Joes. I walk into one of the showrooms and pretend to be a looky-loo browsing the vintage carriages near the back. The showroom's empty, so there's really no need for pretending.

I wander through an employee-only door, which lands me right where I want to be: in the maintenance bays with the scents of old grease, paint, and ten thousand opened bottles of nail-polish remover. I'm surprised no one's even noticed me considering I'm where I don't belong. The men and women are all busy working spells and fixing engines and tires and such. Too busy to notice me. I need to just pick one tinker out, but I'm not sure how I'm going to accomplish this. I hope Mae's having better luck.

I notice one of the tinkers trying to repair a rip in a seat inside the tin she's working on. To complete her patch, she's using a repair spell that doesn't appear to want to hold. There's my in!

"Excuse me. If you use a binding spell after the repair spell, it should hold."

"Who are you?" she asks without turning from her work. "You don't belong back here."

"No, I don't." I figure being honest might benefit me. "My name is Dr. Zelda Harcrow. I was looking for a bit of information, if you have it."

"Harcrow?" Now interested, she turns to look at me. "As in Harcrow Alchemy?"

"Yep, that's me. Well, my family anyhow."

"How can I help you?" The tinker stands tall and lanky, with short, spiky jade-colored hair and eyes to match. "How do you do? My name is Cyan."

I shake her hand. "Your name fits you."

"I know. My parents had no imagination."

I go straight for the questions then. "I'm looking for a car that ran me off the road last evening, and I was wondering if any of the tinkers here might have information they could share with me. It was a black enclosed car with dark-tinted windows, about five meters or more long. It was dusk so I can't be sure, but it may have been an FJ four-door."

"We had a couple roadsters come in after being in some type of hard-boiled ride on the thoroughfare last night. I personally didn't work on those, but Gammell—the one working on the Breezer over there—had his hand in one." She waves her hand, calling the fellow tinker over.

Gammell introduces himself. "Got a gasper for a fella?" Gammell's a big guy with a very deep voice that rattles when he speaks. "Whatcha do ya for?"

Cyan hands him a mullein-and-catnip ciggy, which he promptly puts between his teeth and lights. "Gammell, you worked on that red roadster that crashed up on the Industria 2 thoroughfare. You know anything about the tin that caused the commotion? A black four-door tin, possibly an FJ?"

Gammell takes a long drag from the gasper and speaks as the smoke drifts from his mouth "Yep, sure did. Heard there was some kinda chase going on. Well, seems to have caused a bit of a panic. Whatsit to ya?"

"This is Dr. Harcrow from Harcrow Alchemy," Cyan answers with a growl, "and she's looking for the black car."

"My cousin Quilligan works over at your place," says Gammell. "Likes it quite a bit, he does."

I smile. "Yes, I know Quilligan. He's a good tinker—just got a promotion last string. So what's the dope on the tins?"

"As I 'eard it from Bob—the manager 'ere. Supposedly this black motor was trying to run some iron off the road last night and bashed into his roadster. This motor runs into our customer and forces him into the guardrail and up a light pole. What a mess." He takes another drag from his quickly burning gasper.

Cyan pushes Gammell. "What about the black piece of tin? Quit beatin' your gums and tell her what she wants to know."

Gammell blows the fragrant smoke in Cyan's face. She coughs and punches him in the arm. "Go on."

"I says to Bob, who the black vehicle belong to? He says the coppers were on it. I says ya, he says ya . . ." He goes on and on. I'm losing patience; this bull doesn't know anything.

"Are you bent?" Cyan punches him in the arm again. "Tell the lady what she wants to know!"

"I was getting there," he says, rubbing his bruised arm.

"Yeah, the long way," she replies.

"Fine." He huffs. "Anyways, Bob—ya know, the manager? I says to him, did they get a look at the guys?"

"And . . . ?" This guy is a horrible storyteller.

"He says no, but they got a good look at the carriage."

"Really?" Now we're getting somewhere. It's begun to feel like the longest fishing trip ever.

"Yeah, so I says, what it look like? And he says, it was a black four-door sedan-type motor with dark windows." He takes another drag from the tiny butt of the gasper before throwing it to the floor and stamping it out.

I'm disappointed. I already knew this. Jeepers, I lived through it. "Well, thanks. I was hoping for more."

Gammell smiles. "Oh, there's more."

"Tell her the dope." Cyan goes to hit him in the arm again, and he flinches.

"So I says to Bob, that's all they gots? Bob—you know, the manager?"

I roll my eyes a bit. "Yes, the manager."

"He says that the hood ornament was a funny shape, like a fish girl with wings. I says, I know them tins!"

"Gammell, you know who the vehicle belongs to?" I can't believe my luck.

"Sure do. I grew up over in Portafaran Fisc. My family are fishermen by trade. Me, I showed promise with mechanical stuff and a little magic, so they sent me to apprentice as a tinker. In fact—"

I'm ready to punch him myself, and not in the arm! "Gammell!" both Cyan and I yell. We raise our voices so loud that the rest of the tinkers stop their work for a moment and stare at us.

"Whatcha lookin' at? Go 'bout your business," Gammell yells at his fellow workers. "As I was saying, being from Portafaran Fisc, I recognized the hood ornament."

"You don't say?" I ask, encouraging him to give up the goods on the black motor.

"It really isn't a fish lady with wings. It's more kinda like a—" He's drifting on the waves again, so Cyan punches him in the arm. He flinches and takes a step away from her. "Yea, yea, yea, I know. Cut to it. Anyways, theys got a whole fleet of them FJs, they does. All for their executive types, and sales folks, they gets to drive them."

"Who, Gammell? Who owns this fleet of black vehicles?" I don't think I can take much more. This conversation is becoming a nightmare.

"Oh, didn't I says? Jeepers, sorry about that," he apologizes without giving me the name again. I can't get a straight answer out of this sap. I give him a bit of an *And?* look. Cyan punches him again. "*Ow!* Stop it, will ya?"

Cyan acts like she's going to punch him again; she fakes him out and he flinches. That Cyan's a tough cookie. "The name of the company, you dope."

"Fischers and Sons in Aulde Portafaran, on the docks." He rubs his sore arm. "They're an import-export company; been around for over fifty rotations."

"I'm familiar with the company. I'll check it out. Thanks, Gammell, I appreciate your help. Yours too, Cyan." I give her a wink. "I couldn't have gotten the info without you."

"Not a problem, Dr. Harcrow."

"Please, call me Zelda."

"Zelda, it is. And don't mind my husband here. He may seem like a bit of a palooka, but he's a good man."

Husband? I almost fall over at the revelation. I try not to show my bemusement as I bid them farewell and go off to find Mae.

"Hey!" Cyan calls me back. "How about that binding spell?"

I'm happy to oblige. Mae and Fischers and Sons can wait a few more minutes.

Chapter Ten

The lobby of the garage is empty when I return, except for the two employees behind the counter. Mae is nowhere to be seen. I step out through the double glass doors and peer around. I spot Mae across the street at the trolley stop, waving her hand wildly at me. I wave back and cautiously cross the uneven cobbled street to meet her.

"Well?" she asks. "How did you fair?"

"Not bad. I got the name of—" I'm about to tell her of my windfall of information when she cuts me off.

"Our reservation at the Facere is in a few minutes, and I am starving," she quips. "Let's go over our notes with some iced mint tea and lovely sandwiches."

"Sounds good. Here's the trolley." I step down from the curb, waving my hand wildly.

Facere Tearoom is an elegant restaurant where ladies and gents gather in the afternoon for light lunches and fashion shows. In the evening, the tearoom offers a heavier fare and features a live orchestra that plays delicate music in the background. The vaulted ceilings feature arches that meet square columns, dividing the room with massive gold-leaf sconces shaped in the form of iris flowers.

We're seated at once beneath one of the arches. Gold-leaf-covered wood shapes vertical vines cascading down the columns and glimmering in the glow of the surface-mounted lights. I peruse the menu while models dressed in the latest fashions stop by to give us a turn and tell us tidbits about their outfits.

I'm glad for the distraction from the drama that has entered my life.

Mae immediately orders a pot of herbal-infused mint tea and two blue crystal glasses filled with ice. I take a long sip of tea and direct my attention back to the menu.

Mae's face sours. She tosses the menu onto the table, which is all dressed in white linens to contrast with the black lacquered table and chairs. "Well, everything on the menu seems a bit ordinary."

"They have a salad. Roasted salmon and freshwater prawns over aquatic nasturtium drizzled with a spicy citrus rose dressing."

She yawns. "Typical."

"How about sandwiches?"

Mae waves her hand as if she were swatting at some bug.

"They have roast gammon with mustard seed paste."

"How common. Jeepers, Zelda, I hope the fashions are better than the fare."

"Well." I point to the menu. "There's a Gallus egg with aioli and aquatic nasturtium nestled in a taro root roll. How about that?"

"Darling, you must be joking. I am appalled at this menu. I shall starve!" Like a hot-air balloon leaking air, Mae slumps back into her seat.

"They have cake!" I say, trying to cheer her up. "We could have cake for lunch."

"Darling, how I adore you! Cake, it is!" Mae squeals.

As we wait for our so-called lunch to be brought to our table, we sip our tea and enjoy critiquing the clothing being modeled.

"Well, this looks interesting." Mae leans forward as a dress glides over.

"Number 28," begins the bean-pole model in a high, whispery voice. "This elegant dinner frock by Flap Designs features a low-draped neckline, a handkerchief hemline"—she twirls around—"a drop waist gathered at the abdomen with a ruby buckle that complements the maize spider-silk fabric and matches the buckles on the low-heeled dress pumps." The flatsy finishes with a smile and moves on to the next table.

"I don't like the color," I critique.

"Of course not. It practically matches your skin. Even on my darker skin tone, it would look bland." Mae adds, "The new Autumn Solstice colors are a bit drab."

"I could use it to camouflage. I could let my hair go natural gold, and I would just be one big—"

"Bale of hay!" Mae finishes. She snorts.

Another model glides our way. "Number 30 by Dinner at Eight. This beaded coral party dress can go from dinner to dancing."

I look at Mae. "I found out who owns the car."

The frail model, who doesn't look like she's ever eaten dinner herself, continues. "The drop waist gathers at the left hip in a lovely rosette and the rose design continues in the beading."

"What car?" Mae quizzes me as she turns her attention to the model. "What is the rear view, dear?" Mae gestures for the model to turn around. "What happened to 29? Did we miss her? Or are we out of order?" Mae cranes her neck to see around the restaurant.

The model turns slowly. "Worn with a turban or a beaded hair-net, this number will be the life of the party."

Mae dismisses her and waves over a male model. "Just give us a turn, dear."

The model, in his skinny pants, tight sweater, and driving cap, is about to begin his spiel when Mae waves him away. "Beat it, fella."

He gives Mae a nasty look, sticks out his chin, and struts on over to another table.

"So, what did you find out?"

"Supposedly, the car is one from a fleet of FJs Fischers and Sons owns on the island." I take a sip of my tea.

"Says you!" Mae replies in disbelief.

"On the level," I assure her.

"Why would someone at an import-export company want to bump you off, darling?" She pours out more tea.

I shrug. "I'm all balled up about this one, Mae. It makes no sense."

The waiter finally arrives with our cake. I take one bite and make a face. "It's dry." I slump back hard in the black lacquered chair.

"This joint is going downhill. And how!" Mae pushes her plate away as the next model floats our way.

"What did you get from the Jane at the repair shop?" I ask Mae as the model twirls in front of our table.

Mae ignores the model. "Well, other than that she wants to get to know me better?"

The model continues her speech about the style, color, and designer of her pantsuit. I just talk right over her. "So, she's a bit stuck on you, huh? Wants a little cash and a chance to pet the chassis, does she?" I tease.

The model moves on to the next table and another one sticks itself in front of us.

"She may look like a plain Jane, but she's a bearcat!" exclaimed Mae.

That model leaves, and another replaces her.

"Did this vamp give up any information?"

"Well, she thought she heard Bob—whoever that is—"

"The manager," I inform her.

"Yeah, him. She said that the vehicle in question may have been stolen."

"Bushwa!" I whisper.

"Yes, stolen. Now, I don't know how true it is. I think we should find out."

I stand up. "To Fischers and Sons?" I ask, putting my clutch under my arm.

"To Fischers and Sons," Mae confirms as she stands as well.

"Mae?"

"Yes?"

"I'm hungry," I whine. "Before we start investigating, could we stop at Arthur's Bistro for some fish and chips?"

Mae laughs and nods. "Now you're on the trolley! Let's go!"

We leave the table while another model is still attempting to present another mop-styled dress. I'll have to remind myself not to come back here for lunch again; leaving a restaurant hungry is not a good sign and definitely bad for business. Time for some real food and answers. I head out the door, arm in arm with Mae.

Chapter Eleven

"Doc!" a deep voice calls out.

Shit. "Inspector and DSI—"

"Flynn," the young DSI finishes.

"And *what* do we have here, darling? Do introduce me," purrs Mae.

"Inspector Greyson and DSI Flynn, may I present Miss Mae Griffin."

The inspector tips his fedora and shakes Mae's hand. The DSI takes a big gulp of air, no doubt in awe of Mae and her last name, and then shakes her hand. I give the inspector the once over, and yep, he's still damn good looking. I sigh. Now what?

"How do you do, Miss?" the inspector asks Mae.

"I do just fine, darling." Mae smiles slyly.

"Oh, boy. Come on, Mae. Let's go. I am starving." I shove Mae toward the trolley stop.

"But you just came out of a restaurant." The inspector looks a little perplexed.

"Oh, darling, the food was just ghastly, and the fashions weren't much better," Mae responds.

"Come on!" I grab Mae's arm and start dragging her along.

The inspector and his sidekick follow. "Doc, I have a few more questions for you."

I figure by now he has all the information on the car and has heard about the explosion in my lab. I really don't want to talk with him now, especially not out here, not without my brother, and not on an empty stomach.

"Not now, Inspector." I see the trolley coming out of the corner of my eye. I don't plan to wait for it to stop. "Maybe later, after I finish shopping, okay? Meet you at HA."

I grab Mae and give her a good tug. She looks at me and nods; she knows exactly what I have in mind. We jump on the moving trolley near the front of the car. The inspector and the DSI, surprised by our sudden departure, run and jump up on the back. As they jump on, we jump off and grab a trolley heading the opposite way. The trolley we've boarded will take us the long way around to the bistro. However, the ride will be peaceful with no nosy coppers. Smile.

"What was all that about?" asks Mae as we locate a seat on the trolley near the back.

"He came a-knocking last night, asking questions about the situation on the Industria 2."

"And . . . ?" Mae winks.

"Needless to say, I didn't tell him anything and played the dumb Dora." My stomach is growling. "Are we close to the bistro yet? I am dying of starvation here."

"Jeepers, Zelda, and you say I'm melodramatic. It should only be a few more minutes 'til we get to our stop. Tell me more about this dreamy inspector detective of yours."

"He is not *my* inspector. I'm sure the drones flying around picked up the chase on the thoroughfare last night and that's how he found me. I bet he found out about the explosion too."

"Darling, I know you're hungry, but biting my head off isn't going to satisfy your tummy. Or my sense of humor."

"I am so sorry-ski. Forgive-ski me?" I beg in a high babyish voice and bat my eyelashes.

"I forgive-ski you, my best-ski friend-ski." She mimics my silly baby voice and makes a goofy face. We both are laughing so hard at our own silliness that we almost miss our stop.

Arthur's Bistro at the Rivulet Mall is one of many Arthur's Bistros throughout Tesla. Arthur's is owned by a parent company that leases the bistros out to individuals to run and turn a profit. The menu is the same in all the bistros, except for a delicacy or two, depending on the region. When I was in northern Tesla, they had a mussel chowder that is only served in the Arthur's Bistros up in that region. Here in Rivulet, Fulcrum, and the surrounding cities, the menu is simple: battered, dipped, and fried white fish and prawns, deep-fried terra potatoes, fried masa nuggets, apple or citrus curd turnovers, and a choice of flavored sparkling waters. The food isn't fancy, but it's good and filling and I'm looking forward to sinking my teeth into the warm greasy, crispy goodness.

"Thank the stars we made it. Let's go in and order," I suggest.

"Right behind you, darling."

The quaint bistro is small and smells of burned grease and fish. The inside has an order-and-pick bar in the rear and deep-green upholstered booths lining each wall. Outside, they have additional seating in the form of little tables and chairs under green umbrellas. Mae and I choose to eat inside, even on this pleasant turn, so it would be difficult for the inspector or anyone else to spot us. Mae finds a booth available near the rear, and we sit and wait until our order is up.

"It's getting late. I'm going to have to stop by and see Ephron before driving over to the barrier island to investigate Fischers and Sons."

"Food!" Mae claps her hands together as a smart-looking man in an Arthur's Bistro uniform delivers our fish and chips. Mae takes a bite from her fish and smiles. "Mm . . ."

We sit in silence while we devour our fish. Finally, the conversation continues as we nibble on our chips and sip our fizzy drinks.

"So," Mae says in between bites, "after this, we head back to HA, you have your meeting, and then we head on over to the docks."

"Yes. Oh! I should drop my tin back at my place. Unless you would like for me to drive?" I ask in hopes she will take me up on the offer.

"No, I'll drive."

I cringe at the thought of Mae behind the wheel again. "Are you sure?"

"Absolutely! I don't mind driving, plus we'll get there faster if I drive." Mae smiles and I cringe again.

"Okay, fine, you drive. Just try not to kill us."

Mae sticks her tongue out at me. "Dry up. My driving isn't that bad. Now, back to the subject at hand; tell me about the inspector."

"The inspector is not the subject at hand; the black car is, remember?"

"Is he married?"

"No." I take a sip of my drink.

"Is he engaged?" She pulls the straw from my mouth.

"No," I say, grabbing the straw back.

She takes the straw and bends it. "Do you like him?"

"Change the subject, Mae," I demand as I wave for a new straw.

She steals a chip from me. "Fine. What about his DSI?"

"Stop it, Mae. I am not looking for a relationship." I push my plate of chips toward her because that's what chips are for: sharing with your best friend, even if she is being a pain.

Mae pats my hand. "Zelda, it's been three rotations. It's time to get back out there."

I know Mae loves me; I know she wants what is best for me. But . . .

"Can we talk about this later?"

"Yes," Mae agrees, "but I'm holding you to it. Now let's get you back to HA."

I finish my fizzy. "Sounds good."

Waiting for us outside the bistro is the intrepid Inspector Greyson and his stylish DSI.

"Nice trick," he says.

"I needed to eat."

"I would have bought you and Miss Griffin lunch." He smiles. Jeepers, he's handsome! And the mind needs to stay focused.

"I have to go; I'm late." Yet I just stand there not moving. Thank the stars for Mae. She grips my arm like a vise, and we begin hoofing it toward the valet station two blocks away.

"Doc," the inspector calls after me, "you are going to have to talk to me sooner or later. You can't ignore me forever."

"Just keep walking, darling," Mae whispers as we walk arm in arm. "If he wants to ask questions, he can ask Ephron."

The inspector and DSI Flynn apparently decide to hotfoot it on up to us to continue the questions.

The inspector directs his first question to Mae as the four of us walk. "Miss Griffin, I'm sure you're concerned for your friend's safety, right?"

"I always am, darling," Mae quips.

"So, help me out here; help me keep her safe. Tell her to cooperate," the inspector insists.

"Darling, never tell a Griffin what to do. You want Zelda? Then, darling, that's something for you to figure out." Mae's words are purposeful, and I respond with a sharp look.

The inspector fumbles with his words. "I, uh . . . want, uh . . . wait, uh—I think you misunderstood."

This whole time his poor dressed-to-the-nines DSI is cantering along beside us, trying to take notes.

"Doc, the Safety Council has asked me to investigate—not just the road incident but also the explosion!"

I stop in my tracks and turn toward him. "If you want to investigate, go right ahead. I however have nothing more to add to what you already know." I turn back around and walk to the curb to wait to cross the street.

"Listen. If the National Security Council gets involved, I won't be able to help you, Doc." I can feel him searching for just the right buttons to push. I'm not going to let him sway me. This is a company matter and a personal one for me to solve. Plus, who does he think he's kidding? He's most likely working on behalf of the NSC. So I push my way to the curb to put a small crowd of people between myself and him. Getting a wee bit separated from Mae, I crane my neck to try to spot her within the small congregation of folks waiting to cross the cobbled street.

"Mae!" I call.

"Zelda! Over here!" A white-gloved hand pops up and waves.

There she is! "I'll meet you at the valet desk," I call out.

This intersection is busy at this time of turn; more trolleys run people back and forth between their destinations throughout the mall. The first trolley goes by, then one more, and then we'll be able to cross and get the stars out of here. I can feel the inspector moving closer to me. I also feel another presence—one next to me. I look over to see a round face, a bowler hat, and then the front of a *trolley*! I stumble a bit but manage to stay on my feet.

I hear Mae scream—or is that me? As quickly as I was pushed in front of the trolley, I'm thrown away from it to the hard cobble and safety—or should I say tackled onto them?

I hold on tight to my savior and bury my head in his chest with my eyes closed. My hero grabbed me and held me tight to his body, so when we landed he took the brunt of the fall. Which is a good thing since my pants are light in color and show dirt way too easily. We lie there together for a bit. I'm breathing hard and need to calm down. The curbside crowd is now gathered around us.

Then I hear, "Oh, Zelda! Darling, are you hurt?" It's Mae.

The next thing I hear makes me jolt my eyes open and my head up.

"Sir, are you and the doctor all right? Should I call this in?" a vaguely familiar voice asks.

As I look up, I see my hero: Inspector Chance Greyson. "Oh, boy," I whisper.

Inspector Greyson keeps holding me tight as though he thinks I'll fall into a million pieces if he lets me go. For the moment, I don't mind. I like the way he feels, and damn, he smells good: like starch and heavy musk. Then I come to my senses.

"Are you hurt, Doc? Did you see who did this?"

"Yes—no—I mean . . ." I push myself free of his hold. It's very disquieting to feel so safe in his arms; I don't even know him. "I, uh . . . I fell," I finish.

"You fell." He doesn't believe me. Of course, it's a lie, so why should he believe me?

DSI Flynn has dispersed the small crowd and asks his boss once again if he should call it in. Mae's helping me to my feet and checking me over to make sure nothing's broken. Inspector Greyson and his DSI share a few words as the inspector gets to his feet and brushes himself off. He then directs us over to the valet area to get us out of the middle of the street and to ask us further questions.

He begins interrogating me. "So you say you fell. That's a pretty long way to fall to get to the part of the street where you were. Are you sure you weren't pushed?"

"I fell and I, uh . . . I stumbled," I lie.

He puts his hands around my waist and pulls me to face him. "Doc—"

Mae interrupts. "Darling, if she said she fell, she fell." Mae takes my upper arm and pulls me toward her before chastising the inspector. "Now I would like to get her back to HA to be looked at. Who knows what damage was done by those cobblestones!"

"Mae will drive me back," I assure him. "I'm fine."

"Let's go," Mae says, and we head over to the valet attendant to get her motor.

"Please reconsider your story, Doc." The inspector calls after us. "I can't protect you if you won't let me".

Mae's Jasper arrives, and we hop in. I look over at the inspector, and I can see the frustration on his face.

"So, you fell?" Mae asks. She's taking it easy on the driving. Crap, she must be worried.

"Nope," I answer.

"Pushed?" She gently turns out onto the road.

"Yep."

"Futz," she curses.

"Yep."

"Did you see the torpedo?" She's direct.

"Yep."

"And . . ." She waits for me to respond.

I finally break the small silence. "Bowler Hat Thug."

"Bowler Hat Thug," she repeats.

"Yep."

"You are going to have some nice-sized bruises," she comments.

"Yes, I am."

"St. John's wort," she recommends.

"Works like a charm," I agree.

Her voice goes soft. "Let's get you to HA."

I nod. "Arnica might work better."

"Yes, but I like St. John's wort better."

"Why?" I ask.

"I don't know. Just do." I see that Mae's eyes are full, and she gives a little sniff.

We sit in silence for the rest of the drive to HA. As Mae drives into the parking garage, she breaks the silence. "That was scary, Zelda."

I solemnly step out of the Jasper. "Yep."

Chapter Twelve

"Well, you'll live, Dr. Harcrow." Healer Vaidya's golden eyes twinkle as she smiles at me. "You'll be sore and bruised, though."

"Jeepers, I'm sore already. I feel stiff all over."

Healer Vaidya hands me a tube of white cream. "Arnica cream. It should help with not only the bruising you'll experience but also the stiffness."

"Thank you."

"Also, here's a white willow bark, chamomile, and St. John's wort tea. It'll ease the pain and discomfort and relax your muscles. You can add a little stevia to sweeten it up if you'd like." She pushes her jet-black hair behind one ear.

Healer Vaidya is not only the most talented of healers; she is a stunning beauty. Originally born in Baekeland, she came to Tesla at a very young age. It was a coup for HA to snag such a highly prized healer and magus.

"How often should I drink the tea?"

"It's very relaxing, so I would suggest you only use it when needed and in the evening. You can use the arnica cream as often as you like, though. Just massage it into the area of discomfort. It only takes a few minutes to start working."

I want to go see Clover, but the nurse and medical intuitive are in with her, so I'll have to come by later. I must remember to ask her about her young man.

We take the lift to the main floor; I'm too sore to manage the steps. We head into the executive offices to meet with my father and Ephron. Just wait until I tell them the latest. They're not going to be happy; in fact, they'll probably hire me a bodyguard. I wonder if the Employment Council even has bodyguards to hire out. Jeepers, if their idea of executive assistants are any indication of what they might have in the way of bodyguards for hire . . . crap, I'm dead. Literally.

I take a deep breath. I'm getting way too far ahead of myself.

Mae pats my shoulder. "Darling, relax. You're fine, and we'll find Bowler Hat Thug."

"Okay, Mae, say we find Bowler Hat Thug. Then what?" I am curious about what crazy plan she's come up with.

"I'll let you know," she quips.

"Gr-eat. I look forward to finding out." I shake my head as we pass the now-vacant secretarial desk and enter Ephron's office through already-open doors.

"Hello?" I call out.

Ephron turns his well-worn high-backed swivel chair around. "Zelda, Mae, how was lun—jeepers, Zelda, what happened to you? You look like you were hit by a truck."

"A trolley," Mae corrects.

"*What?*" Ephron stands up and strides around his desk toward me.

"Not quite," I say. "*Almost* is more like it."

"Sit down, sit down. By the stars, now what happened?" Before I can answer, he gets on the horn. "Yes, let me speak with my father." There's a brief pause. "You better come to my office. There's been a development." Another brief pause. "No, the development is in my office." Another pause. "No, Zelda." Yet another pause. "She's fine, I think." He looks at me as he pauses again. "Okeydokey." Ephron hangs up, still looking at me. "Father will be here in a moment."

Titus Harcrow enters—or should I say runs into?—Ephron's office, the worry on his face speaking volumes. He grabs me and gives

me a long hug. Of course, I'm aching all over, so it's a painful but necessary hug.

"I'm okay, Father," I assure him as I ease out of his fatherly vicelike grip. "I promise."

"You're going to come home and stay 'til this is all over. Understood?"

"Father, I have a home of my own," I protest. "I'm safe there."

"No, you have an apartment. Your home is with your family, and
I insist you stay at the house."

"Fine. After the meeting, I'll go to my place to grab some things.
I'll be over in the evening." Behind my back, my fingers are crossed.

"I'll call your mother and fill her in," he says. "Make sure you arrive in time for dinner."

"I'll look after her 'til then, Titus," Mae guarantees.

"So," Ephron says, "spill, dear Sister. Tell us exactly what happened."

"Don't we have a meeting?" I ask, trying to avoid the interrogation.

"Yes, but it can wait for a few minutes," Father responds.

So I tell Ephron and Father in detail about Bowler Hat Thug and
the inspector. I leave out, however, the part about Mae and me investigating. I figure if my father knew I was looking into the explosion
and the thoroughfare incident, he would tell Mother. She would no
doubt read the cards, lock me in my old room, and hide the key.

"I remember he looked at me," I start. "He was shorter than me,
but muscular."

"What color were his eyes?" Mae asks.

Ephron looks at her, confused. "You didn't see him, Mae?"

I answer. "Oh, didn't I mention? We were separated."

"Please continue," Father requests.

"His eyes reminded me of onyx beads," I tell them.

"Hair?" Ephron asks.

"I don't think he had hair, at least not anything I could see. I'm not sure. He had very thick, bushy eyebrows, though. Red like bricks, dark."

"Anything else?" Mae asks. "Like what was he wearing?"

"Jeepers, I didn't notice. Except for the hat; he wore a black bowler hat." That's all I can recall.

"I'll inform the security team here to keep a vigilant watch for him and see if any of the employees remember him," Ephron says.

"Call the Safety Council and update them," Father says. "I want your sister safe; do you hear?"

"It may throw up some red flags with the NSC." Ephron has started making notes on a small pad.

"Well then, dear boy, do it in such a manner that it doesn't raise any red flags, or anything else for that matter. Blame the Safety Council themselves or the local Legere Legalis or the NSC. I don't care, but I want this goon caught and Zelda safe." As he speaks, Father wrings his hands.

"Yes, sir" is the only response from Ephron.

Titus is usually such a jovial, scattered genius of a man. He's always happy, or at least he always seems happy. Not now, though. Not this time. I don't remember the last time he was this upset. "Let's go," my father says quietly. In silence, the four of us file out of Ephron's office and walk to the main conference room.

The main conference room is stylish yet simple, decorated in beige, crème, maize, and chocolate with white floor-to-ceiling marble paneling that dwarfs all who entered. The long chestnut conference table sits in the center of the room, and a massive starburst-shaped glass chandelier hangs above it. There are thirty matching wooden-backed chairs that encircle the oblong table, and all of them, I know, will be filled during this meeting.

Since there are no windows in this conference room, considerably large, square beveled mirrors hang on every other marbled wall paneling. A nice-sized brass beverage cart hides in the front corner, featuring decanters of brightly colored fermented beverages of all sorts and a carafe of hot ginseng tea. I'm thinking I could use a nice fermented beverage about now.

Someone must be a mind reader because at my chair, to the right of Ephron's at the head of the table, is a short yet very full glass of amber liquid with two cubes of ice swimming inside. I smile as I sit down, take a sip, and let the stinging warmth cascade down my throat. I immediately feel the effects of the alcohol on my blood vessels as they relax. Across from me is my father, and on my left is Mae's father.

"Ah," I say, raising my glass toward him in a small toast. "My booze fairy."

The larger-than-life Poppy—otherwise known as Andrew Pierpont Griffin, or A.P.—looks at me. "My dear girl, you look worse for wear. My, my."

"Yes, I have looked better," I agree and take another sip.

"I apologize for our tardiness," my brother begins. "We have had another incident." He looks in my direction, and great, now the whole table is staring at me. There are Professor Ferrum, Dr. Ravenscroft, and their right-hand assistants—whose names I honestly cannot remember. Also attending the meeting and staring at me are the rest of HA's alchemists: Isaac Hermes, Zhang Ostanes, Steven Zozimos, Marie Louise Jewess, Abru Gebber, Dianne Prima, and Winnie Elricki and a few of their assistants. Feeling like I'm in a fish bowl, I shoot my brother a dirty look. He gets the message and moves the meeting forward.

I gulp down the rest of my amber liquid. Okay, maybe it's more like I belt it down.

"We will be putting Dr. Zelda Harcrow on a temporary leave," Ephron announces. "As of today, there have been four separate attempts on her life."

My spine straightens, and I can feel the blood rushing to my head. How dare they put me on leave! I have important projects to complete. I clench my hand around the glass of ice. Who could possibly continue my work? I can't believe it! My body shakes. If I'm unable to work—

A.P. places his large meaty hand over mine and pries the empty glass out of my grasp. Everyone around the table starts whispering to one another.

"Please, let me continue," Ephron speaks up, commanding the room. "At this time, we have no idea which project she's working on may have brought on this sabotage. This means that all your projects are safe and still confidential and you should continue your work without interference."

The room was now still, and all attention was on my brother. "Mr. Griffin is here representing our government councils, and he has assured us his entire support. For now, we will suspend one of Zelda's projects and reassign the other two."

Whispers began again, but this time my father spoke up. "I will reassign the other projects, and only I and the assigned alchemist's team will be aware of their involvement. I will also bring in temporary help in the form of a couple of additional scientists and alchemists to pick up any slack and begin any new contracts we may acquire during this time."

"Please be aware," my brother picks up. "Only Titus will be privy to newly assigned projects. The opportunity for leaks should diminish, so if there is any leaking of information, we will know more easily where it comes from. Remember, my fine, talented alchemists, to caution your teams toward secrecy and discretion."

"How will we find out about these changes?" asks Dr. Gebber.

"I will meet with each of you individually in my office after this meeting," answers Father.

"Where are you getting these so-called temporary alchemists?" asks Dr. Jewess.

Ephron grabs this query. "We have calls out to a few of the universities requesting they lend us professors who specialize in the fields we might need.

"If there are no more questions," Ephron finishes, "then I need to speak privately with Mr. Griffin." He excuses himself, and he, Mae, and her father leave the conference room.

All eyes turn to my father now. "As for the rest of you, please wait here in the conference room. I will have Dottie bring you into my office, one at a time. Please enjoy the refreshments on the beverage cart; I had them brought in especially for you."

As I follow my father out of the conference room, I overhear one of the alchemists remark that he's never seen Titus so serious. I silently agree.

I follow my father back into the executive office suites. Dottie, Father's longtime assistant—too bad Ephron isn't as lucky with assistants—is sitting at her desk, waiting for instructions from her boss. Better known as Dottie, Dorothy Spot is a sweet chubby older lady with keen eyesight and dull gray hair. I've known Dottie my whole life, and I love and respect her. She runs a tight ship, keeps my father organized, and sometimes works hand in hand with my mother to make sure good old Titus is eating and getting home at decent hours.

"Good afternoon, Zelda," Dottie says.

"Good afternoon," I reply. Dottie is efficient and has no time for jibber-jabber, as she calls it. Her niceties go as far as *good morning*, *good afternoon*, and *good evening*. She's focused and takes her job seriously.

"I'll let you know when I'm done, Dottie," Father says as he leads me into his office. He closes the door behind us. "Have a seat, my child."

"Yes, sir."

Titus's office is a messy twin to my brother's. I sit in an oversized leather chair and sink into its old, worn seat. He sits beside me in the matching chair that faces his desk.

"First off, are you all right?"

"Other than some bumps and bruises, I'm fine. I went to see the healer before I came upstairs."

"Okay," he says, "now what about this inspector I keep hearing about?"

I look at him curiously. "What about him?"

"How are you involved with him?"

"*What*?" I lean forward. "What gives you such an idea?"

Father smiles. "It seems he's taken an avid interest in you, that's all."

"I'm not sure what you mean." I truly am perplexed.

"Well, maybe I'm wrong. Of course, I was hoping for another alchemist for you. It has been rotations since . . ." His eyes go blank and his voice trails off.

I shake my head. "There's nothing between me and the inspector. I'm just . . . can we not talk about this now?"

"Zelda, hiding behind your work here, or whatever it is you do to avoid living, isn't going to make you happy."

I cross my arms. "Why not?"

He laughs.

I frown. "What's so funny?"

"Zelda, you have no lab. It'll be strings 'til it's finished. And we're reassigning your workload. How do you think you'll be able to hide in your work when you have none?" He looks at me lovingly. "Take this opportunity to get rest, go to a spa, enjoy. It's time now."

"I love you," I tell him, but I silently refuse to leave Fulcrum or HA. I have nowhere else to go.

He hands me his smartly starched and pressed handkerchief so I can dry my eyes. I have never understood why my mother insists on having his handkerchiefs starched and pressed; they just get balled up and put in his pocket. My father doesn't either, but he loves my mother, so he just goes with it.

"About Clover," I start. "I think we should send her to her parents' in Aladar City to recuperate. If I'm a target, she may be as well. I know I'd feel better knowing she was safe and healing."

"Agreed. I'll have the company purchase her a first-class airship ticket, destination Aladar City."

"Thanks, Father." I get up out of my seat to give him a hug.

He kisses me on the cheek. "Remember, dinner at eight at the house and you are staying with us. No arguments."

I cross my fingers behind my back. "No excuses, I'll be there." As I start for the door, I add, "Should I call Mother?"

"Hmm . . . no . . . better let me. Tell Dottie to get your mother on the horn; I'll talk with her before I deal with everyone else."

I leave his office and give Dottie his directions, for which she starts dialing before I even finish my sentence. I ankle over to my brother's office then, hoping to catch up with Mae.

Chapter Thirteen

"Hey!" I call to Mae as she exits my brother's office and closes the door behind her.

"Poppy is still in there talking with Ephron," Mae says. "They're formulating a plan on how to keep NSC involvement down to minimum."

"Well, that's good." I stop and wait for her to join me. "Now I don't need to investigate."

Mae shakes her head violently. "No, we better speed it up instead." Mae lowers her voice. "Poppy said that if the NSC sends in investigators, then there'll be a complete shutdown of HA."

"Jeepers!" I exclaim. "Why?"

"Shh . . ." She places her finger to her lips. "Procedure," she clarifies.

Dipping my head, I speak quietly. "Did they say what they were going to do?" I take out my munitions and try to fix what's left of my face powder.

"You may not like it—or you just might." She pats my arm. "Let's start toward the garage."

We head on out of the offices and make our way to the lift. Mae seems to be walking a little faster than her usual glide.

"What's the hurry?" I trot to catch up. "And why won't I like A.P. and Ephron's idea?"

She pushes me into the lift. "Come on."

I stumble in before the doors close. "You're not answering my question. Also, I want to stop and talk to Clover before we leave."

When the lift doors open, Mae looks toward the infirmary. "No, you don't."

"Mae?"

"Unplug your roadster, and I'll explain once we get to your apartment. Okay?" Mae pushes me again.

"Stop shoving me!"

I want to stand my ground and get a full explanation as to why she's in such a hurry. Then I see Inspector Greyson and DSI Flynn coming out of the infirmary. I quickly unplug the roadster and start her up.

Industria 2 is clear at this time of turn, so I have an easy time driving to my apartment in Rivulet. I pull into my garage, park, and meet Mae at the curb.

I climb into the passenger seat of the Jasper. "Okay, spill."

I know she gets what I mean: how did she know the inspector was going to be there, even before I could sense him? Mae's only active intentional gift, a.k.a. magic—other than her keen ability to attract any and all, no matter their sex—is her ability to know what a person wants or needs before the person even does. I'm not even sure that's a gift, but it can be handy.

She turns toward me and stares. "Darling, how should I break this to you?"

My head's beginning to pound. "I can't read minds, so quit stalling."

"Fine," Mae answers. "To keep the NSC from starting any formal investigations, Poppy and Ephron have made a deal with the Safety Council to allow the local constabulary to investigate."

"Firstly, how much is that going to cost him, and secondly, is that why I won't be too pleased?"

"Poppy has holdings in HA," Mae says, coming to her father's defense, "and he's involved with the Tesla Space Exploratory Council, so this is important to him, Zelda. He and your brother are only looking out for HA."

I grab her wrists and shake her. "I don't want to squabble over motives. Just answer me."

"He pulled some strings and talked to some people. I don't know how he and Ephron managed it; they just did. I'm not privy to that sort of thing. As for the last question, Inspector Chance Greyson is in charge of the investigation, so you may be seeing a bit more of him." She bites her lower lip as she finishes.

I let go of her and turn away. "Oh, joy."

Mae starts up the Jasper and drives out of the allotment and back onto the Industria 2. We drive up over Industria Island. Once we've passed the island exit, the thoroughfare changes into a four-lane highway that leads directly to Aulde Portafaran. As the highway bridge ends, slower speeds are marked for the sharp turn toward Portafaran Fisc and the straightaway that leads toward the shore and docks. As expected, Mae ignores the slower posted rate of speed. One of these turns, she's going to kill us with her fancy new tin—or at the very least, maim us.

If I were going to see my parents, I'd be taking the first left toward Seaside Village. Instead, Mae drives straight along toward the shore and the docks, where Fischers and Sons is located.

"Let's park and head into the main building and offices." I point toward the pink marbled building. "We'll go straight up to management and ask them about the FJ."

Mae turns into the visitor parking lot. "Are you sure that's a clever idea?"

"If what I believe is true—that the FJ was stolen—then we'll get all the information and maybe even get to examine the vehicle."

I honestly doubt someone at Fischers has it out for me. If they did, then they'd probably just cover it up, lie, and send us on our way anyway. They might try to make a move on me—not that I like the idea—but then I'd at least have information to give to the inspector.

"All right. I like this idea." Mae swerves the Jasper into a parking spot and screeches to a halt.

We exit the vehicle and stroll right into the main headquarters of Fischers and Sons Inc. Mae and I climb the short pyramid of terrazzo stairs to the carved oak doors that are nestled under the decorative arch on the face of the one-story building. We enter the building into a large foyer that leads directly to the reception area. We walk up to the young lady who sits behind the reception station. Around the area are chairs for visitors and tables with literature stacked in upright boxes. They even have a coat rack.

"Hello," I say in the politest voice I can muster. "I need to speak with the person in charge of your fleet vehicles."

"And this is in regards to . . . ?" asks the smartly dressed professional-sounding receptionist.

"To an accident on the—" I start. The receptionist holds up one finger as she answers the switchboard. "Fischers and Sons Incorporated, how may I assist you?"

"Yes, sir . . . no, sir . . . five o'clock, sir . . . yes, sir . . . no, sir . . . I do not have that information, sir . . . yes, sir . . . yes, sir . . . yes, sir . . . no, sir . . . thank you for calling, sir," she finishes.

I lean against the ledge of the reception desk. "One of your vehicles was involved in an incident on one of the thoroughfares last evening. I need to speak with someone about it."

"Any inquiries are to be made to the Fulcrum Legere Legalis or to the Fulcrum Safety Council." The young employee has obviously been schooled on how to respond to inquiries about their company vehicles, so it must mean I'm not the only one who's been inquiring about the FJ. I'll need to come at her another way.

While I'm trying to figure that out, Mae has other ideas.

"Darling girl," she blurts out, "get your management out here now. I demand to talk with them."

"Miss," the receptionist whispers, "please keep it down."

Mae picks up the nameplate on the desk and holds it up. "Cybil, is it? If you want me to keep it down, please tell your boss to come speak with us at once."

Cybil the receptionist grabs her nameplate back from Mae's gloved hand. "Miss, I'll have to ask you to leave. If you don't, I will call security."

I lean over the ledge toward the young Cybil and whisper, "Cybil dear, this is Miss Griffin—A.P. Griffin's daughter?—and she's a bit high-strung. I would suggest calling one of your bosses and just mentioning she's here."

She stands up and slams her nameplate back on the desk ledge. "I'm positive Mr. Fischers won't care who she is, and if you don't leave, I will call security."

"Don't be a flat tire, Cybil dear, and I do hope you have another job waiting. Because if you don't let him know she's here, I can guarantee you'll be out on your fanny." I play along, though it is partially true. Mae could cause a lot of trouble for others if she chose to.

"Well I never!" Cybil says in indignation.

"Never is a long time, darling. Just get your boss on the horn." Mae points at the switchboard with force.

Cybil, the poor bullied receptionist, rings one of the Fischerses. "Mr. Fischers, a Mae Griffin and friend are here to see you about—yes, sir."

I plant my elbow on the ledge and prop my head up on my fist. "Well?"

"Go right in," she says sheepishly. "Mr. Silas Fischers will see you. Second door on the left, down the hall there."

"Thank you," I say. Mae ignores her and glides down the hall with grace toward Mr. Fischers's office.

"Mae, you are naughty," I scold as we approach the executive's door.

"We're in, are we not? Besides, she was getting too comfy with power there behind her switchboard fortress." Mae swings open the door and makes a grand entrance, striking a pose. I follow behind and close the door. I, however, do not strike a pose.

The good-looking young Mr. Fischers greets us warmly. "Miss Griffin, what a pleasure." He puts his hand out, and Mae takes it and gives it a gentle squeeze.

"So wonderful to finally meet you, darling," Mae purrs. "Let me introduce my dear friend Dr. Zelda Harcrow."

"Dr. Harcrow, your reputation precedes you." He shakes my hand with gusto.

"Thank you, Mr. Fischers," I respond, slipping my hand from his and checking my shoulder for injury. "In a good way, I hope."

"Oh, yes. We had your company create for us a new refrigeration system for our warehouse, so now we're able to store goods for delivery for much longer." He smiles and offers us seats. "And please, call me Silas."

"And please call me Zelda," I reply as I sit down. Glancing at Mae, who has draped herself over the other chair, I add, "Silas, we need your help."

"Zelda was the target and victim of your company's stolen vehicle," Mae confides.

"Oh!" Silas exclaims, rushing to Mae's side. "What can we do to help, Miss Griffin? We gave everything we had over to the constables."

I shake my head in disbelief. He's patting her hand and comforting her as if she were the one almost run down.

"Mae," she says, smiling at the handsome man. "Call me Mae, darling."

I butt in. "Silas, I want to know where the tin is now and if any of your employees saw anything."

Without letting his eyes leave Mae's bronze face, he answers, "The FJ in question is in the impound lot of the Safety Council, so I can't help you there. However, the lot attendant who witnessed the theft—you can interview him."

"That would be the berries!" I'm excited; I feel like we're finally getting somewhere.

Silas assists Mae to her feet. "Let me escort you over to the lot, Mae." He takes her arm and wraps it around his.

"Most definitely, darling." Mae bats her eyelashes at her new admirer. They stroll out the door, seeming to temporarily forget about me.

"Zelda darling," Mae calls back to me. "Do get a wiggle on."

"I'm right behind you," I say as I shut the door and follow along.

Chapter Fourteen

S ilas introduces us to a bony young man nicknamed Pike. Pike's a
sweet kid from the local fishing village, Portafaran Fisc. He's
more than willing to offer us any information and help he can. After
all, it was on his watch that one of the company's vehicles was
snatched.

"Sport," Silas booms at his employee. "Tell these two beautiful
ladies everything they need to know about the motor that was pil-
fered and anything else about that turn you remember. Don't leave
anything out!"

"Don't scare the poor thing," Mae says, pulling Silas aside for a
more private conversation.

I wonder what's being said, but the task at hand is to ask the right
questions of this fella. I start with a compliment. "Pike, you seem to
be a darb of an employee, watching over this entire lot by yourself."

He blushes. "Jeez, Miss, yous nice to say soes."

"So . . . tell me . . . did you see the FJ being jacked?"

"Oh, yes sirree, Miss, I did. I saw some thug—short, he
was—getting into one of the tins. I yelled at him and ran over to stop
him." He points toward the lot where the crime occurred.

"Did you catch up to him?" I look in the direction he's pointing,
as if seeing where it happened would make a difference.

"He must have had some kinda master key, Miss; that motor
started right up. And off he went." His hand sails across the lot.

"Did you see what he was wearing? What he looked like?" My
motor's running; finally, we're getting somewhere.

"What he was wearing? Oh, jeepers." He places his hands on his hips and looks to the sky for answers. "I think he was wearing some kinda long trench coat."

I grab his shoulder. "Do you remember what color?"

He looks back at me and nods. "Black as the night, a trench—yeah, and you know what was funny?"

"What was that, Pike?" I shake him a little. Okay, I shake him a lot. I've gotten a little excited. The answers seem so close.

Pike doesn't seem to mind the manhandling. "He had this white scarf wrapped around his neck and the bottom of his face. I thought it was kooky since it was a bit warm yesterturn. And I think he might have been bald, the way he wore that hat of his."

"What kind of hat was that?"

"A black bowler hat," he answers, confirming my suspicions.

So, my Bowler Hat Thug is the torpedo who tried to run me down on the thoroughfare last night. I wonder if he also did my lab and sabotaged my beloved Zenith.

"Didn't the constables ask you these questions?" Pike has acted like this is the first time he's spoken about it to anyone.

"Coppers? They didn't ask noth'n, really. I just answered what those guys asked."

I decide to inquire a bit more. "I see. What else didn't they ask you?"

"Wells, Miss, jeepers. The thief—he was a shadow, Miss. A real shadow. If I hadn't dropped my clipboard, I would never have seen him."

"What do you mean?"

"This thief—thug, yous know—he was like a shadow, yous know. I was scanning the lots with the drone, yous know, and like, I bumped my clipboard and I bents over to get it, yous know, and like, then um . . . I look up and I sees him! I yell, and he looks over at me, gets in the tin, and within seconds—like seconds, I tell yous—he had it started and was gone. Likes a flash, yous know." He waves his hands in the air in front of his face.

"So he had to have had some type of knowledge about motors, then?" Now I know we're dealing with a professional assassin.

"Must have, Miss."

"What time of turn was this?" I need to figure out if the goon had enough time to get to HA to set the bomb and mess with my bike.

"After early morning arrivals."

"Early morning arrivals?"

"Yes sirree, Miss. Yous know, the cargo ships come into the docks and are off-loaded," he says, as if I already should have this information. "Then like, yous know, later like, um . . . the passage ships and submarines come in."

"Do you think this shadow of yours came in on one of the ships?"

"Possibly. I mean, yous know, like . . . well . . . no reason to thinks he did. It's just that . . ." Pike falters.

I understand what he's trying to convey. "He didn't seem to fit here in Tesla."

"Yous got it, Miss! Jeepers, you're a smart gal. Yous pretty keen and has quite a chassis too, if yous know what I'm saying." He shyly smiles and then winks.

Oh boy, the twig's getting all hot and bothered. "Oh, you're pretty swell there yourself, Pike, but I'm not the Jane for you to get stuck on." Maybe I should feel flattered, but he's not my type. Of course, I'm not sure I have a type, but if I did, it wouldn't be him.

He drops his head. "Yeah, I know. Yous too swanky for me."

"That's not what I said, Pike. It's just, I'm always in the lab and you're a Joe who deserves a doll who can give you all the attention you deserve." I have got to remember not to go around pushing witnesses; I might end up getting a marriage proposal.

"Thanks, Miss," Pike says, his eyes half closed. Jeez, he's back to mooning over me.

"Is there anything else you can remember?"

Pike scratches his dirt-colored hair. "Naw, Miss, I can't remember anything else. It was such a crazy morning yesterturn, what with the ships coming in, the cargo being unloaded, the warehouse having some stuff go missing. And of course, I got the FJ jacked, yous know."

"Well, I appreciate all your help. If you think of anything else, you call me, okeydokey?" I hand him one of my business cards, which has my name and the number of Harcrow Alchemy Inc.

He makes eyes at me. "Wow, like, um . . . you're an alchemist?" He speaks as though I'm a celebrity.

"Yes, I am."

"All through, darling?" Mae asks.

"I think we got what we came for," I say, grateful for the interruption.

"Dr. Harcrow, it was a pleasure meeting you." I shake hands with Silas Fischers, who then turns to Mae. "Mae, I am so looking forward to seeing you again."

Mae smiles. "As am I, Silas."

"You'll speak to your father about our conversation?" he asks.

"Of course, darling. Of course." Mae turns and begins to walk away toward her car. Her walk is more of a glide with a small forward tilt of her hips so she sways ever so rhythmically. She's so mesmerizing, even I catch myself staring. Well, that is, until she calls me to catch up.

I try to mimic her walk, but I fall when I trip over my own foot.

"Jeepers, Zelda, just get in the car before you pull something."

Mae pulls on out and drives back to the Portafaran Highway, which she navigates at a good clip while I hang on for dear life. She exits onto Industria Island and takes the small drive to the main road circling the island. Driving along the road that runs parallel to Fulcrum, we head to the Fulcrum Safety Council impound lot, where Silas Fischers informed us the vehicle was being kept.

"So what were you and Silas Fischers talking about while I was questioning the lot employee, hmm?" I wiggle my eyebrows.

"Ugh." She huffs and speeds up. "He's interested in getting out of the family business and into council work. Thinks my Poppy will give him a leg up."

"He wants to get involved in Fulcrum councils? Which one?" I ask, gritting my teeth as she cuts off a motorist.

"No, not Fulcrum—Tesla. He wants to get involved on the national level."

"Really? In which council?" I lean into the curve as she passes another tin.

"Ocean Exploratory Council," she remarks as she honks at another driver.

"You mean the Maritime Council," I correct.

"Nope. There's a new council being put together and the elections will begin next rotation for the Ocean Exploratory Council." She sighs and lays on the horn again in an attempt to get a fellow motorist out of her way.

"Jeez. We have a council for everything. How many more can they come up with? Talk about overkill." I shake my head and clutch the seat for all I'm worth.

"Well, since we're more fully exploring our little universe and looking at colonizing one of our moons, someone decided we should be doing more with our oceans."

"Are they looking at colonizing the oceans? People living under the sea? I don't know about that; sounds a bit hinky." I bite my lip and draw blood as Mae catches the berm trying to get around yet another tin.

Mae sets me straight. "Why, we have ships that travel underwater. People take underwater cruises all the time."

I squeeze my eyes closed tight. "Okay, you have a point. So Fischers wants you to give his name over to A.P.?"

"Pretty much, darling. I have some influence over dear Poppy, but not when it comes to national interests and council positions. But you never know; he may like Silas." She slams on the brake and then just as quickly moves her foot over to the accelerator and speeds up.

My body jerks forward and then back again. "Maybe."

We're just passing HA's direct competitor, Alcazar Alchemy Inc., when I see Clover's beau! He's heading into Alcazar! I scream at Mae, "Mae! Mae! That's him! Pull over! Oh my stars, stop! Stop! Stop!" I keep yelling and slapping her arm.

Mae swerves and cuts off the motor traveling next to us and parks at the side of the road. Of course, it causes a bit of screeching tires, angry voices, and obscene hand gestures, all pointed toward us.

Mae jerks her head in every direction possible. "Bowler Hat Thug? You saw Bowler Hat Thug?"

"No, not Bowler Hat Thug—the boy I saw visiting Clover," I correct excitedly. "I saw him, and he was going into Alcazar."

Mae collapses back into her seat. "What? Start over. You have me all balled up."

"Clover's mysterious visitor in the infirmary—I just saw him going into Alcazar Alchemy. What if it is sabotage?" I pose to her. "And he used Clover to get close to me?"

Mae looks at me. "So do you think Alcazar could be behind these attacks? I know they're Harcrow's closest competitor, but it seems pretty harsh considering the exorbitant amount of time they spend trying to undercut Ephron and buy off company executives."

"Mae dear, jeez, I just don't know. It could be possible, I guess."

"What did Clover say about it?"

"I never got the chance to ask her."

"Jeepers." Mae sighs and covers her eyes.

"I guess when I see her later, I'll find out."

"Promising idea. There's no use worrying about it 'til you have to. Now let's get back on the road and over to the impound lot to look at the biggest clue we do have: the tin."

Mae swerves out into traffic at full speed, changes two lanes, and almost runs over a traffic safety officer, who has been directing traffic. Luckily, he dives out of the way before she can strike him, but there are once again a lot of horn blowing, loud angry voices, and obscene hand gestures directed at us. We don't get much farther, though, before a drone flies into our path, indicating for us to stop. Drones police all of Fulcrum and the surrounding areas, and they're operated by the Fulcrum City Safety Council. Drones operated by the Tesla Safety Council fly higher and don't get involved with local matters, such as traffic violations.

The human sitting in a cubicle somewhere asks through the drone, "Please state your name and reason for reckless driving."

Mae answers dryly. "Mae Griffin, darling, and I wasn't reckless. It's not my fault others aren't skilled drivers. Oh, and darling, why is there some man standing in the middle of the road? Doesn't he know he could cause an accident? I almost hit him. Thank the stars I'm such an excellent driver. You did get my name, right? Mae Griffin?"

I look at Mae in disbelief. I have an incident on the thoroughfare and I get coppers at my door. Mae gets stopped and, well, I bet she'll get an apology.

"I am sorry, Miss Griffin. Please proceed with caution, and I will notify the Safety Council about their officers in the street. Thank you, Miss Griffin." And with that, the drone flies away. Mae starts up the Jasper and away we go, just as fast as before.

My jaw has dropped. "How do you do it?"

"Do what?" she asks, not once slowing down.

"Get in everywhere. Get away with just about everything. How do you do it?"

"Zelda, you do it too—only you don't realize it. It's the name and attitude, of course." Mae tilts her chin up.

"I don't do that," I scoff.

"The Harcrow name carries just as much weight as the Griffin name here in Fulcrum and, believes it or not, all over Tesla. It's just that you have been so unaware of your surroundings. Zelda, Holden has been gone three rotations now. It's time to reenter the world."

"He was my fiancé, Mae, not some stranger. And what are you talking about, anyhow?" I ask defiantly. "Am I not running around trying to solve the mystery of this Bowler Hat Thug who's trying to do me in?"

But my protests can't distract my mind from the topic Mae has broached. Holden Priest was a climate alchemist I met in university—and my fiancé. Three rotations ago, Holden was part of a small group of climate alchemists and scientists sent to study a storm that had been churning and growing for over a rotation in the Southern Ocean. The massive hurricane had been one of several unforeseen weather pattern effects caused by strict weather control across the planet, and they needed to understand it.

But the storm had been worse than anyone expected. Once inside the hurricane, the airship went down. Everyone on board disappeared and was believed to have perished. Rescue attempts were made, but the storm was too dangerous. In fact, one of the airships sent in for a rescue attempt was lost as well.

It hadn't been the first time Weather Workers caused a disaster, but ever since, the Weather Council has limited how much and what kinds of weather are allowed to be controlled. Every country on Gaia, apart from Hyde, has adopted similar policies to avert any more such tragedies.

But such policies could never bring me back Holden. His loss cut me deeply. I had hoped for so long that they would find him; instead, I was left with a hole in my soul.

Mae's voice brings me sharply back to the present. "Yeah, and it only took someone trying to blow you up, tampering with your Zenith in hopes of causing you to have an accident, running you off the road, and attempting to have you crushed under a moving trolley to get you to wake up. The universe is screaming at you to join in, Zelda."

"Then why did coppers land at my door when I had the problem on the Industria 2?" I ask, remembering the original reason for this debate. "Why didn't they just say, 'Oh, that's a Harcrow'? Hmm, Miss Smarty Pants?" I finish my argument by sticking my tongue out at her and crossing my eyes.

"Very mature," she comments. "The universe is so concerned you're not getting any sex that it sent a good-looking mug right to your door. Ha!" She sticks out her tongue and crosses her eyes at me, which is pretty dangerous considering she's the one driving.

"Very funny. Watch the road, will you? Right now, all I can hear is the universe telling me that my best friend is going to kill me with her driving."

"Oh, dry up. You're safe. I'm an excellent driver. Besides, we're almost there." She smiles.

We've crossed over the Industria 3 thoroughfare and exited onto the outer marginal road of Fulcrum near Riverstone Allotment, a lower-middle-class allotment filled with cookie-cutter single- and double-family houses, large apartment complexes, and smaller cluster homes. Mae passes under the on/off ramp for the Riverstone Allotment and finds the Safety Council's impound lot. The impound lot holds everything from stolen or abandoned tins and irons to bicycles, boats, and any other machinery that I could possibly imagine.

Mae parks the Jasper in one of the many visitor spaces outside the gated lot. "Okay," she says, shutting off the Jasper and looking at me. "How do we get in?"

Chapter Fifteen

"Well, this will prove a little more difficult. Let me think . . ." I go quiet, close my eyes, and wait. If I meditate with a clear intention, the answer will come. All great alchemists use meditation as a way of developing ideas. In fact, an entire course is dedicated to the subject of meditation in university.

Mae sits silently, knowing my process and how well it works for me. She takes the opportunity to freshen up her lip rouge. I suddenly open my eyes and grin. *I've got it.* I have an idea for how to get in and roam the lot to find the FJ.

"We're going to keep it simple. We'll go up to the attendant and tell her or him how I left my motor in Fulcrum one night and couldn't find it the next turn. You'll flutter your eyelashes and hand them your card. You and your attitude will open those gates for us." I nod toward the towering fortress of thick iron rods.

"That's it?" Mae complains as she closes the Jasper's shiny door. "That's the plan?"

"Do you have a better one, abercrombie?" I straighten my hat from the rollercoaster ride I've experienced to get here.

Mae blows out a long sigh. "Let's go."

We ankle on over to the lot attendant's shack. It's a little stand-alone office with crystal monitors that display the surveillance videos provided by drones that perform reconnaissance around the yard. A sliding glass window stands open, and a pretty girl a bit younger than Mae and I is seated inside on a tall stool behind a narrow counter.

"Hello," I say. "I hope you can help me. I sorta misplaced my motor last night, and I was wondering if I could see if it was here."

The young girl is dressed in a smart deep-lapis uniform with gold buttons shaped in an SC, and she's no chunk of lead, either. In fact, she's water-proof: she has yellow eyes with hints of green and purple and silky gold hair that's been finger waved and gathered in a low bun at the nape of her neck. She sure doesn't look like she belongs here, hiding behind some desk.

"How did you 'lose it' and where?" she asks politely.

"Well, somewhere in downtown Fulcrum, maybe in the theater district?" I lie. "I was at this joint when I got a bit blind. Had my old man drive me home, and by the morning, I'd forgotten where I'd parked the piece of tin."

Mae leans in. "My poor bunny here had me drive her all over Fulcrum. I finally told her, 'Darling, maybe the tin is at the impound lot.' So I brought her here. Do you have a black four-door FJ here?"

The attendant smiles at Mae, who smiles back. The girl blushes, and I step back to let Mae perform her magic. Obviously, the pretty attendant finds Mae fascinating, with her perfectly coiffed hair under her simple gray woven cloche hat. Mae is a stunner and dresses to perfection every turn. Today she's in her sea-foam-green wide-legged pants and a white satin long-sleeved blouse with wide lapels and wide cuffs that she has buttoned low to reveal her collarbone. Mae screams beauty, intelligence, grace, and money. It's no wonder everyone's attracted to her.

Mae leans farther into the tiny booth window. I hear a little giggling, and Mae saying something about giving her a moment. I hear a buzz, and the pedestrian gate next to us opens. Mae pushes me through.

"Darling, you go ahead and find your motor. I'll catch up. Go." Mae winks at me and I go do what she says.

Unfortunately, I'm not sure where to begin. The lot is huge and just filled to the brim with all kinds of machinery. I scan what I can see of the lot. Everything seems a bit haphazard, but there is a subtle pattern to how they store items. Motors—newer, more pricey ones—seem to be kept near the front and off to the left of the lot. I head in that direction to begin my search for the FJ. The vehicles impounded seem to range from very conservative to flashy, and from very bashed in to pristine.

Within a few minutes, I've located the tin in question. I'm a bit surprised I've found it so quickly, but I confirm it's the correct vehicle not only by the hood ornament but also by the dents and scratches. Well, that and the sticker plastered on the windshield by the employees of the Security Council stating exactly whose it is, where it was found, and that it's part of an ongoing investigation.

I'm surveying the outside of the FJ when Mae finally shows up. She slides up next to me. "There you are."

"Here I am," I reply. "See if the driver-side door opens."

Mae goes around the dented vehicle. "Locked."

"So is the passenger side." I peer in through the window. "I need to get in."

She peers through the opposite window at me. "Aren't you going to ask me?"

"About?" I ask while trying out the other doors.

"The lot attendant." Mae tries the trunk.

"I wasn't sure if I wanted to know or if you wanted to tell. Either way, jeez, you helped us get in here; that's all that matters."

"Okay, well, I got us into the lot. Your move—get us into the tin."

"Let me think . . . give me your hatpin." I put out my palm.

"Why can't you use yours?" she asks, obviously not wanting to give up her silver-and-sapphire hatpin.

"I'll need both and a good spell," I explain as I extend the palm of my hand farther out toward her.

Mae covers her pin with her hand. "Can't you use your telekinesis on these locks?"

"I'm not familiar with these locks, so it would take longer than just picking them."

"Fine, here you are." She hands me the very fancy and pricey pin.

I take both pins and place them inside the lock, feeling around for the tumblers. Once I locate the tumblers, I close my eyes, concentrate on the task, and chant the spell aloud three times: "I charge these objects to be my key, to open this carriage, so it shall be."

I move the pins slowly inside the lock and hear a click. With the driver-side door successfully unlocked, I pull on the handle and swing it open.

"Attagirl! Very nice, indeed," Mae compliments.

I take a bow. "Thank you, thank you, and thank you."

I unlock the passenger door, and Mae goes around, checking out the passenger side of the vehicle.

The driver-side floor is damp, almost soaked. There is a strong smell of fish and a sweet, thick aromatic scent of some kind. The wet floorboards seem to have tiny white drying crystals scattered across them. I reach into my handbag and pull out my magnifying glass—yes, magnifying glass; what kind of alchemist would I be if I didn't keep a magnifying glass with me at all times? Mae pops the trunk to take a gander while I examine the tiny crystals.

Suddenly, I feel someone behind me.

"Mae?" My voice wavers.

"No, not Mae," a deep voice answers.

I get up to turn around so fast that I bump my head on the door-frame and fall back into a pair of muscular arms. Wincing, I look up into a pair of sexy blue eyes.

"Inspector. Hello."

"Hello, Doc," the inspector says, "and nice to see you again, Miss Griffin."

The inspector helps me right myself. "Thanks," I mutter.

"Now, Doc, what are the two of you up to?"

"Well . . ." I begin.

Mae thankfully pipes up. "Silas Fischers asked us to look at the motor to see if Zelda could ascertain who may have stolen it. Mr. Fischers is looking for a possible endorsement from my father, but a stolen vehicle involved in a series of thoroughfare felonies brings up security issues."

"And if I call Mr. Fischers, he'll confirm this story of yours?" the inspector asks, challenging Mae.

"I hope you didn't just call her a liar," I whisper to him.

Before Mae has enough time to boil over, the inspector adds, "Thankfully, that won't be necessary. However, ladies, this vehicle is part of an ongoing investigation and is off-limits, even to the both of you."

Mae slams the trunk closed and tilts her head, signaling to me to get a wiggle on. I give the inspector a nod goodbye and join Mae. The two of us hotfoot it toward the gate, where we pass the friendly DSI Flynn trying to make some headway with the pretty little attendant. It doesn't seem to be going too well. I wonder if I should tell him that he's just not her type. Nah, he'll figure it out. We give them a friendly wave and make a dash for the Jasper. Mae looks over at the attendant, gives her a nod and a wink—which are returned in kind—and holds up a bag.

"Where did you get that fringed bag?" I ask. "And where is your clutch bag?"

"Get in," she answers. "I'll tell you on the way back to your place."

After she has pulled out of the parking lot and begun driving, she tells me about the strange fringed bag.

"Darling, Miss Petunia—the lot attendant—she liked my Gabba clutch and seemingly always wanted one. So we made a trade: my bag and a little pet and play for easy access to the lot and her fringed bag."

"I am so sorry, Mae," I apologize—for the bag, not the petting. I can see that Mae enjoyed the attention. "I know it was one of your favorites."

"Darling, that bag was so last season. I just ordered a new one yesterturn, anyway. Besides, her large fringed bag came in handy; look inside." She shoves the bag toward me.

I open the bag and pull out a white spider-silk scarf that smells exactly like the inside of the car! I hold it up and look at it closely. "Mae, where did you get this?"

"It was in the trunk. When the inspector caught us, I shoved it in the bag."

"This is evidence, Mae. You—we could get in a lot of trouble for swiping this."

"Well, it was already in my hand. And I felt something on it—something gritty, almost crusty," Mae reveals.

"Hmm . . ." I take out my magnifying glass again. "It's the same type of white crystals as the ones I saw on the floorboards. Interesting."

"You can take a better look when I get you home. Hey, you're supposed to go to your folks' tonight, right? I better get you back; you can't show up there like this." Mae speeds up, if that's even possible. I could have sworn the tin had already maxed out on speed, but I guess I was wrong.

"Mae, slow down!" I demand and hold onto the dashboard. "I'm going to cancel for tonight. I'm too tired, and I want to sleep at least one more night in my own bed."

"Oh, boy. Ave is going to be sore, darling. I bet you she's already planned the menu for tonight's dinner."

"I'll ring her up when I get in," I say. "Don't worry; she'll get over it."

"I don't think so. I don't remember her ever being understanding about you skipping out on dinner."

"Well," I say, continuing to brace myself against the dash, "I'll have to take the heat for it then because all I want right now is a stiff drink, a warm bath, and an early evening."

"Well, then, let's get you home. We'll discuss all we found out before I leave for the evening, okay?" It's less a question than a command.

"Sounds fine," I agree as a yawn escapes me.

Mae parks the Jasper illegally right in front of my apartment complex. "You know you aren't supposed to park here."

"Pshaw," she responds.

I shake my head. I'm too tired to argue with her. We head up the stairs, where the evening doorman waits for us.

"Good evening, Dr. Harcrow. Good evening, Miss Griffin. How are you this fine turn?" he greets us.

"Fine, Carston, and you?" I reply.

"Do not let her fool you. She is exhausted and has had quite an adventurous turn," Mae interjects.

"It's Carlton, Miss. And I must say, Dr. Harcrow, I would never have figured you for the adventurous type."

"I am full of surprises, Carlton. What about you, though? What types of adventures have you been undertaking?" I politely inquire, hoping to take the spotlight off myself.

He smiles. "Thank you for asking, Doctor. That's very kind of you."

I smile back. "Oh, not at all. What have you been up to?" Mae taps her foot; she has no patience.

"Well, not much. I have been stepping out with this sweet gal." His face reddens. "I think she might be the one."

"How wonderful, Carton—I mean Carlton. Right. I wish you well. You'll have to let me know how it turns out for you." I hand him a tip and climb the stairs to the second floor and my apartment, with Mae following close behind.

"Thank you, Dr. Harcrow!" Carlton calls after us enthusiastically. "Thank you!"

I wave my hand over the lock. Mae and I enter my apartment, and we each take a sofa and plop down with large sighs. I slip off my sandals, pad on over to the cocktail cabinet, and pour us each a large glass of ruby vinum. Walking back over to the lush carpet and comfy sofas, I hand Mae her drink and sit down opposite her. "Cheers," I say and take a long sip of my sweet vinum.

"Cheers," she responds, taking a long sip herself.

"Okay, what have we got?"

"What's with the tête-à-tête with the doorman?"

"I was just being friendly," I respond. "You and my father keep telling me to get my head out my test tubes."

"Darling, you are hopeless. I applaud you for trying, though."

"Thanks, I think." I take another gulp of vinum. "Back to our investigation."

"Okeydokey, let's start at the beginning. First your lab blows up." She raises a finger.

I wave my hand and shake my head. "Wait, wait. Start at Bowler Hat Thug's beginning, instead."

"How do we do that?"

I take another long sip, look at my glass, and decide I should just bring over the whole bottle. I shuffle over to the cabinet. "I think we should extrapolate what we think his movements were based on the information we've collected."

I bring the bottle back to my luxurious shaggy carpet and cozy sofas and pour myself another glass. Mae clears her throat and puts out her glass for a refill as well. With both of our glasses replenished, we're ready to speculate on the torpedo's movements.

Mae begins. "Well, we know the early part of the turn: he stole the car from Fischers and Sons at the dock. We can't assume, though, that he came from that area or that he came in on a ship."

"You're right," I say. "If he works for Alcazar Alchemy, he could have come from Industria Island."

"What next?" Mae asks.

I shrug. I'm too tired to think straight. Then the wireless starts buzzing, and I know immediately who's calling. Picking up the receiver, I say, "Mother, how are you?"

"Why are you not on your way, Zelda?" my mother's voice calls loudly through the receiver.

I pull the receiver from my ear, wincing. "I'm sorry. I was just about to call. I can't come tonight."

"Zelda, this isn't about dinner planning. You are not safe there!" she insists.

"Mother, I have a doorman and locks on my door. Nothing's going to happen to me, I promise."

"I read your cards," Mother states.

"*What*? No! You know I don't like it when you scry or read for me." Ever since she foretold Holden's disappearance, I've refused to let her read for me. I can't face any bad news; for me, obliviousness is the way to go.

"This was not for you, Zelda; it was for me." Mother's voice cracks. "I needed to know what I could do, and the cards said to keep you close."

Mae interrupts the conversation. "Zelda, tell her I'll leave my zephyr shockgun with you for added protection."

I relay the message to Mother. "See? Added protection."

"I would feel better if you were here," she reiterates.

"I know. I love you. Thank you for worrying about me."

My mother sighs on the other end of the line. "Fine, but promise me you'll be careful, you won't leave the apartment, and you'll come stay with us tomorrow."

"You're reading my cards right now, aren't you?" I accuse.

"Yes, yes, I am." I can hear the pride in her voice. "Just do what I ask, Zelda."

"I will do as you ask," I assure her, hoping to relieve her fears.

"I hope you will. I love you. See you tomorrow." I repeat the last back to her before I hang up.

Mae pours another glass of vinum. "Well?"

I hold out my glass. "Fill me up." I'm beginning to feel a little buzzed now. A few more glasses, and I'll be passing out. I take a sip and put my glass on the table. I better slow it down while I can still use all my brain cells.

"Where were we?" Mae asks, following my lead and setting down her glass as well.

"Before the unrivaled Ave Harcrow called?" I slouch down against the back of the sofa.

"Yes. Hey, your mother is just worried, that's all. She has every right to be."

"I know," I say. "But back to Bowler Hat Thug. We have him stealing the FJ in the morning, so he must have come straight to HA."

"Sets the bomb," Mae adds.

"If he was the one who planted it," I agree. "Of course, it's logical that he'd be our bomber."

"Bomb doesn't go off as expected," Mae continues, "so he sabotages your iron while everyone is busy with the explosions and waits."

"That would make sense. Then I fix the bike, so the torpedo tries to run me down," I logically conclude.

"You lose him on the thoroughfare, so he ditches the vehicle on the other side of Fulcrum, according to that impound sticker."

"Okay, so he's failed three times." I pick up my glass for a nice long swallow. "He must not know where I live, because no attempts have been made here."

"Thank the stars for small miracles," Mae says as she puts her feet up on the lounging sofa and looks up at the ceiling.

"He knows where I work. And he must have picked up another piece of tin to follow us to the mall." I slump back down on the sofa. "Bowler Hat Thug is getting desperate."

"Why do you say that?" Mae asks.

"He risked exposure. A bomb, sabotage, and use of a motor as a weapon, and then he gets right up next to me and pushes me? He could have easily been caught exposing himself at the mall. During all the other attempts he was hiding." I look over at Mae, who is still staring at my ceiling.

Mae turns her head away from the ceiling to look back at me from across the table. Her face has gone quiet. I know then that we better solve this and fast. Desperate folk are dangerous folk. He could get sloppy and someone besides me could get hurt.

"Tomorrow, I'll take that scarf to HA and get it under a microscope and take a sample of the spider silk to determine the smells. We need more clues to figure out who this goon works for."

"How will looking at the scarf help?" Mae asks.

"If I can determine where the scarf has been, I'll be able to conclude where the torpedo has been," I explain. "If we know where he's been or know where he lives, then we can give the information to the inspector and he'll be caught."

Mae grabs her glass. "Sounds like a good plan. What about Alcazar Alchemy and Clover's friend?"

"I'll have a conversation with Clover tomorrow when I get into work."

"Isn't she leaving for her parents?" Mae asks. Then, "Wait, how are you going to work if you have no lab and no projects?"

I grab my glass off the table. "I want to go in and check on the reconstruction of my lab. I think I'd like to make a few changes to the floor plan. Of course, while I'm there, I'll see Clover and get this bit on her friend straightened out. As far as I know, she isn't leaving for another turn."

Mae empties the last of the vinum into her glass. "What if Alcazar Alchemy is involved? What then?"

"Then I'll let Ephron know, and we'll let him, Father, and A.P. handle it."

"So we won't know anything 'til tomorrow, then?" She downs her vinum in one gulp.

"Exactly."

"Well then, believe it or not, I have had quite enough excitement for today. I'm going." She puts her shoes back on. "I'll give the shock-gun to your doorman to bring up to you. Do you know how to work it? It's pretty easy: just make sure it's charged, keep the safety on when it's not in use, and if you need it, just point and click."

"Thank you, Mae," I say as I walk her to the door. "For everything today. Be careful driving."

She gives me a quick hug. "That's what best friends are for." With that, she exits through the door.

Chapter Sixteen

I make myself the tea blend Healer Vaidya prepared for me. Then I grab some parchment and a pen and head to my rarely used veranda. I sit down and take a sip of the warm smooth tea before placing it next to me on a small white filigreed iron side table. Looking out on the beautiful sky that's slowly darkening from the setting sun star, I marvel at the stars—millions of kilometers away—presenting themselves one by one. There really isn't a need for streetlights with the way the moons and the billions of stars light up the sky. Even so, the small clear glass-crystal leaves that adorn the iron and steel trees lining the walkways begin to emit a low delicate yellow glow to light the walkways they shade.

I close my eyes and let my mind clear to nothing. I let the emptiness of thought wash over my consciousness.

There it is! A spark, an idea, a formula!

I quickly open my eyes, pick up my pen, and scribble on the parchment paper. I address an envelope to an old colleague. Since I have no clue as to which project is the reason for our current trouble, I need to get this almost complete formula to someone outside of it, someone I can hopefully trust.

Afterward, I stand in front of the icebox, holding the door open and staring at its lack of contents. There are only two prepared meals left and some leftover seaweed salad. Neither choice seems appealing to me, so I head back out to the main living area. I look at the addressed envelope that I left on the entry table. My stomach is swearing at me, and the letter needs to be posted today. I decide to drive over to the marginal road right outside Rivulet Mall, post the letter, and grab some food from one of the small vendor stands that litter the area. Grabbing a blue woolen duster, my hat, my clutch, and the letter, I leave the apartment.

"Carston, I'm stepping out for a few minutes. I'm not expecting any company. However, should anyone happen to pop by, just inform them I'm not receiving guests tonight and that I retired early." Just in case my mother decides to check on me. I hand him a decent tip and head for the back to get my roadster from the garage.

"Yes, Doctor," I can hear him saying as I exit the building. "Thank you, Doctor. And it's Carlton."

Tesla's postal and delivery stores are open all twenty-four hours of each turn. I park along the curb in front of the Postal and Delivery Service building. Sliding over to the passenger side of the roadster, I exit the vehicle, hustle over to the drop box, and slide the letter through the narrow slot. The sooner it's out of my hands, the better. Thank the stars they pick up every four hours for delivery; it should reach Capital City tonight.

After I've posted the letter, I start feeling nauseated. It must be the tea and all that vinum; I definitely need nourishment. Without warning, the ground begins to move out from under me—or is that just me? I stop to steady myself. The air feels dense, but as quickly as the experience appears, it disappears.

Wow, I really should save that tea for right before I go to bed.

I've resumed my quest for food when my shoulders tighten. I hold my breath. It feels like someone is following me. I walk faster toward the food vendor. As I do, I reach into my clutch to retrieve the zephyr my doorman delivered after Mae left. I lay my finger on the smooth, thin trigger, ready to pull it out and shoot.

The feeling of being followed is strong; the hairs on the back of my neck stand straight up. I'm about to turn around when muscular hands grab me around the waist. I spin around quickly and point the shockgun right at my stalker's gut.

The hands tighten around my waist. "And what are you going to do? Shoot me?"

It's Inspector Greyson. I hit him in the chest.

"What were you *thinking*, sneaking up on me like that? I could have pulled the trigger! You could have several volts of electricity pulsing through you right now."

"Relax, Doc. What are you doing out by yourself? Are you trying to get yourself killed?"

I put the shockgun back into my clutch. My face screws up into a weird frown. "If you must know, I had to post an important letter, and ... well, I was starving and had nothing to eat in my apartment."

"Haven't you heard of food delivery?" His hands are still around my waist, apparently with no intention of leaving.

"I thought I would kill two birds with one stone. I was only planning on being gone for a brief time." I turn to pull myself from his grasp and head for one of the street vendors.

The inspector grabs my arm, puts it through his, and walks me over to one of the shacks. The smells of the independent chefs cooking their delicacies waft through the air and mix, creating a sweet, sour, and spicy fragrance. I choose the vendor serving grilled vegetables on flat bread with a creamy borage-flower dressing. I order one sandwich and a bottle of fermented birch ale.

The inspector watches me as he pays the vendor for my dinner. "Are you ready to go home now?"

I look up at his perfectly chiseled features. "Thank you, and yes, I am ready to go home. But aren't you going to order anything for yourself?"

He doesn't answer me. Instead, he waves, signaling someone over: the well-dressed DSI Flynn.

DSI Flynn jogs over to us. "Yes, sir."

"I'm going to take the Doc here back to her place. You follow in our vehicle," he instructs.

Flynn whines, "But, sir, what about our dinner?"

"Really, Flynn, grab us something and pick me up at the Doc's, okay?" He motions with his thumb toward the food stands.

"Yes, sir. Sorry, sir. Doctor." He tips his hat as he mumbles apologies and acknowledgments.

"I'm parked over there." I point at the yellow roadster. "But you really don't have to see me home. I am quite capable of driving home safely. And it seems to me that the only person following me is you."

"Let's go," he says, ignoring my protests. We walk quickly to the shiny yellow tin. "And I'm driving."

"It is *my* motor; I should drive."

"I won't argue with you, so no, I am driving." He opens the passenger-side door for me. "Get in."

"You're a royal pain," I say as he climbs into the driver's seat and starts up the quiet motor.

He chuckles and pulls me in close to him. "You don't say."

"I say," I smart back. "I say!"

He is an excellent driver, I must admit, though only to myself, of course. No need to get him thinking too highly of himself, although I think he already knows. We take the short drive in silence, and I catch myself staring at him a few times. Yes, he's damn hot and sexy, and it seems like there's much more to him than just his ruggedly handsome looks.

"Where do I park her?" he asks me as we reach the apartment building.

"In the garage. You can see my parking spot just there." I point to my spot as we slowly enter the garage.

"I can guarantee we were not followed, so all should be good. No harm done, but please do not go out on your own again." The inspector plugs the roadster back in to finish charging.

"I promise I won't leave 'til I go into work tomorrow, and after that I'll be spending some time at my parents' in Seaside Village."

"Good. Now let me walk you up to your apartment and make sure you're all locked in." He follows me up and through the back door into the lobby.

Carlton greets us. "Dr. Harcrow, you're back."

"Carlton, this is Inspector Chance Greyson," I introduce.

"Carlton and I have met," the inspector says.

"Oh, that's right." I look at the inspector sideways. "The night you came barging into my apartment."

"I'm sorry about that, Doctor," Carlton apologizes.

"Not your fault," I say to him while still looking at the inspector.

"Yeah, yeah, yeah. Let's get you settled. Flynn is gonna be here anytime now to pick me up." The inspector slides past the verbal jab and escorts me upstairs.

I wave my hand and unlock my door. "Did you want to wait inside for your DSI?"

"No, thanks. He should be here soon." He smiles. "Nice trick with the door."

"Goodnight, Inspector."

"Goodnight, Doc." He pulls me in close to him. I close my eyes, certain he's going to kiss me. He releases me and whispers, "Make sure you lock up."

I stand there like a dumb Dora. When I open my eyes, he's gone. My face is burning hot. "What an ass."

Once inside, with my door locked behind me, I peel off my coat and kick off my shoes. The aches and pains of the bruises I received from my unfortunate stumble earlier are rearing up. I eat quickly and down my birch ale so I can wash up and rub on the arnica cream to relieve the pain. I finally settle myself in bed with a cup of the prescribed tea and the shockgun under my pillow.

My sleep is restless. Tossing and turning, with the sheets on and then off, I dream of running—only I'm not getting anywhere—while a shadow gains on me threateningly. I sit straight up in bed, awakened by the nightmare. Then I hear a strange soft noise coming from the other side of the boudoir door.

Was it the bad dream that woke me, or a noise?

I sit there, listening intently to be sure it wasn't my imagination working overtime because of the nightmare. There it is again! I grab the zephyr from under my pillow and take the safety off. Pointing the barrel toward the door, it rattles in my hand. I steady the cold steel with my other hand and wait.

Nothing. No sound, no movement. I wait in the silence.

Slowly and noiselessly, I slip out from under the silk sheets of my bed. Standing, I face the door and wait some more.

Still, I hear nothing. It must have been my imagination. I go to the boudoir door and gradually open it. The door creaks as it opens.

I hear a sound, some rustling, and then silence. I peek my head out into the main living area. That's when I see the source of the noise. The veranda accordion door is ajar, and the willowy sheers waft on the incoming wind.

I shake my head at my overworked imagination. "I could have sworn I shut those before I left earlier."

I look around the room and see nothing amiss. Just in case, though, I keep the shockgun ready as I close the veranda door.

The hairs suddenly raise on the back of my neck, a shiver cutting up my spine. A strong smell of fish and stogies assaults my nostrils. *Oh crap!* Before I can react, a rope finds its way around my neck. The gun falls to the floor as I manage to get my hands between the thick cord and my neck.

He pulls me backward.

I scream.

My hearts pound in my chest.

He's short, but he's so strong!

The rope pinches my palms as my hands are crushed against my neck. He grunts and the rope tightens.

My eyes cloud over with water, and I gasp. I won't go down without a fight. I throw my head back but hit only air, causing me to fall backward into my attacker, and we topple to the floor.

I hear a crack.

He loses his grip on the rope.

I scramble off him and throw the cord from around my neck. It hits the wall with a thud.

My throat spasms for air as I struggle to crawl away. A hand grips my ankle like a vice and yanks me backward. I roll and swing my free foot, hoping to make contact with his head.

I miss. His grip tightens, and he drags me along the smooth wood of the floor.

I bat at the air and wriggle as he pulls me under him. I'm on my back, kicking and hitting as hard as I can. He fends off my defenses and pins me to the floor.

"Get off me!" Dang good construction! The walls in each of these units are basically soundproof; none of my neighbors will be able to hear me. Regardless, I keep screaming.

He's on top of me and I can see him now: Bowler Hat Thug.

I continue flailing around, to no avail. He maneuvers his thick hands around my slender neck, the fringe of his smelly scarf dangling above my open mouth.

Pulling his hands off my throat isn't an option; he's too strong. I'm getting light-headed. I don't have much time before I pass out and the torpedo will be able to finish me off.

I scratch at his face and grab at his neck. *I'm dying!* His neck is slimy, and there are deep slits on the sides. My mind races. *He has gills!* I must act now.

I shove my hand into one of the gills and pull. His grip loosens slightly, and I gasp quickly for breath. I hear a crash and the sound of wood splintering. Did someone hear me?

His grip tightens.

It's too late. Everything is going black.

Chapter Seventeen

As my lungs fill with warmth, I open my eyes to a blurry fig-ure—a face! My eyes fly open and I grab at my neck as I gasp for a full breath. Everything's a bit hazy; my eyes are consumed with tears. My lungs burn as I gulp air.

"There you are," a voice says, prodding me to consciousness on my living room floor. "Thought we might have lost you there."

Get away! Get away! I flail my arms around wildly, trying to es-cape the threat. I try to cry out but nothing comes. Still, I keep hit-ting and kicking.

"Doc . . . Doc, it's me!" the deep voice calls. "Calm down, Doc—Zelda. It's Chance. I've got you. You're safe. He's gone."

My eyes clear, and I can see his face now. It is indeed the inspec-tor. I put my hands gently around my neck and cough, gasping for every little bit of air I can get. Slowly, I sit up.

My throat hurts and I feel very weak. "I . . . what . . . thank you." My voice comes out scratchy and barely audible.

I look up into the face that accompanies a warm embrace. "In-spector." I cough, trying to clear my damaged throat. "Did you catch—" *Cough! Cough!* "Get him?"

His lips press against my forehead. "Try not to talk. You may have damage to your esophagus."

I try to swallow and find it difficult. I cling to the inspector as he barks orders to the coppers swarming my apartment.

"Let's get you over to the sofa and wrapped in a blanket." He lifts me up; I feel like a feather in his arms. He carries me over to the sofa and then secures a blanket from my boudoir to cover me. "There you go," he says. "The healers should give you a once over."

I look around. My place is crawling with coppers, and DSI Flynn is shouting orders. Chance—Inspector Greyson—still has his arms wrapped around me, holding me very close and tight. Normally, it would bother me, but not now. I'm needy, scared, and still shaking like a leaf, and my throat and body hurt like a bird on a wire.

"I've called the Care Center to have them come pick you up and take you to the healers. You really should be checked out." The inspector speaks gently as he pulls the blanket snug around me.

I shake my head and croak in a raspy voice, "I'll be fine. How . . . did . . . you . . . know?" My voice cracks. I put my hand on my throat and ask again. "How did you know to come back?"

The inspector is still holding me close. "When I left earlier, I had a few words with Carlton, your doorman. I told him that if he saw anything suspicious to call me immediately because I was concerned another attempt would be made."

He puts his lips to the top of my head.

I shiver.

He squeezes me tighter. "Carlton called me and said that when he was making his outside rounds, he saw a man staring at the apartment building. When he went to confront him, the man ran away. Being a good guy, Carlton called me just to ask if I could send a patrol around. I decided to turn around myself and come back just to be safe."

"I . . . I . . ." Smiling, I manage to squeak out, "I'll have to give Carlton a big fat tip."

"Well . . ." The inspector looks toward my splintered door. "Doc . . . I don't know how to say this . . ." His face grows grim.

My eyes follow his to the door and I wait.

"When the patrol and I arrived . . ." He takes a deep breath. "The main door was open and the lobby empty. I found Carlton behind the reception counter."

I put my hand to my mouth as my eyes widen.

He gently rests his chin on my forehead. "I am so sorry, Doc. Carlton was bludgeoned from behind and then strangled. He never stood a chance."

"But . . . I was just starting to remember his name." I begin to cry, burying my head into the sturdy chest of my protector.

He draws a breath and continues. "I raced up the stairs to your apartment when I found him." He scratches his head. "Sorry about your door. Anyways, I pulled the assassin off you and we wrestled." He gives me a squeeze. "And sorry about your entryway chair. The assassin bolted. I got off a few phaser shots as he fled out the veranda—oh, also, sorry about your curtains."

I look up at him and put my hands to his lips. "But did you catch him?"

The inspector takes my hands. "You weren't breathing, doll; I had to get you taken care of first. He couldn't have gotten far, though. We're combing the area now."

Great.

DSI Flynn enters the apartment through the busted doorway. "Sir, can I have a moment?"

Inspector Greyson leaves me with one of the female constables. "I'd like to clean up," I tell her.

"I'll help you to the bathing room. Will you be okay, or do you want me to come in with you?" the empathetic constable asks.

"I think I'll be able to manage on my own. Thank you, though."

She walks me slowly over to the bathing room door. "I'll wait right outside the door for you."

I close the door behind me. I peer into the mirror. What a sight! And I should say, a fright! My eyes are red, teary, and swollen; my neck is red as well. I look down at my hands; there's blood on them, though not my own, thank the stars.

As I stare at my hands, they begin to tremble. I almost died tonight. I need to be less stupid, I need to be smart, and I need to help find this torpedo before anyone else dies like poor Carol—I mean Carlton. What can I do?

I turn on the sink's spigot to wash my hands, but then I stop. The blood could give me the last bit of clues as to who this thug is, where he's from, and who hired him.

I open the chest of drawers behind me that I use to hold my linens and other bath essentials. Searching the top drawer, I find a compact mirror and a metal nail file. Opening the compact, I scrape the blood and other foreign substances off my hands and out from under my fingernails with the file.

The female constable knocks. "Are you all right in there?"

I open the door a crack. "Yes, I just need a few more minutes."

She nods as I close the door. I put the evidence on the mirror of the compact and put it back in the drawer. Tomorrow, I'll get the sample to HA and get it analyzed. Then I'll be one step closer to solving this nightmare.

I jump into the tub for a quick rinse under the shower, towel off, and head into the boudoir to put on a fresh nightie. I think I'll just throw the other one out; I doubt I'll ever want to wear it again.

The inspector dismisses the female constable, sending her back to the precinct with bags that I assume contain the evidence they've gathered.

"Doc, let the Emergency Health and Safety folks give you a once over—make sure you're healthy." The inspector motions over the duo who have just arrived.

I nod and let the twosome examine my neck and throat. They use a portable THR scanner to ensure there are no internal injuries. I receive a somewhat clean bill of health. Other than bruising and a little hemorrhaging around my eyes, I appear to be okay. No real damage was done to my esophagus, although they warn that I'll feel as though I have a sore throat for a while. I also have a bit of neck strain and swallowing might be a bit difficult for a couple of turns.

"Doc, let me drive you over to your folks," the inspector insists as the emergency duo are packing up.

"No. I want to stay here tonight; I'll head over in the morning. It's late now and I don't want them unsettled." It burns to talk.

"Don't you think they're going to be upset if you don't?" He signs a few forms DSI Flynn hands him.

"Let them be upset tomorrow. I'm going to bed." I go into the kitchen to take some valerian root extract to ensure my ability to sleep.

"Your call, Doc. Get me a pillow and a blanket, though," he calls after me as he dismisses DSI Flynn. "I'm not taking any more chances; I'm sleeping on the sofa."

I retrieve a blanket and an extra pillow from the front closet and lay them on the couch. "Suit yourself."

I retreat into my boudoir, climb into bed for what will be the last time for quite a while, and drift off into a heavy and thankfully dreamless sleep.

I'm nudged awake by the warm smell of deliciousness coming from my kitchen, which is strange considering I have no food to cook.

I slide out of my comfy bed, taking a moment to put on my dressing gown, and make my way to the kitchen. I avoid looking in any mirrors along the way. No need to scare myself so early in the morning.

My kitchen holds not only the surprise of cooking food—without any burns or explosions—but also the handsome and shirtless Inspector Chance Greyson. I lean against the edge of the archway, watching him. Dang, he looks delicious without a shirt. I must say, I'm impressed by his well-toned muscular chest. As I gaze at him lustfully, it dawns on me again: just where in the stars did he get the food?

"I made you a pot of the prescription tea I found on your kitchen counter," he says without looking up. "It's on the table in the alcove."

I wonder how long he's known I've been standing here admiring his half-naked body. "Thanks," I whisper. I drag my body to the icebox. I pull the handle and am met with a cold, stark, empty space. Maybe it's a magical refrigerator? I close the heavy door and then give it a yank. Nope, still empty.

"I called Flynn to get some food for me to cook. Don't you ever eat?" He flips something in the pan, something that resembles a wheat cake.

"Don't know how to cook." My voice cracks. It's still scratchy from the night before.

He chuckles and shakes his head. "Well, maybe I need to teach you." He hands me a cup. "I would have made you something, but I figured your throat would be a bit too sore to swallow anything but some nice warm tea."

I nod as I sit at my small table in the kitchen's bay window alcove, which overlooks the river Fyrest. It's sunny and the weather looks mild. Last night just seems so far away right at this moment. However, when I go to swallow my tea, I'm quickly reminded of the viciousness of the attack I endured last night. The food the inspector is making smells so appetizing and I'm so hungry, but my throat is too tender to even think about taking a single bite. I'll have to be happy with my tea.

"Oh my, oh my, oh my." The words are spoken in a familiar voice coming from the outside hall. "Ephron my boy, what a mess. She has no door. Zelda dear, Zelda dear," my father calls out.

I raise my brow at the inspector.

He takes a bite of food. "I had Flynn call them this morning."

Ephron and my father enter the kitchen. "Oh dear, oh my darling Zelda, are you all right? I heard what happened. Your mother's hearts are just broken to pieces over this."

I get up and go give my father a nice long hug. "I'll be fine," I whisper, trying not to strain my already fragile vocal chords.

"We're taking you straight to the house," insists Ephron.

My father wrinkles his brow. "Why doesn't Inspector Greyson have a shirt on?"

"He stayed the night, Father."

Father snorts. "Don't you think we should get to know him a little bit, my dear, before he starts spending the night with you?"

I raise my brows "*We?*" I let out a sigh. "Father, he slept on the sofa." I give my brother a hug then. "Tell him there's nothing going on between me and the inspector."

"Nope, this is your mess. You explain it to him." Ephron takes my seat at the table and helps himself to a plate of breakfast.

I give my brother a dirty look. "Father." I swallow the pain. "Inspector Greyson stayed to make sure I'd be safe. He slept on the sofa. No cuddling whatsoever happened last night."

I look over at the inspector to find his face turning a nice rosy shade of embarrassment. To make things worse, my father adds, "Well, that's not what your mother told me. She was very clear about it." Then he shakes a finger at the inspector. "And he has no shirt on."

Ephron mouths at me, *Cards.* Great, now mother is reading tarot for Greyson.

"Sir." The inspector moves his plate away. "I promise you I was a true gentleman last night."

"Father," Ephron finally interjects. "I think the assassination attempt would have been a bit of a fire extinguisher, don't you think?"

"Well, I still think we need to get to know him much better if he's going to be courting her. Zelda, get dressed. I'm taking you home." Father shoos me toward the bathing room.

My head starts to pound. I look at the inspector. I really wish he could read my mind.

Inspector Greyson looks at me and gives a quick nod. "Sir, it is nothing but a professional relationship between your daughter and me." His chair scrapes the floor as he pushes away from the table. "Now if you'll excuse me, I think I'll go put that shirt on now. I'll have my officers finish up here and secure the premises. It was nice to see you both again, Dr. Harcrow, Mr. Harcrow." With that, the inspector leaves the room to pound out orders to his minions, while my mouth hangs open at the possibility that he can, in fact, read my mind.

My father's eyes narrow as the inspector passes him. "Zelda, dear." My father leans into me. "I don't know that I want him as a son-in-law."

The palm of my hand hits my forehead hard as I shake my head. My dear brother bursts out laughing so hard that food spits out of his mouth and travels across the table. I don't know where Father gets his ideas. Actually, yes, I do. Ave and her tarot cards. I trot off to the bathroom to get myself ready and to pack up to go to my parents' home. So much for my independence.

As I wash up and begin to put on my munitions, I can see the red dots of broken blood vessels all around my eyes. I don't think there's enough powder in all of Tesla to cover these babies up. The whites of my eyes are red as rubies. I sure look a sight. I decide to put a scarf around my neck to cover the bruises the brute's hands left when he attempted to kill me last night.

As I pack several outfits, nightclothes, and a few of my undergarments, I bring down my hatboxes, into one of which I place Bowler Hat Thug's scarf, which Mae confiscated from the stolen car, and the compact that contains his physical skin and blood. I'll take them into HA to have them examined properly. I need to know where this torpedo came from and who sent him.

"All set to go," I struggle to call out. Even with the warm, soothing tea, my throat is still a bit coarse and raw.

"Ephron, get your sister's bags and take them down to the car," Father orders.

My brother huffs and grabs my bags, heading out through what was once my front doorway.

"I've arranged for an escort to follow you to your home, sir," the now-dressed inspector informs us. "I want to make sure the doc gets there, nice and safe. I'll be by later to get additional statements."

The inspector takes me by the arm and pulls me aside. "Doc, please be careful. No more crazy chances; I'm afraid I may not be able to get to you in time if it happens again."

"I didn't know you cared so much," I kid, smiling and giving him a wink.

He tightens his grip on my arm. "Doc, I'm not joking. This is serious."

I pry his hand off my arm. "Attaboy. It's all copacetic; I'll be okey-dokey."

I don't think he believes me, not for a moment. He's right not to, but I must take the chance to stop this before it goes any further and anyone else gets hurt or loses their life. However, this time I'll be much more careful.

With a police escort, I leave my apartment and go back to my childhood home. I grew up in a grand house in Seaside Village, with a view of the sea. A beautiful large older mansion with lots of wood, lots of brick, and lots of windows, it is categorically in need of a modern update.

The butler, George, who has been with our family for quite a number of rotations, opens the door for me. "Young Miss Zelda, how good it is to see you."

"Zelda!" My mother comes sweeping down the stairs and envelops me in her arms. "Oh, my dear girl, my dear girl. Oh, I told you. Did I not tell you to stay indoors? You should have come here last night. You shouldn't be out there on your own." My mother continues to babble. "Get right—get right upstairs. Ephron, take her bags upstairs, right upstairs. Zelda, you take a nice long hot bath, and then I'll get you some warm soothing soup, and I believe Mae is on her way over too."

After all that, my mom flits off to bark orders at our kitchen staff as I head up to my old room.

"I'm not sure how I got stuck carrying your bags again." Ephron stops midway on the stairs. "Why am I taking up these bags when we have housing staff for that?"

I shake my head. "You know George has a bad back and can't really lift anything." I wave for him to continue the climb.

He takes a few steps before stopping again. "Then why do we have him?"

"Because he and his wife have been with our family for so long that what else would he do? Where else would he go? He's like furniture: he belongs here, just like the dining room table. Now put a sock in it and just take my bags up to my room."

His shoulders slump as he finishes the climb.

The housemaid brings up a small bowl of soup. I'm so hungry, I just down the whole thing.

"Zelda, Zelda dear," my mother says as she enters my room. "Now, I put a small sleeping spell on the soup. It might be a bit strong, though, so I wouldn't eat the whole thing."

My eyes widen. "What?"

"I said I wouldn't eat the whole thing, dear. Did your ears get hurt in the struggle? Are you okay?"

"You did what to the soup?" I slowly ask.

"I put a small sleeping spell on it. I put a little bit of herbs in there and said a little spell. It should relax you. But it might be a bit strong, so I wouldn't eat it all."

"Jeepers!" I hit the floor, sound asleep.

Chapter Eighteen

The sun star's rays shimmer through double glass doors, etching out rectangles on the thickly carpeted floor as I lay in bed quietly. I note the doors that lead out to the sunny balcony of my childhood bedroom as I slowly awaken from what seems to have been an endless sleep.

"Hey, Starshine, nice of you to join us," Mae says without even looking up from the fashion rag she's reading.

I rub my forehead. "Hey. Oh, my. Level with me; how long have I been sleeping?"

"Darling, you know, I think I could do a much better job of designing today's fashions. Some of what they have out this solstice is horrid. I mean, what were they thinking? We should be wearing—look at these hems!" The magazine pages crackle as she turns the magazine around with fervor to show me. "They're way below the knee and completely off the cob. I think the hem should be brought up above the knee. I mean, knees aren't that attractive, but they're not ugly, either. I think a girl has a right to show her knees. Oh, and the colors! The colors should be brighter for this solstice, not so drab."

I struggle to sit up. "Mae, how long have I been sleeping? It seems like forever."

"Darling, you've slept an entire turn." Mae's eyes glance up at me, and then she stuffs her head back into the rag.

I rub my eyes, urging them to stay open. "Men don't show their knees."

"That's not the point." She cocks her head to one side. "What's that noise?" Mae asks without looking up.

"Stomach. I'm starving. I haven't eaten since that soup my mother drugged me with." I swing my legs over the side of the bed and slowly stand up. My stomach grumbles again. "I'm going to get washed up. Would you be a doll and call down to the kitchen; have them send me up a tray? Thank you, dear."

I shuffle to my en suite bathing room. The warm water cascades down over my body, relaxing my sore muscles. The towel, sadly, feels like sandpaper against my skin. I take a gander at myself in the mirror and frown. I'm taken aback by the red dots of broken capillaries still showing around my eyes. The good news is that the swelling has gone down. The bruises around my neck, however, are still purple. Boy, I just look horrendous.

I choose a coral accordion pleated skirt with a hem that grazes my legs just below the knee. Mae's right; it sure would be aces if the hem was a bit shorter. I add a bone-colored high-necked blouse, with a matching coral necktie to help hide the bruises. Putting on stockings that match my blouse, I decide my hair needs to match my skirt. I go model my outfit for Mae.

"Darling, its marvelous! What a perfect choice!" she says, bestowing her blessing on my choice of outfit and matching hair color.

"Mae, could you do me one more favor? Could you call HA and ask Ephron when Clover is going to be leaving? I really want to talk to her about her boyfriend before she leaves for her parents' house. Okeydokey?"

"My pleasure, darling. My pleasure. Now go put on some munitions. I'll make the call."

I cover the red blotches on my face with powder. Hopefully, all this makeup will be enough to camouflage the blood-red dots and weird blotches shaped like misshapen overripe fruit that now litter my complexion. I blend charcoal shadow around my peepers and put a coral color on my lids to accent my new hair color. Then I brush on some mascara and make sure my eyebrows are filled in. Just because somebody is trying to kill me, there's no need to have sloppy, unfinished eyes. I'm ready; all I still need are lip rouge and a hat.

"The hatbox!" I must remember to bring along the evidence. I pull out the hatbox that contains the scarf and the mirror compact.

"Bad news, pally," Mae calls from the boudoir.

"What's up?" I step out of the dressing room, placing the evidence in my bag.

"Clover has already left for the airship. She's heading for downtown Fulcrum now." As the words part from Mae's lips, my long-awaited food tray of fruit, pastries, and tea arrives. My stomach calls for them.

Mae grabs my wrist. "No time to eat now. We've got to blow."

"But—but—but let me just grab a pastry, at least."

Mae pulls me out of my room and right down the sweeping staircase, out the oversized oak doors, down the cement steps, and smack dab into one of Fulcrum's finest.

"Whoa, ladies. Ladies, ladies, where's the fire?" the constable asks.

"No fire, darling, just an airship we need to catch," Mae responds.

"Airship?" He looks perplexed.

"Yes, an airship," I add. "I need to get downtown and fast. I need to talk to my assistant before she leaves."

"Well, I'm sorry, Doctor. I have strict instructions from Inspector Greyson: you are to stay put."

"What's your name, darling?" Mae diddles around with one of his brass buttons.

"Hodge," he says, his voice rising an octave or two. "Constable Ethan Hodge."

"Darling," Mae says. She doesn't use the name she just asked him for, most likely because she probably forgot it as soon as he said it. "You have a choice. You can either get out of our way or come with us."

"I'm sorry, Miss. I have my orders." Obviously, Constable Hodge has no idea who he's dealing with. Mae, as far as I can remember, has never taken no for an answer, and she isn't going to start now.

So I let Mae handle him.

"Darling, darling," she purrs. "What are your instructions?"

"M-m-my job," he stutters, taking in a gulp of air like it's courage, "is to make sure the doctor stays safe, Miss."

Lucky for him, he called her *Miss* and not *ma'am*. "Darling Constable, nowhere in those instructions does it say that Zelda can't go anywhere, just that you need to protect her. So again, either you come with or we go without you. Your option." Mae pushes him out of her way and struts over to her motor.

"I don't think you're going to win this argument," I kindly inform the bewildered constable.

"I'll drive," Hodge says, gesturing toward his Legere Constable tin that sits parallel to my parents' home.

Mae and I slide into the backseat as the constable gets behind the wheel of the sedan. We pull out and head off the island, over the bridge onto Industria 2, and toward the heart of Fulcrum city.

"Could you speed it up?" I whine. "We'll never make it in time, and I've got to speak with her."

"Doctor, I'll get you there, and I'll get you there safely. I can't take any chances, and I can't speed. I have to uphold the law, you know," he claims proudly.

"Bushwa, darling." Mae leans over the front seat and yells in his ear, "Put the pedal to the metal, and let's blow."

I pull Mae back down beside me. "Seriously, Hodge, I've got to get to my assistant. We must go faster. I'm sure going a little bit over the speed limit won't get you into any trouble." I fold my hands together and shake them in the air, begging him.

However, he takes his duty very seriously. "I'm sorry, Doctor, but I must obey the law. I'll get you there, and hopefully the traffic will be light. We'll be there in time."

Mae isn't going to take this sitting down—at least, not in the backseat. She straddles the front seat and rolls herself up and over into the front seat next to the constable.

The tin swerves with Hodge's surprise. "Miss, what are you doing?"

"Switch spots with me, flatfoot, and let me drive. I'll get us there. I don't mind bending a few rules." Mae elbows him hard.

"I need to make it there in one piece!" I yell from the backseat. "What are you doing?"

"Darling, if this dolt continues to drive, you'll be there maybe tomorrow, if you're lucky. Put an extra hatpin in; we have an airship to catch." The constable refuses to switch with her, but Mae doesn't let that stop her. "Let's go, baby." She slams her foot on top of the constable's and pushes the pedal down to the floor.

The tin rears forward and almost swerves into another motor. The constable screams, I scream, and Mae laughs.

Mae and the constable struggle with the steering wheel, weaving in and out of traffic and avoiding every tin they came upon.

Thud.

My body hits the door. I roll first to one side—

Smash.

And then into the other door—

Whump.

My body catapults back into the first door again. Grabbing the armrest, I hold on for dear life. Great, now my bruises have bruises.

The motors swiftly blur by as we keep going, back and forth, in and out, swerving this way and that, that way and this, faster and faster. My stomach is in my throat, and I close my eyes for the rest of the frightening ride.

Finally, the battling duo pull up to Griffin Tower. "Oh . . . I think I'm going to puke!" I cry. Of course, even if I do upchuck, there isn't anything in my stomach to come up. I'm hungry. I don't know which is worse: the nausea or the hunger pangs.

Constable Hodge stumbles out of the driver's side, and Mae, completely composed, exits from the vehicle like she just took a leisurely ride in the country. I seriously don't know how she does it.

"We're here. Let's get a wiggle on. Come on, Zelda." Mae leads as the constable and I whimper along behind her, still trying to grab back our composure from that horrific trip. We walk through the large gold-and-glass doors of Griffin Tower. Griffin Tower was built and named for Mae's father, A.P. It holds offices, apartments, and at the very top, an observation deck and concourses where passengers wait for airships to dock.

We enter the golden-brass building and head toward the elevators that lead to the top observation deck and concourse. There's quite a line, which is unusual, but that isn't stopping Mae; she pushes right through. Dirty looks and obscene gestures follow us from those we pass, and I'm beginning to think we might start a riot. Constable Hodge trails after us, holding up his badge to keep the peace.

The three of us approach the departing elevators and saddle up to the counter where passengers and baggage are checked in. "Excuse me, Miss. Excuse me, Miss." I flap my hand back and forth, trying to get the attention of the service attendant.

"Yes, ma'am. May I help you today?" she offers politely. Her eyes move to our chaperone and his shiny badge. "Oh, you must be here about the incident."

"Yes," Mae answers.

"Wait, what?" I lean into the counter. "What incident?"

"The body they found shoved into the baggage hold of the airship coming in from Trade City." The attendant raises one eyebrow at us. "You're not here about the body, are you?"

"No, ma'am," Constable Hodge pins his badge back onto his uniform. "We're here on another matter."

"I need to check a flight." My voice cracks with agitation. "It was leaving today for Aladar City."

The attendant responds, "We did have an airship flight leaving for Aladar City today, but it has already embarked on its journey. You're sure you're not here for the body?"

"No. Thank you." I sigh and turn toward Mae and Constable Hodge. "We missed her."

Mae moves me aside to talk to the attendant. "What kind of body is it?"

"A dead one, Mae, and if we don't start finding answers, I'll be joining him." I look to the constable for answers and then remember the poor Joe is just along for the ride.

"Fine." Mae turns and sways off through the mumbling, grumbling line of waiting passengers. "Let's regroup. Darlings, come on and let's ankle on out back to the tin. I'll let you drive this time, Constable."

I'm deep in thought when a wave of nausea washes over me and I crash right into an arriving passenger. "Oof! Oh, dear, I'm sorry. I'm so sorry. Excuse me, please; I wasn't watching where I was going."

"No problem. It was my fault as well," he mumbles as he turns and quickly exits the building. I notice how tall he is and the way his dark hair brushes his shoulders as he turns away. A funny shiver went up my spine when he spoke. I brush it away, though. I have more important things to think about.

The three of us are standing on the sidewalk outside the building, thinking about our next move, when who should pull up but Inspector Greyson. Boy, this isn't going to be pretty.

"Doc, I'm surprised to see you here. Hodge, Miss Griffin." He acknowledges each of us, but he looks directly at Hodge.

"Sir, I-I-I know you said to protect the doctor, but she insisted on coming." Poor Hodge's shoulders slump as he stammers.

I push Hodge aside and plant myself in front of the inspector. "I know you wanted me to stay put, but I really needed to speak with Clover, my assistant. It was very important."

He looks right past me. "I actually hadn't heard about your escapades yet. I'm here on other business, and I would suggest you go back to your parents' home."

I move to get back into his line of sight. "You're here about the dead body."

He grabs my shoulders, picks me up, moves me out of his way, and struts into the building.

Mae looks at me with raised brows. "He's fuming. I think I actually saw steam escape from under his collar."

"Yep, I think we better head back."

Just as I'm about to get into the backseat of the constable's motor, though, I see him. Bowler Hat Thug.

I yell.

Bowler Hat Thug's eyes bug out of his head, and his jaw drops.

Yelling again, I start to run without even thinking. My legs head straight for him as my hand grabs the shockgun from my purse. "Stop, you! Stop!"

So much for being careful.

Constable Hodge grabs at me, but only catches air. "Dr. Harcrow, Miss Griffin, stop! Stop!"

"Zelda!" Mae screams as she tries to keep up with me. "No . . . !"

There's no stopping me.

Bowler Hat Thug takes one look at me charging at him, and his eyes widen in disbelief, as if I were throwing him a curveball. He turns and runs the other way. Running against the flow of pedestrians walking down the sidewalk, he tries to lose me in the commotion.

"You!" I shout. "You bimbo, stop!"

I run and jump, trying to keep my eye on him. He's so short, he's getting lost in the stream. I lose sight of him. I get to the corner of an alley and turn to keep chase, but he's nowhere to be seen. Mae and Constable Hodge finally catch up.

"What were you thinking?" Mae yells, shaking my shoulders. "You could have gotten yourself killed!"

"Doctor, exactly what were you planning on doing?" Constable Hodge doubles over, supporting his hand on his bent knees. "And how in the stars do you run so fast in those heels?"

I look down at my shoes. "I gotta be honest with you: I don't know what my logic was. I can't fathom what I would have done if I had caught him." I turn to face them both. "I guess shoot him."

The three of us are standing in the alley at the corner of the block when I catch sight of the tall, long-haired gentleman I'd bumped into earlier. My stomach flips. He's standing across the street, and it looks as if he's staring at us.

Correction: staring at me.

"Zelda, Zelda!" Mae is calling to me, waving her hand in front of my face. "What are you looking at?"

The dark stranger gets in a taxi and drives away. I shake my head. "Nothing," I say, bringing my attention back to Mae and Hodge. It's time to head back to the car, before I make any more idiotic decisions.

"Ladies." Constable Hodge directs us toward his vehicle.

"We should get you back home, Zelda," Mae says, a worried lilt in her voice.

I slide into the vehicle. "No, not yet. I need to get to HA. I have one more thing to accomplish today."

Chapter Nineteen

"What was that?" asks Constable Hodge. Mae eyes me. "I heard it too."

"My stomach, okay? I'm starving; I still haven't gotten anything to eat." I'm like a little whiny child, and I don't care. I just want food. "Maybe we can stop to pick up a little something on our way to HA? I won't take too much time; I just need something to hold me over."

"I'm sorry, Dr. Harcrow. We won't be taking any more chances. We can't stop someplace when it's possible we're being followed. It's best to be safe and go straight to HA." He keeps driving.

"But I'm famished! If I don't get something to eat, you won't have to worry about the assassin killing me because I'll have already starved to death." I'm being melodramatic, of course, but if it gets me food, I'll lay it on as thick as I possibly can.

"No, Doctor, I can't do that. We'll get you something at HA." Constable Hodge has found some courage. I can't really blame him; he's trying to hold onto his job.

"I'm sure they'll have something there for you to munch on, and then afterward, we'll go out. We'll get some food, a late lunch. You'll be fine, I promise." Mae crosses her hearts with her fingers.

I sigh. "Fine." My stomach rumbles again. "Ugh." I sit in silence except for the rumbles of my stomach.

"I want to check on my Zenith," I say, breaking my short silence. "See how she's coming along and if those parts came in. As soon as this is all over, I'm taking a drive. A nice long road trip, maybe."

"Right, like you'd ever leave your lab for such an amount of time. Soon as this is over, you'll be right back in there, blowing things up again and skipping out on lunch dates with me."

I stick my tongue out at her. "Oh, dry up." My stomach grumbles again.

We arrive at HA, go in through the front entrance, and pass through security. We enter the main hall and decide to take the stairs down to the tinkers instead of the lift.

"Tick! Tick!" I call out for the old tinker.

Tick appears, all greasy and grimy. I smile and laugh. "What have you been up to?"

"Can't tell you," he says. "Let me guess, you're here about the Zenith."

"Yes, I'm here about my Zenith." I pout. "Have we gotten the parts in yet?"

"Sorry. Probably in a couple more turns. I can put a rush on the parts; maybe we'll get lucky. When the parts come in, I promise we'll have her up and running and ready to go." Tick looks around. "What's that sound?"

"It's just my stomach. You wouldn't happen to have any food lying about, would you?" My stomach jazzes up a few more notes.

"None down here. Sorry, pretty one," Tick empathizes.

"Ugh." My stomach rumbles again.

I drag Mae and Constable Hodge to the lift, and we travel up a couple of floors. My next stop is to see one of the assistants to one of our house alchemists. Dr. Steven Zozimos is a chemist and a physicist, and he employs two assistants: his wife, Cora, and a brownnoser named Orin Needs. Needs is an idiot and a rat; Cora, however, is a true soul.

I need to employ Cora's help. The three of us enter Zozimos's lab. "Zelda," Zozimos says. "To what do we owe the pleasure of your visit? We're quite busy, you know; don't have time for chitchat."

I think Dr. Zozimos is an idiot and a poser; I never have figured out why Cora married him or why we employ him. "I just need to tug on Cora's ear for a moment. Girl stuff, you know."

"She's over there," Dr. Zozimos says dismissively. This is fine by me; I don't want him nosing around about why I'm here and blabbing to Ephron. We hop on over to visit with Cora.

"Cora, how are you?" I ask.

"I'm doing fine, though how are you? I've heard about your troubles. Are you okay? Is there anything I can do?" Cora smiles and gives me a pat on the shoulder.

"Well, now that you mention it." I look over at Constable Hodge. "This is a delicate matter, and I would prefer Inspector Greyson not know about what I'm doing. He would trivialize it, and this may just help us crack the case."

"What do you mean?" he asks.

"Well, I need a little science." I slap Mae's diddling hand away from the microscopes on the table.

"You mean criminal science."

I stare at Hodge, surprised. "Yes, criminal science."

"Forensics is something I'm quite interested in," says the constable, "but they don't do very much of it here. It's not very popular."

"But why?" asks Cora.

"Well, in this country, most scientists are also alchemists," he explains. "Magic, and any uses of it, can taint evidence, so many criminals would go free on technicalities. Nonmagical evidence can be used in a court of law or even an eyewitness, but otherwise, there'd be no conviction."

Mae stops playing with all of Cora's little gadgets, now interested. "Well, I don't know too much about that. I mean, there's barely any crime in all Tesla."

"There is crime—a lot that you don't see, that you don't know about. Criminals go free due to lack of evidence. I'm involved in a group of non-alchemists, nonmagical people interested in science and its uses in solving crimes. Right now, the club—Forensics Club—we have meetings and seminars, but there's no formal teaching. We're trying to get some of the universities interested, but nobody wants to get involved without having some type of financial or council backing."

Constable Hodge is quite an interesting fellow. Kind of cute too, with his fine-pressed uniform and not a hair out of place.

"I'll keep your secret as long as you keep mine," he finishes.

I cross my hearts. "Ab-so-lute-ly." I turn my attention back to Cora.

Mae interrupts. "We're going to use science to figure out who the Bowler Hat Thug is?"

I pull from my bag the scarf and the compact. "Cora, I need you to test this."

"I'll do it," Cora agrees, "but it might take me a turn. I got to be honest with you, if you're looking for nonmagical science, I'm going to have to do it on the QT. I'll call you when I figure out the isotopes."

Mae cocks her head to one side. Cora adds, "They'll tell us where the scarf has been. The blood and tissue will tell us who this person is or where he lives, what he eats, where he grew up. I'll be able tell all kinds of things about him."

Cora suddenly stops and looks at me. "What's that sound?"

"My stomach." I hug my middle. "We're done here for now. Let's go down and see Father and back to the house for food." I look at Mae, who seems lost in thought.

"Mae, Mae . . ." I call.

"Hodgey darling, could you get Zelda back?" Mae asks. "I've got something I need to take care of."

"Mae, what are you up to?"

"Nothing, darling, nothing. I'll tell you later. I'll stop by tonight, okay? And we'll talk all about it." Mae waves to us as she trots off.

"You're up to something." My stomach grumbles again as I call after her, "What about your car?" This is not a good sign. I have a foreboding of disaster. However, that could just be my stomach talking.

Hodge, the ever-increasingly attractive constable, and I travel back downstairs and into the main executive offices. I lead Constable Hodge straight toward Father's office. I look across the reception area and notice Ephron's new assistant. I wonder what's wrong with this one; she's very beautiful and very pale, and she has blue eyes with hints of pink flecks, rosy cheeks, and a red bow-shaped mouth. Her hair is golden and finger waved. Interesting.

As we enter the office, my father comes flying from behind his desk. "My dear, how are we feeling? You slept an entire turn away. There's so much occurring, so much."

"I just came to check on when I could get a gander at my lab."

"Why don't you come back by tomorrow and look? Also, the help I requested for some of our ongoing projects will be here tomorrow. You should be here to meet them." He suddenly notices my companion. "Who's this? What happened to the inspector fellow? Zelda, is he a new beau?"

Poor Constable Hodge turns several shades of red before I can save him. "No, Father, this is Constable Hodge. He was assigned to me today as protection."

Father looks Hodge up and down. "Is it working?"

The constable squirms in his uniform. "I'm doing my best to ensure your daughter's safety, sir."

Father gets right up in his face, and Hodge begins to perspire. "Pretty, isn't she? My pride and joy, she is."

Hodge clears his throat. "Yes, sir."

I finally dive in to the rescue. "Father, I wanted you to meet the fine constable. He's interested in forensic science, and he's a nonmagical."

Grabbing the overwhelmed constable's hand for a firm, frenzied handshake, my father begins excitedly, "Titus. Call me Titus."

Hodge meekly smiles at the overly animated man in front of him. "Nice to meet you, sir."

"Father!" I raise my voice, bringing him back into focus. "Why don't we all sit down and chat."

"Splendid idea, Zelda," he agrees and waves us over to worn leather chairs that have seen many ideas and fascinating secrets.

I share with Father and Constable Hodge my concept for giving the university an endowment to teach forensics. After a brief—and I would say successful—meeting, I have the constable take me back to my parents'.

Once we arrive, the constable tips his hat. "Thank you, Dr. Harcrow. I surely do appreciate all you're doing for me."

"Not a problem. Forensics is something that interests me too," I say as I walk up the stairs, leaving the constable behind. I stop briefly at the top of the stairs and take a good look at Ethan Hodge. I notice his eyes; they are kind and generous, and in an instant I am glad we've become friends.

My stomach rumbles again. I missed breakfast and I missed lunch; I am not missing dinner. I head upstairs to draw myself a nice hot bath, call down for some food, and be done for the turn.

After my soak, I find a tray waiting for me on the table in my room. With its warm inviting smells, all my senses are just running amok and my stomach growls. "Don't you worry, baby. We're going to get you all taken care of."

My bedside line suddenly begins to ring off the hook.

"Zelda . . ."

"Mae? Mae? Is that you calling?"

"Can you hear me?" Mae whispers over the dim connection.

"Mae? Where are you?"

"I'm sort of, kind of stuck, darling," she says, continuing to whisper. "I need you to come and get me. I'm kind of in trouble."

So much for dinner. My stomach rumbles again.

"Ugh."

Chapter Twenty

"Zelda, are you there?" Mae's voice whispers.

"Mae, where are you?" I listen for a response.

"I'm at Alcazar Alchemy."

"Where?" I can't believe what I'm hearing.

"Alcazar Alchemy," she repeats.

"For crying out loud! What are you doing there?"

"Trying to help you get the goods."

"Help me do what?"

"Never mind. Just come and get me before I get pinched," she begs me.

"Fine. Where are you?"

"Fifth-floor records room. Hurry up before the guards do their rounds."

"Stay put; I'm on my way."

I disconnect and rummage through my closet for some type of disguise. How can I infiltrate the company without being noticed or seen? I pull out an outfit and give it a once over as the corners of my mouth curl up slowly. Maybe I need to be noticed and seen.

Like HA, Alcazar Alchemy is closed for the night and all that should be left is a security detail. In my old closet, I find a costume I wore over three rotations ago when my fiancé and I went to a party. The theme of the party was "Dress like Your Favorite Alchemist." I went as Betty Budnick, an inventor and alchemist who developed popular lubricants. Her most famous was a personal lubricant. I bet she was popular in her turn.

I stand in front of the mirror and take a good look at myself. I have donned a gray wig with long braids, a corset with a lab coat over it, a long skirt, and laced-up shoes. I put on a pair of cheaters so thick, my eyes look massive. I look a little old-fashioned, but I think this will do the trick.

Before I head off to save Mae, I stop by the kitchen and grab some cleaning products and some empty apothecary bottles. All I need to do is create a distraction.

The solarium is the easiest room to access without being noticed. The window rattles and makes a sharp squeaking sound as I lift the sash. I hesitate and listen for footsteps, but none sound. Swinging one leg over the sill and then the other, I shimmy down the trellis, careful to avoid both snags in my stockings and my protection detail. Staying in the shadows, I dart out and jump into one of the dark discreet tins my father happens to own but doesn't drive.

Off I go to rescue Mae.

I don't want to pull up directly in front of Alcazar Alchemy, so I hide the car far away behind some bushes and I walk the rest of the way. Brazenly, I enter the main doors of the building with the household items I brought and a little spell I'm going to use to rescue Mae.

A security guard station sits in front, just like at HA. I make myself known in a very high, squeaky voice.

"Ahem. I am Dr. Fliberterber . . . bee." I really wish I thought up a name before I got here. "I am here to drop off some products for Dr. D. Scumme."

"Who?" the young guard asks.

"Dr. Fliberberterber . . . to see Dr. Scumme," I mumble in what hopefully sounds like some kind of unrecognizable accent.

"I'm sorry, Dr. Fli . . . um, ber . . . um . . . Dr. Scumme isn't in. We're closed for the turn."

"Oh my, I came all this way. I really need to give him these products. I'm catching an airship out of downtown Fulcrum tonight. There's a conference in Capital City that I just can't miss. I know Dr. Scumme was going tomorrow, and he needs his product for his talk."

I'm not completely lying. There is a Dr. Scumme and there is a convention in Capital City, but if Dr. Scumme is going to be speaking at it, or even attending, I have no idea. I just need to get in and get to a lab.

I know Mae's located in the fifth-floor records office. I have to get to at least one lab so I can create a distraction and escape with Mae. I cross my fingers and hope the guard buys my story.

"Well, ma'am, I don't know . . . I don't think I can really let you go through, not without an escort," he claims.

"Well, poopsy. Why don't you escort me?" I ask in my very bad, ever-changing fake accent.

"I can't leave my post, ma'am," says the wide-eyed young security guard.

"Oh, such a shame, such a shame. Well, I tried. You let Dr. Scumme know tomorrow that he won't get any of my products." From what I have heard of Dr. Scumme, he is bad tempered. If things aren't done the way he wants them done, heads roll. He's abusive, he's mean, and he drinks too much—a regular boozehound. His work shows it, as does the way he treats people. I use this to my advantage.

"Wait, wait, wait, wait, wait," stammers the young security guard. "Let me get my relief to come, and I'll escort you up there myself."

I smile. "Sounds ducky."

Now I have to figure out a way to ditch him.

We arrive at Dr. Scumme's lab on the second floor. There are three floors between me and Mae; I had hoped this would be easier. The guard lets me into the lab and stands outside the door, I immediately get to work mixing items together. When placed over a small continuous laser, the mixture will give me enough time to get out of the way before it goes bang.

I work quickly, mixing as carefully as I can. After wiping off my fingerprints, I place the bottle on the burner. "Water, fire, air, and earth, give this mixture of mine birth." As I chant, the mixture begins to stir itself. I decide to run around a little bit to make it seem like I'm doing something.

Luckily, the guard receives a call on his transmitter; it seems somebody has noticed evidence of Mae coming in and they need to do a quick search of the building. "Ma'am, are you about done? I need to do some rounds."

"I'm going to be a few more minutes; I want to leave a small letter for the doctor. I'll wait right here. Come and get me when you're done." I thank my lucky stars as the words dribble out of my mouth.

"Thank you, ma'am," he says, leaving me.

As soon as the guard leaves, I grab my things and hotfoot it right out the door, taking the nearby stairs up to the next floor. I need to buy time and keep the guards busy while I make my way up to the fifth floor and retrieve Mae. I find an open lab and set up another little timed explosion. Sneaking out of that room, I take the stairs up another floor to the fourth floor. I need to get the last explosion as far away from the records office as I can. I'm not sure exactly where Mae is, so I'll have to take a chance. I find the last lab on the floor open; it'll have to do. I place up another little device, making certain I wipe down my prints before I head up to retrieve Mae.

That's when the first device explodes, most likely causing minimal damage and a small fire, just enough to get the guards' attention. They're going to start looking for me. I have to move fast.

I make it up to the fifth floor and find the records room. It's locked. Banging on the door and hoping no one else will hear me, I call, "Mae! Mae! It's me, Zelda!"

Mae cracks open the door. "It's about time! Took you long enough! What's the plan?"

I offer her a blank stare. "Plan?"

Mae pulls a crazy curly white wig from her head. "You know how to get us out of here, right?"

"Well, I thought maybe I'd figure it out when I got here." I cock my head to the side and ask, "Who are you supposed to be?"

"Does it really matter?" She hits me with the wig. "A cleaning lady. I dressed as a cleaning lady!"

"Hey! Don't hit me with that thing!" I say, batting at the wig.

We stand staring at each other.

"You plan a caper and don't have an escape route?" Mae's eyes bug.

"Look who's talking," I yell back. I'm starting to panic. "You broke into a building with absolutely no plan."

She throws the wig at me. "That's why I called you! You're supposed to be the genius!"

"Fine!" I shriek, tossing the white curly mess back at her.

Bang!

I jump. That might have been just a little bit larger than it was supposed to be—too much ammonia.

Have I mentioned I have a penchant for blowing things up?

Alarms are sounding now. The guards are screaming and running around like cicen hens with their heads chopped off. "Mae, we've got to get out of here!" I look up and down the hall. I remember seeing a garbage chute and a dumpster on the side of the building. "Let's go!"

The clacking of our shoes is lost amid the blaring sirens and shouting security. We run down the hall to the garbage chute.

Mae shakes her head violently. "I'm not going in there!"

"Oh yes, you are! We've only got one more explosion." I open the trash chute and push Mae through.

I wonder then if the garbage lid is up.

I can hear Mae scream as she slides down five stories of metal shoot, with me howling down right behind her. We hit the dumpster; thankfully it's open. Unfortunately, it's also full of waste.

We crawl out of the dumpster, covered head to toe in I-don't-know-what, and to be on the level, I don't really want to know. "The tin is behind the bushes across the parking lot. Run!" I start sprinting toward the car, pulling slime from my coat and reaching up for my wig.

It's gone!

"Go ahead! I've got to go back; I dropped my wig."

Thankfully the wig is outside the dumpster. I don't think I could have taken one more jump into that filthy mess. Just as my hand clasps the wiry wig, security comes around the building. "Fuck." I dive behind the dumpster, my stomach growling.

Large shoes clomp up to the dumpster. "Who's there?" I'm done for! I squeeze my eyes closed and suck in a breath.

Bang!

The last explosion rings out, and I open one eye. The shoes turn around and pound back from where they came. I blow out my breath; the coast is clear. I run full force toward the motor; looking back, I can see the commotion around the building. I take a dive right into the bushes.

The tiny branches and tough little leaves snag at my costume. Mae pulls me out. "Come on; let's blow."

The stench of the smelly garbage-encrusted costumes hammers our senses. Stripping down, we dump everything into disposable bags and make our getaway in only our skivvies.

Chapter Twenty-One

Leaving Mae to dispatch the disguises, I enter the mansion in the same manner I left it. In only my undergarments, I quietly tip-toe through the solarium and the dining room to the front hall and foyer. As I reach the main stairs, I hear voices. I freeze on my tippy-toes, hunched over and arms out, ready to creep up the stairs.

I hear my mother's voice coming from the front parlor. "I understand your concern, but it is late and Zelda has been through enough. I'm sure this can wait 'til tomorrow."

The next voice I hear seems to be coming toward me. "Mrs. Harcrow, I must insist on speaking with her. For us to find the assassin that has been hired to kill your daughter, I need to get some details about the attack of the other night."

"Maybe you should have gotten those details when you happened to be staying at my daughter's apartment all night." The parlor door opens.

A small chuckle comes from another voice, and I finally recognize the first voice as Inspector Greyson's. *Crap, he's here!* I begin to creep toward the stairs again when my mother walks through the parlor doors, the inspector and his DSI tagging along.

"I insist that you leave and come back tomorrow. My daughter's tired."

"She's looking pretty good to me." The inspector smiles at me.

Mother turns around. She stands in shock for a brief moment upon seeing me sneaking around in my unmentionables, but she quickly recovers.

"Zelda," she yells, "you're sleepwalking again!"

I'm dumbfounded. Here I am in my skivvies, creeping toward the stairs on tiptoe after I have just broken into and set off several explosives at a rival alchemy company. Ducky, my mother is covering for me! I wonder what this is going to cost me.

"You're exhausted. Go right upstairs . . . go right on up and get right back to bed. See, Inspector, she is so distraught over all of this that she is wandering the house. Surely you can come another time. And call first." My mother is direct.

The inspector walks over to me, bends over a little, looks at me, smiles, and takes something from my hair. "Hmm . . ." He looks at the twig he's pulled from my hair, looks at me and then my mother, and says, "Goodnight, ladies. I'll contact you late tomorrow."

As soon as the door closes behind the inspector and his DSI, my mother speaks. "Zelda love, I don't know where you've been, and I don't care, but you look like you haven't eaten all turn. Go get cleaned up and come down to the kitchen. I'll have something made for you."

I would say there's no arguing with my mother, except—well, okay, there is no arguing with my mother. I turn and go upstairs. I screw up my dumpster-smelling undergarments and toss them into the trash because, well, I don't think I'll ever want to wear them again. Wrapping myself in my satin caftan—after a shower—I head down the back staff stairs to the kitchen.

Not many things have been updated in this old mansion; however, the kitchen has been one of the few that has received a modern makeover. It has a new refrigeration system, an eight-infrared-burner stove, and all the latest gadgets and gizmos a kitchen could ask for. I sit at the prep table, where my mom has laid out for me a fried fish sandwich topped with lettuce and a slice of purple tomato. Sitting next to this warm, wonderfully smelling plate of food is a tall glass of lightly fermented citrus tea.

"Sit down and eat something already," Mother orders.

Mr. George Georg and Mrs. Georg also sit down. George Georg has been with us for as long as I can recall, as has his wife, Mrs. Georg. Mrs. Georg runs the household; she takes care of the rest of the staff and makes sure that everything runs smoothly. She even acts as a personal secretary to my mother.

"Good evening, young Zelda," George warmly greets me.

"Good evening, George." He calls me young Zelda because I am named after a great aunt on my mother's side. She was an eccentric lady and the most adventurous person I have ever heard of, but that's another story.

"Is the sandwich satisfactory, young Zelda?" Mrs. Georg asks.

"Oh, yes, it looks scrumptious!" I waste no time and dig right in. I practically inhale the sandwich. Boy, I'm famished!

My mother pulls out her cards.

"Aw, applesauce! Mother, really?"

"Yes, Zelda, really. Do not argue. We need answers." She pulls out the Queen of Wands and sets it down on the table in front of me. She shuffles the cards and hands them to me.

Now that the sandwich is safely inside my tummy, my hands are free. I shuffle the cards and hand them back to her. After cutting the deck, she deals out the first one.

She covers the queen with the Fool. "This is you." Then she flips over the Magician. "What you do. Your adventure has just begun. Choose wisely, my love. The Magician is the card of the alchemist, your power of manifestation and magic. Here you are . . ." The next card is placed on the table. "Standing ready to defend your territory. There are a number of outside influences around you . . . interesting."

Another card is turned. "A force has been dealt with. Maybe the person who is after you is gone."

I don't see how he can be.

"The card shows that he, or his influence, has left. Wait, I see something coming. It doesn't make much sense. I see your attacker leaving, yet I still see a man—a man whose intentions are evil and malicious." She turns over the King of Swords, reversed. "He is deceitful."

She holds up the King of Wands. "I also see a man who is honorable, calm, and powerful."

Next off the deck: "The Wheel of Life. You'll have success; everything's going in your favor.

"I also see great counsel from your friends and family; take their advice, Zelda. Although, as is typical, you will do what you want to do.

"I see here that you're seeking justice."

"What's the outcome?" I ask.

She pulls the last card from the deck. "Journey, my darling, a journey. What kind of journey? It could be physical, it could be emotional, it could be professional, or it could even be spiritual. I see a journey, a great journey. It's one you're going to be taking, for the good or the bad. This is your outcome."

"Are you sure?" I ask, eyeing the Chariot.

"See for yourself, Zelda. It's in the cards." My mother gathers up the cards and hands them to Mrs. Georg. She shuffles the cards and hands them back to Mother. Mr. Georg gathers from a cupboard candles, incense, and a red cloth.

Mrs. Georg sits down next to my mother and, in a monotone voice, begins chanting. Mother continues to rummage through her deck as Mr. Georg lights the incense and the candles. Placing an amethyst crystal on the red cloth, along with the candles and incense, he steps back behind my mother.

Now, magic is an interesting thing; it can be more accurately described as a vibrational intention. Whatever you put your attention to, you will attract. Magic is not really a manipulation as many believe. Everyone has an ability; it is simply that some of us are so connected to the universe in a way that we can create or manifest what others cannot. Some believe it is because we have two hearts; others believe our brains are wired differently. Whatever the reason, some can wield magic while others cannot.

Now, magic cannot make a person do something; there is a law of free will that we all must follow. There are some who use magic in an attempt to influence the way things are perceived. That is Black Magic and dangerous.

But magic allows me to move energy in a positive way. With the addition of my mother and the Georges' positive vibrational energy, I will have a boost to my already impressive powers.

Out of the deck Mother pulls the Moon, the Star, and the Magician and places them on the cloth in front of her. Mr. Georg sits down, and the three of them close their eyes, hold hands, and affirm:

"Now this time, now this place, we reach forward into time and space. We surround ourselves and young Zelda with protection and light. We send her power; we give her knowledge and might. So shall it be."

After some time spent in silence, the candles are put out and the table is cleared. Mother gives me a small amulet, which she hangs around my neck, and sends me to bed.

I sleep peacefully.

Chapter Twenty-Two

"Pally, it's me, Zelda. Hightail it over here; we have some work to do." I hang up and call down to have tea and snacks ready on the back terrace for Mae and me.

Once she arrives, we sit in the warmth of the beautiful sun star, with the salty breeze blowing off the ocean. Tiny sandwiches are served on a tiered serving tray, along with tea. "Mae, I was thinking we need to call Clover and just get the scoop on her mysterious visitor."

She huffs. "Well, I wish you would have come up with that idea yesterturn, before I went to Alcazar."

"I never told you to break in there," I scold.

"Well, our caper last night yielded nothing," says Mae, brushing aside my comment, "except bruises and smelly hair."

I just shake my head and make the call.

"Hello?" Clover answers.

"Dr. Harcrow, Clover," I say. "How are you doing?"

"I'm doing much better, Dr. Harcrow."

"Attagirl! What did the healers say about your recovery?"

"I should be able to be back at work in a couple of strings. Will you be ready for me?" The phone connection is so good, she sounds like she's just in the next room.

"Yes, Clover, I'm planning on it." Not that I've been doing much more than chasing and being chased. "When you were in the infirmary, I saw you had a visit from a young man."

"Yes," Clover says and waits for me to continue with my question.

"Can I ask who he is?"

159

Clover responds, "Oh, sure! That's my cousin Albert. He's a tinker's apprentice over at Alcazar Alchemy. He came to check on me for my family."

"I didn't know you had family here in Fulcrum." I feel a bit stupid now for thinking Clover let in a saboteur.

"Yes. Albert's my only relation in Fulcrum, so when the accident happened, the family sent him over to check up on me."

"Well, that's wonderful of him." I have what I needed. "Well, I don't want to keep you. I want you to recover and get back here as soon as you can."

"I will. That I will. I sure do miss Fulcrum, and to be honest with you, my mother is a little overprotective right now and is hovering a lot."

"I understand that one, Clover. I understand that one. Don't worry; all is copacetic. You come back to us as soon as you can." I ring off with Clover and turn my attention back to Mae. "I'm sure you heard all that; the visit was from her cousin."

Mae pours the tea. "One suspect scratched."

"Only suspect." I pop a teeny sandwich into my mouth. "You remember that lot attendant told me about a break-in at the Fischers warehouse? Do you think the break-in might have had something to do with the FJ that was stolen by Bowler Hat Thug?"

She hands me a napkin. "How can we find out?"

An idea flashes through my head. "What about Silas Fischers? He wants into you and Poppy's good graces. Maybe he'll spill on what went missing."

"On it." Mae winks and makes the call.

Mae connects with Fischers and Sons. "Silas Fischers, please . . . well, of course, darling, this is Mae Griffin—yes, I'll hold." She covers the mouthpiece. "I'm going to take the snap out of that Cybil's garters yet!"

"I don't think Silas's receptionist likes you, Mae," I say.

"That's fine by me. I don't fancy her a bit, either, darling." Mae sips her hot tea while she waits to speak to Silas. "Silas darling, how are you? Of course I did. Poppy is so excited about meeting you. He has—oh, really . . . wonderful . . . wonderful . . . wonderful . . ." Mae makes a yapping-mouth motion with her hand and rolls her eyes. "Wonderful . . . darling—Silas—I have a little question for you. About my friend Zelda. Remember we came over and talked about that stolen car? Yes—did you get it back? No? Well, that scrawny attendant said something about a break-in at your warehouse that morning too." Mae begins jotting down a number of items and hands me the paper. "Thank you, darling. Oh, you're such a gem . . . I guess . . . Ta-ta . . . bye-bye . . . so long . . . okay . . . goodbye . . . I got to go . . . bye." Finally, she disconnects.

"I'll have to confirm the list with the tinkers at HA, but some of these items could be used in a bomb. I guess we should get this list over there." I fold up the piece of paper and toss it onto the table.

Luckily, I have a direct number to Tick's office. "Tick, Zelda."

"Zelda," Tick answers, "what can I do ya for? Zenith's not ready yet."

"Actually, I'm calling on another matter. I have a list of items. I'd like to see if they match any of the remnants of the bomb that exploded in my lab."

"Sure. Glad you're in the loop now and not over the line, doll. Send it over."

"You're such a good egg," I tell him.

"How are you doing?" His voice sounds concerned now.

I pull my lips tight. "Now? Doing fine. I'm healing and my ire is up. So . . . everything is copacetic."

"Glad to hear it," he says, but he doesn't sound convinced.

"Ring me up when you get it." We say our goodbyes and hang up.

I quickly call a messenger service to deliver the list, and then I turn to Mae. "Well, we have to wait for Tick to call. Do you want to grab a swim in the ocean?"

"Sounds berries, if I can borrow a suit."

"Not a problem. Come on." I motion her toward the pool house.

We walk off the terrace and down past our pool to the pool house, where extra swimming gear is kept. The suits are very last Summer Solstice yet still fashionable. I choose to wear a two piece; the blue-and-white-striped scoop-necked tunic top hangs down past my upper thighs like a skirt, and the solid-blue shorts show my knees and six inches of my thighs. I clasp the decorative belt around my waist and look up to see what suit Mae has chosen.

Mae's a bit more adventurous with swimming suits, just as she is in life. She wears a solid-red form-fitting jumper, the shorts end far more than six inches above her knee, and thin straps hold up the low-cut top of the suit. It is definitely a daring suit, which Mae seems pleased with.

The ocean breeze has a beautiful aroma of fish and seaweed. The red sand is soft beneath my feet. The spray from incoming waves salts my face. I lick my lips and taste the saltiness of the deep green-blue water. I wade into the ocean as a foamy wave approaches me. I dive into its embrace. I swim parallel to the shore for a few meters and then turn around and head back. Mae just wades in to about her waist and splashes around. She likes it better when she can sit in the shallows and let the waves roll in and push her to shore. As I re-join Mae, I spot George waving from the boardwalk. He stands there with soft fluffy towels and embroidered woolen wraps for us.

"A call from HA waiting for you on the veranda, young Miss Zelda," George informs me.

"Thank you, George. I'll be up in a moment."

George nods and walks back up to the house.

Cuddled in the warm robe, I answer the line. "This is Zelda. How can I help you?"

"Zelda, this is Tick. That list you sent over does match components of the bomb. What is going on?"

"Thanks, Tick. I'll fill you in later." I disconnect quickly and turn to Mae. "So the warehouse was a convenience. He didn't bring the bomb with him. He had to create it from stuff he found here. He's not from Tesla, Mae. He came in on one of the ships or subs, stole the components and then the sedan, and drove to HA!"

"We have to figure out who hired him," Mae adds.

"Well, I think I'll have that answer soon by way of Cora, but we're not going to wait for her to contact us. I already have an idea where he hails from." I stand up. "Let's get dressed. We're headed to HA."

Chapter Twenty-Three

Mae, having decided to drive herself, is waiting at HA for me and my protection detail when we arrive. Today my chaperone is a middle-aged woman who looks like she can handle any torpedo coming her way.

As soon as we arrive, I go straight to see Tick Croft. On my way, I catch a glimpse of my Zenith in the garage; it appears that the cyclone engine has been removed. Tick must have gotten the parts in. *Yipee!* Finally, something good is happening for me.

"I have some of my best tinkers working on it," Tick says, seeming to appear from thin air. "It should be ready for you in the next turn or two. I'm sure you miss her."

"Oh yes, I do! I'm so grateful for all your help with repairing my girl." Mae and I follow him to his office.

"No problem. Anything for you, sweetie." He smiles as he closes the door behind him. "So, this list that you sent me—you know where the bomb came from?" Tick inquires.

Mae edges me out. "It appears that our Bowler Hat Thug stole them from Fischers and Sons' warehouse and brought them here."

"You're kidding." He wipes his greasy hands with a towel.

"No, I'm being square. The torpedo is not from Tesla," Mae whispers, as if the information were a national secret.

"You better tell Titus and Ephron right away," he advises us.

"Soon," I say. "First, I have to get a little bit more information." I give him a peck on the cheek "Tick, you're the berries for looking after the Zenith."

We pick up my shadow outside Tick's office and head upstairs.

I decide to go see the progress of my lab, to see how it's coming along. My lab is located on the third floor and takes up most of one side of the long hallway. As I pass Dr. Ravenscroft's lab, she just gives me a look.

"I think she's mad at me," I say.

"Why?" Mae asks. "The explosion wasn't your fault."

I shrug.

We walk through the open doorway to find that everything is virgin white. The new walls are up, along with shatterproof glass windows. The office and new lavatory are framed out. It looks promising, but I'm not impressed with how far the workers have gotten.

"I expected more." I sigh. "Some of the rafters are even still exposed."

Mae puts a comforting hand on my shoulder. "There was a lot of damage, darling. I'm sure it'll be ready sooner than you think."

"Let's go see Cora."

Other than Cora, the lab is empty. Zozimos and his brownnosing assistant, Needs, are nowhere to be seen. *Does Zozimos ever work?* runs through my brain.

"They're at lunch," Cora says when she sees me scanning the lab, excusing her hubby's lack of work ethic.

"I came by to see if the results were in on those samples." I wink at her and give her a nod.

"Your timing couldn't be better." Cora led us toward her desk. "I just finished with the last of the samples. Is there something wrong with your eye?"

Clearing my throat, I put my hand up to caution Cora not to say anything more. Obviously, my nodding and winking weren't clear enough. We have my one-woman protection detail right on my heels. I turn and look at my babysitter.

"Excuse-ski for a minute. Could you step outside for a moment? This is HA business."

As she leaves to stand outside the lab, she shoots me such a dirty look that I think I might need to go wash my hands.

Once the protection detail is out of the lab, Cora begins. "I ran the scarf through COORS."

"Darling, what in creation is Coors?" asks Mae.

I can guess the results, but I need solid evidence to bring to Ephron and my father. "COORS. It's a chemical and organic odor recognition system."

Mae gives me a look. "A what?"

"It's a smell sensor," Cora simplifies.

"Well, that makes sense," says Mae, who starts fiddling with knobs.

Cora briefly tries to explain it to Mae. "Basically, a sample is placed inside a box filled with sensors that respond to certain known chemical and organic molecules that attach themselves to objects. The information is then projected onto a crystal screen, where the scientist, in this case me—"

Mae cuts her off. "Okay, darling, sounds fascinating, but let's cut to the chase. What did *we* learn?"

"Thank you for your explanation, Cora." I give Mae the stink eye for her rudeness. "So what did you find out?"

"The scarf is a fine virgin spider silk, hand loomed. The white residue is salt, but not from the mines up in northern Tesla. This is from saltwater. The distinct heavy aroma is from a cigar made in Elione. Those are imported to Tesla, but with the facts found in your blood and tissue samples using a monazite crystal isotope reader, it looks like he came from the swamps of Abalone originally. I surmise that he only recently arrived here in Tesla; he was born and raised in the swamps of Abalone, Elione."

"Darling," Mae says, "how does this help us determine who hired him?"

Cora hands me her report. "Sorry to say, gals, but all my nifty crystals, pretty boxes, and microscopes aren't going to tell you that. As for who hired him, that's for you to figure out."

Mae and I pick up our shadow and head straight down to the executive offices to see Father. I see, to my surprise, that Ephron still has the same assistant as he did yesterturn. I look at Mae. "Maybe he's finally found someone?"

Mae looks at me and scowls. "Maybe he just likes to look at her. You must admit, she's a doll."

We introduce ourselves to the doll and ask to see my brother.

The doll kindly nods and shows us into my brother's office without a word. She looks and seems normal. I wonder if something's wrong with this one. Ephron gets up from behind his desk and greets us with warm hugs and loving words.

"Sit down, sit down," he says, looking me over. "How are you feeling?"

"Other than some bruising, I'm fine." I give him a peck on the cheek and take a seat.

"You have got to stop taking so many chances, Zelda." He turns his attentions to Mae. "And how is the beautiful Mae Griffin doing?"

"Fabulous, except for all this business of a torpedo trying to kill my best friend, everything's just absolutely copacetic." She dramatically waves her hand.

"I see you have new assistant," I tease my brother.

His eyes crinkle as he smiles. "Miss Trick is actually quite competent. Not only is she pleasant to look at, but she's efficient."

Mae's face sours. "Well, good for you, darling." She purses her lips and adds, "We also have some news."

Ephron walks over to his large wooden office doors and makes sure they're closed. "What's up?"

"Well, we kind of got ourselves—we kind of came into possession of—some evidence." I stumble over my words.

"We have the goods, darling!" Mae claps and rubs her hands together. "Call Titus in, and we'll give you the scoop."

"What goods? What evidence? What have you been up to?" Ephron jumps on the horn and calls Father before I can answer.

After Father joins us behind closed doors, we briefly tell them about the gathering of the scarf and the tissue samples from when I stuck my fingers in the gills of the torpedo during the attack. Ephron slumps down in his chair and looks at us.

"I'm not sure if I should congratulate you or reprimand you. Do you know what kind of chances you were taking? Not just with the local Legere, but with that assassin with the bowler hat?"

"I know, but it paid off big," I answer sheepishly. "With this evidence, we can figure out who hired him by what projects I was working on."

My father sits with his fingertips pressed together, tapping his thumbs against each other. His eerily quiet presence abruptly changes with a smirk that appears above his goatee. "Oh, what beautiful girls!" He bounces up and gives me a kiss on the forehead. "I think I know who sent the assassin."

I nod. "I think I do too."

Mae shoots forward in her seat. "Who?"

"Are you talking about the imitation spider silk?" Ephron asks, looking for confirmation.

"Yep, and they're too late," I say. "The project is in final production. The formula is finished, and the specs for the machinery are with the tinkers."

"So . . . let me get this straight . . . " Mae surmises. "An incompetent agent from Elione was dispatched to Tesla to stop you from creating a fake spider silk that you have already created?"

"Pretty much," I say.

"I guess they felt that it would tank their economy should our version of spider silk hit the market." says Ephron.

"It wouldn't even affect their market," Father remarks smartly. "Those fools! The imitation spider silk is to be marketed to those who cannot afford real spider silk. Spider silk is unrecyclable, cannot be repurposed, and is too expensive for those with a smaller income. Fools!"

"What are we to do?"

Mae raises her hand. "What if you're wrong about who hired him?"

"Call that detective of yours, Zelda, and have him come here and meet with me. I have a call to make." He gives me another kiss on the cheek and one to Mae. "See you at the dinner party," he says and promptly walks out.

"He's an odd bird, your father," Mae comments.

"Yes, but a genius."

Mae scrunches up her face. "What did he mean, the dinner party?"

"What did he mean, *my* detective?" I look at Mae, she shrugs, and we both eye Ephron inquiringly.

"The three visiting alchemists have arrived, and there's a dinner party for them tonight," Ephron informs us. "As for the comment about the inspector . . ." He just laughs and sits back down behind his desk.

Chapter Twenty-Four

The drawing room of my parents' home holds a stone fireplace that is the centerpiece of the room. The immense fireplace—carnelian-colored marble inset with black and gold veins—contains a small fire crackling away behind a gilded-iron peacock screen. There's a large gilded mirror above the fireplace, flanked by a pair of lighted sconces. The sconces, along with the two chandeliers hanging from the ornate ceiling, give light to the long room.

Many paintings of historic Teslian figures, as well as those of the Galfry and Harcrow families, adorn the grass-cloth walls. Large, neatly upholstered sofas face each other as bookends around the fireplace. Chairs are smartly scattered throughout the room, placed in conversational positions. Large floor-to-ceiling windows that face the front of the mansion are adorned with heavy velvet curtains hemmed with gold fringe.

The only thing modern about this room is the cocktails being prepared for the guests. The guests have arrived one by one and are announced by George as they enter. My mother looks upset; my father is nowhere to be seen.

Mae arrives fashionably with Silas Fischers on her arm. A.P. trails in behind them.

"Does Mother know Mae was coming with a date?" I look at a perturbed Ephron, who is usually Mae's dinner partner.

"I don't know." He gulps down his highball. "Mother hates a lopsided dinner."

It's true, even though more modern ways have given in to more relaxed rules on the subject.

"Quit fretting, Ephron. Silas Fischers is only interested in the seat on the Ocean Exploratory Council that A.P. can provide," I sort of lie. Fischers is interested in the position, but it appears to be a position that also includes Mae.

"I have no idea what your implying, Zelda." Ephron stares into his empty glass. "I need a drink." His shoulders droop as he walks away.

"Zelda, dahling!" Mae dramatically drops her *r* and sweeps toward me in a full-length sateen gown beaded with glass and pearls and adorned with rhea feathers. She even wears a large matching headpiece with rhea feathers pluming from the top. She looks like a bird.

"Zelda, you remember Mr. Fischers?" Mae reintroduces her dinner companion.

Silas shakes my hand. "Silas, please."

"Silas, it is, then. Please, try one of the cocktails. I'm drinking that new one, Bees Knees."

"Thank you, but that's a little sweet for me. I'll stick with a highball, if you have any."

"I'm game, darling!" Mae looks around the room. "Why is Ephron sulking over by the card table?"

I smile as I wave over one of the servers for drinks. "I couldn't begin to speculate."

"Well, that just won't do." She grabs her cocktail and excuses herself.

"Are your brother and Miss Griffin an item?" Silas fishes.

"No. At least, they don't think so. Don't let it bother you; it has been going on like this for rotations," I say, soothing any proverbial ruffled feathers there might be.

Although I'm in conversation with Silas, I can still hear George as he announces the guests.

"Dr. Chase, Dr. Shamm and Miss Trick, Dr. Carnot," George's old deep voice broadcasts.

The visiting alchemists have arrived. I don't know what I'm more surprised about: that Dr. Shamm is the man I bumped into at Griffin tower, that he is escorted by Ephron's new secretary, or that Dr. Nickolas Carnot is one of the visiting alchemists.

"Oh . . ." I let out a whimper.

Both Mae and Ephron dash to my side.

"I'm sorry I didn't tell you, Zelda," Ephron apologizes. "I really thought Father would mention it."

Mae elbows my brother. "You idiot, Ephron, you should have warned her."

Standing there greeting my mother was Dr. Nickolas Carnot. He was my first crush, my first unrequited love, and my first heartsbreak. Yet after all these many, many rotations, my hearts still skip beats when I see him.

Mae leads Silas away. "Darling, come, let's see about more drinks, shall we?"

My eyes are welling up. "What's he doing here?"

Ephron puts his arm around my shoulder. "He came to help."

"He wasn't supposed to come here," I mumble.

Ephron leans in closer to hear. "What did you say, Zelda?"

"Nothing," I say softly and shake my head.

"Zelda, beautiful as ever." Nickolas approaches, takes my hand, and gently kisses its back. A warm feeling comes over me. Nickolas was an employee of HA and a friend of the family, but he left to teach at one of the universities before I returned from my studies to work alongside my father and brother at HA. He's still so handsome, and his short dark messy hair, gray at the temples, now sports streaks of steel gray throughout.

"Nickolas, what a surprise" is the only thing I can muster. My mind wanders back to when I was younger, before university and before Holden. I idolized Nickolas; he was handsome and a genius alchemist. He used to let me assist him in his lab, and he even taught me spells and how to code my formulas against prying eyes. He thought he was mentoring me; I thought I was in love.

One evening, I showed up at his door in only a long, feathered coat I had borrowed from my older sister. I professed my love for him, dropped the coat, and threw myself into his arms. It didn't turn out like I had imagined. I had imagined him admitting that he had always been in love with me and making love to me all night long.

Instead, to my utter humiliation, he was an icy mitt. He grabbed the coat from the floor, covered me up, and told me that I had misinterpreted his interest in me. He'd told me he was sorry, that I was too young, that I would find someone else, that it was a crush, and so on and so forth. He sent me away.

I was *devastated*. I cried and cried. I even locked myself in my room for turns. I made the decision to leave early for university and never saw him again. Now he was here, right in front of me.

"A pleasant one, I hope." He's still holding my hand.

I can't help staring. "A pleasant what?"

"Surprise," he repeats my earlier word. "A pleasant surprise."

Before I can answer, my hand is snatched away by another. "Dr. Zelda Harcrow, how lovely to meet you. I am Dr. Shamm."

I'm relieved by his rude interruption. "We have met before, sort of." His blue-black hair is slicked back into a ponytail, making his triangular face seem harsh.

"I am sure I would have a remember such a meeting." His voice carries a thick accent that seems to add letters and turn his *w*'s into *v*'s.

Ephron jerks his head back. "You've met?"

"At Griffin Tower," I tell them. "I don't remember you having—" Before I can finish my thought, my father arrives. He doesn't arrive alone.

George announces his companion. "Inspector Chance Greyson."

Mae comes flitting over. "What is the flatfoot doing here? And who would have guessed he'd own a dinner tux. Attaboy!" She elbows my side.

The inspector, I must admit, does look handsome in his tux. "Hmm . . ." I lean my head back to get a better look.

"An inspector at a dinner party. How rich," slurs the heavily accented Dr. Shamm.

The inspector makes a beeline for our ever-widening circle. "Doc." He nods at me. "Miss Griffin, Ephron . . ." He shakes my brother's hand. "Nice to see you again."

"Inspector Greyson," I acknowledge. I start to introduce him to Dr. Shamm and his date, but they seem to have faded out of the circle to join Dr. Chase. "Ah, well. I'm sure you'll meet them later. This is Dr. Nickolas Carnot. Dr. Carnot, this is Inspector Greyson."

Nickolas shakes the inspector's hand. "Please, Nickolas. Use my first name, as Zelda does."

Inspector Greyson stands a little straighter and plants himself next to me. Surprisingly, he places his warm hand firmly on my back. "Thank you, Nickolas. And please, call me Chance."

Ephron is smiling like he has a secret of some kind. And since when is my brother on first-name basis with the inspector? I look at Mae, who shrugs. She's just as surprised as I am. I hate secrets, especially when I'm not in on them.

"Dinner is served," George announces.

Both Nickolas and the inspector offer their arms to escort me into the dining room. How do I choose? Mae comes up behind me and whispers, "Why choose, darling?"

Taking Mae's advice, I accept both offers. The three of us exit the drawing room together and head across the hall and foyer toward the formal dining room.

"Zelda!" Bounding down the stairs is my younger sister, Phrennie, home from Trade City University.

"What are you doing home?" I ask.

She shrugs. "Oh, who knows! Mother rang me up, gabbing about how Father wanted me at the dinner, so here I am. Who's the hotsy-totsy hotty? You're a fresh one; you really got *It*." Phrennie talks so fast, it's difficult to keep up.

"Inspector Chance Greyson, may I introduce you to my sister Phrennie Harcrow. Phrennie, this is Inspector Chance Greyson, and I'm sure you remember Dr. Carnot." I present Phrennie to my two handsome escorts.

"Inspector? You're jiving me. On the level? A real-life dick, flat-foot, copper? Whoopee, a regular bull!" Phrennie chats furiously.

The inspector flashes his gorgeous smile at her. "On the level, baby, a real-life copper."

I push my sister. "Quit flapping your gums and get a wiggle on."

"My, you have grown, Phrennie," Nickolas begins. "You're in university now—"

"You're on the trolley there, Joe. I'm having a bash being a frosh; it's a real hoot. Come on; let's head on in." Phrennie talks quickly, taking Nickolas's arm and dragging him away. "A gal could crush on you, daddy . . ." I can hear her continuing to jabber away.

"It looks like Nickolas's ear is going to get a workout."

"You have no idea." I laugh as I enter the dining room, arm in arm with my attentive companion.

The dining room features a long wood table with matching wood chairs and rich leather seat covers. The table is covered in a white damask cloth and each place setting has matching napkins. A smaller version of the drawing room fireplace is located on the back wall. The large floor-to-ceiling windows are dressed in drapes that match the ones in the drawing room. The fireplace wall has an archway leading to a less formal sitting and dining area and a butler's pantry, which leads directly to the kitchen.

Though the dining room is as outdated as the drawing room, the dinnerware is thankfully more modern. Bordered with a fine blue-and-gold curlicue motif, the china is the one thing about this dinner party that's thoroughly modern.

Well, there is a second: me. I wear a simple white satin gown adorned with white scalloped fringe and a low-cut cowl-draped neckline. My headdress is beaded with crystal and pearls, and white feathers drop in a curve from top to bottom on the left side, framing my face. Unlike Mae, I don't look like a bird.

Delicately handwritten place cards lead me to my designated seat. Nickolas sits across from me, and the inspector is seated next to me. A frown comes over my face. I'd like very much to know who arranged the seating. The menu is simple; the conversation, not always. We start off with grilled oysters in champagne vinegar, while the conversation centers on the Ocean Exploratory Council and its new plans for undersea studies, exploration, development, and colonization.

I listen intently as Silas begins the conversation. "The Marine Council has no interest in charting our ocean floors. Not only does it play a significant role in our climate, it also plays a role in our food supply, and they're missing out on an area of development."

"Exactly what do you mean?" A.P. sounds intrigued.

"Colonization and mining minerals—so much can be done in our oceans," continues Silas.

"People living in the ocean?" Dr. Chase slurps at her oysters.

"Well, I don't know if I'd want to live on an ocean floor." Miss Trick chimes in in an obnoxiously nasal voice. She's nice to look at, but boy, that voice! Geez. I notice Dr. Shamm slide a glance toward her that clearly says, *Shut your trap.*

"I have been counseled that much-needed minerals can be found by mining in the oceans," My father confirms. "Silver, gold, copper, zinc, and many others can be found below the ocean's surface."

"Would not all this damage the ecosystem?" I ask, attempting to both enter the conversation and keep my mind off the handsome inspector sitting next to me and my first yearning sitting across the table.

"Hence why we need an Ocean Exploratory Council," bellows A.P.

"If we mine, then we are also looking at colonization. Is that correct?" Dr. Shamm's small almond-shaped eyes narrow to slits as he says, "It sounds like it's a long way off."

Silas leans forward with great passion. "I would say there's a lot of work to be done and that it may require worldwide cooperation."

The conversation doesn't end until the oysters are finished and the smoked ham hock and pea suppa is served. A conversation begins then on the International Trade Council's decision to not expel the country of Hyde for trade infractions. It starts out benign enough. However, it quickly becomes a hot issue.

"Ideas are an important part of trade," Nickolas argues.

"Benefiting society as a whole and being able to expand on work already created—I agree," adds Dr. Chase.

"Sharing ideas and trading on these ideas created this advance society," I note. "We are so much more advanced than the world Tesla himself traveled from." I sip my vinum.

"Tesla!" Dr. Shamm seems to have taken offense from my innocuous comment. "The mythology of Tesla has no bearing on Hyde!"

Good old A.P. comes to my rescue. "We have advanced technology that would not have been possible if we all kept our discoveries under lock and key."

Everyone seems to have some sort of opinion on this matter. My mother, of course, feels that politics are never a good thing to be discussed at a dinner party and, over all, cause indigestion. Miss Trick is the only one who doesn't share an opinion about the subject, which doesn't surprise.

The person that does surprise is Dr. Shamm. He himself has created and shared his inventions and wisdom with others. I'm shocked by his statements, my sister looks confused, and my father's face has become ashen. Thankfully, the conversation switches to a newly discovered element when the warm kale salad with porto dressing is served.

"Dr. Strom from Baekeland," Ephron chimes in. "I was trying to get him to come here as well. I'm interested in learning more about this supposedly new malleable metal."

The inspector leans into me and puts his hand over mine. "Titus and I spoke."

"Oh . . . ?" I look into his protective blue sparklers.

"We should have your attacker under wraps soon." He squeezes my hand, and I swear I almost have an orgasm. Of course, it has been a while, or it might just be the vinum. I think of pulling my hand away, but his warm hand over mine seems natural.

"How much longer?" I lean in, keeping my voice low.

He takes a sip of his vinum, dabs his lips, and turns to me, his lips almost touching my ear. "Trying to get rid of me?"

Heat rises up to my cheeks. I take a deep breath. "No."

"Something else bothering you?" He gives my hand another squeeze.

"No, just a feeling." There's something more than just my unmanageable attraction for my dinner companion that I'm sensing at this table.

Nickolas notices the odd hand holding. When he clears his throat, staring at me, my hand retreats into my lap.

"I'm looking forward to reading more on Dr. Strom's new discovery," I say. From the corner of my eye, I watch the inspector's face sour over Nickolas's interruption.

Venison roast with boiled root vegetables and an aioli is served next. Another political conversation is being avoided; every subject seems to go back to politics. Poor Mother. My father, however, sits quietly as though in deep contemplation and doesn't enter the conversation.

Next, meringue floating in a sea of custard and fresh berries is served. I must make sure that I compliment Mother on her menu choices.

My sister starts the new conversation free of politics, which no doubt makes Mother happy. "The clam bakes at the U are the berries. I'm just dizzy with listening to the cob pipe. Just hot, I tell you, with canaries scat singing. The riffs on the horns are the cat's meow. Oh, the joints are hopping! Whoopee!" Phrennie's gums are flapping so fast, I think she might spew fire at any moment.

We all sit quietly for a moment, staring at Phrennie and trying to translate in our heads what she has said.

It's the inspector who does the honors. "So, Phrennie, you enjoy the parties at the university? I agree, the saxophone is quite an instrument; you really can feel the music. I heard some of the singers were making it on the fly with the lyrics; takes a lot of talent. The bands are great. I'm glad there are many places you can go to have fun."

Phrennie frowns at the table of guests. "Isn't that what I just said?"

I let my face widen with a smile. A little giggle escapes, and I quickly add that I just heard this terrifically keen new song.

My mother is beginning to look like she's staving off a headache. Luckily, dessert arrives. Aluha cake—one of my absolute favorites: dark cacao, cerasum-fruit-infused cacao covered in a thick cacao-nut-cream frosting.

The rest of the dinner conversation remains light and centers on the weather, the upcoming season, new motors, and fast music.

Chapter Twenty-Five

The party adjourns back into the drawing room for digestives and conversation. I sit on one of the heavily upholstered sofas with Dr. Chase and Mae. It's rude to leave right after dinner; all guests are expected to stay at least a few hours. Brandy and herbal liqueurs are served with conversation that is usually meant to stay light and steady.

"Phrennie plays the piano beautifully." I've never practiced, so my musical skills are practically nonexistent.

Mae, herself musically impressive, adds, "She certainly has Nickolas, Chance, and Ephron captivated."

"Your mother seems to have Silas and A.P. captive as well," Dr. Chase comments, taking a deep gulp of her brandy. The three mentioned are deep in conversation on the other side of the long room, probably discussing A.P.'s pet project, the Ocean Exploratory Council.

Feeling a bit bored of punching the bag, I begin to wander away from the conversation. I notice my father standing off to the side of everyone else, his face pinched as though he just ate sour candy. He just seems to stare into the nothingness that surrounds objects. Noticing my lack of interest in the current subject, Mae follows my eyeline. "What's eating Titus?"

Father seems to notice something that no one else in the room can see. "I'm not sure, but I plan on finding out." I excuse myself to join him, when he appears to wake up, so to speak. My eyes follow him as he makes his way to Dr. Shamm. My curiosity is piqued. I can feel my father's suspicion emanating from him as I draw closer.

"I have no idea what you are implying, Titus," I overhear. Before I can reach them, Dr. Shamm abruptly excuses himself and exits the party, pulling Miss Trick along.

Father looks very pensive, so I go ahead and ask, "Where did Dr. Shamm go?"

He strokes his goatee and then, without warning, snaps at me, "He had another appointment."

I'm shocked. Father is never short with me. "Okay."

Mae abandons Dr. Chase too. "What's going on?"

"I don't know what you mean," he says and walks off.

"I don't know. Something has his lather up."

"He does look upset." Mae's voice lilts as we watch him leave the drawing room.

"Who?"

I jump in surprise as Nickolas comes up behind us. Holding my hand to my hearts, I answer, "Father."

"What did he say?" Nickolas asks.

"Who?" Mae responds, adjusting her sheer shawl hemmed with feathers.

"Father," I answer, "and I'm not sure."

Mae looks up at me, confused, as if she's just entering the conversation. "Not sure of what?"

Nickolas smiles that warm beautiful smile of his. "Not sure what he said?"

Mae puts the back of her hand to her forehead. "My head is spinning. I think I need a drink."

"Stiff?" asks Nickolas.

I wave over the server, and we each take a new glass of warm liquor.

"So?" Nickolas inquires.

Mae takes a sip of her liqueur "Who said what?" She raises her eyebrows at me.

"I couldn't hear much. Shamm left as I approached."

"And Titus left when I came over," Mae adds. "Said it was nothing."

"Something's going on," I remark.

"Hey," Nickolas greets Ephron. "Ephron, what's going on?"

He looks perplexed. "With what?"

"No," Mae corrects. "Who."

Ephron shakes his head. "Okay. Who?"

"Titus," Nickolas answers.

"Actually, with Father and Dr. Shamm." I relate the exchange I saw between the two.

"Well?" Mae prods.

"I'm confused," comments Ephron. "I didn't think there was a problem."

"Then this is something new," I conclude.

We stand in silence for a moment. The rest of the room is lively with conversation.

Mae is the one to break the silence. "I see Poppy waving me over. Please pardon me." She joins her father. She looks over at Ephron and slips her arm under Silas's. She's really trying to get a rise out of Ephron tonight.

Ephron huffs. "I don't know what she sees in that guy." He's never understood his feelings for Mae. It's most likely best if he never does.

"It seems you're being summoned as well, Nickolas," I point out. Nickolas reluctantly shuffles over to the large group.

"We are now alone, Brother dear. Tell me what is going on between Father and Dr. Shamm."

"I honestly have no idea, Zelda." He puts a comforting arm around my shoulders and gives me a squeeze. "I wish I had witnessed what you saw myself."

"Maybe you could look into it tomorrow at the office?"

"He doesn't confide in me, Zelda. He really doesn't confide in anyone. Father keeps everything close to the chest 'til he's ready to share. He would talk to you about it long before he would me. However, I'll make some inquiries into Dr. Shamm."

I lay my head gently on his shoulder. "I wonder how Father came to the decision to bring the doctor to HA."

"I'll find out tomorrow." He kisses me lovingly on the forehead and pats me on the shoulder.

Inspector Chance Greyson locks in on me from across the room. His crystal-like eyes give me a melty feeling all over. Phrennie has retired from the piano, freeing the inspector from her enchantment. As he makes his way across the room toward me, my hearts quicken. Why do I feel this way whenever I look at him?

"Ephron, Zelda, I've had a most interesting time," he says, indicating his impending departure from the party. "Your little sister is a hoot; I've never come across anyone who could talk that fast."

"I'm glad you could make it, Chance. Zelda, be a dear and see Chance to the door. I see Dr. Chase is sitting by herself, and that just won't do." Ephron shakes hands with the inspector before excusing himself.

As I take the inspector's arm, a warm feeling comes over me again. We walk the short distance to the hall together. I listen for him to say something; instead, I hear a metallic sound as my foot kicks something across the floor.

"What was that?" he asks.

I walk over to where the metal object has stopped, bend over, and pick it up. It's a silver eye-shaped brooch with silver spikes adorning the upper emerald-studded lid. The middle holds a strange stone with a glimmering swirl in the center that appears to resemble an eyeball. "Miss Trick wore it. It must have come off when she left with Shamm. I'll give it to Ephron to return it to her tomorrow."

At the door, George helps the inspector on with his coat and hands him his hat. The inspector leans over and plants a kiss on my rouged cheek. I'm a bit surprised, and it leaves me with a hot sizzle down to my satin slippers. In fact, I think I might need to check for smoke coming from my feet. He smiles, puts on and adjusts his hat, and exits out the door.

I put my hand on my cheek and turn to see Nickolas standing in the door of the drawing room. I'm not sure if he saw the kiss from the inspector, but he must have. His face appears sad somehow, and he stands there staring at me for what seems like forever. I'm not going to make a big deal out of this; why should I? He's the one who turned me away all those rotations ago. I've led a life since then and loved since him. Did he think I would pine away? I stand a little straighter and walk back toward the drawing room, toward Nickolas. He turns to retreat into the room before I reach him.

"Just ducky," I mutter and hold my head a little higher. "Ephron," I call. "It appears your new assistant has lost a piece of jewelry."

Chapter Twenty-Six

I wake up oddly refreshed after the late night. Mother and Phrennie are still asleep, no doubt tired from the night before. I lie there in my sateen pajamas under the warm overstuffed comforter, missing the coziness of my own bed in my own apartment.

My stomach twangs with hunger. The one thing I do enjoy about staying at my folks' is the easy access to tasty food. I stick my arm out from under the bedding, fumble for the receiver, and ring down to the kitchen. Luckily, the kitchen is awake, and so is Mrs. Georg.

"Have a breakfast tray brought up to my room. Thank you." I hang up, close my eyes, and take a deep breath. Then I spring out of bed and smile. I have made the decision that I will go into HA, even if I have no lab. I rub my hands together. I want to work with the tinkers on my Zenith motorcycle. Today will be a good turn.

I hum a fast tune as I run my hands through my wardrobe. Head bopping to my own melody, I find the perfect outfit. To work on my iron, I decide to go casual: dark-lapis dungarees, a light-colored blouse, and a necktie to match the pants. This means I can't wear the amulet my mother gave me, so I leave it on my dressing table next to Mae's charging shockgun. I tuck my dungarees into a pair of knee-high laced boots that I use for riding my bike, and I put a blue cotton cap on over my pink-tipped golden tresses. With charcoaled eyes, rouged cheeks, and stained lips, I'm ready to go.

I look in the mirror. Jeepers! My eyes widen, and I give my reflection a nod. I'm a regular doll. Just because a gal is working on machinery doesn't mean she can't wear fashionable gear.

I'm still under a protective detail, even though we've identified the threat. Deciding to ride with my father to HA in his chauffeured motor, I gallop outside and down the front steps. A chill goes through me. The mornings are beginning to get nippy; as such, the evenings already are. Tesla is entering the cooler temperatures of the Autumn Equinox, leaving me to question if I should have worn a coat. As I'm contemplating my choice of outfits, Father joins me on the walkway outside.

I greet him with a kiss on the cheek. "Good morning, Father. I hope the morning finds you better than the evening did."

"I'm sorry, my dear. What did you say?" Father looks a bit queer, as if he's in another world.

"I said, how does this morning find you?"

"Decidedly better, my dear, decidedly better." He smiles and gives me a comforting little wink. He's acting more himself.

"Well I'm glad to hear it," I say as we walk together toward the car. My father's driver stands at attention at the rear of vehicle with the door open, and our escort is already in the front of the vehicle.

Suddenly, I start feeling queasy.

I stop dead and turn toward Father, who looks at me strangely. "What's wrong, Zelda?"

My head tilts and I look past him. I can see air moving. The landscape is still there, clear all around except for a large oval-shaped area. A wave of nausea overtakes me. Everything behind my father is hazy and wavy. I squeeze my eyes shut tight and quickly reopen them, but everything behind him is still a blur.

My whole body begins to sway. He grabs my arms and shakes me. "Zelda! Zelda!"

My jaw goes slack; all I can do is stare. My stomach flips again, and my breakfast attempts to escape. A blaze of lightning flies through the wavy, distorted landscape. It's some sort of gateway, a portal. I've heard of them before, but I've never seen one. The foudroyant attack of nausea comes again. Like a slap in the face, it wakes me; I clasp Father's arms and push him behind the motor, covering him with my body. I fumble for the zephyr and groan; I forgot it upstairs. My arm swings up over my head for protection, and I wish I had the gun and the amulet.

I hear shouting and the low pitch of an EP weapon. Our constabulary escort screams for everyone to stay down as he continues releasing electromagnetic pulses from his weapon at the mysterious disturbance. The portal, or whatever it was, disappears along with my nausea. I cautiously lift my head and turn in time to see a white spider-silk scarf floating gently to the ground.

At first, I think it's Bowler Hat Thug, but the attack seemed to have targeted my father and not me. And what about the portal? The thug has never used one before. This attack was different. Reinforcements are called in, and one of the officers checks us over for any physical damage while another guards us until we can be questioned. My leg is restless, bouncing up and down while we wait for Inspector Greyson.

Our property is searched for the perpetrator. "Fools!" my father blurts out. "They will find nothing!"

"What was that?" I'm anxious for this experience to be over.

Father's voice drops. "Something dangerous."

"What do you mean, dangerous?"

Before he can answer, Inspector Greyson arrives on the scene. "Doc, Doc, are you all right?" He runs swiftly to me.

I put my hands out to stop his closer advances. "I'm fine. I'm fine."

His brow furrows and his face twists as if he's confused or hurt by my refusal for comfort. "What happened?" His tone flattens.

"I don't know," I whisper. Physically I'm aces, but mentally this last attack has thrown me a little off.

"What do you mean by 'I don't know'?" he demands, his voice rising.

I begin talking fast. "It was like a portal." My voice strains. "Like a hole in the space behind Father." I begin shaking. "A shot of lightning came out, directed right at him." Tears are now escaping. "The chauffeur dove into the motor, and I pushed Father behind the back bumper."

My hands are trembling. He places one strong hand over mine and instantly it calms me.

"A portal would be impossible, Doc. It must have been something else." His eyes shoot over to my father and then back to me. "Relax and tell me what you saw, first." His voice has become warm again.

"Nothing, Inspector. She saw nothing." Father pulls me close into his embrace and whispers, "Say nothing about what you thought you saw. I'll handle it." Father kisses me on the cheek as he releases me.

"Well, Dr. Harcrow, I believe your assassin from Elione hasn't gotten the message that your daughter's experiment is done and finished." Inspector Greyson's voice rises. "They seem to still be after her!"

"But it seemed like the attack wasn't directed at me. It was directed at my father."

"I'm sure that's what you think," he replies, pushing aside what I recall. Speaking more to my father than to me, he adds, "We do have a lead on the assassin, and you know we'll keep you apprised of the situation."

As they continue to talk, I leave their company to watch the coppers work the scene. I walk over to where the portal opened. Squatting down, I peer closer at the curious evidence that was left. My nose wrinkles. I pick up the scarf that still lies on the walkway, put my nose to the material, and inhale. I jerk my head away at the foul stench. It smells different. It no longer holds the heady scent of a savory cigar or even of salty fish; it smells like decay.

"Doc, that's evidence. You shouldn't be handling it." The inspector crowds close to me.

I step back and hand him the scarf. "Something's not right."

He moves closer to me. "This scarf shows that the assassin is still after you."

Standing my ground, I tell him, "It doesn't smell right."

He chuckles. "It doesn't smell right? Listen to yourself, Doc. That doesn't make any sense. I understand you've had quite an experience, but you're getting worked up over a smell," the inspector says judgingly as he bags the scarf and hands it to DSI Flynn. "Look, I'll send it down to the Legere Legalis headquarters, and I'll take a look at it." His placating doesn't decrease my anxiety any.

Father clears his throat. "Inspector."

"Yes, sir?" The inspector stands straighter as he addresses him.

Dr. Titus Harcrow's stature is smaller than the inspector's; somehow though, his presence is larger. "Could you take my darling daughter over to HA? Make sure she gets there safely? I have some things to do." He walks promptly back into the mansion without saying another word. I'm perplexed by his ever-changing behavior, and he doesn't seem concerned that he might now be a target.

I grab the inspector's arm. "Let me take this scarf to the HA labs. I have someone who can test it properly. I'm telling you, something's not right. It smells like decomp, not fish or cigar."

He pulls his arm from my grasp, annoyed "You're telling me that because it doesn't smell of fish, something's wrong?"

"Yes." Then I smack my head. I never did tell him about the scarf we found in the stolen car, and I'm not sure I should now. Mae and I could get in a lot of trouble for it; Constable Hodge too.

The inspector removes his hat and combs his fingers through his hair. "If there's something up, *we* will figure it out. Meaning law enforcement, not you. Understood?" He raises an eyebrow at me. "Besides, I already have a lead on the assassin." He flashes a smile. "We'll pinch him up, and everything will be copacetic."

Pacifying me is not the way to go. "Are you listening?" I hold my breath for a moment and then exhale forcefully. "The torpedo could not have pulled off an attack like that."

He motions for one of the constables. "Take the Doc to HA, no stops."

"Yes, sir." The nondescript constable salutes.

I growl, stomping off after my new driver. How I wish Hodge was back to being my driver. Working on my Zenith might actually be the only thing that will keep me from exploding. Whatever feelings I may have been fostering for Inspector Chance Greyson just flew away with the warmer weather.

I check in at HA and head down to the tinker area to begin working on the Zenith. *Cl-ump, cl-ump.* My boots make a rhythmic, determined sound on the marble floor of the main lobby area. The lobby is buzzing with employees and visitors jabbering and chattering before the start of business. No gossiping for me; I'm on a mission. I'm not exactly sure of my mission; all I know is that I'm still a bit steamed at the inspector.

Inspector Chance Greyson and his rejection of my ideas takes a backseat when I see Dr. Shamm talking up Nickolas's assistant, What's Her Name. "What a cake-eater." First Ephron's assistant, now Carnot's. This guy gets around.

"Darling, Zelda, yoo-hoo!" calls a voice most familiar. I smile and turn around. There is Mae in a pure-white shift dress, long beads, white cloche hat, and white Mary Janes, with white stockings to match.

"You look like snow."

Mae frowns and puts her hand on her hip. "Really, darling, snow?"

"You're all white, head to toe!"

She fluffs her hair with one hand. "I am dark, darling, so white looks fabulous on me."

"Seriously, white? You know you'll spill something on it," I tease.

Mae twirls her beads like a windmill. "I am not eating or drinking today. Easy enough." She smirks.

I grab the beads midflight. "Stop that before you put somebody's eye out!"

Mae pulls her beads back. "Darling, tell me what has happened. I can see the stress on your face. If you keep frowning like that, you'll look like an old woman, a regular face stretcher."

I feel my forehead for any premature wrinkling. "We had another attack."

"Bowler Hat Thug? I thought Titus took care of that?"

"Honestly, Mae, I'm not sure. Something is off; I can feel it." I look over to see if Shamm is still cozying up for a cuddle with Nickolas's lab assistant. Both are long gone, so I turn my attention back to my pal.

"Go in and see your brother. I'm sure he can help."

"Huh?"

Mae curls her lip. "You weren't listening. Where did your mind fly off to?"

"Just across the room; it was nothing." I sigh. "I am sorry. Where were we?"

"I was thinking about the dinner party last night and Titus."

"Oh, like something came to his attention?" I'm on the trolley now.

"Exactly." Mae nods. "Right, let's go talk to Ephron." Arm in arm, we trot off to the executive offices.

Miss Trick is still employed as Ephron's assistant; as long as she doesn't open her squeaky mouth, she should last. "Miss Trick, I'm here to see my brother. Is he available?"

"Oh, I'm sure for you he is. I had such a lovely time last night. So many interesting people." Her vocal chords have found a new high pitch, and I cringe a bit at her attempt at articulation.

"Did Ephron return your brooch? I found it on the hall floor last night."

"My brooch?" She looks at me, puzzled, and then seems to acknowledge the strange piece of jewelry. "Yes, the watching eye." She pulls it out of the desk drawer and pins it on the faux lapel of her dress. "Yes, he did." She pats the oddly enticing piece of jewelry. "Thank you for finding it." Miss Trick abruptly deserts her seat behind her desk. "I'll announce you."

Mae pulls me into her side and whispers in my ear. "That was odd, don't you think?"

I nod at Mae in agreement as Miss Trick shows us into the office.

"My two favorite girls!" My brother seems to be in a good mood. He walks swiftly to us and gives us each a hug. "Sit down, sit down." He's grinning from ear to ear.

"Ephron, what's got you so hopped up?" Obviously, he hasn't heard about the recent attack.

Mae's eyes widen. "You're not on dope, are you?"

"What? No!" Ephron flops down in his chair. Apparently, Mae just took the wind out of his sails.

"Don't get in a panic. I just received some swell news."

"We came with news too." I push my hair behind my ear. "Tell us your news first." I could use some good news right about now.

Ephron can obviously sense that something is wrong, though; he leans forward in his chair. "What's up, Zelda?"

Mae glances at me for a moment, smiles, and takes the lead in the only way the ever-eccentric Mae can. "You show me yours, and then I'll show mine." She smiles seductively and winks.

"Oh, please." I roll my eyes so hard, my head goes along with them. "Seriously?" I slouch back into my chair. "Just spill already, will you?"

"I just landed an additional deal with the Space Exploratory Council!" He jumps from his seat in enthusiasm, knocking his hot tea all over his desk. "Oh shit!"

Mae runs to Ephron's side to help move his important papers. I run out of his office to get something to wipe up the mess from Miss Trick. I swing open the office door and am confronted with Dr. Shamm leaning over Miss Trick from behind, whispering in her ear. I stand there for just a moment, staring at the pair. Dr. Shamm whispering and Miss Trick staring straight ahead—it doesn't seem like much of a lovey-dovey situation, so I don't mind crashing in.

I loudly clear my throat. "Ahem."

"Dr. Harcrow, how nice to see you again." Dr. Shamm's dark almond-shaped eyes glare at me, sending shivers up my spine.

I ignore Dr. Shamm's false pleasantries and speak directly to my brother's assistant. "Miss Trick, my brother has made quite a mess of his desk. Could you please bring in some rags to help clean it up?"

Blinking rapidly, she looks up at her aristocratic admirer nervously before bolting from her desk to help. I think she might have broken the sound barrier.

I move slowly toward the tall alchemist. "Dr. Shamm," I start, looking into his dark eyes. "You left so quickly after dinner last night that we didn't get a chance to talk."

"I am sorry that I was so abrupt." His words flow like tar out of his mouth: hot, smelly, and sticky. "The food was a bit rich for my delicate digestion. I was not feeling too well."

I narrow my eyes. "It's hard to believe a handsome, virile man such as yourself would succumb to something as innocuous as a rich dinner." I cast my line to see what I might catch. I'm curious about what went on between my father and this man standing in front of me.

Shamm cocks his head, lets out a small chuckle, and smiles. "Titus said something similar last night, without the lovely compliments you bestow upon me. I would have stayed and ignored my unfortunate condition had you been my companion for the evening."

That's not quite the reaction I was looking for, but I play along to save myself any possible embarrassment. "That would have been lovely. Maybe another time?"

"It would be a delight, Dr. Harcrow." He glides toward me and brings my hand to his mouth.

"A delight." His voice oozes as he kisses my hand before slowly releasing it.

I pull my hand away. "You may call me Zelda."

"Zelda it is," he says.

I turn my head toward the door when I hear Mae calling for me. "Doctor . . ." I turn back to excuse myself; however, the puzzling Shamm is gone. I shrug, wipe my hand on my dungarees, and head back in to Ephron and Mae.

"Thank you, Miss Trick," Ephron says, dismissing his assistant. "Close the door behind you."

"Yes, sir." My brother's good-looking aide bops out the door.

"Okay. What's up?" Pressing forward, I ask, "The new deal?"

"We have just been placed in the catbird seat. Our very special company has been asked to head up the entire Moon Exploration Phase 1 project." His voice squeaks with excitement.

"Oh, Ephron, how exciting!" I run around the desk to hug him.

"Congratulations! We will have to celebrate!" Mae claps her hands and trots over to the cocktail tray. "Where's the bubbly?"

Ephron pats the air with his hands to quell our excitement. "It hasn't been made public yet, so keep it under your hats. However, with everything going on, I wanted to share something positive."

"I am so proud of you, Brother. Excellent job!" I then add, "Does Father know?"

"Not yet. I was going to give him the news this morning. I thought he would be in by now."

Mae pours herself a drink and gives me a look.

I nod. "It's hard to explain things."

Ephron's smile has left his face, the excitement of his news deflating like a balloon. "What now?"

Mae waves the back of her hand toward me. "Go on. Tell him."

I proceed to fill Ephron and Mae in on the perplexing assault that took place this morning. "It was like a portal opened up."

"Portal? I didn't think anyone still had knowledge of portal magic." Ephron leaves his desk to kneel beside me and hold my hand. "Continue," he urges.

There's not much else to convey. I shake my head as I describe the inspector's decision to focus only on the Elione assassin. "We need to get hold of that scarf or some other evidence."

"What about Titus and the dinner party?" Mae asks. Ice clinks in the glasses she brings over to us.

Ephron pinches his lips together and walks back behind his desk. "Whatever is going on with him, he is keeping me at a distance. Chance probably knows more about our father than any of us." He shuffles papers on his desk and sighs. "I agree that something is up, and with this latest attack, the new contract may be at risk."

So I'm back to trying to help save the family business. I rub the back of my neck. "I think I need to find out more about portals."

"How are you going to manage that?" Mae asks.

There is one person I know who might have my answer, but can I stay steady in front of him or would I melt in his presence? I excuse myself from Mae and my brother and head upstairs to visit with Dr. Nickolas Carnot.

I knock on the glass door of the laboratory that the visiting alchemist is using. His bright-eyed assistant lets me in. I hold out my hand. "Hello. We haven't met yet. My name is Dr. Harcrow."

She lets my hand dangle there in the air. "Yes, I've heard of you. Put on goggles; we've had a few minor setbacks."

A small explosion rocks the lab, and my goggles go up over my eyes in a flash. "I see," I say as I follow the rude little vamp.

Nickolas looks up from an infrared burner. His eyes sparkle and he gives a wide grin. "Ah-ha! I'm onto something, Zelda!"

"Attaboy!" I'm transported for a moment back into the past as I run over and embrace my one-time mentor. I freeze and my cheeks flush. "I'm sorry. I got caught up in the excitement." Clumsily, I back away.

"Don't apologize." His voice has softened. "It was nice. I forgot how much I missed that."

I can feel my ears burn, and I'm sure they're as red as my face. "You must miss creating new formulations."

He lifts my chin with his hand and stares into my eyes. "Among other things." The space between us becomes smaller.

The stillness is broken by the loud coughing of his lab assistant, whom I have decided not to like.

"Sir, what do you need me to do?" the sourpuss asks.

"Clean up the lab and put my notes in my office safe before you head off to lunch." Nickolas removes his goggles and then mine. "Lunch, Zelda?"

The answer comes tripping and tumbling out. "Yes, that would be swell." I give Whatever Her Name Is a smug smile as I stroll out of the lab with Nickolas's arm around my waist.

Chapter Twenty-Seven

Once I have checked in with the tinkers and my Zenith cycle, I send a note up to Ephron and Mae about my lunch plans. Nickolas and I pick up the fire extinguisher, a.k.a. my constabulary bodyguard, and drive out to Seaside Village Town Center. The afternoon has warmed up, and the sun star's rays feel like a warm blanket on me. I close my eyes and let the warmth continue its comfort.

Nickolas reaches over and puts his hand on my shoulder, bringing me to the present. "Are you okay?"

"Yes, I'm fine." Not really. I have someone trying to hurt my family and, by extension, our business. I look out the passenger window again and close my eyes. I smile up at the sun star; the big fiery ball of gas is on my side, and for just this moment, everything feels all right.

Restaurant by the Sea is on the wharf at Seaside Village Town Center, located before Seaside Village, where I grew up. I've eaten here many a time throughout my life. In fact, I've done so many a time with my current companion, even. I look at Nickolas as we walk to the entrance. If I were to close my eyes, it would almost feel like nothing had changed. Time would feel like it was standing still: he and I taking in lunch after a big discovery in the lab, venturing here to this place as a celebration. Things have changed, though; rotations upon rotations have gone by. I'm no longer that young drunk-in-love girl. Now, with my life in peril, Carlton's death, and possibly the lives of others in danger, I can see that I'm changing again. Nothing will ever be the same.

The hostess ushers us to a table, our very noticeable chaperone trailing behind. "Officer, would you like to join us?" I'm only being polite, hoping he'll say no. How am I supposed to grill Nickolas about portals if this flat tire is hanging about?

The nondescript constable tips his uniform hat. "No, thank you, Dr. Harcrow. I'm on duty. I'll be taking a position at the entrance to the patio."

"Okeydokey." I salute him as we take a seat on the patio overlooking the crisp blue sea. I dodged that one. Good. Now I need to ease into the whole magical portal topic without getting sidetracked by the dreamiest alchemist in all of Tesla. Crap, I am a lost cause. Stay focused.

The restaurant's patio is done up in a very rustic seafaring way. Carved driftwood tables and benches adorn the warm-gray weathered deck that looks out over the red sand dunes and crashing surf. The hostess hands us the one-page menu and takes our drink orders.

"Thank you for agreeing to have lunch with me." Nickolas smiles as he takes a quick sip of his barley beer.

Jeepers! He has the most engaging smile. His smile is broad and curls up into shallow dimples on his cheeks. His eyes crinkle ever so slightly at the corners to reveal happy wrinkles. I begin gazing at him like a silly infatuated schoolgirl.

Then it hits me like great black clouds rolling in over an ocean. I remember my past embarrassment with Nickolas, and without thinking, I hug my middle, trying to keep myself from dashing away. I smile shyly back at him and take a massive nervous gulp of my beer. I begin to gasp as my tiny smile of embarrassment leads to liquid rushing up through my nose. I keep coughing and choking as the beer burns and stings my nasal cavity.

"Zelda! Are you okay?" The bench flies back as Nickolas dashes to my side.

I keep hacking and coughing as Nickolas pats my back. I've never understood the whole patting someone on the back thing. It doesn't do anything. I mean, I'm coughing because I just put fermented liquid up my nose and now I have someone pounding on my back. Yep, not helpful. I hold my chest with one hand and wave him away with the other.

"I'm fine. Just embarrassed a bit, and I could use a glass of water." I continue to wave him back toward his seat.

"Miss, I brought you some water." My shadow detail has come to my rescue. I cough out a "Thank you," but he's already returned to his post at the patio entrance.

"You shouldn't be embarrassed. You are not the first person that's happened to. You won't be the last!" Nickolas chuckles and hands me a napkin to wipe up the snot-infused beer that has landed all over my dungarees. I clean up my pants and blouse while he tells me a story of a time he was giving a lecture on how silicon could replace fluorocarbons in solar panels and a small sip of water catapulted out of his nose and onto a visiting member of the Energy Council.

I start feeling a little better. I have finally composed myself a bit. After checking my compact to be sure no stray snot is affixed to my face anywhere, I return my attention to the table. "I think we should order."

"Sounds good. What do you think? Seafood tower?" He tosses aside the menu and holds up his glass.

"I'm game if you are!" I smile and tap his glass with mine.

We sit and chat over our drinks, avoiding any subject of importance. While we wait for the massive amount of food that we both know we couldn't possibly finish, I bring Nickolas up to speed on what I've been up to over these many rotations.

I take a large gulp of beer, taking care to let it slide down my throat instead of swallowing. Once up and out my nose is enough for me. "As you know, my fiancé, Holden, died investigating a storm." I take another gulp for courage. "Since then, I've been buried in work." I update him on some of my published work and successful experiments that have already been made public.

The hostess interrupts our unimportant conversation with a large sheet of butcher's paper. "Let me get this down for you, and the server will bring out your lunch." She goes straight to work, covering the length of the driftwood table with the brown paper. As soon as she has the ends secured, the food is carted over to the table. A large tray piled high with every imaginable type of seafood is set between us. Napkins, hot clarified butter, and a pitcher of barley beer are delivered as well.

Nickolas dives right in and pulls out a very spiny crab leg. *Crack.* He opens the hard shell and retrieves the sweet meat. "I miss the fresh seafood here in Fulcrum. We don't get this kind of spread in Capital City."

I pull out a bright-red lobster tail. The shell has already been cut, revealing the white and pink tender meat. "I must admit, I haven't been here in over a rotation." I dunk the meat into the butter sauce. "Mmm . . . so good."

"I know you've been busy; I've kept up with your career."

"Really?" I briefly look up from stuffing my face. I study his expression, searching for a clue as to what kind of reaction he's expecting from me in response to his little revelation. I can't read him. I grab a prawn and pull it from its shell. I inhale sharply and ask, "What can you tell me about portals?" I've gone for it; no turning back now.

"What?" His mouth drops open and the clamshell he was shucking falls and tumbles onto the deck. He stares at me intently and then lowers his head and voice. "What brought this on?"

I lower my voice to match his hushed tone. "Why are we whispering?"

"Nobody practices it." He kicks the abandoned clam off the deck after a quick look around to see if anyone is watching.

I check around too. "Is it a secret?" I lean toward Nickolas so as not to be overheard.

"I don't think so." He's still whispering.

"Then why are we whispering?" I grab a crab leg and sit back on the bench.

Nickolas sits up straight and a wave of puzzlement stretches across his face.

I return his look of befuddlement. "Well?" I ask.

"I have no idea." His normal volume returns as he squirms in his seat. "So tell me why you asked about portals?"

I suck in a breath, close my eyes, and let the air slowly leave my body through my nose. A good cleansing breath always calms the anxious mind. I take a moment and begin my "bland" tale of adventure, mishap, danger, and intrigue. I skip over the Chance Greyson parts and a few of his heroic exploits on my behalf, because I'm still mad at the inspector. I go into detail, though, on the latest attack and what I saw.

"Wow! I'd heard about some of what you've just told me, but I thought it was all over now. Titus and that inspector contacted the Elione government to reach out to the spider silk farms and factories." He leans his chin into the open hand covering his mouth and shakes his head. "Wow."

"Yeah, wow." I nod. I avert my eyes and then my head toward the open waters of the sea and the gentle puffs of wind coming into the coast.

Nickolas stands and leans over the table and the mound of seafood, takes my chin, and tenderly turns my head toward him. "Tell me what you want to know."

Okay, I blush when he touches me. Jeepers! He still has such an effect on me. I shake my head free and ask my first question, acting as though his simple touch is not affecting me. "What is a portal, really?"

Nickolas retreats to his seat and takes up his role of teacher. "Simply put, it is a doorway that connects two locations. You enter one side and end up in your destination of choice."

Well, that sounds simple. "Is it a physical doorway?"

"No. It's all mind-thought and manifestation." His dimples appear at my naïveté.

Damn those dimples, I need to stay focused. I clear my throat. "Just like spells or telekinesis, then."

"Yes and no." He finishes his beer and pours another glassful from the pitcher. He holds up the pitcher to me. I shake my head and urge him to continue.

He takes a long drag of the dark amber liquid. "First, you have to know where you're going, and I mean *know*. In theory, not visualizing your destination properly could get you stuck in an in-between space."

My body tenses. I need more than a preschool tutorial. "I understand that. Now how are they created? And . . . who is still out there practicing this?"

"To answer you . . ." He dips his head and looks up at me with his lips tight. "It's like opening a curtain and pushing up a window sash."

"And . . . ?" I start to drum my fingers with force.

"And . . . I don't have any idea who could still be using magical portals. I mean, they're dangerous. They haven't been used in fifty rotations, and for good reason." He takes another slug of beer and refills his glass again.

With a huff, I hold out my glass. "Fill 'er up." Nickolas obliges and fills my glass. "Sorry. I get that you're worried. How am I going to protect myself, my family, and HA if I don't understand what is happening?"

Nickolas catches my hand as I set the glass on the table. "Just promise me you won't try to use one."

"Sure, I promise." I cross my fingers behind my back.

His speech is slow and deliberate. "Once your destination is held in mind, focus on a point of space."

I nod my head, and he continues. "Take this point and sweep a line out horizontally each way from that zero dimension. Now you have one dimension."

Seems simple enough. I nod again, encouraging the flow of information and secretly hoping he'll speed it up a bit.

"Move the one dimension perpendicular to itself 'til it becomes a two-dimensional square. Move the square in the direction perpendicular to the plane of the space, and you now have a three-dimensional cube. See where I'm going with this?" He stops to take a bite of food and a long drink of beer.

"The one I saw looked more like an egg." I scratch my head, wondering if there is more than one kind of portal.

"Nope, that is what they call bending; it's actually square. Now, you have a cube. Move that cube into itself and push it forward to create the four-dimensional hypercube otherwise known as a tesseract. That's your doorway. Then you just place your destination in the last cube you made."

He stops and waits for me to respond. And I do, but with a question that takes him aback.

"What about time?" I'm not sure why I ask about it, but it feels important for future information.

"Zelda!" His voice booms loud enough to catch the constable's attention. Nickolas waves the constable back to his post and lowers his voice. "Time travel is illegal, Zelda. Besides, moving through time would require one to create additional dimensions. In theory, you would need to create a great number of vertices, edges, and facets; it's not any easy task to hold all of that and hold your exact time and place in mind."

"Why do you have to have intimate knowledge of your destination?" I ask. "Couldn't I use a picture?"

He finishes his beer and proceeds to fill me in on the small details. "Say you wanted to go to a tropical spa on the Island of Nani, but you've never been there. Imagine what it's like with palm trees and sand. That could describe any place with sand and palm trees, and you could end up anywhere with that landscape." Nickolas goes on to explain, "You could use a recent picture in theory, but not one with people. You could never be sure where the people are currently or if they actually are in the place in the picture."

I close my eyes for a moment, contemplating the information he has passed on. When I open my eyes, I take a bite of food and a small sip of my beverage. "Nickolas, you make it sound so easy."

He simply says, "If you have a keen mind, yes, it can be easy."

We sit in silence, eating the unending tower of seafood. I'm going to need to be rolled out of here if I keep shoveling in the grub. Just as I shove another piece of crustacean into my kisser, Inspector Greyson slides up next to me.

"Okeydokey, Doc, where is it?" he demands.

I look at him and then at my lunch companion and shrug. Nickolas mirrors my shrug. Together, we look at the inspector, confused.

"Come on. You know exactly what I'm talking about!" The inspector seems a bit peeved, for which I wish I could have claimed responsibility.

"Sorry, I have no idea what you're going on about. I've been here having lunch with Nickolas. Plus, your constable hasn't left me for one instant. So whatever I'm being accused of, it wasn't me," I respond smartly with as much venom as someone like me can muster.

Nickolas rises to my defense. "Chance, you ask your man; he has been with her all turn."

"I need some answers. A piece of evidence from this morning is missing." And the inspector has obviously attributed the vanished clue to me. With him coming to blame me, I can only conclude that it must be something like the scarf.

The inspector slams his hand down on the table. "I'm not buying it. If you didn't take it, you must know who did."

"What was this evidence that has you all in a tizzy?" I know it isn't nice to egg him on like this, but I'm still miffed at him.

His eyebrows unfurrow. "Are you on the up and up? You didn't take it?"

I nod. I would have liked to keep him on the rocks. Unfortunately, my stomach has other ideas and does a bit of a flip. I turn my head to Nickolas sitting across the table from me; he's still shoveling in oysters. He stops suddenly, mid-slurp, his eyes widening a bit. I look back at Inspector Greyson, who gives me a similar look. A large belch rumbles from deep within my belly, and I swiftly lift my hand to cover my mouth.

Inspector Greyson is the first to comment. "Doc, you're looking a bit green around the gills."

"Zelda, are you feeling all right?" Nickolas inquires.

My stomach begins to turn and churn, and it takes everything I have not to puke all over what's left of the jumbled heap of seafood.

Nickolas gets up from his seat and holds out his hand. "I think I better get you home—now."

I reach out to take his hand, but Inspector Greyson catches mine instead. "I got this, Nickolas."

Nickolas backs away. "Fine." He then waves my chaperone over to assist. "Zelda, drink some ginger-and-mint tea; it will help with the upset tummy. It looks like you had way too much food and drink."

With assistance, I make my way off the patio, but not before Nickolas gives me a gentle kiss on the cheek. "Take care."

Greyson pulls me away. "Don't worry. I said I've got this."

The short trip back to my folks' house seems longer than it should, though I'm not sure if that's because of my stomach or the deafening silence inside the tin. Even after we arrive, the walk from the curb to the front step seems far. Jeepers! Climbing the stairs is like scaling a mountain. George opens the door as I struggle with the last step. I muster a weak smile of acknowledgment.

"Young Miss Zelda, are you all right?" George asks, holding the door open for me.

"It seems the doc ate a bit too much, George," the inspector says as he hands me over.

"Thank you, Inspector Greyson, for bringing her home. We'll take care of her." George helps me into the hall. Greyson lets go of my waist, but not before kissing me on the forehead.

Once I'm in my room, Mrs. Georg closes the drapes to darken the room, prepares a hot water bottle, and makes me a steaming hot cup of ginger-mint tea. Another perk of staying at my parents' is the whole getting waited on, hand and foot. I still miss my apartment and my privacy, but I miss it less in instances such as this.

Chapter Twenty-Eight

I wake with a start and sit straight up. For a moment, I'm a bit disoriented as I have a ringing sound in my head. Slowly, I remember that I'm at my folks. I also remember the huge seafood tower and my bellyache. I shake my head, but it keeps on ringing.

It takes me a moment to realize the sound is coming from my phone, not my head. I fumble for the receiver. "Hello—hello?" I continue talking, and the phone keeps hollering at me.

Crap, I picked up the house phone. The ear piece finds the cradle after a few tries. Then I answer my wireless. "This better be good!"

"Jeepers creepers, darling! What's eating you?" Mae's voice calls out from the other end. "And where did you disappear to after lunch yesterturn?"

"Sorry, Mae," I apologize. "I came home with a stomachache, and I was lying down. I must have fallen asleep and just slept through the rest of the turn."

"You're forgiven-ski, darling," Mae purrs through the airwaves. "Why the tummy troubles?"

"Seafood tower and a lot of beer," I complain, rubbing my stomach.

"Seafood tower would do it. So how was the lunch, other than the hangover?"

I give Mae an abridged version of the conversation with Nickolas and the interruption by Inspector Chance Greyson. I decidedly leave out details like the inspector kissing my forehead before leaving. "So that's the scoop boop be doop."

Mae laughs. "Who do you think would have absconded with a piece of evidence?"

"Inspector Greyson wouldn't know what to do with a clue even if directions were attached."

My conversation with Mae drifts to more mundane things, like the upcoming Winter Solstice season's colors and fabrics. We revisit the idea of raising hemlines and knee socks; I'm enjoying talking about something other than assassins, magic portals, and sabotage.

Without warning, the door to my room swings open, creating a hole in the plaster of the wall. My head turns before my body does, and the wireless slips from my hand. There stands my mother, frozen in the doorway, her face lacking all color. I bite my lip as I shift around to stand up. I can hear Mae shouting through the wireless. I bend down to pick it up. "Mae, let me call you back." I stare at Mother as I disconnect the call with my best friend.

Mother's hand rises to touch her face, as though checking to make sure she's here. "Zelda." She swallows hard. "Your father . . ." A single tear escapes the corner of her eye, releasing the flood gate on her sobs. Her hand covers her mouth as she inhales sharply.

"What happened?" My body starts to shake uncontrollably, but I manage to hold back the tears. I'm not going to fall to pieces until after I have found out why.

My mother takes a deep breath and holds it. "There was an attack on Titus at HA." She exhales so hard then, her body goes limp for a second.

My hands clench. "Is he . . . ?" I close my eyes tight. I can't finish the sentence.

"I don't know if he is . . . Zelda, please take me there." My mother rubs her face dry with her hands and then smooths her dress. With a sniffle, she turns and heads downstairs.

I stand there frozen, unable to move. If I take a step, just one, I will surely collapse and shatter upon the floor. There's ringing again, coming closer to the forefront of my consciousness. *Ring, ring, ring.* Nonstop, it keeps coming, bringing me back to the present like I'm being shaken awake. I peer down at my hand; it's my wireless that's heating up with an undeterred ringing. Slowly, I bring the handset up to my ear, and without listening for any response, I say, "Mae, I'll call you back."

I have my protection detail drive us to HA as I'm in no shape to be behind the wheel and Mother doesn't drive. Rather, we don't let her drive. Tortoises are faster than Ave on the road. And even at the slowest speed possible, she still manages to return the vehicle with unexplained scratches, dents, and dings. Mother has said countless times, "If I want to go fast, I'd take the train, but why would anyone want to go that fast, anyhow? You miss too many things along the way." That actually probably clears up the mystery of the dents and dings.

Mother and I rush into HA and straight toward the executive offices. Security guards stand diligently at the doors of the offices. When they see my mother and me running toward them, they promptly hold open the doors for us. They must have been told to be ready for our hurried arrival.

What we enter is complete chaos. Mother is screaming "Titus!" at the top of her lungs. Security is scurrying like startled mice, and medics from the infirmary are checking employees for any injuries. I try to spot Ephron and Father, but there are too many people going in too many directions.

Mother keeps hollering, "Titus! Titus Harcrow, where are you?"

"Here I am, my sweet."

Father's voice calls out from behind one of the sofas. A sofa that is now adorned with a very large burning, gaping hole. Titus's head peers through the hole in the sofa, and then he slowly rises to greet us. "Nothing to fret about. I'm fine."

Titus stands there with his shoulders back, his hands on his hips, and a smile on his face. I am sure that's intended to signal to us that all is copacetic. However, the fact that his hair is standing straight up and still smoldering gives my mother and me other ideas.

I'm so relieved he's unharmed. I dash into his arms, grateful he's okay beyond his new unwanted hairdo. Father squeezes us in his arms, holding my mother and me as tightly as he can muster.

"What happened?" I ask. "Was anyone hurt?"

"I don't know if anyone was hurt besides the sofa and my pride, my dear." He kisses me on the cheek. I close my eyes and send out a silent *thank you* to the universe. Father nods toward my brother as Ephron joins us in our little family huddle.

"Well?" I ask Ephron, my tone turning accusatory. "What in the stars is going on?"

Ephron frowns. "I'm fine, thank you very much."

"I'm sorry," I apologize, giving him an extra sisterly squeeze. "Are you all right? What happened?"

"Never seen anything like it." Ephron shakes his head. "Bolts of lightning were coming out of nowhere, shooting all over the offices, and trying to hit Father."

"The attack didn't come from nothing, my son," Father says quietly.

We stand in our huddle for a pensive moment when Mother blurts out, "Like in the cards!"

Great, she foresaw something specific and now she tells us. "Was it—"

"A portal," my father finishes.

My mouth goes dry, so I just nod. He kisses me on the temple and lightly rests his head alongside mine as he confirms my theory.

After a few more moments of the stillness among the chaos, we break our huddle. "Listen," says Ephron. "I've got to check on everybody and make sure the building is secure." He swiftly returns to the fray to find our head of security, Jep.

My mother and I look to Titus to fill us in on the details of the mysterious shots of lightning. He obliges.

According to my father, he was exiting Ephron's office with Dr. Carnot when large bolts of electricity began emerging from the center of the room. My father's voice is surprisingly even as he just gives us the facts, nothing more. There's no trembling voice as he describes running from the onslaught of lightning barreling down on him or when he describes Dr. Carnot's bravery when Nickolas pushed him seemingly out of the way of a stream of lightning. His voice never wavers from the calm tone as he recounts his mad dive behind the sofa as the last bolt barely missed him.

"Really, Titus, are you all right?" Mother tries to smooth his still smoking hair back into place.

He pats her hand. "Yes, my sweet, I'm fine now that you're here." Father looks at me. "What we should be asking is how Nickolas is."

My brow knits, and I feel like I have somehow been lied to. "I thought no one was hurt."

"Calm yourself, Zelda. All I know is that he pushed me and I fell out of the way. Why don't you go check on him?" He looks back at my mother, smiles at her, and states, "We'll stay here for a few more moments, if you don't mind."

"No problem." I surely don't want to be subjected to their canoodling.

I begin walking slowly through the large room, scanning it for signs of Nickolas. Our security people and other employees are dashing about, making my search a bit more difficult. My feet stop moving abruptly, my body stiff with anxiety. Usually when I catch a glimpse of Nickolas, my hearts race, the blood rushes to my face, and I get all giddy. Not this time, though. In this instance, my hearts sink and my blood pools toward my feet. My one-time mentor and first real crush lies on a gurney with healers surrounding him.

"Oh, no!" I cry softly, just above a whisper. As if on autopilot, I put one foot in front of the other toward Nickolas. The jumble of bodies dashing around the room seems to magically part as I make my way across.

I'm close now. I stop and snatch a breath of air, and my hand flies to my hearts as I catch sight of Nickolas sitting up and conversing with the medics and healers at his side. Letting go of my tightly held breath in relief, I easily ankle my way over to one of the handsomest and most amazing alchemists I have ever known—besides my father, of course.

Nickolas's head turns my way, and a smile runs across his face. I hope the smile is for me. My hand reaches for my hot cheeks; my grin must be a kilometer wide. I quicken my step and close the gap between us. Once at his side, I can't help but wrap my arms around him.

"Ow!" he yelps. "Careful there."

I promptly release him. "I'm so sorry! Are you hurt? Did I make it worse? Are you going to be okay? Where did you get hurt? Did the healers take care of you?" Words are flying out of my mouth while I look him over.

Nickolas puts a hand to my mouth, cutting me off. "I'm just fine; no real damage done." He lowers his hand and grasps mine. "Now I know why you were concerned about portals and Titus."

I look him over. He's sitting up on the gurney with his legs dangling over the edge. His shirt is off, revealing his well-toned arms and chest. A bandage is wound around his arm and shoulder.

"What's this?" I ask, pointing to his injury.

"Nothing. Don't worry." He squeezes my hand to alleviate my concern. "Now you can see that messing around with portals is dangerous. You need to forget what I told you."

I look at the medic who is gathering up the medical supplies used on Nickolas. The older gentleman answers my unspoken question.

"Yes, he will be fine. Some bumps and bruises from falling and a scorched flesh wound from the lightning." He continues to pack up. "The healers performed a standard healing spell, and the intuitive said there were no internal injuries."

"Is that it?"

"He'll be a little sore, but that's about it. Keep the wound clean and let the spell do its job. In a turn or two, the doctor will be right as the rain the Weather Council grants us."

I murmur a thank you and nod at the departing medic. Turning my attention to Nickolas, I smile. "I'm so happy you are okay." He reaches up with his free hand, grabs the back of my neck, and kisses me.

Chapter Twenty-Nine

Wow! Nickolas releases me from the unexpected yet most keen kiss.

"Zelda," he begins. "I wanted to talk to you about . . ." His voice slows as he loses my attention to some new arrivals.

I pull my hand out of Nickolas's and step back when the office doors open and in saunters Inspector Chance Greyson with an entourage of constables and his ever-loyal DSI Flynn. He barks a few orders, and his constables disperse to all corners of the already busy room. One of the constables is my new friend, Officer Ethan Hodge, who quickly dashes off to my father. My brain flashes to what Ethan might have to speak to my father about, but the thought is quickly replaced with the desire to give the know-it-all inspector an earful.

"I warned him my father was in danger, but he just gave me the bum's rush on the subject." Steam is coming out of my ears.

"Hey." Nickolas grabs my arm and turns me to face him. "Forget about him. Let's you and me talk." He lets go of my arm. "Privately," he adds.

My body still faces him, but my head turns to watch Inspector Greyson walk toward us. "Sure," I say apathetically, not really listening to Nickolas's requests.

"You're not going to forget him, are you?" Nickolas's voice goes flat. "What is going on between the two of you? Zelda—"

"Nothing is going on," I mumble as I walk away from Nickolas and toward Inspector Chance Greyson.

The distance between the inspector and me grows smaller as we make a straight line for each other. Without warning, I can't move, and I become nauseous and lightheaded. The words *Oh, no* stay in my head, as I find myself unable to vocalize them. My stomach churns, and time seems to elapse slowly; everything moves at a tortoise-like pace. I can hear voices trying to bash through the cloud in my head. Was that Father yelling for me to run? Maybe it was Ephron; they can sound alike. My ears are trying to make out all the different muffled voices that are demanding action from my hazy brain.

One voice cracks through the others—Mother's. "Watch out, Zelda! Run!"

Yes, run. I must get away. My feet scrape the carpet in an attempt to free myself, but it's too late. My arm flares with pain, a vicelike grip on my upper arm. It grows tighter and pulls me closer to the rip in space. I pull in the other direction, my body turning away from the dizzying conjured doorway. The hold on my arm grows even tighter, and a shriek bolts from my mouth.

Without thought, I turn my head toward the cause of my agony. It's a hand! I try to look up to see the man attached to the offending appendage, but there's nothing but a hand! Whomever this member belongs to is still inside the swirling vortex of the portal, and the hand is pulling me in to join its owner. What takes only seconds seems like hours of struggle.

A sharp scream rushes at me and shakes me awake with its arrival. I struggle against the pull, the nausea, and my impending doom. Then, without warning, I'm wrenched free of the grasp that has held me so tightly and thrown to the ground. A familiar scent of comfort enters my nostrils as my savior lies over me. The portal has closed, and I lie on the ground, crying from excruciating pain, as my rescuer cries from relief, covering my body and protecting it from any further attack.

My mother—the "I don't leave the house without scrying first" worrier—saved me.

Soon she and I are encircled by everyone else asking if we are okay. What a ridiculous thing to ask, really. I was just manhandled by a magically conjured doorway, and my mother just tackled me to the floor. No, I am not okay, and I would have chewed out everyone for the inane question had I not been in such a ludicrous amount of agony.

I go to move my arm, but it's filled with pain, so that's not happening. I fling up my good hand and grasp my shoulder. "Fuck!" My hand runs along the bump at the front of my shoulder, and I scream again in distress. My arm has been dislocated. Crap!

Inspector Greyson shoos away the bystanders to let the medics examine me. My father helps Mother up and holds her close to him while Ephron shouts orders at anyone and everyone.

Me? I'm begging for something to knock out the all-consuming pain.

Thankfully, I get my wish. I feel a poke in my good arm. "Ouch!" A wave of warmth comes over me, bringing an absence of pain and numbness. I close my eyes, and everything just goes away.

Chapter Thirty

I wake up with my arm aching for more opium to ease the pain. I feel my shoulder with my free hand; my shoulder is back where it belongs. Someone leans over me and says something, but it's all faint. I close my eyes and drift away.

I'm unsure how long I've been out. Was it just an afternoon? Or has it been a turn or maybe two. Everything seems hazy as I lie there, trying to focus on the ceiling tiles above me in the infirmary. I slowly move my head to the side and strain a bit to see who the figure is that is slumped in the cushioned chair by my bedside.

"Hey, you're finally awake. Jeepers, you were sleeping a long time." Mae sits up. Her curly hair is smooshed on one side, and her bangs, which usually sit straight on her forehead, are pushed to the side. She looks a sight!

"How long have I—you been here?" My voice is small and tired. I try to maneuver myself up to a sitting position, or at least a decent incline. Then I notice my arm is in a sling and I'm no longer wearing my own clothes but cheap nightclothes supplied by the infirmary.

"Darling, they had you hopped-up big time. You've been on dope for two turns."

Wow. I rub my head. Mae bounces up and over to the side of the bed and helps me into a sitting position. "They've got you under twenty-four-hour guard, and they're out there looking for the torpedo." She attempts to fluff up the flat, unfluffable pillows. "I made up an overnight bag for you. I brought you some glad rags and some munitions. You look like a chunk of lead."

"Gee, thanks. You don't look so swell, either." I grab the bag of goodies she offers.

"What do you mean? I always look spot on." Mae grabs a compact mirror from her handbag. A shrill shriek explodes from her mouth. "This just won't do! I look hideous! I look worse than you!"

"Settle down. It isn't that bad." I hand her a comb.

"Really? You may be used to looking like that, what with things exploding around you on a regular basis. No, darling, Mae Griffin is always perfect."

I raise my eyebrows at her unbelievable claim. "Mae, fix your hair and give me the scoop. What's the dirt on the whole portal attack, and why have they kept me hopped up for turns?"

"Don't know much myself." She fluffs her hair and brings it back to life with her hand and my rat tail comb. "See that baby grand outside your door?" She points the comb toward the door and a brick house resembling a man—or vice versa. "He's not letting anyone—and I mean anyone—get near you." Mae drops her compact back into her purse and hands me back my comb.

"On whose orders?"

"Well, your father's, Ephron's, and Inspector Chance Greyson's, I guess." She shrugs.

"Really?" I exclaim. "They haven't found him yet?"

"Bowler Hat Thug?" Mae pulls a very attractive pantsuit from the overnight bag. "There's been neither hide nor hair of him, and the Elione government is denying any involvement or knowledge of the ongoing attacks."

Mae drops a silky chemise over my head, and I carefully remove my arm from the sling to slip it through the armhole. It's a bit painful, so of course I complain.

"Careful, darling. You're still healing." Mae lays out the pantsuit in front of me.

"Come on, give it up. What's the scoop?" I lift the jacket of the suit. "Is this new?"

"Of course it is. You're in need of something new after what you've been through." She helps me on with the jacket. "Everything has been very hush-hush around here. They really battened down the hatches." Mae frowns. "Poppy—he won't even talk to me."

My hair is brushed, my eyebrows are filled in, and my mouth is drawn red. I'm almost dressed and ready to go. But go where? I'm not sure. Should I go back to my parents? Should I go back to my apartment? All I know for certain is that I miss my life: I miss working in the lab. I miss discovering things. I even miss when things go a little haywire and we have a small explosion.

Mae aids me as I maneuver out of bed and step into my fancy new slacks. I pull them up just in time, as Inspector Greyson saunters into my room. I slip one of my feet into a mule and give him a sideways glance. "And to what do I owe the pleasure of your company?"

"Are you supposed to be out of bed?" he asks, ignoring my question.

Balancing on one leg, I set my other foot into the matching shoe. "It was only a dislocated shoulder, nothing life threatening. Certainly nothing that required me to be unconscious for two turns." My annoyance spews forth from my mouth.

He puts his hands up in surrender. "Hey, not my idea. You can take that one up with your family."

"Believe me, I will." I put my hand on my hip. It would have looked more decisive having both hands on my hips, but the other one does have to stay in a sling for now. I think he gets the gist of my attitude, though. "Mae said she doesn't know anything. How about you? What's going on? Have you located the source of the portals?"

The inspector looks down at the hat he's holding. He plays around with the brim and looks up. "I'm sorry. There's no news yet on the assassin. He seems to have disappeared into thin air, so to speak."

"Are you pulling my leg? That bimbo, conjuring up a portal?" I laugh.

"Listen, I know you have some strange theory that the Elione assassin is somehow out of the picture, but there are no other suspects. Understand? Unless you have an idea?" He rocks back and forth on his heels.

"What are you saying?" I press my lips together and narrow my eyes. "Well?"

"Have you pissed anybody else off recently? Of course, besides me."

I grab a floppy pillow, and with my good arm, I fling it in his general direction. "I'm beginning to hate you. You know that, right?"

"I think not. I think not." With that, he picks up the pillow and tosses it over to Mae's vacated chair. Smiling, hat in hand, he exits the room.

Mae steps forward. "Do you really think Bowler Hat Thug is no longer a threat?"

My face softens, and I scoot onto the bed. "I wish I could get my hands on that scarf."

"Say you do, darling. What would that prove?"

She's right, of course. Without Bowler Hat Thug, the Legere will continue to chase shadows. I rub my head and groan. How do I prove that the maker of the dangerous doorways is someone other than the assassin from Elione? Mae pats my leg and sits beside me. Our legs dangle above the floor, and our heads are lowered, just like my spirit.

Mae breaks the silence. "When was the last time the torpedo attacked?"

I scrunch my face and lift my head. "The last time I saw him was when I stupidly chased after him. The next attack was the first portal."

"Isn't that when the scarf was left?"

"Yes, trying to throw us off."

"Or maybe to send a message." Mae cocks her head. "When did you lose him?"

I'm still stuck on the idea of the scarf being some sort of note. Mae clears her throat. "Oh, sorry." I tuck my hair behind my ear. "That's what happened: I lost him." I blankly stare across the room.

Mae clears her throat again. "And?"

I bring my focus back to the present. "You know, when I chased him at Griffin Tower."

Mae presses on. "No, I mean yes. On the corner by the alleyway?" She falls silent for only a beat. "Isn't that where the Old Vick Hotel is?"

"Umm . . . yep, it's being modernized—refitted from steam and gas."

Mae stands up and brushes the creases from her pants. "It's abandoned, right?"

I shrug my shoulders and then wince from a twinge of pain.

"Darling, let's see about getting you sprung from this joint." With a swish of her wide-legged slacks, she turns on her heel and flits out the door, past the very large bodyguard shadowing my door.

Hopping off the bed, I pace the room. Jeez, what's taking Mae so long. Finally, voices come from the hall.

Healer Vaidya enters my room with clipboard in hand. "Well, it seems you're healing up nicely. I don't see any physical reason to keep you any longer."

I blow out a sigh of relief.

"Just give your arm some time. No overexertion." I shake her hand, gather up my overnight bag, and head for the door and the bimbo guarding it.

I stop before crossing the threshold. "Healer, where's Mae?"

"Not sure, Zelda. She asked if I would release you and headed out."

"Thanks." I step over the threshold and right into a brick wall.

"And who might you be?" I ask the very large and intimidating baby grand in front of me.

"My name is Zeper Jo, but they call me Big Jim."

"Really? But your name is Zeper."

The very large man shrugs his shoulders. He stands at about two meters tall. He's bald, though I think that's because he shaves; I can see a little stubble regrowth on the back of his skull. His suit seems so ill-fitted that if he threw a punch, the seams of his jacket would probably split. Big Jim looks like a fighter. His arms are as big as my waist, his muscles a reservoir of power. He's a regular tank. Not sure how this guy is going to stop the formation of a portal with lightning shooting out of it. Maybe he's lightning-proof; otherwise, I see him being absolutely no help.

"Okay, Big Jim, let's blow." I step onto the lift. When Big Jim steps on, it kind of shakes a bit. "You know, there's a weight limit on these things. Maybe we should take the stairs." He looks at me and nods in agreement.

The last time I was in the executive suites at HA, it was utter chaos. Now it looks as though nothing occurred; even the sofa with the large burning hole in it has already been replaced. Dottie bolts from behind her desk and gives me a squeeze. "I'm so glad to see you're all right."

I flinch from the exuberant hug. "Thanks. Is my father in?"

"He's in with Mr. Ephron, dear."

I give Dottie a squeeze of the hand and a quick smile, and then my shadow and I cross the floor to my brother's office. There, sitting behind the desk, is the vocally challenged Miss Trick. "Nice to see you again, Dr. Harcrow."

I know I should be happy that Ephron finally found a capable assistant, but I just can't get myself to like her. "Nice to see you too, Miss Trick. I'd like to see my brother, please."

"Yes, I'll announce your arrival."

Miss Trick gives Big Jim the once-over up and down before she knocks and waits for permission to enter the office. In a bit, she comes back out and tells us to go right in. I open the door slightly, making a small gap between the doors, before turning to the brick house behind me.

"Wait here."

I squeeze in and shut the door. There stands my father, leaning over Ephron's shoulder. My brother is fingering a stack of papers. The door bangs shut, and Father looks up and smiles. "Zelda, my dear, you look terrific."

Ephron and Father round the heavy wood desk and rush to me. I flinch again from the well-meaning embraces, and my hand flies to my shoulder to rub away the dagger of pain.

"Sorry, Sister dear. I'm just so glad to see you up and about."

"Well, Brother dear, I would have been up sooner had someone not had me all doped up." My eyes shoot back and forth between my father and brother. Ephron steps back, his chin drops down, and the smile leaves my father's face.

"It was for your own good, Zelda. You needed time to heal, and I knew you would want to try to get involved in the investigation again. Your mother and I felt that you needed to be protected."

"Protected? You knocked me out. What if a portal had opened up? I wouldn't have been able to defend myself."

"Now, now, that's not true. We hired that nice young man to watch over you."

"You mean the brick building?" I swing my good arm around to point at the door.

Father looks at Ephron, a little confused. "Father, she means the bodyguard is very large."

"You slay me, Zelda!" He looks back to Ephron with raised brows.

Ephron's eyes roll up as he nods. "Yes, Father, you used the word correctly."

Father grins. "See, I can learn."

I release a deep sigh, close my eyes, and shake my head. I can never stay mad at my father. He's always such a jovial fellow, and deep down, I know he thought he was doing the right thing.

"So where is Mother? Back at the house?"

"I sent her to join Phrennie at your sister Ava's place in Capital City. They will be staying there until this situation is over."

We take seats to discuss what has happened and what is next. "Everything leaves a trace, Zelda, even magic," Father says. Nodding in agreement, I stay silent as I listen. "That nice Constable Hodge assisted Dr. Ravenscroft in collecting samples from the area where the portal opened twice."

Ephron leans back into the leather sofa and looks to the ceiling. "Hopefully, we will hear something in the next turn or so."

I move to the edge of my seat. "Why was Ethan Hodge assisting one of our people?" I inquire.

"Nothing for you to concern yourself with, Zelda. Right now, you need to keep yourself safe and out of trouble. Besides, your mother will have my head if something happens to you."

I look toward my brother, who clasps his hands and lowers his eyes. "We got this, Zelda."

My insides twist. I'm being frozen out. I open my mouth to protest when Dottie dashes into the office unannounced. "Miss Zelda, there's an urgent call from Mae Griffin."

Great.

Ephron stands up. "Dottie, is Miss Griffin okay?"

I butt in. "Relax. She's probably having a shopping crisis or banged up her new ride." I lift myself out of my chair. "I'll take it at your desk, Dottie." I look back at my brother and father before I exit the office. "Don't think we're done here. I want to know everything that's going on; this concerns me too, you know."

I feel something under my foot as I exit the office. Lifting my foot, I find that ugly pin of Miss Trick's. Picking up the brooch, I leave my father and Ephron. As I make my way over to Dottie's desk, I toss the pin at Trick.

"The clasp broke," I say in a trance-like tone. Nickolas has entered the reception area, and my attention lies on him alone. I think a squeaky voice says something, but I just wave it away and make my way toward him.

"Zelda, it's so wonderful to see you up and about. How are you feeling?"

I shove Big Jim toward the outer office door to wait for me. "Oh, I'm just ducky." I smile shyly. Ugh, I can't believe I still get all aflutter whenever he's around. The lump in my throat proves challenging. "How shoulder?" *My stars!* "Shoulder doing?"

I jab the air with my finger. My face has begun to roast; I wonder how many shades of red have come and gone in this brief few seconds. "How is the burn on your shoulder?" I finally articulate.

He flashes his dimples. "Healing just fine. The bandages come off today. Aren't we a matching set?"

My hearts leap to join the lump in my throat. It's getting a bit crowded up here. "Matching?" my voice scrapes out, barely audible.

"Our shoulders," he explains. "Both wounded?"

"Oh, yes!" I giggle like a schoolgirl. I'm about to say something else completely stupid when, to my luck, Dottie interrupts to hand me her phone receiver. Thank the universe for small miracles.

"Mae, what's the news? Wardrobe malfunction? Barrels of paint in your tin? Shoes not matching your purse?" I laugh.

"Not quite, my darling. I'm in a bit of a pickle."

The connection is a bit soft. "Mae, I can barely make out what you're saying." I press my ear harder against the headset. "Mae, you didn't break in somewhere and get stuck again, did you?" I can barely hear her, but I can hear the trembling in the words she speaks. Something is deadly wrong.

"Mae, talk to me." I hush my voice so as not to call attention to my conversation. "Mae." The hair on my neck stands up, and a soft breath warms my exposed ear. I swing my head around.

Nickolas.

"What's wrong?" he whispers in my ear. I cover the mouthpiece. "It's Mae. She's in trouble again."

Then I hear a whimpering from the other end of the line. "I found him."

"Found who, Mae?" Nickolas cocks his head to one side and mouths *Who?* I call into the receiver again, "Mae, who did you find?"

Mae's voice cracks. "Bowler Hat Thug!"

Chapter Thirty-One

I can't believe my ears. My jaw drops open, and I whimper her name. Every horrid scenario runs through my skull in seconds. I should have known she would do something stupid trying to help me. Oh stars, what has she done?

"Mae," I call into the phone again. Nickolas places his hand lightly on my shoulder. "Mae, are you okay? Are you in danger? Where are you?"

"Darling, I'm sorry," she answers. "I'm fine, but I can't say the same for Bowler Hat Thug."

"What?" My brows furrow in my confusion.

"I'm not in any danger. You were right; Bowler Hat Thug is gone."

"Where did he go?" I ask.

"Zelda, he's gone. You know . . . out of business, done for, finished, expired, bereft of life, no longer alive. He's dead."

"Are you sure?"

"Well, he isn't moving. He hasn't blinked once, and the knife sticking out of him leads me to believe he has, by all accounts, kicked the bucket. He's deceased."

"Oh." I look over at Nickolas and mouth, *He's dead*. The tension I've been holding for so long escapes in a large exhale.

"What should I do now?" Mae asks.

"Call the inspector," I say.

Nickolas rips the receiver from my hand as if it were a weapon. "Before you call anyone, go through his pockets."

"Are you crazy? He's dead, remember?" Her voice shrieks over the line. "He smells too."

"You have to. Come on," he begs. "Check to see if he has any papers or objects."

"Why can't the Legere do this?"

After these new attacks, a nagging feeling has been plaguing me. I don't have the whole picture, and others have been personally keeping me in the dark. Maybe before all this started, I would have been happy being left out, but things are different now. I'm different now, and I want to know. I pull the handset to my kisser.

"Because, that's why. Please-ski?" I use my best whiny voice.

"Ew-ski," Mae complains. "I am going to puke."

"Anything?" Nickolas is impatient.

"Yuck, yuck, and gross," Mae fusses. "No scarf."

I place my hand over the mouthpiece. "No scarf?"

"Look harder!" Nickolas spits into the speaker.

"No papers, either, just some weird . . ."

I slide a confused look to Nickolas for his out-of-character pushiness as I pull the receiver away from him. "Call the Legere while we come meet you."

"Sounds reasonable. I'm at the Old Vick Hotel. There's a joint across the street, Mack's Bar and Grill. I'll meet you there."

"Dandy." I write the name of the place on a piece of scratch paper on Dottie's desk. I tilt my head toward the paper. "Can you take me there?"

Nickolas seems preoccupied with whatever Ephron's assistant is doing. It doesn't look like she's doing much from where I'm standing, just flirting with that dummy Needs and playing with the clasp of her pin.

I shake my head and direct my attention onto more important matters. "When you call, leave an anonymous tip," I firmly instruct.

Mae drops her voice. "What was that?"

"What was what?" The tension in my body is back.

"I heard something. I think I have company."

"Mae, hide or, better yet, beat it!" I try not to raise my voice. Several folks in the reception area are already looking at me. I smile and turn away. No need to draw attention to our newest predicament.

Nickolas leans in to whisper in my ear. "What's happening?" I shrug my answer.

"Oh, my stars!" Mae's voice vibrates from the other end.

"Mae?" I'm going to explode. "What is happening?"

"Aren't you just the sweetest little thing."

"Who are you talking to?"

"Elephantus's eyebrows! Don't eat the bad man's face! That's just icky."

"Mae!"

"That's it, precious. Come here. Don't be afraid. No, don't eat his hat; you might get bad dead man cooties."

I raise my voice. "What is going on?"

"Zelda darling, it's a little dogacorn. It must be hungry. Poor little one, don't worry. I'll take care of you."

"You scared me, Mae. I thought—"

Mae's voice shakes as she interrupts me. "He's growling, and it's not at me."

"What do you hear?" I ask.

"Sounds like footsteps, I think. It's too hard to tell."

"Make tracks. I'm on my way."

"Okeydokey. You shred it—wheat!"

The line goes cold. I put the receiver back in the cradle and take a deep breath. I jab at the paper frantically. "Nickolas, will you drive me there?"

"Yes." He seems to be back to normal. He grabs my hand with calm strength. "Relax. Everything will be fine. But what are we going to do about our very large company?"

"Easy. We take him with us; we may need him."

I peer toward Ephron's office. Needs is gone, Miss Trick is on the horn, and the office door is closed. No need to bother Ephron with this.

Getting a tank into a car that really doesn't have a backseat is not an easy task. "Does this tin have a rumble seat?"

"No. Maybe he can run alongside," Nickolas comments as he pulls the bodyguard's arm from one side of the vehicle while I pushed his backend on the other side.

"Big Jim doesn't run," he says, squeezing one leg into the tin.

"I can understand that," I remark.

"He's not fitting in the car; he's too large." Nickolas puts his foot on the tin to gain some leverage, to no avail.

"That's why they call me Big Jim." Big Jim is half in the small motor now, one leg hanging out one side and his head sticking out the other.

"Maybe we could cut a hole in the roof?" I scratch my head and take a couple of steps back to get a better vantage point of the apparent conundrum.

"We are not cutting a hole in my roof!" Nickolas puts all his weight into pushing Big Jim's oversized melon into the car. "Don't you have a spell or something for these kinds of occasions?"

"First off, I am an alchemist, not a miracle worker. Secondly, why would you surmise that I would have many occasions such as this?" I push at Big Jim's backside. "I think the back tire went flat," I holler over the carriage to Nickolas.

Big Jim moans.

"Zelda, this isn't working." Nickolas stops pushing on Big Jim's head.

"Well, my roadster is back at my apartment, so I don't have any wheels."

Big Jim clears his throat.

I duck my head into the carriage. "What?"

"I have a vehicle." Big Jim attempts to shift his body. The tiny tin rocks back and forth.

I poke my head out. "Big Jim's got a tin."

Nickolas leans through the opened passenger door. "You have transportation?"

"How do you think I got here?" Big Jim tries to shift again, and the other back tire blows out. "I think my leg is asleep. I can't feel it no more."

"Why didn't you tell me you had a vehicle?" I ask.

"You didn't ask," he says bluntly.

Nickolas throws his hands up in the air. "Great. Now how are we going to get him out?"

I frown. "I need vegetable grease and a spatula."

Big Jim groans again, and Nickolas starts pulling at Big Jim's head.

Chapter Thirty-Two

Finally in Big Jim's sedan, I sit in the roomy front, while Nickolas is relegated to the squished backseat. Big Jim has the front bench seat pushed so far back to make room for the tree trunks he calls legs that the backseat is mostly moot.

Big Jim starts the motor. "Where to?"

"Crap, I forgot the piece of paper on Dottie's desk." I punch my leg.

"I think it was Joe's Bar and Grill." Nickolas spouts out, trying to find a place for his legs.

"No, not Joe's," I say. "It started with an M."

Big Jim shifts into drive and heads out of the front lot. "Would that be Mack's Bar and Grill?"

"That's it!" I snap my fingers. "Attaboy!"

"I'm familiar with the joint." The bimbo heads out to the Industria 2 and straight toward the center of Fulcrum.

We drop off the thoroughfare a couple of exits from the city center. The shiny Griffin Tower sparkles in the midafternoon sun, and in its shadow is the abandoned Victoria Grand Hotel, which has garnered the name Old Vick as the city has grown and modernized around her old bones. Big Jim drives down the street and past the old girl, turning down an alley catty-corner to it.

"Stay in the car 'til I clear the parking lot," Big Jim orders. He proceeds to walk the small lot behind the bar, checking all nooks and crannies and in-betweens, as well as inside parked vehicles. The big guy gives us a wave. I give the amulet my mother gave me a squeeze before I slide out the driver's side. Nickolas squeezes out of the backseat headfirst onto the pavement.

"Quit fooling around," I say to Nickolas as he makes it to his feet and brushes off his trousers.

"How else was I going to get out?" he asks, falling in behind me.

"Feet first." I smile. I have my back to him, so my confidence, false as it is around him, has revived.

We stop at the alleyway and the corner of the building. Big Jim holds one hand up. "Stay behind me. Wait for my signal to move." He peers around the edge. He gives a nod and waves us forward. We follow closely, and I suppose we look a bit silly walking into the bar single file. Big Jim stops abruptly, his hand rising swiftly as we enter. Unfortunately, I don't stop quite fast enough. I plow into what feels like a stone wall and land on my fanny.

"Ow!"

"Let me help you." Nickolas attempts to lift me off the sticky bar floor.

"I got it; I'm fine." My ego and my ass are both bruised. "Can you see Mae?" I turn my head away. I don't want him to see the crimson my face is surely turning.

"I can't see anything past Big Jim here," Nickolas says, moving side to side to try to look around my bodyguard.

I jump up and down trying to get a look-see. "Me neither."

Mack's Bar and Grill resides in one of the older brown brick-and-stone buildings that still stand among the youthful towering steel-and-glass structures. The joint is not like modern clubs. Newer clubs have large bandstands and equally large dance floors, cloth-covered tables, waiters in tuxedos, and lots of bubbly vinum. Mack's is a neighborhood dive, where everybody knows everyone else. It doesn't have a large orchestra, just a quartet that plays ballads and drinking songs in the evenings. People come here for the camaraderie and to play nine-ball on the back tables or a hand or two of pinochle. The food here is simple, and so is the liquor.

I hear a definite "Yoo-hoo!" from the back of the dimly lit room.

"This way." Jim turns sideways and gestures toward a teal glove waving from behind the tall-backed bench seat of a far corner booth.

We hustle on over and slide in to join Mae. Big Jim gives the bartender a nod and takes up position outside the booth, keeping guard over our powwow.

"Are you all right?" is the first thing I ask. The second is "What are you wearing?"

"This is my incognito investigation outfit. What do you think?" She turns her head to the side, fluffs up her hair, and strikes a pose.

"Incognito?" I study her outfit. She wears a black cloche hat that has bright teal feathers extending from the hat's band on the right side. She wears an ebony modern long-sleeve shift with a teal neckerchief tied high around her neck. Long gold chain necklaces, teal gloves, and gold bangles on her wrists finish the outfit. Definitely not incognito.

Nickolas says nothing; he just sits there stupefied. He raises his hand, gaining the attention of the bartender, and calls for a drink. I yell over to amend his signaled order. "Make it two."

"Whiskey?" The bartender lifts a bottle. Nickolas's thumb goes up.

"Whiskey, it is."

Mae takes a gulp of whatever concoction she's having. "I heard that in Baekeland they are all teetotalers and that alcohol is illegal. Can you imagine: no liquor?"

A small scream escapes my mouth. I creep up the back of the booth's bench seat. Nickolas jerks back and falls on the floor. Big Jim turns to see what is going on, and his face becomes a mirror of horror.

"I know it's frightening, but I've heard there are underground clubs that serve alcohol. You're really taking this to heart." Her head cocks to the side, and her eyes widen.

"It's not that!" I squirm.

Nickolas jumps to his feet. "What is that?"

Big Jim points a quivering finger at Mae, backing away.

"What?" Mae lifts a ball of mange-ridden matted fur. "You mean this precious little guy? It's the dogacorn I rescued."

I slide back down to sit on the bench. Nickolas shakes his head, though he seems to prefer to stay standing next to Jim. "That's a dogacorn? How can you tell?"

The animal looks my way. The horn protruding from its forehead is off center and crooked. The large crossed eyes—one yellow, one blue—bulge out from their sockets. The dogacorn's underbite sticks out so far that its canine fangs show prominently outside its muzzle, forcing its tongue to hang out slightly.

By far, it's the ugliest dogacorn I've ever laid eyes on. To be honest, it's the ugliest animal I have ever seen. The mutt sneezes, and one eyeball floats to the side and then back. Then he yips, and his tongue slips out the side of his muzzle, dripping drool.

Mae brings it up to her face and nuzzles the creature. "Isn't he just the sweetest?" She gives it a kiss and tries to hand it off to me.

"Ah, no. No, thanks, dear. He's all yours." I wave my hands in front of myself in refusal.

"Don't you worry, precious pup. Mommy loves you." Mae hugs the horrid-looking creature. The thing turns its head toward me, makes a growling noise, and sticks its tongue straight out.

"He stuck his tongue out at me!" I point at the mongrel. "And he growled!"

"Don't be silly, Zelda. He's just a dogacorn. They do not go around sticking their tongues out at people."

Then that thing smiles. "He just made a face at me."

"Really, a face? My goodness, we better solve this case. I think you're losing it." She pats its head.

I stick my tongue out at the dogacorn. It starts crying and buries its head into the crook of Mae's arm. Mae shakes her head at me. "Now look, you hurt his feelings."

I smack my palm against my head. She's right; I'm falling off my rocker. My life as I've known it is in shambles and I am worried that an ugly little dogacorn is making faces at me.

The bartender brings over our drinks. I grab one and shoot it back. Grabbing Nickolas's, I finish that one off with a gulp as well. Nickolas says nothing; instead, he goes to the bar to order another. Hopefully he'll order one for me too; I have a feeling I'm going to need it.

"Do you want to hear about my adventure or not?" Mae puts the little mutt back on her lap and out of sight.

"Sorry. Yes, please," I say.

Mae begins to recount the movements that led to her discovery of the body: How she figured out how he disappeared at Griffin Tower when I chased him. How she found a garbage chute leading into the basement of the Old Vick. How she found another way into the building—because once was enough with garbage chutes—and began searching for clues floor by floor. It was an accident that she even ran across the body.

However, we now know these latest attacks couldn't have come from the torpedo; it appeared to her that he had been dead quite a while.

Nickolas brings over more drinks and some chips. "I wasn't sure if you were hungry."

"Thanks." *Like, when am I not?*

"Did I miss anything?" Nickolas asks.

"So why did he run?" I toss a chip into my mouth.

Nickolas slides in next to me. "Who ran?"

"The torpedo, the other turn on the street. He looked surprised to see me."

The outside door, most likely original to the building, squeaks and creaks, and a familiar voice calls out to the bartender. "Mack, give me a hard cider and a shot."

"Yous got it, Chance," the bartender calls back.

My hearts quicken when I hear the familiar voice. I grab my glass and shoot back another whiskey. Before I can get my hand around Nickolas's drink, he roughly seizes the glass.

"Not this time." In one fast swig, the whiskey is gone and the glass slams down on the table.

"Maybe he won't notice us, darling," Mae says quietly.

No such luck. He walks over like he's known we've been here the entire time.

"Inspector," I greet.

Nickolas rises to shake the inspector's hand. "Chance."

"Nickolas." The inspector slips his hand into Nickolas's, turning them both as he shakes it. Then he releases the handshake, sits down, and slides up next to me. In one quick movement, Chance has unseated Nickolas.

Nickolas's face sours. "What can we do for you, Inspector?"

"I'm sure it's just happenstance that the inspector dropped in while we were all here." I lean toward him as if he were magnetic. When I'm around him, my body completely disregards what my brain tells it.

"I don't think so, darling." Mae narrows her eyes, leans forward, and assesses Chance Greyson's expression. "He has someone following you."

I turn toward my bench partner. "You have someone watching me?"

"I'm not surprised," Nickolas interjects.

The inspector's attention turns to my mentor. "What is that supposed to mean?"

Nickolas puffs his chest out at the inspector. "You know exactly what I'm implying."

"Wait, stop." I grab the inspector's arm and yank his attention back to me. "Am I being followed?"

He places his warm hand over mine "As long as there is still a threat, my job—our job—is to keep you safe."

"I have a bodyguard," I say, nodding toward Big Jim.

Things go quiet fast as I look into his eyes to search for the truth. I get a little lost in those celestial blues for a moment too long.

"Sir. Ahem, sir," DSI Flynn interrupts. I immediately pull my hand away and look around for Nickolas. He's nowhere in sight. Shit.

"Well?" the inspector asks his assistant.

"Nothing, sir."

"Nothing?"

"Yes, sir."

Mae knits her eyebrows together and gives me a look. Something is going on—something significant.

Inspector Greyson lifts his fedora just enough to run his fingers through his hair. Replacing his hat, he stares hard at Mae. "Miss Griffin . . ."

DSI Flynn yelps. The inspector's words freeze. The little mongrel has popped its head up from Mae's lap.

"What . . . ?" is all that makes it out of Flynn's kisser.

The dogacorn sneezes, its eyes uncrossing before floating back to their unfortunate positions. It looks my way, sticks its tongue out, and growls before placing its head back on Mae's lap.

"I don't think that dogacorn likes you," the inspector finally says.

"I told you he doesn't like me," I nag Mae.

Mae pets her new companion. "Don't be silly."

The inspector gestures with a wave toward the mutt. "Where did you find it?"

"You could tell it was a dogacorn?" I interrupt.

"The horn gave it away." His finger circles his forehead to indicate the obvious. His attention turns back across the table. "Now, Miss Griffin, making false statements to a safety officer is a crime."

Mae gives me a puzzled look. I shrug my shoulders and shake my head. I have no clue what is going on.

"Darling, I do not make false statements, unless it's about my weight, age, or dating status." Mae sticks her nose up in the air.

The inspector is direct. "Did you or did you not call claiming you found a dead body?"

I let my foot fly under the table to connect with Mae's shin.

"Ow!" Mae grabs her leg. "What was that for?"

I scrunch up my nose and narrow my eyes. I can't believe she gave her name! It was supposed to be an anonymous tip!

"Don't you give me that look." She wags her finger at me. "I did exactly what you said." She turns her head away from me and crosses her arms.

"Well, then how would he know who called?" I point at her accusingly. "Huh?"

She turns her head back toward me and sticks out her tongue.

"You did not just stick your tongue out at me!"

Mae turns toward me again and out comes her tongue. I lunge across the table. "I am going to rip that thing right out of your mouth!"

She swats at me like a bug. "Oh, yeah? You and whose army?"

"Ladies!" Inspector Greyson's hands clasp around my waist and pull me back down beside him. "Settle down." Big Jim comes over to make sure Mae stays seated. The inspector anchors me down with one arm around my waist. He grabs his hard cider with his free hand and chugs it down.

Mae, much calmer now, looks at me. "I didn't leave a name."

I try to pry the inspector's arm from my waist. "How did you know Mae called?" His arm is not going anywhere, so I quit struggling. "Wait, you said false statements."

Mae's eyes go big. "Where's the body?"

The inspector releases me from his grip, and Big Jim goes back to standing guard. I move a few centimeters away from the inspector, enough to turn and capture his facial expression. His face holds no clues; I surely wouldn't want to play cards with him.

"There is no body," he states.

"I'm lost," Mae says. "I saw his stinky, smelly decomposing remains."

"How did you know it was Mae who called? Are you following her too?"

"No, I am not following her too. And no, I won't tell you how we know it was her."

"Well, that's crap," Mae complains.

The inspector leans forward. "What is it you think you saw?"

Mae looks at me for permission. "Go ahead, spill," I say.

"I found Bowler Hat Thug, expired, at the Old Vick."

"What made you think to look there, and how did you know he would be dead?"

Mae leans forward, excited to tell her tale again. "It was something Zelda said."

"Me?"

"She said that she lost him at the corner alley when she was chasing him the other turn. He had just disappeared."

Chance leans back and crosses his arms over his wrinkled trench coat. "Go on."

Mae repeats the story she told me, though with a few added embellishments. "There you have it, Inspector. I didn't lie; I found the body. It is not my fault you lost it."

The inspector leans toward me. "She's not serious about us losing the body, is she?"

I laughed. "I'm afraid so."

The creature lifts its head and gives its support in the form of a yap and a sneeze that makes its blue eye spin.

"You still haven't told me why you thought he would be dead."

"Because, darling, Zelda believed it to be so," she said with such certainty.

"Did you think about what would happen if he hadn't been?"

Mae may not have, but I have. "Mae, the inspector is right. If anything had happened to you . . ." My emotions roll up into my eyes. "Don't take any more chances like that again." I reach across the table, take her hand, and give it a squeeze.

She squeezes my hand back. "I won't, darling, I promise. I just wanted to help."

Inspector Greyson slides out of the booth. "Doc, Miss Griffin . . ." He pauses for a moment before continuing. "I think it's best for you both to head home now."

The inspector turns, pats Big Jim's shoulder, and says something to him that I can't make out as he passes toward the bar and his patiently waiting, lonely shot. Big Jim approaches the booth and gestures toward the door.

"How do you know the inspector?"

"When I'm not moonlighting as a bodyguard, I'm a copper." He holds up his hand and motions for us to get behind him.

I let out a long, slow sigh. "What did he say to you?"

Big Jim doesn't answer my question. Instead, he orders us to wait near the door as he scans the street. Mae and the mutt go first. I begin to follow when I start feeling nauseous again. My body wobbles a bit. I try to move, but my feet seem to stick to the floor. I can hear my name being called, but everything seems muffled and far away. My vision blurs a bit. Through the haze, I see the inspector's face.

"Doc? Doc?" He shakes my good shoulder.

Suddenly, everything clears and I feel fine. "Yep, I'm okeydokey."

"Are you sure?"

"Ab-so-lute-ly. It must have been the three drinks on an empty stomach."

"Okay. Go home and get some rest, Doc." He walks me to the front.

Big Jim ducks his head in the door. "Problem?"

"No, I'm fine. Ready to go." I put one foot in front of the other and follow Big Jim out the door.

We head back toward the sedan. All the while, I keep a look out for Nickolas. Where could he have gone? I'm not sure if I should be hurt, mad, or worried.

"Horsefeathers!" Mae swears.

"What?"

"I forgot to give the inspector that tie-clip thingy."

We stop at the tin and I turn to Mae. "Please no more adventures for you."

"Not to worry. I'm not running off to find any more bodies. I promise." She crosses her hearts with a wave of a couple of fingers. "Besides, I need to get rid of the smell of decay, dirt, dust, smoke, and whatever else I picked up in that derelict building."

I give her a hug. "Call me later?"

The dogacorn growls at me and then sneezes, its tongue flopping out the side of its snout. "Oops, I think we smooshed him." Mae readjusts it in her arms.

"What are you going to name him?"

"I think Pip. Yes, Pip it is." She scratches it under the chin. "Do you like that name?" she asks in a baby voice. The thing yaps and gives Mae's hand a lick.

"Seems he likes the name." The mutt gives me a look and sticks out its tongue. I'm about to point it out when Mae speaks.

"Darling, I think Pip and I are going to head over to the Spa on the Shore. Pip needs fumigation and some grooming. I need a good soak, massage, and some rest after tonight's events." Mae pats Pip's head. "We'll be incommunicado for a turn. Will you be okay with that?"

I smile and nod. I watch her head back to the bar. Pip peeks his head around and sticks his tongue out again, his yellow eye looking straight at me. Then he smiles before tucking his head into Mae's arm.

Big Jim steps up next to me. "I'll take you home. If you don't mind me saying, I don't think that dogacorn likes you much. I'd keep my eye on that one."

I agree with him.

Chapter Thirty-Three

After a fitful sleep, I sit at the edge of my bed and stare at my toes. The bright red lacquer coating my toenails is beginning to chip and wear. While I consider whether I should repaint them red or go with another color altogether, it hits me that I'm bored. I've always had an experiment or two bubbling away on some burner and a few more percolating between my ears.

I fall with a flop atop my tossed-aside comforter and stare at the ceiling. "Is this what the unmagical feel like? Tons of thoughts in their heads with no way to direct them?" I roll onto my stomach. "How can they live like this? It's just too depressing."

I gallop lightly down the back stairs to the family area of the mansion where more informal rooms preside. I enter the kitchen to a lovely deluge of appetizing smells. Stirring a large pot in front of the stove is mother's chef—the same chef who makes me the reheatable wonders I keep in my fridge at home.

"Good morning."

No response. I move forward, putting my hand on the counter as I lean in. "Good morning."

She stops stirring and turns around. Wiping her hands on her apron, she asks, "What can I do for you?" She doesn't look up.

"I was wondering if my father has been down yet for breakfast. I was hoping to join him."

"Haven't seen him." She goes back to her stirring.

"Okeydokey, how about Mrs. Georg? Is she about?"

"She left this morning to join Mrs. Harcrow in Capital City."

"What about Mr. Georg?"

She stops stirring and turns, placing her hands firmly on her hips. "I have no time for idle chitchat. It's none of my business where people go." She walks over to a chafing dish, lifts the lid, and scoops some sort of billowy yellow food out onto a plate, adds some root vegetables from another dish, and slides it across the counter to me.

"Is this for me?"

Her jaw is set straight when she looks at me. Instead of uttering a word, she grabs utensils and a cloth napkin and marches them over to me.

"Thanks," I mutter. I grab my plate of goodies and skedaddle to the informal dining room.

I use the fork to fiddle with the mystery glop on the plate, moving it this way and that. I half-heartedly take a bite. There's too much turmeric, and I still can't tell what it's supposed to be. Chef must be losing her touch. The silverware rattles against the plate as I push it away. Slumping back in my chair, I let out a moan.

"Ahem." George stands behind me in the doorway that leads out to the informal sitting room.

Like my thoughts in boredom, I slowly turn. "I didn't see you there. Is my father home?"

"He has left on a small trip." George offers no additional information.

"Where to?"

"I haven't been privileged with that information."

"When is he returning?" Jeez. Trying to get information out of him is like trying to get unobtainium to boil.

"He didn't say, young Miss Zelda." He stands in the doorway like a statue, not moving a muscle, just waiting.

"Okay, I'll bite; what can I help you with?"

"Nothing, Miss. You do, however, have a visitor."

Maybe he should have opened with that one. "Thank you, George. Show them into the drawing room."

"Excellent, young Miss Zelda." He turns to leave.

"Whoa." I stop him. "Are you not going to tell me who's calling?"

"You didn't ask, Miss."

"Well, don't keep me wound in the sheets."

"Sorry, Miss?"

I crack a smile. "Who, may I ask, has come calling, George?"

"Dr. Shamm has come to call."

"For me?"

"Yes, Miss."

I give a shrug and go to meet my uninvited guest.

Mr. Georg has preceded me to show Dr. Shamm into the drawing room, and there he waits for my entrance.

I confidently strut into the room, hand extended, ready for a strong greeting. "Dr. Shamm, to what do I owe your visit?"

He grasps my hand and holds its back tightly to his full lips. "My dear Dr. Harcrow, please call me Monki."

"Zelda." I pull my hand back. "Monki, would you care for some tea?" I motion to one of the sofas bookending the cold fireplace.

Nodding to George to bring tea for our guest, I lead Shamm to our seats. "What can I do for you?" I shift back and forth on the cushion.

"I came to see how you were doing." His arm slides along the back of the sofa like a snake. I straighten my spine, smooth my slacks, and clear my throat, all while attempting a smile. "I see your family has all but abandoned you during this very stressful time." He shifts closer to me, his words hot and his stare burning.

I stumble over my words. "I—I'm not sure what you mean."

"Your mother and sisters are in the capital, your father absconded in the night, and your brother is buried in—"

"Everyone is exactly where they need to be Dr. Shamm. I—"

"Monki."

"Monki. I am far from being forgotten."

He moves into my space. "It is heartbreaking for me to see such genius being sidelined."

"Well, I've been having some roadblocks keeping me from my work."

"Your roadblock is gone. The lab may yet be unfinished, but your work should continue."

His aroma is intoxicating; I never noticed it before. "My father has turned my unfinished work over to our other house alchemists."

Monki's eyes avert to my chest. "What a unique adornment."

"My mother gave it to me." My hand covers the protection amulet around my neck. I haven't taken it off since I left the infirmary.

"May I?" His long fingers take hold of the amulet for a closer inspection. "Interesting."

"Thank you." I study his face. I can see why women are drawn to him. His features are well-defined and remarkably symmetrical. His skin is a light olive in color and flawless, like a river rock worn smooth and polished by the ever-running water. If I had one word to describe him and his expressions, I would use *unreal*.

"Not all of your work has been handed off." The glint of silver specks in his dark almond eyes seem to move, spinning toward me.

"You're correct, but that is no secret." I scoot away from him.

"Given the opportunity and a safe place, would you want to continue it?"

"I'm not exactly clear what you're asking." I turn my body to face him, spine straight and eyes set on him.

"You are remarkable; no wonder the threat of an assassin has failed."

Monki's face softens and his voice changes. His face is different somehow, as though a veil has been lifted for a moment and I see someone else. My head tilts, and I search his eyes for a hint of what I have just experienced.

"Zelda, I want an opportunity to work side-by-side with you. When I arrived here in Fulcrum, I had no idea what an intelligent, smart, brave, magical alchemist you were." His breath is hot on my face.

How did he get so close? I can't breathe. I can't look away from his swirling eyes. Is he saying something?

"Ahem. Tea is served." George rattles the silver tea service as if the cream and sugar containers were pots and pans and Shamm were a fox to be shooed away from a cicen hen house.

My eyes drop to Shamm's hand on my upper thigh. Interested in my work, my ass! Good old Monki Shamm is looking to put another line on his beaker. Grabbing his hand none too gently, I say, "Tea? I'll pour."

"Only half a cup, please." The corners of his mouth curl up like he has a secret that only he knows.

He keeps looking at me like he's a bobcat and I'm a canaria bird. I feel for the amulet around my neck. Nothing.

"Something wrong?" Shamm places his tea down.

It's not in the sofa cushions. Down on my hands and knees, I search the surrounding area. Monki Shamm stays planted, the stupid, unhelpful cake-eater. I collapse back onto the disheveled sofa.

"Young Miss Zelda, is everything all right?" George is back to being stealthy. "DSI Flynn, Miss."

"Dr. Harcrow, pardon the interruption. I was actually looking for the elder Dr. Harcrow."

I don't move a depressed muscle. Honestly, I think my slouch even gets slouchier and a little deeper into the sofa. "He's not here."

The darling DSI fiddles with his hat brim. "Oh, he's left already?"

My back goes rigid and I shoot upright. DSI Flynn knew my father had travel plans!

I'm not the only one who appears shocked. The pitch and speed of Monki Shamm's usually slow, articulate, and syrupy voice rise.

"You are aware of Titus's whereabouts?" His voice cracks and he clears it. His eyes close. "Where, pray tell, is the great Titus Harcrow?"

DSI Flynn ignores Shamm. "Doctor, you have your arm out of the sling. Are you feeling better?"

My hand rises to my shoulder. "Right as rain on the Weather Council's turn off." I push past Shamm. "Flynn, do you know where my father went?"

"Oh, no." He looks down at his hat as he rotates it by the brim, round and round. "Maybe he went to the capital?"

Monki slithers up beside me. "Young man, if you know where he is, I think you should inform Zelda. She is his daughter." Shamm's vocal performance is back to wet and sleazy. However, he does have a point; I should be told where the old bird is.

"I—ah . . . I—ah . . ." The blue-haired deputy second inspector swallows hard, responding slowly. "I really . . . really—I honestly have no information."

He's holding back. My head teeters back and forth as I attempt to catch his eye and learn the truth.

"I should . . . be . . ." He takes a step back.

Dr. Shamm's upper lip twitches, and then he pulls out his pocket watch. "I'm sorry to hurry off, but I just remembered something." His upper lip twitches again.

An irritated grimace spreads across my face. "I hope nothing too important."

"I hope not, either." He snaps his watch closed and pockets it. "I shall see you very soon, my dear Zelda."

"Nice to see you again." I am such a liar.

"Remember my offer, Zelda. You and I would be unstoppable together . . . in a lab." His face widens with a smile so large that for a moment I believe if he opened his mouth, he could devour me in one bite.

"Creep," I say under my breath, though not quietly enough.

"I'm with ya there, sister," mumbles the DSI.

"Please have a seat, DSI Flynn, and let me see if I can be of assistance." I gesture to the sofa I haven't ripped apart in search of my amulet. "A cup of tea?"

"No, thank you, Doctor. I'm sorry I broke up your meeting with Dr. Shamm."

"Ah, no apologies necessary. He was just chewing gum in my ear."

The young man bows a bit, swivels, deftly flips his fedora onto his head, and heads toward the door. A shrill whistle tweets from between my puckered lips. "Hold on—not so fast there, fella."

He screeches to a halt, and his head droops like he's a naughty little dogacorn caught chewing its master's favorite slipper.

"Turn around." I plant my hands on my hips. "Start talking."

"Dr. Harcrow, I honestly don't know where your father is." His hat is in his hands once more, and he fiddles with the brim again.

"Cut the crap. You know something, and you're going to spill." My chin hits the nod hard. I mean business.

"We found him."

I look around the room. "Found who?"

"Eli Darko, the unidentified body."

I shrug. "The body in the airship? You figured out who he is?"

"Yes—no, I mean, not that one, the other one." He's back to fumbling with the brim of his hat.

Could he be any more cryptic? "Flynn, what body?"

"Eli Darko."

My shoulders hunch as I squeeze my eyes tightly closed. My head is starting to pound. "Who is Eli Darko?"

Flynn looks confused. "The assassin from Elione."

"Bowler Hat Thug, then. Where did you find him? Was there any evidence on the knife?"

"Knife?"

"So, no knife. What else can you tell me?" I turn toward the fireplace and pinch the bridge of my nose. Finally, I'm getting somewhere. I swing around to find that DSI Flynn has flown the coop. "Crap," I mutter and slam my foot against the ground.

My vexed attitude comes out loudly and booms through the mansion. "George!"

Poor George. He really doesn't deserve my wrath, but he's the most convenient body. "Young Miss Zelda?" His voice remains even.

"George, get on the horn with that bodyguard of mine. I'm going out." My mules clack loudly as I stamp out of the room like a spoiled child.

"Yes, Miss" is barely audible as I continue to my room.

I smooth my low-denier spider-silk stockings up my legs, securing their welts in the garter clips. I shimmy a black-and-white asymmetrical skirt up over my hips and pull over my head a black form-fitting knitted top with long white rippling diagonal overlay. *Screw the hair.* I grab a black loose-knit cap and pull it over my straight gold hair. After powdering my face and fastening on some jewelry, I head down the back stairs to mother's study.

Ave keeps her study—or sitting room, as some of the old fuddy-duddies call it—very tidy. I'm surprised when I see some modern furnishings. I wonder when she began redecorating.

I walk in through the side door and make a beeline for the bookshelves that line the opposite wall. The bookcases hold more than just books, including everything I think I'll need for a very particular spell.

Suddenly, I feel something catch at my foot. Flinging my arms out in front of me, I attempt to catch myself as I fall. Crushed blue velvet jumps toward my head as I fall into the back of the sofa sitting in the center of the room. Old sofa, new furniture arrangement, and a rug burn compliments of the new rug I didn't notice. Horsefeathers! There goes a perfectly good pair of stockings. Using the back of the sofa to assist me to my feet, I survey the room so I won't fall to any more surprises.

"I really need to pay more attention to things around me."

The chandelier centering the room is still the same, as is the sofa, but to my surprise, most everything else has been replaced with more modern fare. The desk that sits in front of the three floor-to-ceiling windows—all now draped with stark-white curtains—is gorgeous, I must admit. I move toward it to get a closer look; it's mahogany, inlaid with aventurine panels in the desk cabinet doors, across the blotter area, and along the edge of the desktop. "Just gorgeous." I run my fingers along the cold stone as I bring my attention back to why I came to Mother's study.

The bookcases are filled with old and new books on a variety of subjects, sculptures, jars filled with herbs, minerals, and multiple stones and crystals, as well as other items important to a magical diviner.

I scour the shelves, looking for just the right book. And there it is: yellowed parchment pages bound in smelly old leather, the Galfry Family Shadowbook. Given to my mother by my Great Aunt Zelda—as Mother was the eldest of her siblings—the book has been in my mother's family for generations. I believe there are others, but this is the oldest.

My fingers gingerly turn each page so as not to damage some of the brittler sheets. On some pages, the ink has faded with age, and on others, more current notes line the margins of the ancient codex. I skip the beginning of the shadowbook, not just because of its age and fragile condition but because it is written in an unused form of language that I cannot be bothered with. Instead, I turn to the last few pages of the tome; I know what I want.

"There you are." I smile as I lay my hand over the page and caress the words.

I position the thick, ancient grimoire on mother's neoteric desk. I run my fingers down the list of components for the spell.

"Let's see: white candle, apophyllite crystal, licorice root, sea sage, and fawn lily." Being present so I won't trip on the rug again, I briskly walk to the far end of the floor-to-ceiling shelves and begin collecting the ingredients for the formula that will garner me what I need.

Arranging the items on the desk, I prepare myself for the incantation that will yield me my desire: the truth.

I station an abalone shell with the correct measurements of roots and plants to my right and light the dried concoction. The flame recedes and the incense begins to burn and smoke. I light the white candle next and settle into a meditative state with both a bowl of sea water and the crystal placed to my left.

Truth spells can be tricky. There are many forms of truth invocations, depending on what the conjurer is actually trying to accomplish. Sometimes the spells don't have the exact outcome the conjurer may be looking for. This spell should help me see the naked truth and move on it. The lucidity of truth comes in many forms, but I'm hoping for the practical ability to recognize it and the mindfulness to absorb and analyze it in ways that favor me.

"Layers of darkness
Obscures what is real
Light is shed upon the concealed
To see the truth
To know the way
To unseal secrets that hide away
I cast this spell for me
The truth I only see."

I repeat the incantation three times. The cool crystal feels like glass beneath my fingers as I pick it up and glide the crystal through the candle's flame. "Fire." I hold it over the smoke of the burning incense. "Air." I dunk the crystal in the seawater. "Water."

I have one last thing to do, which is to bury the candle and the ashes of the incense. I meditate on my intention for the truth as the candle burns down, almost finished. The smile that begins to cross my face is quickly shut down by a knock at the study door.

Chapter Thirty-Four

M y eyelids shoot open. "Crap."
The knock comes again.

"Yes."

George slips his head into the study. "Young Miss Zelda, Mr. Zeper has arrived."

"Who?" I tilt my head in confusion.

"Your bodyguard, Miss."

"Zeper . . . Oh yeah, Big Jim." I stand up and pocket the apophyllite. "Tell him I'll be right with him."

George nods and slips back out, closing the door behind him.

I hate leaving a spell not quite finished. One never knows what one will get, if anything. The incense needs to burn out and the candle needs to cool before I can bury them and finish releasing the intention.

I join Big Jim in the hall.

"Where to?"

"Take me to the Legere Legalis building in downtown Fulcrum." I pull on my gloves. "I want to see Inspector Greyson."

The trip into Fulcrum seems shorter than usual. My arms cross and uncross constantly; I can't seem to keep still. Big Jim pulls into the parking lot and finds a place to dock his tin.

"I can make it inside by myself. Stay here and wait for me."

Big Jim says nothing as he slams the passenger-side door closed behind me. I stop midway to the large metal-and-glass structure, take a deep breath, and check behind me. My bodyguard leans up against his motor with his arms crossed. I give him a small smile, and he gives me a nod in return. I turn back toward the building, set my shoulders, and climb up the marble steps.

Loud, bustling voices reverberate off the granite-lined walls and the terrazzo floor. Coppers and suits move here and there, shuffling papers and cons as if they were interchangeable. Trying my best not to plow into those constantly crossing my path, I finally move catawampus across the room to the constable sergeant's counter, constantly starting and stopping to avoid the bodies that clutter my path.

The older woman behind the elevated counter looks over her spectacles at me. "How can I help you?"

"I need to speak with Inspector Greyson."

"Can I have your name?"

"Dr. Zelda Harcrow. It's important that I speak with him." I'm planning on finding out some truths, even with my spell unfinished. I stick my hand in my pocket and give the crystal a rub.

The spectacled constable speaks into the headset that adorns her gray-haired head. I'm not sure how she can hear whomever she's talking to; the longer I stand in the vestibule of the station, the louder it seems to get.

"Dr. Harcrow, if you wait by the double doors over there," she says, pointing to the frosted glass doors down a short hall from where I'm standing, "someone will be down to escort you to his office."

"Thank you." I hustle over to the doors to wait impatiently for my escort.

I don't have to wait long for a constable to arrive and show me to the inspector's office. It's much quieter behind the glass doors. My heels click on the terrazzo floor as we cross a large open area and head to the stairs that take us to the second floor and to Chance.

The constable knocks on the closed office door to announce my arrival.

"Enter." The inspector's voice seems short and gruff.

Oh boy, this isn't going well already, and I haven't even seen him yet. My gut shakes and flips. Did I make a mistake coming here?

The door is opened for me, and I slowly walk over the threshold and stop just a meter inside the door.

The inspector looks up from behind a desk littered with stacks of manila file folders. "Doc, this is a surprise. To what do I owe the pleasure of your visit?" He stands and motions for me to move farther inside.

The door shuts behind me, and my escort has disappeared. "I'm here to get some information."

"Oh? What information would that be?" He waves his hand toward a chair in front of his desk. "Sit, please."

"Thanks." I remove my gloves and place them in my clutch. Before I sit down, I steal a moment to squeeze the apophyllite that still lies in the pocket of my outfit.

Chance makes his way around the front of his desk to face me. He leans back on the desk and crosses his arms. "What is it you want to know?"

"Just the truth of things."

"Just the truth of things," he repeats.

"Yes."

I stand up and lean on the desk next to him. "Flynn said you found the assassin's body."

"Yes, we did."

"Where did it turn up?" I toss my clutch onto the chair I just vacated.

"Under the Industria 2 overpass."

"That's quite a ways from where Mae found the body."

"Yes, true. By the way, where is your cohort?" He flashes a teasing smile.

"At a spa. Too many cobwebs and dust." I return the smile. Mine's more like a smirk.

He scoots a little closer to me, his arms still crossed. "Good, I don't need any more bodies."

"I don't think she'll pull any more stunts like she did the other turn."

"I can hope."

"Wouldn't hold my breath, though."

He unfolds his arms and gives me a little nudge. "Wasn't going to."

I need to get back on track. I take a short breath, readying myself for my next question. "Flynn mentioned the knife was missing."

"Flynn is going to be demoted if he keeps spilling." He sounds a bit annoyed.

I nudge him back. "Don't take it out on him. I think I scared him."

Inspector Chance Greyson's eyes sparkle as he laughs at my revelation about DSI Flynn.

"Whoever moved the body removed any evidence that would lead us to his killer." He's being very forthcoming with the information. Maybe my unfinished spell was completed enough to give me an assist in asking the right questions and listening closely to the answers.

"Where's my father?"

"Honestly, I'm not sure."

"Did he tell you why he was leaving?" *Spell, don't fail me now.*

"Not really. He said he had to confirm something and when he was sure he would contact me."

"Truth?" I stare up at him.

He returns my stare. "Truth."

I tilt my head to get a better look at him. By the stars, he is good-looking. The gold strands scattered throughout his hair glimmer under the artificial light in his office. I have the urge to run my hands through his short, shaggy hair. Truth spells can be tricky, eyes opened and all that.

Everything goes still. I can't move and I don't want to. His hand reaches across and cups the back of my neck. My lips part as if I'm about to speak, but I have no words. The heat races up and down my body; both my hearts begin to race. He brings his face down toward mine until our foreheads touch, and I close my eyes. Then his mouth covers mine and everything else disappears.

My mouth drops open, an invitation he eagerly accepts. His mouth is warm, his tongue eager to explore. I fling my arm around his neck to pull him closer. Moving away from the desk, he faces me and grabs my thighs. Lifting me up, he sets me with care on the edge of his already cluttered desk. He leans into me and I don't pull away. I want him closer and he knows it.

His hands slide up the top of my thighs, pushing my skirt up to my garters. Our tongues dance with each other, a dance that becomes deeper and more frenzied. Under my skirt, his hand holds my hips against his. Things are moving fast and I don't care. I feel a moan rumble from my abdomen straight up and out of my otherwise-engaged mouth. Chance responds, pulling me closer. Things are hot, heavy, and purely physical—perfect.

"Sir?" a voice calls, accompanying a loud knock on the door.

Chance moves his mouth off mine and shoots over his shoulder, "Go away, Flynn." His mouth finds mine again very quickly.

Flynn knocks again. "Sir, it's important."

I push Chance back. "You better take care of it."

"That, Doc, is not what I want to be taking care of right now." He pulls at my bottom lip gently with his teeth.

I smile. "Go take care of business."

"I'm trying." His voice is a murmur against my lips. He puts me down. "Fine."

I smooth out my skirt and pull out my compact to touch up the old munitions. I give him a nod to let him know it's okay to let Flynn in.

"Dr. Harcrow," Flynn acknowledges and then whispers something to Chance that makes Chance look back at me.

"Doc, I'll be right back. Don't go anywhere; this won't take long." With that, he and his DSI leave the office.

I sit back down, trying to figure out what just occurred between the inspector and me. I run my hand down my stockings to smooth them out, stopping at the run. I know he's a looker and sexy as all get out, but that was out of character for me. I caress my lips, thinking about his heated kisses. I don't think I have ever had such an intense physical attraction to someone before.

I shake my head—like that's going to get my brain working again. My fingers go back to the run in my stocking before I pull them off. Removing the stockings seems freeing, somehow. Like when nothing is going as expected, so one just throws one's hands up, says "Fuck it!" and means it.

I turn my head back toward the door. "I wonder how long he's going to be." I glance around his office. It's simple and nothing very personal is displayed. There's his desk, the chairs in front of his desk, a couch with a flannel blanket neatly folded at one end, several filing cabinets, and a credenza.

I make my way around his desk: no pictures, just files, notepads, and a desk lamp. I shuffle a few things around, just being nosy to see what kind of guy I just let stick his tongue down my throat. I move one of the large notepads, and there is a manila file with Eli Darko's name on the tab.

"Hmm . . ." Curiosity can be my worst enemy. Setting down my silk stockings and purse, I open the file. Inside, there are a few forms and some notes. Eli Darko was born in the salty swamps of Elione thirty-one rotations ago. There's a physical description, which I don't need to read, considering I've had up-close and personal experience of how he looked.

I turn the page. "Assassin for hire. Mostly works out of Hyde." A scribble—"No known associates. Victims listed." I peer at the brief list of victims known here in Tesla: me, my doorman, Carlton, and possibly one other unidentified victim. I wonder who that could be. My father and the portal attacks aren't listed. "Huh."

I look for other information in the file that I don't already have knowledge of. In a pocket is a flat crystal. I glance around the office, but there's no crystal reader. I won't be able to access the information.

I close the file, which is when I see two other files underneath it that immediately catch my attention. One tab has Harcrow Inc. and my name on it. The one on top is labeled "Unidentified male victim 5614F." I quickly flip it open. A short written report is inside, along with another crystal file in a pocket.

"Unidentified male victim found in utility closet in Arriving Airship section of Griffin Tower." Why was this file with mine? Who was this victim, and how did he figure into what was happening to me and my family?

I open my file to find a report of everything I'm already aware of and another crystal disc. I really wish there was a reader in here with me. I can't take the chance of leaving with it. Greyson would definitely know it was me. I flip through the file, looking for clues—something, anything, that might be able to tell me what is going on.

On one of the last pages is a list of alchemists and their assistants, all of whom are employees of Harcrow Alchemy Inc. One name has a star next to it. I have to sit down. I read it again, but I'm not seeing things. There it is in black and white: Dr. Nickolas Carnot.

I have to get out of here. I quickly close the file, put everything back the way I think I found it, and leave.

Chapter Thirty-Five

My eyes dart back and forth, keeping an eye out for the inspector as I hotfoot it down the stairs. The last thing I need right now is for him to catch me sneaking away. My chest tightens. If I can get on the other side of the frosted glass door, I can get lost in the swarm of bodies and make an easy escape.

Once I'm in the sea of the lobby, I hustle to the exit. With my palms sweaty, I rub the back of my neck. Right or wrong, I decide to ditch Big Jim. I don't see him by his vehicle. I scan the lot—nothing. My eyes jump to the taxi at the curb. Taking the stairs two at a time, I leap into the taxi and rattle off Nickolas's address before I have too much time to think and change my mind.

I soon find myself looking up at the high-rise Nickolas now calls home. I feel a twinge of guilt that he left his cushy job at the university to help my family and me, just to become a suspect in this mess that decided to curse us.

With a deep breath and a shrug of my shoulders, I tuck a bit of hair behind my ear and put on an air of false confidence. Entering the building, I take the lift to his apartment.

Shifting from one foot to another, I ruminate on my decision to come here. I cover my face with my hands and take another deep breath as I stand in front of his door. *I can do this.* Finally, I knock on his door.

My ears pick up the sound of footsteps getting louder; he's home. The lock clicks, the door swings open, and there he is. His white starched shirt is untucked and unbuttoned down to his waist, and his well-toned upper body peeks through the gap. My breath catches. He smells of sandalwood. Old feelings begin to rise again.

"Zelda, what are you doing here?" He moves back to invite me into his temporary lodging.

I step across the threshold and into a large loft-style flat, one large, brutal space. Gray concrete makes up the floor and huge, unadorned windows look out over the city. "Wow," I say, verbalizing my impression.

"Like it?"

"Love it." I'm amazed he can fund this on a university salary.

"Let me take your things." He stretches out his hands.

"I've got it." I remove my gloves and place them and my clutch on the entryway credenza.

"This is quite the digs," I say as I move forward, looking about to take in the space. "The view is amazing."

I stare out at the skyline of Fulcrum. I glance away, though, when I notice his reflection in the window, staring at me. Turning around quickly, I scan the room. Simple but useful, the sitting area is designated by a grouping of furniture on a large rug, with the sofa facing the windows so its occupants can appreciate the view.

Toward the back of the flat is a concrete island with stools that fronts the open kitchen. Only two areas are closed off: the bathroom and the bedroom. Due to the partial floor-to-ceiling glass walls, though, the bedroom offers no privacy and doesn't interfere with the 180-degree view of the skyline.

"Drink?" Nickolas moves to the bar cart near the sitting area.

"Sure." I could use some liquid courage.

He pours us each two fingers of amber-colored booze. "No ice?"

"No ice." I meet him in front of the sofa, accept the glass of whiskey he offers, and take a sip of the smoky yet smooth liquid. It stings the back of my throat a bit as it goes down. I squint my eyes and shake it off. I raise my glass to him and take another sip. The second always goes down easier than the first.

"Please." He gestures to the sofa.

I take a seat and a sip. A little larger this time, the third sip goes down even easier than the second.

"Tell me, to what do I owe the pleasure of your company?"

"Let me ask first: why did you leave the bar?"

He gulps down his drink and gets up to get another. "Seemed to me Inspector Greyson had everything well in hand—especially you." He pours the drink and sits back down, looking at me with accusing eyes.

Is he jealous or am I just reading something that isn't there? The truth spell is just not working, or the alcohol is affecting my ability to see it. "I'm not sure what you're implying."

"He looked pretty cozy next to you."

My face turns red. Here I am, acting as if there's nothing personal between Chance and me after I just came from playing tongue tango with the man. "We left soon after you did. Or rather, soon after the lecture on how we were taking too many chances." That was the truth, basically.

His face softens, and he sets his drink down on the black-lacquered gold-trimmed coffee table. "Did they find the body?"

"Yes. Well, really, no."

He pulls his head back and cocks it in confusion.

"The body disappeared from the Old Vick and popped up the following turn under the Industria 2." I finish up my drink, which by now is going down like silk.

He grabs my glass and holds it up. "Another?"

I nod my answer.

He comes back with my refill. "Tell me why you're here."

"Why did you come back to Fulcrum?" I take a large dose of courage. "You haven't set foot in Fulcrum for rotations. Then suddenly you pop up. I know you weren't on Ephron's list of alchemists."

He doesn't answer me. He averts his eyes and gazes out the windows at the slowly darkening sky. "Do they know how the torpedo's body got from the rundown hotel to under the overpass?"

"No. Answer my question." The booze is starting to take effect.

"Are you seeing Chance?"

"No." I'm being truthful, despite almost having sex with the inspector on his littered desk. "He and I have not been dating, or anything else for that matter." A twang rises in my abdomen, but I decide to ignore it.

"I came here for you."

"For me?" My eyes almost pop right out of their sockets. "I didn't ask you to."

"After—" he starts and then stops. The words come more slowly and deliberately then, rehearsed. "I called Titus and asked if I could come."

"He said yes?" My voice squeaks, my annoyance with my father coming out.

"I wanted to be part of everything again." He takes my hands in his. "To be with you again."

Whoa, Nelly! "What?"

I abruptly pull my hands from his, grab my glass, and make my way over to the bar cart and the bottle. This revelation from him makes me ill. I humiliated myself in front of him proclaiming my undying love all those rotations ago. Now suddenly, he's acting as though I drove him away, when in fact it was quite the opposite.

"I've made you angry." He comes up behind me, his hands warm on my shoulders. "I should explain."

"Don't bother." I knock back my drink and slam the glass down on the cart, almost shattering the bar cart's mirrored top.

Nickolas spins me around to face him. "Don't you know I've always loved you?"

I raise an eyebrow.

"It is true. I relive that night you came to me repeatedly. It plays constantly in my head, like a scratched record." He shakes me.

"You're lying! You sent me away!" I scream. I'm the young naïve girl again.

"Zelda." His grip tightens on my shoulders. "You were young, going off to university. I couldn't be anything more to you than a mentor."

I struggle to free myself. "You are lying! Why are you saying these things?"

Nickolas pulls me into his chest, wrapping his arms around me. I wish I never tried that spell; it's backfiring. It must be. None of this can be true. Tears roll down my cheeks, and my hearts feel as though they've dropped into my stomach and are swimming in the booze.

He speaks more softly. His words are warm against my ear. "Darling," he calls me. "You can trust me. We can be together and work together again."

My knees buckle underneath me. "I need to sit down."

Nickolas helps me to the couch. Once he gets me settled, he brings over another drink.

My head is reeling, overwhelmed by all the truths. I push the drink away, wipe the tears from my face, and sit up. Why must the men I choose get me so wound up that I don't know up from down?

"When you left for university, I thought you would come home eventually and that we'd talk. That I could tell you after a bit." He clears his throat. "But you got engaged, Zelda."

Oh, boy.

He takes the drink I refused and downs it in one gulp, shaking off the sting of the alcohol.

"I knew I had waited too long. Your father wanted you at HA; you had become a most exceptional alchemist. The best. You could create things others could only dream of." He set the glass down gently.

What can I say to this? Nothing, so I just listen.

He continues. "Titus arranged a teaching position for me, so I left. I did hear about your fiancé, and I am sorry for your loss, Zelda. Truly."

"I believe you." I'm calm now, though I'm still not sure what to do with the revelation placed so heavily upon me. So I change the subject. "Can I trust you?" I push aside any doubts the inspector's star next to Nickolas's name placed in my head.

"I told you, you can," he reaffirms.

"Why do you think I was targeted? Or should I say, what project is the target?" I lean forward and use my thighs to support my elbows.

"Elione, maybe for the spider silk?" Nickolas suggests.

I shake my head. I no longer believe that. The imitation silk formula was finished long ago. "It's something else."

"What about the formula you were working on right before the explosion?"

"I'd already discovered which elements will work for the shatter-proof glass for the moon ship."

His hands rub over his face. "What about—"

I hold up my hand. "The fuel cell experiment has been suspended. You would know that if you had talked my father into bringing you here."

"Maybe the plan changed."

I knit my brows together. "Whoever hired the torpedo may be the one who murdered him."

Nickolas shrugs. "Why kill him?"

I stand up and begin to pace. I'm firm on my feet once again. "What about the portal attacks, and why try to kill Father?" I stop to look out at the dimly lit city. The sun star has finally finished setting.

"I don't know, Zelda. Is it possible whoever is behind this thinks your father is in the way?"

"In the way of what?"

His reflection shows in the window; he stands tall behind me. "You, Zelda. Titus stands between you and . . ."

My hand rises to my face. My reflection in the glass is one of pure terror. I hug myself, and Nickolas wraps his arms around mine. "Zelda, you now have something they need."

I turn into his embrace and clutch his shirt in my fists. I'm scared. He lifts my chin and our eyes meet. Pulling my chin down, he kisses my forehead. Guiding my face, he kisses one cheek and then the other. I softly close my eyes. Gently, he lays kisses on each lid before he kisses my nose. A tingle zips from my face down to my toes and back up again.

"You know how I feel about you," he proclaims before he draws in a long breath and places his lips on mine.

His kisses are so different from what I experienced with Greyson. Nickolas is slow and gentle. His kisses aren't feverish; instead they're slow, methodical. He leaves my mouth and trails down my neck. I take in a sharp breath of ecstasy, and a tiny moan floats out of me.

"I will keep you safe. I promise. Always." He scoops me up and carries me to his bed.

I could care less if he means his promise. As I feel the weight of his strong, lean body on top of me, I think that this is the way it was meant to be.

Chapter Thirty-Six

The morning sun star encroaches on my sleep as it floods through the windows. Nabbing the corner of the pillow, I roll over and pull it over my head.

Sandalwood. I inhale, and a small smile creeps over my face. *My stars, what a night.*

I reach out my arm and feel for my companion. I trace the muscles of his arm with my hand. His skin is smooth. My hand moves to his chest. I run my fingers through the gray hair that covers his well-toned muscles.

"Mm . . ." Nickolas's eyes open and squint against the morning light. He lifts the pillow off my head and kisses me. "Good morning."

"Good morning."

His arm reaches under the sheets, and he pulls me to him. Our bodies lock together as we roll over and I lie on top of him. It doesn't look like he's going to make it into the lab anytime soon. At least, that's what I'm hoping.

After an energetic evening and an equally energetic morning, my stomach is now crying out for food. Correction: my stomach is *screaming* for food and quite loudly.

Nickolas caresses my tummy. "Sounds like someone needs some breakfast."

"I am starving." I giggle. I feel alive and happy. "What are you going to make me?" I tease.

"You laugh, but I make a mean piece of toast." Nickolas kisses me again before sliding out of bed and into a robe. "I can pour a glass of juice like no other as well."

I toss a pillow his way. I roll over onto my back and close my eyes. "I could stay in bed forever."

"I surely wouldn't mind that," he calls from the kitchen.

I sit up in bed as Nickolas returns to the bedroom with our breakfast. As he lays the tray between us on the bed, I notice that separating the toast and the glass is a small crushed-velvet box. My eyes zero in on it before I lift them to my bedmate.

"Open it," he instructs.

Picking up the small square box, I study it for a moment. It's only a few centimeters wide. I run my hand through my hair and look up into his eyes. "What is it?"

"Something I've carried around with me for more rotations than I care to admit." He cups my face and kisses me. "Now open it."

My hands shake as I pull the box open. "Jeepers!" There sits the most beautiful ring I have ever laid eyes on. The center stone is a two-carat round-cut garnet. Surrounding the dark blood-red center stone are diamonds cut like the petals of a flower and set in a platinum filigree ring.

"It's beautiful."

"I have hoped for the turn when I could present this to you." Nickolas leans in and kisses me again. "Zelda Harcrow, marry me."

I sit straight up and pull away. "What?" I cannot be hearing this correctly. He just came back into my life. My feelings become muddled. I stutter. "I—ah . . . I—oh . . . I—what to say?"

"Say yes, Zelda." Moving the tray, he scoots closer to me. "I know it seems sudden to you, but for me, I've waited forever."

"Nickolas, the ring is beautiful." I slip it on my finger and admire it. "I'm just not sure if I'm ready. We've been apart a long time. I'm not same as I was when I left for university. In fact, I'm not the same as I was a string or so ago when my lab was blown to smithereens and someone started trying to do me in."

"Then don't answer me just yet." He holds my hand to admire the ring. "It fits perfectly."

"I promise to think about it." I start to remove the ring so I can return it to him.

"No. it's yours. I had it designed specifically for you." He seems a bit miffed. "No matter what, it belongs to you."

Grabbing the back of his neck, I pull him to me. He definitely is not going to make it into the lab this morning. "Kiss me again," I say as I wrap my legs around his waist.

I'M DREAMING OF A GREEN field when I hear water running nearby. I'm searching for its source when suddenly it stops. The sky darkens and I feel fear. I begin screaming, but no sound emerges from my throat.

I sit straight up. *Fuck!* A nightmare. I've drenched the sheets with sweat, my pulse is fast, and my breathing has quickened. I look to the other side of the bed, but Nickolas is not there. I stumble out of bed and pull the sheet up around my naked body. I'm heading out of the boudoir when he emerges from the bathing room.

"There you are."

"I was just taking a shower." He pulls me against him. My sheet drops, and we stand there in our naked embrace. He pushes my bangs aside and presses his lips to my forehead. "I have to get into HA. I'd like to take a crack at that formula myself."

"Oh, yeah? Did you figure it out? Or are you just tired of me already?" I lick his lips.

He bends down to engage my tongue with his. He feels so good. He pulls away. "Join me. It'll be like old times, but better."

"I'd love to, but I think I should head back to my folks' and get some clean clothes."

"Meet up with me at HA later. We'll finish this together." He kisses my forehead. "Now, I have to get dressed."

Rubbing the back of my neck, a thought stops me. "Hey, Nickolas, you don't think this mysterious enemy knows about—"

He pulls me in for a tight hug and softly kisses my lips. "Everything is copacetic, Zelda. No worrying."

Nickolas and I part ways, him to the lab and me in a taxi back to my folks' home for a shower and a change of clothes. When I arrive at the mansion, pulling up behind my taxi is Big Jim.

"Jeepers, Big Jim! I'm sorry about yesterturn. I am fine, though, and if you want to hang out, I'll be heading over to HA later. I promise I won't ditch you this time."

"You didn't ditch me yesterturn, either," he claims.

"You followed me?"

"Waited for you too." His eyes go to my hand and the ring that adorns it.

For some reason, I feel incredibly guilty. I hide my hands behind my back and slip off the ring.

"Please don't squeal to Inspector Greyson."

"Not my place." He turns and heads back to his tin. He stops and calls to me, "Let me know when you're ready and I'll drive you over."

"Thanks." I wave and head up the steps to George.

Waiting for me inside is a package I've been anxious for. I rip open the box, and there it is! My new lock and handle have arrived for my apartment's new door. The brass plate of the lockset is engraved with stems, leaves, and flowers. The latch set, however, is a large brass bird perching on the knob—truly a work of art. I know I'm supposed to be heading to HA now, but I can't help but take this opportunity to get to know this beautiful lock and be able to open it with a wave of my hand.

My fingers eagerly plug in Nickolas's extension, but unfortunately I get his assistant. "Dr. Carnot isn't available. Would you like to leave a message?"

"Yes, please. Let him know that Dr. Harcrow won't be coming in and to call me when he's free."

"Yeah, sure." And the insipid girl hangs up.

I stick my tongue out at the receiver. An unwarranted shiver of dread runs up my spine. "Everything is fine," I say, shaking away the feeling. Seizing my new lock and latch, I head upstairs for a nice long soak in the tub.

"Nothing beats bubbles, a stiff drink, and alchemy." I'm thinking of my new treasure and how long it might take me to memorize and move the tumblers when I remember my unfinished truth spell from the night before. "Oopsy," I mumble. I climb out of the tub, towel off, and dress.

Pocketing the ring and the crystal, I bring my drink and my lock down to the study. My new piece of jewelry makes soft clunks as it tumbles gently onto the desk. Hanging onto the more important crystal, I grab the unfinished candle stub and the ashes of the incense, along with the sea water, and I venture out to the back garden.

"Gaia."

With the one word, I bury the candle and the ashes, pour the water over the ground, and put the crystal back in my skirt pocket. Once I feel the spell has done its job, the crystal can be cleansed and reused for another purpose. Hopefully that will be soon.

Chapter Thirty-Seven

"Darling," Mae answers when I call. "My turn at the spa was delectable."

"And Pip's?"

"Like a new dogacorn," she replies.

"When can we get together? I have news." I'm itching to tell her about Nickolas and the ring. I sit at my mother's desk, tinkering with the lockset and chewing the fat over the wireless.

"What news?" Mae's voice hits a high octave. "Did someone try to abscond with you again through one of those vortex thingies?"

"You mean portal? No, I'm perfectly fine," I assure her.

"Then what's this all about, darling?"

As I begin to answer, George enters the study. "Young Miss Zelda, Inspector Greyson is here to see you."

"Shit! I forgot about him," I say.

"Forgot about whom?"

"Didn't mean to say that out loud. Sorry," I ramble into the receiver to Mae. I cover the mouthpiece and whisper to George, "Tell the inspector I'm indisposed."

Mae's voice echoes through the wireless. "Inspector Greyson? What does he want?"

Obviously, I didn't cover the mouthpiece well enough.

"I don't know, Mae."

George clears his throat.

"Just get rid of him," I spit at George.

"Zelda!" Mae screams through the earpiece.

"Sir!" George's gruff voice bellows.

"Mae, meet me at HA. I'll take you out to dinner." I hang up on Mae midsentence, distracted by the uninvited entrance of Inspector Greyson.

"Beat it, George," his voice growls.

The old butler pulls his shoulders straight back like a young buck. "Miss Zelda, should I have this . . . gentleman removed?"

"You and whose army? I have business with your mistress here." The inspector doesn't even look back at George as he speaks. His gaze stays firmly planted on me.

"It's fine—I'll be fine."

The door clicks closed behind George as he exits in a huff.

I chastise the inspector. "You shouldn't have yapped at him that way. It was rude and he didn't deserve it."

"I could say the same of you, Doc." He moves toward me and flings his hat at the sofa. It makes a safe landing as his hands flatten on the desk and he leans accusingly toward me.

I could play dumb with the "Whatever do you mean" crap, but I know it wouldn't wash with a man like him. Instead, I just let my mouth hang open, no explanation forthcoming.

His hand slides up under my chin and shuts my mouth for me. "What's the excuse, then? Had to go home and wash your hair? Or . . ."

His voice trails off and changes from his usual strong confidence to that of a boy who just lost his best bumboozer shooter in the Ringer playing marbles. "I see." He picks up the ring Nickolas gave me, which I so nonchalantly tossed aside on the desk and forgot about.

I stand up and walk around to face him.

"It's not what—"

"What?" He pushes his hand off the desk with such force that the desk screeches against the floor. "It's not what I think? Is that what you were going to say?"

Crap. I drop my head down and look up at him. He steps back away from me and crosses his arms. What am I supposed to say?

"Why did you come to my office yesterturn?" His voice rises. "Were you just playing me to get hold of the investigation files?"

"What? No! I didn't go to spy on you!" I lift my head and take a teeny step toward him. I'm shaking. Why am I shaking? "I just came to find out the truth."

"The truth? I don't think you would know the truth if it hit you in the ass." The inspector cocks his head and stares at me.

"What?" I sputter.

He tosses the ring back on the desk. "You have been purposefully evasive and deceitful since I first met you."

My mouth opens to spout something about my stellar integrity, but I stop myself. He's right. I don't know when I have ever been completely straight with him. I never felt I could trust him, or maybe I've never felt I could just trust, in general. Plus, he makes me all tingly every time I'm near him, which kind of throws me. I want to throw myself right at him.

I set my jaw and ready myself to apologize when the moment passes and I realize something. I'm like a teakettle with steam building inside. I'm ready to blow. I can feel my eyes widening, and my voice becomes shrill.

"Look who's talking, mister!"

He gives me a dazed look.

"Don't act like you don't know what I'm talking about." I think my voice has hit a new high note.

He opens his mouth to respond. "Doc—"

Oh, no, I'm not finished. "Don't 'Doc' me! You and my father have been keeping things from me and probably from Ephron too," I scold. "You come in here all high and mighty when you're just as guilty of keeping secrets. My work is secretive; I couldn't risk telling you company business. Besides, you obviously know everything now, anyhow. I'm the one being kept in the dark."

"I don't know everything, evidently." He nods at the ring that has been cast aside. "And you need to be careful." He takes a deep breath. "As for secrets, my job requires me to examine the evidence and not make public what my investigations bring forth 'til after the bad guys are caught."

I ignore his gesture toward the ring. "But those secrets involve me. I have the right to know what you and Father are holding back from me." This could be my opportunity to finally get the whole picture.

"Your dear old pops plays it close to the vest and doesn't let me in on anything 'til he's ready." Chance moves slowly toward me as he lectures me. "The only reason I know what I know is because I promised I'd protect you." His finger jabs my chest.

I hold my ground and grab his finger. "Protect me? I don't need your protection; plus, you are doing a really lousy job of it."

"If you would quit dodging your protection detail, listen, and stay in one place, I might be able to solve this case without having to spend every second worrying that something is going to happen to you." Chance is right on top of me, but I still hold onto his finger.

"So you're here because of my father?"

"For one of the smartest people in the world, you can be a bit of a dunce," he whispers.

"Oh" is the only thing I can get out before he kisses me.

Just like before, the kiss is feverish and rough. When he finishes counting my teeth with his tongue, he pushes me away. "Doc." He turns without another word and starts for the door.

"How did you know I looked at the files?" I ask his turned back.

He reaches into the pocket of his trench coat, takes out the rolled-up pair of stockings I forgot on his desk, and tosses them onto the sofa as he retrieves his hat on his way out.

I clench my teeth until my eyes begin to water. I stand so still as I watch him leave that something inside me begins to well up. My physical stillness ends when my arm flies up and straight out to the side. I hear the sound of metal scraping against wood, gouging as it moves swiftly toward the window. Only when I hear the sharp sound of a windowpane shattering and then an odd splash do I realize what I've done.

"Crap." I let my eyes follow the line of my extended arm. "Shit." The beautiful dark wood and dark-green stone of my mother's new desk have deep scratches in them. "Futz." My eyes continue up to the large gaping, jagged hole in the middle of the window behind her desk. I timidly move around the desk to stare out through the shattered hole. "Fuck!"

I turn my attention back to the top of the desk; the new lockset I was practicing locking and unlocking with telekinesis is gone. I turn and peer out the broken window again toward the pool. "Well, that's new." I have never moved anything unintentionally with my mind. I have never even moved anything intentionally with my mind without constant practice.

I stand up straight. "George!" I call at the top of my lungs. "Be a good egg and get the pool skimmer."

Chapter Thirty-Eight

T ea flies out of Mae's mouth. "You did what?"

I hand her a napkin. "Then the lockset flew out the window and landed in the pool."

Pip lifts his ugly but well-groomed head from Mae's lap. "Grrr . . . yap . . . humf," he articulates before shaking splattered tea from his head.

"I see that thing is still quite attached to you," I say.

Mae pats herself dry with the cloth, then Pip. "Well, I did rescue him from that dingy wreck of a building." She gives him a scratch behind his floppy ear. "Doesn't he look handsome?"

I almost choke on her question. It's like a dry biscuit got caught in my throat and all I can do is hack and cough.

"Are you okay?"

"You're serious." I look at the mutt of a dogacorn. Although he's now clean and tidy, his horn is still crooked and off-center, the different-colored eyes are still bulging and crossed, his underbite is still prominent, and his tongue hangs out the other side of his mouth now.

She just stares at me.

"Yes, he looks like a brand-new dog," I lie.

Mae smiles and lifts Pip to give him a nuzzle. "Such a good doggy," she says and plants a kiss on the tip of his horn before placing him back on her lap, where he proceeds to glare at me.

"Well, I didn't change our dinner plans to late afternoon tea to talk about Pip and his pulchritude and appeal." Mae sets her tea down and takes her time adjusting her gloves, smoothing the points on the back of them. "Zelda darling, let me give you some advice."

She looks up for a moment, as if she's arranging the thoughts in her head before speaking, which is very unlike her.

"Jeepers, just let me have it."

"Fine, darling, but remember, you asked." She fluffs up her curly hair with one hand and clears her throat. "First off, you have someone trying to do in either you, your father, or the company. Secondly, you have a lab under construction because someone blew it up, not to mention a lab assistant on the mend, two dead bodies, and you back to living at your folks."

"What are you trying to say?"

She pinches the bridge of her nose, closes her eyes, and shakes her head. "Dar-ling, you are in no position to start a committed relationship or even to contemplate commitment of any sort."

"You're the one who told me I needed to get back out there," I say, my voice rising. A few heads turn my way in the café, so I lower my voice. "You said—"

"I meant you needed *sex*." Her words cause a few more heads to pivot our way. "Yes, you old fuddy-duddies, I said sex. Now mind your own beeswax." After a few "I nevers" and some overly done huffs, our fellow patrons return to their tiny sandwiches and milky tea. "Now what are you going to do?"

I blow out a breath of air in relief. "I guess I'll head over to HA and tell Nickolas I'm not ready to even consider his proposal of partnership of any kind 'til this whole dangerous problem is solved."

"And what about the virile Inspector Chance Greyson?"

"Virile? Really?"

Mae lifts a brow and smirks. "What would you call him, then?"

I stick my tongue out at her. The mutt lifts his head and growls at me, his left eye moving to look at me. It must cause him great strain to straighten his eye; he gives such a sneeze that his eye whirls around twice before taking its original place. His tongue now resides on the opposite side of his muzzle.

"Don't upset Pip. He is very sensitive." Mae caresses the thing until it settles back into a ball on her lap.

"Good grief." I take a deep breath and attempt to continue the already odd and off-track conversation. "Chance—Inspector Greyson and I have no real relationship. We have an attraction; that's it."

"You sound disappointed."

I lower my eyes to my teacup. "I'm not. Besides, the way we—or should I say he—left things today, I should think we have nothing more to talk about."

"If you say so." Mae rises, pup in arm. "You need to go take care of business, Zelda Harcrow. I love you and do be careful."

I give her a hug, trying not to squish Pip. He still growls at me, though. "I'll call you."

"You better," she says.

Grabbing my very large bodyguard, I make my way out of the little café and into Big Jim's motor.

"Where to?"

"Take me to HA." I've decided to take Mae's advice and start confidently forward. I have something of a plan, but I'll have to delay my project until I can talk to Father and Ephron. Won't they be surprised when I tell them my discovery? Biota, here we come! Then everything will just fall into place: my lab, my work, and my love life.

Finally feeling confident that everything is working out, a broad smile covers my face when we arrive at HA and I spot my Zenith finished and ready to go. Big Jim has barely pulled into a parking space before I'm jumping from the tin and running to my beloved cycle.

Big Jim joins me. "What's the hurry?"

"This," I say as I caress the smooth cool steel and chrome of the Zenith.

"Baby of an iron you've got, Doctor."

"This is proof that everything is going to be copacetic." I walk around the bike, admiring her.

"If you say so," he says.

"I say so." For the first time in over a string, I don't feel all grummy.

Since the brick house is too heavy for the lift, we clomp up the stairs. "First stop, Ephron's office. I want to know if he's heard from Father."

"Right behind you." Big Jim abruptly stops and checks me; I stumble forward, turn, and give him a glare. "Take a gander," he finishes with a nod.

Furrowing my brows, I pivot in the direction of his nod. I'm befuddled for a moment as to what I'm witnessing. "Not good."

Dr. Shamm and Nickolas's pill of an assistant seem to be in an intense conversation. Shamm grabs the girl by the arm and shakes her.

"I wonder what's got him all in a lather," I say. They're too far away for me to hear the conversation. "I'm going to try to get closer."

I start over. I can see tears running down her face as Shamm leans in with an angry expression. I whisper to Big Jim, "If I could just move a little bit more without being too obvious."

Too late, though. Dr. Monki Shamm swings around and makes tracks for a lift to carry him upstairs.

Big Jim leans. "Wonder what that was all about."

"Not sure, but I plan on finding out." I begin to march toward Nickolas's assistant.

"Zelda!" my brother's voice calls out.

I turn my head to acknowledge him, along with a sisterly annoyed "What?"

Ephron jogs over to us. "Have you heard from the old bird?"

"Father? Naw. You?"

He just shakes his head.

I can see the frustration all over his face. "Jeepers, are you going on a long trip?"

A befuddled Ephron scratches his head. Pointing at his face, I razz him. "Those bags under your eyes look pretty heavy."

"Very funny. This is serious." Without another word, he tilts to one side, turns, and begins plodding his way back to his office, planting his feet one in front of the other as if it's of great effort.

Big Jim takes a couple of heavy steps forward. "Are we supposed to follow him?"

"I think so."

We both trail Ephron across the atrium and into the executive suites, catching up with him in his office.

"Miss Trick," I lightly acknowledge as I sweep past her and close the door behind us.

"You're giving me the heebie-jeebies, Brother. Level with me; what's eating you?" I stand behind him, rubbing his shoulders. He sits at his desk with his head in his hands.

"You want some privacy?" Big Jim asks, standing ready at the door.

I shake my head. "Take a seat. I may need backup."

"You mean, someone to call Chance," he says.

I look up at him, but I don't need to give him an answer.

I wrap my arms around my brother's neck and lean over, giving him a peck on the cheek. "Spill. What has happened?"

"Everything—nothing . . . it's all falling apart." He hangs onto my arms, keeping me close.

"Ephron, you're being cryptic," I say.

Big Jim brings over a rocks glass filled three-fingers deep with some strong amber liquid. "Neat."

"Thanks." Ephron lets go of me, and I stand back as he downs the alcohol in one gulp.

I wait until my rumpled brother gives the drained glass back to Big Jim for a refill he doesn't necessarily need. "Lay it out for me."

He takes a breath and wipes his face with his hands. "I have no idea where Father is or even Mother and Phrennie. Customers have been leaving us in droves after someone leaked the story of the attacks on our company. The Space Council is talking about pulling out as well. I don't know if I can fix this."

I put up my hand to halt another glass of hooch being passed to him by my silent yet fully present bodyguard. Big Jim nods and steps back. Kneeling next to Ephron, I speak as quietly and calmly as I can fake.

"First off, Mother and Phrennie are with Ava in the capital. They're safe. As for Father, I'm sure he'll show up soon with all the answers." My voice wavers, but it's my turn to be the strong one.

"Call A.P. Have him calm the Space Council and tell them that even with everything going on, we are still on schedule for Biota. As for the other clients, get our customer procurement team on it and find out where they're going." I stop, stand up, and smooth out my slacks. I am such a good sister.

"Jeez, Zelda, don't you know?" His eyebrows furrow as water fills his eyes. "Phrennie and Mother aren't in Capital City. Ava had no idea they were even supposed to stay with her."

"I don't understand."

"Father carted them off somewhere for some reason, and I have no clue where." His arms fly up in the air. "Zelda, Zelda, Zelda . . ." His voice trails off as he gets up and snatches the booze-filled glass from Big Jim.

"Where could he have sent them and why?"

"Your guess is as good as mine."

"We've got to fix this, Ephron."

He somberly shuffles over and reaches out, putting a hand on my shoulder. With a bitter tone, he spits out, "And how, may I ask, are we, you and I, going to do that?"

Pushing his hand off, I straighten my shoulders. "Ephron, I have something I've discovered."

"What? When?" my brother inquires with befuddlement. Big Jim takes the empty glass from Ephron and helps him back into one of the leather chairs.

"It's something I've been playing around with for some time. The rest came to me—well, almost the rest came to me one evening."

"This formula?"

"It could revolutionize travel—space travel." I grab his hands and look up at him, urging him with my eyes to understand the gravity of what I'm telling him.

He gets it. "This . . . this could save us."

"Now you're on the trolley!" I say as I watch his face fill with hope.

"Does Father know about this?" Ephron asks as he motions for Jim to get him another belt.

I stand up. "Unless Nickolas told him? No."

"What does this have to do with Nickolas? You haven't seen him in rotations."

"I coded the formula and sent it to him to keep it protected 'til this whole threat on the company was solved."

"But then he showed up?" Ephron downs another glass.

I pause, cock my head, and bite my lip. "Unexpectedly."

"Can you fill in the missing piece?"

"I can use Nickolas's lab."

He slams the emptied tumbler on his desk. "What are you waiting for?"

"Making sure you're okay."

He stands up and attempts to smooth his wrinkled suit. "I have phone calls to make, and you have a miracle to deliver." He grabs a discarded tie to put around his neck.

Big Jim stands at the door. "Ready, Doctor?"

I give Ephron a hug and join my muscle at the door. I turn back and watch Ephron for a moment as he straightens the scattered papers on his desk, picks up the horn, and shouts out orders to someone or another.

"One more moment to watch him get back on his feet won't hurt."

"I'll wait outside."

I nod in acknowledgment as I take a bit more time to witness the transformation of Ephron from depleted and dismayed back to his old ahead-of-the-game, prosperous self.

Outside his office door, I find Big Jim waiting and eyeing Miss Trick. "She's a looker, I'll agree," I say, "but ooh . . . her voice."

"You got the wrong idea."

"Really?" I take a gander at my brother's assistant. She's covering an ear with one hand while taking a call. She also has her legs crossed and her skirt is hiked up to reveal her garter. "Uh-huh." I chuckle as I walk away.

He rushes to catch up. "I just can't put my finger on it."

"If you did, you'd probably get slapped."

"Why would I get slapped?"

We gallop up the stairs to the floor above my new laboratory. "No need to be embarrassed. I'm sure almost every Joe and Jane has been ogling her garters and anything else they could lay their eyeballs on."

"Dr. Harcrow, that's not what I meant."

I turn to him as we walk into Nickolas's laboratory. "What did you mean, then?"

"Dr. Harcrow, I want you to move outside the door," he commands.

"What? Why?"

"Now!" His voice is stern and low, like the growl of a large animal.

I knit my brows together and defy his request, stepping backward, away from him and into the lab.

"Nickolas, what is Big Jim worried about?"

"Doctor, please." Big Jim's voice is gentle now.

My heel catches on an object on the floor. A kilometer of expletives run from my mouth as my rear hits the cold, hard cement.

I freeze.

Then I scream.

The object is a slumped lifeless body lying on the cold, callous cement floor. An avalanche of tears flows from my eyes as I wail, "Do something! Help him!" Nickolas's eyes are wide and drained, as if his soul was pulled out of him suddenly.

"Dr. Harcrow—Zelda—there's nothing you can do." Big Jim pulls me up into his arms and carries me out as I continue my howling. My big old towser sets me on the cool terrazzo outside the lab. I can hear the door slam as he shuts it. I crush my eyes tightly closed against my new reality, but the hope I had is gone like a burned-out bulb. My ears can't block out the truth of things: Big Jim's feet pounding past me, the crack of glass, and the shrill sound of the alarm.

"Zelda, can you hear me?" Big Jim's voice booms above the alarm.

I shake my head. Not because I can't hear him, but because I don't want to.

"I have to guard this door. I'm right here; just hang tight." His voice bellows at me. Even if I wanted to shut him out, I couldn't.

I must look puny, a sack cowering in a bundle on the harsh floor.

I become aware of the rhythmic chant of the heavy-soled shoes of the HA security team invading my skull, and it continues to echo there long after they arrive.

"You must be Zeper. I'm Jep, head of security here. What's the status?"

"The body is in the lab. No one has been in or out since we arrived."

"Zelda." A voice tries to reach me. "Zelda!" the voice yells. Familiar hands shake my shoulders. "Zelda!"

I push my hands angrily over my ears. "Go away." My body rocks back and forth. I can still hear them talking; they keep talking with the same unyielding volume even though the alarm has ceased its screaming.

"I think she's in shock," I hear my brother say.

"Then let's get her downstairs. You—yeah, you, the big guy, pick her up. Let's go." It's Olga Ravenscroft who is shouting orders at Big Jim. I wonder why she's here.

"Big Jim, take her to my office; you can lay her on the sofa." Ephron's voice starts to lose some of its volume.

I keep my eyes closed and let my bodyguard lift and carry me. I push everything from my mind; I've done it before, when I lost Holden. I escape into my mind until I fall unconscious.

Chapter Thirty-Nine

The cool wet cloth patting my face is not enough for me to open my eyes. I don't even flinch. I lie on Ephron's couch, pretending to still be out like a light. I can't face anyone. The grief clenches tightly around my chest like a vice—or is it guilt that's slowly suffocating me?

Rough, round, chubby hands continue to pat my forehead. It isn't one of the healers; they're known for their soft, smooth, and gentle touch. I lie there, unmoving but eavesdropping on the congregation of voices coming and going in Ephron's office.

"Miss Trick, have you gotten hold of A.P. and Mae Griffin?" Ephron belts out from behind his desk.

"Yes, sir. They're in the building." Miss Trick's voice cracks.

"Put together a drink cart and wheel it in here," he directs her.

"Yes, sir."

I hear the door close briefly before it bangs open, crashing into the credenza behind it. There's a wobble and a thud, probably from the modern stylized brass sculpture of a woman's head that I gave to Ephron falling to the floor. There's a miniscule amount of silence. Someone is making a dramatic entrance, and I need only one guess as to who that may be.

"Oh, darling Ephron, where is my dear Zelda?" I can hear the swish of Mae's taffeta coat as the stiff fabric brushes against the tender silk of her stockings. It must have gotten colder out since I arrived today. "Zelda!" The swishing becomes fervent and louder. I feel her gloved hand take mine. Then there arises a yap and a deep growl. She's brought the damn dogacorn; that thing hates me. I'm certainly not going to open my eyes now.

"Ephron, I think you had better fill me in, Son," thunders the gruff voice of A.P.

"Have a seat, A.P. This is Zeper Jo, though everyone calls him Big Jim. He found Nickolas, along with my sister. And you know the head of our security."

"How do you do? Thank you for taking such diligent care of our girl." I'm sure there's a handshake involved.

Ephron's voice comes next. "Where is Miss Trick with that beverage cart?"

I strain to hear what they're saying over Mae's constant calling of my name. "She's not waking up. Do something!"

Without a word of warning, a snap reaches my ears and a vicious odor assaults my olfactory nerves, catapulting me up into a sitting position. "What the fuck!"

"Oh, Zelda!" Mae wraps her arms around me and begins to hug me with an enthusiasm that includes a rapid rocking back and forth. Pip is up on his hind legs, his head tilted so he can lay one of his eyes on me. He yaps, growls, and then begins sneezing so hard that he falls over sideways. Mae finally releases me to rescue Pip.

I look over and see Olga Ravenscroft—round, short, and soured—sitting on a stool next to the sofa. Olga has been the one attending me all this time and the one who opened the ammonia capsule under my nose. Olga's chubby little hand reaches into her lab pocket and pulls out a little flask. Into the cap of the flask—about the size of a shot glass—Olga pours a black slow-moving goopy substance. I'm really hoping that isn't for me.

"Drink this. It'll set you right as rain on the Weather Council's turn off." She shoves the cap into my hand.

I pull my head back with a frown. "What is it?"

"You, with the creepy dogacorn, go get me some whiskey," Olga blasts.

Mae doesn't utter a word. She just wrinkles her nose, sticks out her tongue, and picks up Pip to go grab a bottle and glass from Ephron's small liquor cabinet. She brings them over.

"Don't be a big baby. It doesn't taste bad." Olga aggressively presses the concoction toward my lips. I grudgingly put the gross-looking syrup to my mouth and sling my head back, pouring the gloopy foul-tasting goop down my throat.

"Ew! You said it didn't taste bad." I motion for the whiskey. Mae offers the glass, but I grab the bottle and chug away the putrid gunk. "You lied!"

"Everybody lies," Olga says calmly and without remorse. "How else was I going to get you to take it?" She gets up, swoops up the stool, and waddles off to talk to A.P. and Ephron.

"She's a real humdinger, isn't she, darling?" Mae sits next to me at the edge of the couch, while Pip chases what's left of his tail. "She scares me."

"She is a force, I must agree. And she brings her own stool." I set the bottle on the floor.

Mae pats my knee. "How are you, really?"

"Numb." I sigh. "And not from the booze, either." We sit in silence, just mindlessly watching Pip fail over and over again to capture his nemesis, The Tail. I turn my attention to Olga, who is arguing with A.P., while Ephron is on the horn stressfully talking to someone or other. Luckily, Olga and A.P. are loud enough that I don't have to strain to hear their heated conversation.

"Listen, A.P., my guy knows what he's doing." She pokes him in the belly with her finger. She was probably aiming for his chest but couldn't reach that high.

"He's wet behind the ears. Don't we have someone here to take care of this?" A.P. leans down to shout but can't stoop low enough, so he shouts at the top of her tightly finger-waved jet-black hair.

She jabs him again. "What are you implying?"

I bow my head toward Mae and whisper, "Wonder who or what they're talking about."

"Don't know, but I've never seen Poppy lose a debate before." Mae cups a hand over her mouth. "I think she might hurt him."

The office door opens once again. I suddenly find myself on my feet, having kicked Mae in the behind while getting vertical.

"Hey!" Mae squeals, rubbing her butt. "Ow!" She stops and looks at the new guests. "I see," she adds.

Inspector Greyson marches in, followed closely by Flynn. Tagging along is an unexpected soul: Constable Hodge.

"Here he is." Olga walks past the inspector and his sidekick, making a beeline for Hodge.

My mouth hangs open. "Hodge is her guy?" I ask Mae.

"Apparently."

"What would Hodge be doing on this case?" My confusion mixes with the tragedy of losing both Nickolas and an opportunity to save the company, and I'm too defeated to move or really care.

The inspector has to shake everyone's hand as he enters and makes his way toward Mae and me.

"My condolences, Dr. Harcrow." The inspector's eyes are distant and detached. He looks at me as if I were a stranger, with none of the warmth of before.

I nod at the inspector and acknowledge his DSI, who has pulled out his handy-dandy notebook and pen.

Mae puts her arm around me. "Inspector darling, I don't think Zelda is up to any of your questions right at this time. Could you just go figure this out on your own? That is what you do, isn't it?"

"Dr. Harcrow, to find out who killed Nickolas Carnot, we're going to need your help."

He called me Dr. Harcrow. He never calls me that; he's always called me Doc. Things truly have changed. "I'll be okay, Mae. Let him ask us questions."

DSI Flynn begins to scribble in his notebook. "Ready, sir."

The inspector's questions begin simple. "When was the last time you saw Dr. Carnot?"

I take a small breath. "This morning."

"Can you tell me what his attitude was like?"

"Good, I guess."

"I see." His voice has become quiet. I go ahead and let the inspector misunderstand my answer. "When did he arrive here?"

I shake my head "Don't know."

He tilts his head, looking confused. "You said you saw him."

"No—I mean, yes."

"Dr. Harcrow, I'm trying to establish a timeline. I understand you are grieving, but I need you to recall what he did and said the last time you saw him."

I don't like that he isn't calling me Doc. The distance between us seems to grow as I answer these questions. My knees begin to buckle under the weight of my guilt and sadness. Mae pulls me closer to help prop me up. "Do you need to sit down, darling?"

I shake my head no and straighten my spine.

"Are you okay to continue?" Mae asks. "Would you like some water?"

I shake my head, and my brain seems to rattle inside. Mae nods to the inspector, urging him to speed it up.

The inspector begins again. "When you're ready."

"I—" I close my eyes. "I don't know the time; it was midmorning." I stop, open my eyes, and look at Chance. "It's my fault, you know!"

"Now, darling, it isn't. Don't be silly," Mae interjects.

"If I had said yes or hadn't sent him my formula—if I hadn't gone home."

Chance's eyebrows rise and then lower. "You didn't say yes?"

I nod.

The silence between us is deafening. It's DSI Flynn who pushes aside the quiet. He steps forward out of the inspector's shadow for a moment. "What formula?"

The inspector slides Flynn a look. Flynn steps back into the inspector's shadow and continues taking notes, his head lowered.

"I told him I needed to go home and change, and he said he was coming here."

Chance tries to get me to clarify my answer. "So you went home to change?"

"I received a package—my new door handle and lock—so I decided to take a bath. I took my sweet old time." I cover my mouth with one hand and close my eyes. Maybe I could just restart the turn. "I told his assistant that I wasn't coming in."

"So you weren't expected?"

"I had to fish my lockset from the pool, and then I met up with Mae."

Flynn steps forward again, holding up his pencil as though he were asking a question in class. "Why was the lockset in the pool?"

I look up at Chance. "I was mad at someone."

A smile covers Flynn's face, and he steps back smugly, as if he just scored some points against his boss.

Chance's chin drops, and he breaks eye contact with me. "Let's move on to your arrival here."

My body feels heavy. I'm tired—not sleepy tired, but as if something has drained me dry of any energy I had.

"Darling, I think you need to sit down." Mae isn't ready for my body to just finally give in.

"Hold on." Chance's strong grasp stops me from hitting the floor. Flynn drops his pad and rushes to my side.

"Okay, boys, let's lower her back onto the couch," Mae directs. "And I think the rest of the questions can wait."

"Miss Griffin—"

"No, Inspector. Besides, at that point, Big Jim was with her, so you can talk with him." She waves Olga to come look me over.

The inspector and DSI Flynn back off. I watch them walk away. It's strange; I feel like an observer watching a play or story being acted out on the stage for my entertainment.

Olga Ravenscroft is a clever alchemist, always leading with her head. Leaving nothing to chance, she values prudence over everything else. "To the stars with those sleepers." Olga refers to anyone she finds dull-witted as "sleepers." "Take a deep breath and close your eyes."

I do as I'm told, but all I can see is Nickolas's body and all I can think is that I could have prevented his death.

"Stop thinking so much, girl. Nothing you said or did would have made one iota of difference."

Mae pats my hand. "She's right, Zelda." She kisses me on the cheek and says softly, "The only one to blame is the evil person who killed him."

"Take another slug of that whiskey." Olga moves from side to side and cranes her neck. "Where's the bottle?"

"I put it on the floor here." I lean over to grab the bottle, but it's not there. "It was here; I swear."

Olga pats the floor. "The carpet is all wet."

"I must've kicked it when I stood up." I rub my forehead. "Maybe it rolled under the couch."

Mae stands up and gives the immediate area a once-over. "Where's Pip?"

Olga, already on her hands and knees, is grimacing as she peers under the deep leather couch. "Found them."

"Them?" I repeat.

"Pip?" Mae calls.

"It'll be a while 'til he's up and about." Olga snickers.

Mae reluctantly gets down on her hands and knees and peeks under the sofa. Her head pops up for a moment with a stare of disbelief before she heads back under couch.

Curiosity gets the best of me, and I join the two ladies on the floor. "Jeepers, Mae! Pip's a lush."

There lies Pip with the half-empty bottle cozied up to his body, his front legs lying across the amber bottle. His bulging eyes are closed, and his tongue now hangs out over his misshapen muzzle. I'd think him dead if not for the sudden disruptive belch that erupts from his belly and the rasps, snorts, and grunts of snoring that come immediately after.

"Pip, how could you?" Mae whines.

I reach under to grab the bottle and am met with a sudden growl. "You're on your own with this one." I pull my hand out and sit back.

Olga wobbles slowly to her feet and dusts her hands off on her lab coat. "He's just going to have to sleep it off, I'm afraid."

"I have a sap for a dogacorn."

"A regular boozehound," I joke.

"Not funny."

"Yes, it is." I'm feeling better.

Mae's hands are planted firmly on her hips. She slides me a glance as her mouth tightens.

"A hooch pooch."

"Zelda!"

"What?"

Her face relaxes into a small smile, and she shakes her head. "You're too much."

While Mae and I are giggling, Olga bravely retrieves the bent Pip and his bottle of brown juice. "Let's get this ragamuffin onto the couch."

Olga shoves the bottle of booze into my hand. I hold up the bottle and look at the meager amount left. "Do you think he might need a little hair of the dog later?"

"Stop it, will you?" Mae snatches the bottle from my hand and marches across the room to toss it in the can.

The entire room goes quiet as everyone watches the dramatic Mae cross the room with proverbial fire coming out of her ears. "And what are you all looking at? Haven't you ever seen a dogacorn have a snort too many?"

Quickly, the room goes back to buzzing over the latest clues as Mae regains her composure and makes her way back, holding her chin high.

"Sorry."

She sighs. "He is a mess of a dogacorn, isn't he?"

"Yes, but he's your mess and he adores you."

"He does, doesn't he?"

"Too bad he won't take a shine to me."

"You're being silly, Zelda. He likes you just fine."

Olga finishes up with Pip. "He may want to lose his stomach when he wakes up, so make sure he gets plenty of water. If you need to, find me and I'll take another look at him."

"Thank you."

Olga nods toward the door. "Excuse me, ladies." We watch as she leaves us to talk to Hodge, who has reappeared in the office. This time, he has several bags, which Olga takes and brings over to Inspector Greyson.

Chapter Forty

"I wonder what they found?"

"Looks important," observes Mae as she goes back to fretting over her inebriated pet.

I wander over to the gathering of bodies, each trying to talk over the others. They look like a gaggle of geese waddling and squawking at each other. I approach the agitated bunch and quietly make myself part of their circle. I look at each member of the group as they pass the evidence around and give their uninformed opinion on it.

A.P. spouts with great authority, "It is obviously some sort of letter."

"It is a fine parchment," Jep says, taking the paper from A.P.

Chance holds up the torn piece to the light. "What are these markings?"

"Looks like a code," Ephron surmises.

"It is a code." Olga grabs the evidence and shakes her head at the cluelessness of the men surrounding her.

"Dr. Ravenscroft," Chance says, bowing to her superior knowledge of the evidence. "What kind of code?"

Olga passes the paper on to Hodge. "Alchemist code."

"What does it say?"

Olga shrugs her shoulders. "I have no idea, Inspector Greyson."

"I thought you just said it was an alchemist code?" bellows A.P.

"I did." Olga huffs. "Every alchemist has their own code."

"So with Carnot dead, we have no idea what it says." The inspector sounds exasperated.

The piece of torn parchment finally makes its way to me. I raise my hand. "I do."

All eyes are on me like I'm a gate-crasher.

"Doc, you can read this?"

"Of course. I wrote it."

"I thought it was Dr. Carnot's code?" A.P. scrunches up his face, still trying to sound like he's in command.

"It is, but it isn't." I look at Ephron; he would understand.

"It's the one you used when Carnot worked here," Ephron interprets.

I nod.

"You better explain," Ephron says.

Time to put my big-girl pants on and get back in the game. "Before I headed to university, I was an assistant here. I worked with Carnot. This was the code we used then."

Chance runs his fingers through his streaked locks. "I'm still not following. How did this end up with him?"

"Remember the night you found me out mailing a letter?"

The inspector nods.

I tell my story to the group. Ephron just stands there with his arms crossed and his head down, listening. Flynn's pen can't seem to keep up with me. A.P. keeps clearing his throat, but I think that's directed at Mae and her ossified dog, not me.

"I thought it would be safe, and if anything happened to me, it would make it back here."

I look at Ephron and he picks up the story. "Then, as you know, he called and spoke to Titus." Ephron refers to Father by his first name, which I find telling.

The inspector nods, like there's some secret knowledge between him and Titus that Ephron isn't aware of.

I examine the fragment. "Where's the rest?"

It's Olga who speaks up. "Officer Hodge found it grasped in Nickolas's hand."

"Someone ripped it out of his hand?" I ask in disbelief.

"It appears so," she confirms.

"He was killed for the formula." Guilt rises inside me like a tsunami.

The inspector puts up his palms as if to stop traffic. "We don't know that, Doc."

"He's dead and the paper is gone," I say.

Dr. Ravenscroft answers, "He was most likely dead when the paper was ripped from his hand."

I may be a great alchemist, but dead bodies are not my thing. "How can you tell?"

Everyone listens with great interest as Dr. Ravenscroft explains. "It appears as though someone tried to pry it from his hands postmortem. There was bruising on the hands, and the body was stiff but still warm."

"The body—you mean Nickolas?" I correct her.

"Yes, I mean Nickolas."

Chance's fingers form a stiff pyramid against his mouth as he listens to Dr. Ravenscroft, dropping them mindfully to speak. "If that's true, then he was killed almost as soon as he got here."

Dr. Ravenscroft wiggles her chin. "It would seem so."

I'm confused. "But if he was killed for the formula, why wouldn't they wait 'til it was finished?"

"You never finished it?" asks the inspector.

"Well, no. I thought Nickolas came here to finish it. But he said he wanted me to come in today to complete it."

Inspector Greyson turns toward my brother. "Ephron, what was Nickolas supposed to be working on?"

"Titus controlled all the experiments," Ephron answers. "Not that Carnot was that great of an alchemist."

"What are you talking about, Ephron? He was one of the greatest," I declare, defending Nickolas's memory.

Ephron shakes his head. "You were the talent, Zelda. It was always you. When you left, he couldn't cut it and Titus got him a position teaching."

I stand there stunned into silence by disbelief.

The inspector drives the conversation back on track. "Only Titus knew about the experiments?"

"Because of the attacks, he felt it was safer if only he, the alchemists, and their teams knew," Ephron confirms.

"So we don't know what Nickolas was actually working on, if anything? Was it Doc's experiment, or was it something else?"

I break my brief silence. "His assistant would know."

"We'll track her down." Ephron walks with purpose to the door. "Miss Trick, Miss Trick—where in the stars is she?"

Ephron heads to his desk to make a call. Hodge reappears and waves a bag in the air. Olga backs away from the group and meets Hodge at the door. I'm a bit nosy; I mean, this does concern me. They whisper back and forth. Hodge looks in my direction and gives me a nod. I smile back, but I don't think he notices; he's thick as thieves with Olga.

"Ephron!" Olga's sharp voice calls my brother to her side.

I screw up my face, a little peeved that I'm being left out of both conversations. Although I'm not really paying attention to anything Jep, A.P., and Chance are debating.

Letting out a frustrated huff, I shrug my shoulders and go to see how Mae is faring with her ossified pooch.

"What's going on?" Mae doesn't look up as she continues to pet Pip's wiry fur.

"Not really sure."

"Weren't you listening?" She places Pip on the floor. He gives me the eye, growls, coughs, and passes out. "All this stuff is giving me the heebie-jeebies, Zelda."

I collapse on the sofa.

"And stop feeling guilty," Mae commands.

"It was my formula."

"That's not what I mean."

I rub my forehead with force; inside my head is a marching band.

"Zelda, you didn't love him."

"Did too," I flatly insist.

Mae scoffs. "Who are you kidding?"

"I slept with him, remember?"

"Sex and love are two different things."

"Not in this case," I argue.

Mae gives me a little shove. "In this case, you slept with a fantasy you created when you were a naïve, wide-eyed, hero-worshiping young girl."

I open my mouth, but no words come.

Mae continues to lecture me. "Now Holden—that was attraction, respect, mutual admiration, and deep love."

I sit forward and put my finger up so as to say something that seems important, but I quickly fall back into a slouch again.

"You are not responsible for his death. You do not have to feel guilty for not loving him."

"Why do I feel so horrible?" I moan.

Mae puts her arms around me. "Because you're a good egg. I love you."

"I love you too."

The office door bangs open, jarring the rest of the figures off the credenza. Led by Constable Hodge, two other constables drag in a struggling male figure.

Chapter Forty-One

I stand to see around the gathering. "Who is that?" I ask.
"Can't tell. Let's move forward. Come on, Pip." Mae speeds
toward the group with Pip at her heels.

"Jeepers." I hustle to catch up. The figure is dragged to a chair and
shoved into it. I push through and past A.P. "Needs?"

There sits Orin Needs, Dr. Zozimos's assistant. His normally sal-
low okra complexion seems yellower and paler than usual.

I look at Hodge. "What's he doing here?"

Needs's narrow body melts into the chair, his bland eyes filling
with pools of tears. Neither would be noticeable if it weren't for his
bushy eyebrows cringing together above his peepers. "I didn't do it, I
swear!" he blubbers over and over.

"Then how did you end up with Zelda's formula?" Ephron demands.

I stand there, head spinning. *Needs? It makes no sense.*

Ephron screams in his face, "Answer me!"

Needs keeps blubbering unintelligible words strung sloppily together to form gobbledygook sentences.

Chance pushes Ephron aside and takes over the interrogation.
"Needs, answer the question. What were you doing with the parch-
ments?"

I stand as silently and still as I can for fear that Needs will bolt
like a scared rodent if I make any sudden moves. The rest of my com-
panions concentrate on him and occasionally whisper to each other.
Chance goes at him a bit stronger.

"Listen, buster, you're in deep. Why did you kill Dr. Carnot?"

Needs just keeps blubbering and shaking his head.

"Was it for the formula?"

"This isn't happening . . ." Needs tosses his head into his hands.

"He wouldn't decipher it and so you killed him?" Chance grabs Needs's collar and tears his head away from his hands."

"No!" Orin Needs is bawling like a baby.

The inspector's voice is deep, fast, and furious. "What did you use? Poison? We will find out; he's with the cutters now." Chance places his hands on either armrest of the chair, boxing Needs in. "You're going down, you measly bug, for the murder of Dr. Nickolas Carnot." Chance directs his men to lift Needs to his feet and take him to the station.

As Needs is forced to his feet, I feel strongly compelled to start beating the life out of him.

So I do just that.

I rush toward the brownnosing weasel, and my fist finds his left eye, then his nose, and then his other eye. I'm pulled back by my brother, but not before another punch connects with his chin. With my arm still free, I wind up to clobber Needs once more, but a vice clenches around my arm and pulls me back from the subject of my fury.

"Hot dang, Doc! Cut it out!"

"Needs, you asshole!" I scream. "How could you?"

"I'm sorry." His voice is barely audible.

"Sorry doesn't cut it, weasel!"

"Doc!" Chance pulls at me to step back.

Wriggling and wriggling, I free myself from the inspector, and my hands collapse around Needs's scrawny neck. "Why were you trying to kill me and my father?"

The inspector grabs me around the waist, lifting my legs up into the air. Ephron pries my hands from Needs's throat. The inspector now has to have help pulling me off the little brownnosing vermin.

Needs falls back into the chair and begins to spill it all. "I didn't do any of it."

"Didn't do what?" Ephron demands.

"I didn't kill anyone!"

"Keep talking," Chance says, stepping in front of Ephron and me.

"I just found him. I saw the form—formu—formula, and I took it. That's it." Orin Needs starts wiping the snot and tears from his nicely bruised face.

"Why?" Chance speaks more smoothly and calmly so as not to spook the now-cooperating suspect.

"Steven—I mean Dr. Zozimos—hasn't done a thing in over a rotation. He hasn't discovered or created anything, and his time is coming up. Then I'll be out of a job."

All eyes move to Ephron, who nods. "Dr. Zozimos would have been let go."

"If it wasn't for Cora, he would have been long gone by now." Calmer than before, Needs continues. "I saw the formula in Dr. Carnot's hand. I thought, 'This could be it!' I didn't know it was Dr. Harcrow's. KayAnne, his assistant, didn't tell me that."

Chance puts his chin forward and looks down at Orin. "His assistant knew about the formula?"

Needs nods.

"More!" Chance motions with his hand.

"KayAnne told me she could get me a job with her employers. As soon as they got what they wanted, they'd be out of here, and I could go with them. She said they needed smart, willing assistants."

"I don't understand," I pipe in, pulling myself out of my brother's arms.

Chance continues his questioning. "Who is her employer?"

"I don't know. I just know there were two of them, one being Carnot." He rubs the top of his head as if trying to erase the memories of this turn. "KayAnne will know. I was supposed to meet her in Carnot's lab."

I stand there in disbelief that anyone could think Nickolas a saboteur.

"Then what?" Chance asks as he looks back at me in empathy.

"That's when we were all supposed to leave."

"All?" Chance prods.

"I got there, but KayAnne was nowhere to be found. Dr. Carnot was just sitting there, holding the formula. I couldn't leave empty-handed, so I pulled at the formula. It ripped and I ran."

I walk calmly up to the chair. "You just left him sitting there? You called no one?"

"He was dead. What difference would it have made?"

I haul off and punch him in the mouth again. As my fist hits his weak jaw, I hear a crack.

"Get her off him," orders Chance.

I'm pulled away again.

Everyone goes silent, even the whimpering Needs, as a very loud "Ack!" fills the room. A terrifyingly putrid smell wafts under our nostrils.

"Mae!" A.P. hollers.

All heads turn toward A.P. as he raises one expensive, vomit-covered shoe. Pip finally tossed his cookies—all over A.P.'s shoes.

"Poppy, so sorry! Pip didn't mean it. His tummy is poor."

"Get this mutt out of here and take Zelda the boxer with you!"

"Poppy!" whines Mae.

"Now!" A.P.'s voice trembles in an angry baritone pitch.

We don't argue. Needs cowers behind a constable, his arms flying up to protect his badly bruised head as I pass him on my way out.

"Now where?" Mae asks, cradling the sick Pip.

"Let's take a gander at my new lab and get Pip some water and a little sodium bark-carbonate," I suggest with a giggle.

Mae rolls her eyes at my horrid pun. "That was terrible, but I am sorry."

"Sorry for my stinky pun?"

"For getting us kicked out of the office."

"I'll admit, Pip's timing is poor, but I think me clobbering Orin Needs may have been the reason for our dismissal."

Mae looks over at me as we walk. "Are you mad?"

"Furious."

Pip belches.

I wave away the smell of booze emanating from the dogacorn's crooked snout. "I hate that I'm constantly being kept in the dark over something that's entirely to do with me." We clomp along to the lift to take it up to my laboratory. "I feel like I'm being manipulated by everyone around me."

"I hope that doesn't include me."

"You are the one person I can say for certain is on my side," I say.

"What about Ephron?"

"Him too," I agree. "It seems he knows just as much as I do, and that isn't much."

We walk in silence down the hall to my lab. "Excellent, the door's on now; that's an improvement." The door swings quietly open. I move the door back and forth on its hinges, inspecting the work.

Mae steps into the darkness. "Where's the light switch?"

"I got it." My hand falls to the smooth plaster of the walls in search of the knob to illuminate the empty room. "Finally, the walls are finished, but it seems they moved the switch to turn on the ceiling lamps."

"Hurry up, it's getting creepy." Pip yaps in agreement from Mae's arms.

"Found it!" The knob clicks, and the large room becomes bright. I look straight up and frown. "The rafters are still exposed. Jeepers, are they ever going to finish the ceiling?"

"That's the least of your worries," Mae says, her voice cracking.

My gaze turns toward Mae, who stands frozen, her eyes fixed across the room. Pip's ears are at attention. My eyes follow Mae's stare.

Crap. There, dangling from the rafters of the unfinished ceiling, is a figure.

"Isn't that . . . ?" Mae stammers. "Nickolas's assistant . . ."

"It's What's Her Name," I say flatly as I stare at the body swaying from a joist. Her head is slumped against her chest, concealing the rope tied around her neck.

Mae steps forward to stand next to me. "I guess we better call someone to get her down."

I make a quick scan of the room. "The line's not installed yet."

"Okay, then." Mae takes a deep breath. A scream so high, so long, and so loud that I nearly jump out of my skin spews from her mouth.

"Jeepers, Mae!" I yell. "What was that for?"

The room quickly fills with alchemists and their assistants from across the hall. A few security personnel follow soon after. Mae tucks Pip under one arm and waves the other dramatically about as she looks at me with perfect composure. "I called someone."

I drop my head into my hands, defeated by her logic.

Soon, Inspector Chance Greyson, Ephron, DSI Flynn, and Hodge push through the crowd.

"Everybody, back to your labs," Jep calls from the hall.

Once security clears everyone out, Ephron addresses the obvious issue. "Jeez Louise, Zelda, what in the stars is going on?" He dramatically points to the dangling corpse. "Why is there a dead body hanging from the rafters?"

"Why are you asking me?" My hands fly to my hips as I take a defiant stance. "It's not like I put What's Her Name up there."

Ephron swings his head around to the inspector. "You're not going to leave her up there, are you?"

Chance walks around the body, examining the floor. Every so often, he makes a comment to his tagalong, Flynn, who diligently writes everything down.

Mae edges up to me and whispers, "What's Hodge doing?"

"It looks like he's getting bags of some sort of out of his case."

"What are they for?"

I raise my brow at her. "I don't know. Never really saw a murder scene after the fact before." I go back to watching the Legere work. "Until today, I'd never seen a murdered body before."

Ephron gets impatient and begins to pace. Mae leaves my side to tend to him for a bit. I watch intently as Chance and Hodge become methodical in each of their moves. Hodge gingerly wraps each of Nickolas's assistant's hands, then each of her feet, in cellophane sacks.

"Hodge, you can sweep up now." Chance waves at the constable. Hodge begins sweeping with a small bristle broom and dustpan.

Chance, with Flynn on his tail, makes his way over to me. I motion for Mae to join me.

"What can you tell me about her?" He nods back toward the still-swaying body.

"Other than that she was Nickolas's assistant?" I shrug.

"Is this the KayAnne Orin Needs spoke of?"

I feel a small twinge of guilt. "I have no idea."

His gaze moves to Mae, who looks appalled. "Darling, why on Gaia would I ever know her name?"

"Never mind." With that, Inspector Chance Greyson turns on his heel and covers the short distance back to the victim. "Let's get her down." A ladder is hustled forward, and a constable quickly loosens the noose. The assistant's lifeless body flops as it falls toward the floor, but it's caught before it can touch the cold cement. "Check her clothing before she's taken away—and someone find out exactly who she is," Chance continues, managing the room.

Hodge pulls several items out of her pockets and lays them on a cloth beside her body. The glint of one of the items catches my eye, but Mae nudges me.

"Darling, I must skedaddle down to the infirmary. Pip is looking peaked. All this excitement isn't good for him in his condition."

"You mean his hungover condition?"

Mae sticks her tongue out at me as she sashays out of the room, Pip in arms.

"Hey!" I hustle over and bend down to pick up the little piece of unique jewelry I noticed.

"Dr. Harcrow, you cannot touch the evidence," Hodge scolds.

"Sorry." I hand it over to Hodge. "It's just that it looks similar to Miss Trick's brooch."

"Who is Miss Trick?" he asks.

"Doc, please stand back." Chance's hand clasps firmly around my upper arm and pulls me back. "No offense, but that Dr. Ravenscroft scares the bejeezus out of me and I really don't want to get on her bad side."

"What does Olga have to do with this?"

Hodge joins us. "Titus took your advice, and Dr. Ravenscroft is overseeing my training in using science to assist the Legere."

"Oh." Something else I wasn't told about. My eyes widen as I look over the other items lying on the soft lint-free cloth. "How did she get my amulet?"

"Maybe you dropped it in Carnot's lab when you found the body," Chance deduces.

"No. I swear I lost it at my folks'." My eyes dart back and forth. "DSI Flynn, you were there. Remember? I was tearing apart the couch when you came looking for my father."

Chance scowls at his DSI. "Flynn?"

"Sorry, I didn't know why you were rummaging through the couch. I thought maybe Dr. Shamm had lost something." Flynn goes back to his notebook. "Although his face does always look per- turbed."

A deep frown forms on the inspector's face. "What was Dr. Shamm doing there?"

"Looking for my father—a seemingly popular pastime of every- one's lately," I complain. *Well, my father and a few other things.* I think about the pass Dr. Shamm made at me, and a shiver runs up my spine.

"I don't like it." Chance grabs the evidence bag from Hodge, al- most hitting DSI Flynn in the chest. "Now about this." The piece of jewelry, now safely ensconced in a see-through container, is present- ed to me.

"This looks a lot like that weird watching-eye brooch Miss Trick keeps losing." I examine the small tiepin through the transparent film of the pouch.

Chance grabs the container. "Maybe they just go to the same store?"

I grab it back to take a closer look. "It has no metal lashes and no setting."

"The stone is similar to the one Miss Griffin found," he says to Flynn, who writes the information in his handy little notebook.

"Mae found?" My voice goes up an octave or two.

Hodge takes the pouch back and packs up his gear. I wave slight- ly as he passes. "Explain, Inspector." I'm a tad miffed that Mae didn't tell me about the clue.

"When Miss Griffin found the assassin's body, she found a tie clip with a similar stone next to the body," Chance explains.

"Was it his?"

"At the time, I thought so."

"And now?"

"Sir," Flynn interrupts.

Chance acknowledges his DSI with a raised eyebrow and a nod. "I have to accompany the body to the wagon." He shouts orders at one of the constables. "Nothing and no one in or out without my permission."

The constable salutes. "Yes, sir."

Chance's attention returns to me. "Go back to your brother's office. I'll be there as soon as I'm done." He moves out with the rest of the coppers, leaving me standing in the large now-empty space.

"This is giving me the heebie-jeebies." I spin around and quickly make my way back to Ephron's office.

I sit.

I sigh loudly.

I tap my foot.

I stand.

I sigh loudly again.

I drum my fingers.

I huff.

I pace.

I huff again.

"Stop it." Ephron looks up at me from his huddle with A.P. at his desk.

"How about a drink?" A.P. asks as he saunters over to the drink cart.

"Sure." I look over at the cart. "So Miss Trick finally made an appearance?"

Ephron lifts his head in annoyance. "No. Still no sign of her. I'm not happy." His head drops back down into the mounds of papers that are stacked on his desk.

"Who—"

"I had Dottie put it together."

"Well, bite my head off, why don't you?" I gripe.

"Sorry." He doesn't even look up.

A.P. hands me a tumbler of cloudy booze. I put the thick glass to my lips. The strong smell of alcohol is more like turpentine. "Jeepers! This is a bit strong, even for this alchemist."

"Should I pour you something else?" A.P. looks up from some report he's perusing on a crystal tablet.

"I'll get it." I'm lifting myself and the gross drink out of the deep leather armchair when the glimmer of a sparkle hits the corner of my eye. Setting the heavy glass on Ephron's desk, I lower myself to the floor. My knees pop on the way down.

"What are you doing?" Ephron, annoyed at another interruption, leans over his desk.

I inch forward under his desk. "I see something."

"Where?" He joins me on the floor from the opposite side of his desk.

A.P. must have gazed up from his crystal screen. "By the stars, what are the two of you doing crawling around?"

I reach for the metal object and bring it out from under the desk. "When was the last time you saw Miss Trick?"

Chapter Forty-Two

E phron stands up and comes around the desk to join me. A.P. joins us, apparently intrigued by my question. "What is this?" he asks, pointing at the piece of metal and glass on Ephron's desktop.

"Miss Trick's brooch," I respond.

"Her brooch?" A.P. leans over to get a better look.

"And . . . it's broken," I add.

"She's always losing it," Ephron complains to A.P.

"Yes, but now the front is cracked." I point at the strange stone that gives the brooch the appearance of an eye. I snap my fingers repeatedly. "I need my handbag."

Ephron hustles over to the couch, where my purse has lain since I was brought in after the discovery of Nickolas's body.

"Open it up and hand me my magnifying glass."

"Here," he says, handing me my glass.

A.P. stands back. "Are you going to look at the crack?"

I hold up the magnifying glass and examine the watching-eye brooch. "Interesting . . ." I grab the twig-thin magnetic-hematite-tipped utensil that A.P. uses to move information around on his crystal tablet and begin to pick at the top of the center stone. "It's not solid."

Ephron looks over my shoulder. "What do you see?"

I brush him away. "I'm not sure." I move the cracked piece with the point of the stylus. "It seems like some kind of receiver."

Ephron peers back over my shoulder. "We better get the inspector."

"I agree, and someone better locate your assistant too." I continue to dissect the piece of jewelry.

"I'll go." A.P. ankles over to the door and quietly closes it behind himself.

"You don't think Miss Trick ran afoul of whoever . . . you know . . . did in Nickolas's assistant?"

I shrug and continue to study the wires in the mesh and film. "It appears Miss Trick has been spying on us—on you."

"What? No—how—when . . . ?" Ephron stumbles over his words, his hands clenching in his hair.

"I suggest you get Tick up here pronto." I point the stylus at his wireless.

"Yes." He walks out of the office to make the call.

"What do you have?" asks a familiar deep, rough voice from behind me.

I jump.

I squeal.

I smack the inspector on the arm. "Don't sneak up on folks. You scared the bejeezus out of me."

"Sorry, Doc. I came in as Ephron headed out." He rubs his arm as he leans in to get a view of the pin. "So what is it?"

"Looks like a receiver of some kind." I hand him my magnifier.

"I've heard of them but never seen the insides of one up close."

"They don't use them in your line of work?"

"Nope. We leave that kind of stuff to the NSC," he says, handing me back my glass.

"I see. Did Miss Trick work at the secret council?"

His breath is hot on my neck, making it hard to concentrate. "No, according to the NCS, they've had no agents at work here at all."

"So who is she spying for? And . . . why did Nickolas's no-name assistant have a similar stone?" I try to move aside. I still feel guilty about being attracted to him.

"And why did Miss Griffin find one just like it next to the assassin's body?" He pulls out of his pocket the bag that holds the smaller, almost identical tiepin found on Nickolas's assistant.

"Good question." I take the bag from him to get a better look at the tiepin.

"Better question: where is the high-pitched Miss Trick?" He leans into me, taking the evidence bag back from me.

"Is she really missing?" I ask as I turn my attention away from Chance and back to the spy brooch.

Chance nods.

"What device do we have here?" Tick asks, wobbling over.

I move aside. "Take a look."

The rotund tinker pulls down his many-lensed eyeglasses from atop his balding head, adjusts them on his bulbus nose, and flips glass lens upon glass lens over the eyepiece until he receives a magnification that makes him smile. "By Tinker's Magic, what a unique device! Much smaller than I've ever seen or made."

I look down at my little handheld magnifying glass that pales in comparison to Tick's fancy spectacles. I have magnifying glass envy.

"This technology is not Teslan." Tick places the object in a small mesh box designed to block electrical waves. "Just in case it's still active."

Chance runs his hand through his unkempt, shaggy hair. "Then who—"

"Sir," Zeper Jo interrupts.

"Well, don't you look spiffy," I say, eyeing Big Jim. The hulking copper blushes. "Never seen you in your copper's uniform."

He adjusts his bulging brass-buttoned jacket over his trunk-like frame. "Thanks."

"This mean I've lost you to your turn job?"

Chance is the one who answers. "We need Big Jim to help with the search for Miss Trick. This place is big."

"Looking for a body?" I ask as I slip my magnifier back into my purse, secretly wishing I had corny glasses like Tick's.

"Possibly," Chance half answers as his attention moves away from me.

The room has begun to fill again with coppers and security, and I'm being pushed aside again. This time I don't mind. I really have no intention of finding another dead body today. I check my munitions and almost fall over. My eyebrows are uneven and the mascara under my eyes make me look like I went ten rounds in the ring. I need a drink, and unfortunately that dang dogacorn drank all the good whiskey.

"If I'm needed, I'm going to find Mae." I know my best bud will have a flask on hand, and she has excellent taste buds when it comes to booze.

"I don't want you wandering about without a chaperone," Ephron scolds as he walks back into the office filled with teeming fish.

"You are not going anywhere, Doc." Inspector Chance Greyson doesn't even lift his head from the report Flynn has handed him.

I scrunch up my uneven, overly arched brows. "Mae's down in the infirmary with the hungover mutt." I tug on Ephron's rolled-up shirt sleeve. "Come on. It's a straight shot down there."

Ephron wavers. "I don't know . . ."

"Thbpt!" I blurt out, sticking out my tongue.

Ephron looks at Chance and receives a nod. "Okay, but go straight down and stay there. I'll be down in a moment."

"Aww . . . you're aces! A real darb of a brother." I pucker my red-stained lips and blow him a kiss. "See you in a skinny minute."

I walk to the outer offices, leaving behind the commotion of bodies all waiting for orders. I'm hit by a wall of quiet as the door clicks softly closed.

"What are you doing out here by yourself, Zelda?" A.P. appears with papers in one hand and his flask in the other.

"Oh, hi there, A.P." I look around to see if Mae is about.

"Mae's still in the infirmary with that thing. You'd be wise to take someone with you."

"Everyone is organizing to do a search or whatever else they have up their sleeves."

"And . . ."

"I'm not included, and I need a diversion."

"I see." A.P. bends over and gives me a fatherly kiss on the cheek. "Straight down."

"Yes, sir." I salute, click my heels together, and start off to the lift.

"And Zelda love . . ."

"Yes?" I stop and lean my head back to one side.

"Keep my dear daughter out of any sticky messes."

"Gotcha." I give him a thumbs up.

He holds up his hand as he steps into the office.

A shiver runs up my spine—a feeling that A. P.'s farewell might be the last time I'll ever see him. Wrapping my arms around my middle, I steady myself. My legs seem heavy as I step forward with a sense of dread clinging to my heels. Closing my eyes, I stop and take a breath. I'm being silly, giving myself the heebie-jeebies. "Ish kibibble." I take a more hurried step.

"What the stars?" I mutter under my breath as I catch sight of Monki Shamm creeping around the corner and slipping into one of the conference rooms. "What is he doing wandering around? He's supposed to be in lockdown in his lab like everyone else."

Turning on my heel, the balls of my shoes make muted sounds on the tile as I tiptoe to the solid double doors. "What is that cad up to?" I whisper to the cold steel lever of the door handle.

I grab the handle and slowly push down, hoping I don't make a sound.

Chapter Forty-Three

I stop before opening the door. He probably has some creepy liaison going on. "Why do I care?" I begin releasing the pressure on the handle. "And . . . why the stars am I talking out loud to myself?" I let the handle go, and my foot pivots away from the door.

However, I still feel the smooth metal of the lever in my hand. Looking over at it, I give in, push down on the handle, and release the door silently from its latch. So much for minding my own business. I slip into the room, trying not to allow the door to open wide enough to attract attention.

This particular conference room is large and void of any furnishings or decorations—just smooth crisp-white laminate walls. Since it's primarily used for demonstrations, it has a small foyer and arched entry into the main room.

Continuing to tiptoe, I hustle up behind the partial wall and faux pillar framing the archway. Tucking my hair behind my ear, I attempt to peek around the corner. I'm suddenly swept away with nausea. Clutching my stomach with one hand and covering my mouth with the other, I flatten my back against the wall and close my eyes. I'm stuck, frozen. Dang! Mechanically, I move my hand off my stomach and flatten my palm against the wall the way my back is.

Steady girl.

There's only one explanation.

I open my eyes, but I know it before I even dare to look.

A portal!

Is Dr. Shamm party to this or another victim, like Nickolas, his assistant, and possibly Miss Trick?

I have to look.

I have to witness.

I have to be a dumb Dora and an absolute idiot.

My head turns slowly, and I peer around the corner. My jaw drops. A portal is open, spinning the air around it, and standing in front of it are Dr. Monki Shamm and Miss Trick. I can just barely make out what he's saying to her.

"Your assignment here has been cut short." He extends his arm toward the portal. "I'll finish up."

Miss Trick only nods. Then she disappears into the space of nothingness.

My hand is still at my mouth, now there to quiet my instinctive reactions rather than my nausea. I watch him speak a few words in a tongue I don't understand and make several manipulations and gestures with his hands that close the portal.

I should have left when he was busy with his magic!

The doctor turns, mutters something, and waves his hands back and forth.

I don't know if he's seen me or sensed me; maybe he's just singing and dancing. I do know I can outrun him.

Leaping for the door, I grab the handle.

I push. Shit!

I pull. Futz!

My hearts are racing faster than a runaway cicen hen from a farmer's axe.

I jiggle the handle as a feeling of dread overwhelms me. There are no locks on the conference doors. This is a spell and I'm in the poison now.

"It's no use. You aren't going anywhere, baby." His voice edges closer and closer from behind.

I push harder; I pull harder. I push, I pull, and I cry out. "Help! Someone, help!"

"No one can hear you; they're all in lockdown, remember?" His voice is smooth and even.

I know the search for the recently departed—and certainly not dead—Miss Trick will be underway soon. At least, I hope so.

"Now, now . . ."

I stop and slip a bit of hair behind my ear, turning to face Shamm. What the stars! I stare into a face that seems familiar but is not the one I've known as Monki Shamm. "Who . . . what . . . ?"

He reaches out long fingers and releases the hair from behind my ear. The backs of his fingers feel like fire as they trail down my cheek to my neck and then my collarbone. He smiles and abruptly pulls his hand away.

"I should introduce myself." His long black hair falls forward as he bows. "Alexander Textrix from Void Dynamics, of the great empire of Hyde. At your service." He stands. His jaw is triangular, his eyes, still shaped like almonds, are like obsidian, and his skin is the color of burned sienna. He's a stranger.

"What happened to Shamm?"

He takes my hand and gently kisses it. My face scrunches up in disgust at the smell of burning sulfur. Textrix leads me into the large presentation area.

"My dear Dr. Shamm had a rather unfortunate accident getting off the airship."

"The body they found . . . you bumped off . . ."

"Yes."

"I collided with you at Griffin Tower."

"I wasn't expecting that." He kisses my hand again. "I wasn't expecting you."

A shiver runs up and down my spine, making my brain tingle with electric shocks of warning. "You used a masking spell on yourself." I try to act as cool as helium. "How did you get it to work?"

"You mean, how did it work on an animate subject?" That he feels it necessary to correct my question would have annoyed me was I not scared shitless.

I pull my hand back and step backward, away from my captor.

He follows. "Practice."

I step back again. "The dinner party . . ."

Moving forward again, he sneers crookedly. "Your father saw through me. Somehow, he knew I wasn't Monki Shamm."

My father put it together and didn't warn me. He is so going to get a piece of my mind—as soon as I figure out where on Gaia he is. "What did you do with my father and my mother?" I step back once more. "Where is my sister?"

"I have no idea where the old bird got off to." He slides toward me. "It seems you have no idea what he is up to, either. Intriguing."

"You're finding this way too amusing." Stumbling back, I scramble to stay vertical. "You killed your own assassin. Why?"

"Not my assassin and . . . I had dear Nickolas take care of that piece of nasty business."

"Liar!"

His eyes glint with the excitement of revealing truths. "If it weren't for you, the assassin from Elione would be alive and most likely on his way back to his family."

My voice shakes. "But . . . the . . . tie clip . . ."

"Nickolas was so worried when he lost it that I had to try to retrieve it for him." The enjoyment in his voice is sickening. "Miss Griffin is very lucky she ran. Had I known she had the clip . . ."

I take another step back, and my heel smacks into the baseboard. I'm up against the wall. "How is it my fault?"

Textrix moves in; only a breath of space remains between us. "Poor bunny, kept in the dark." His thin, muscular frame presses against me.

I turn my head to the side, clenching my eyes closed. "Please stop."

His finger traces back and forth along the line of my collarbone. "Such a brilliant mind. Nick knew it, but then when you sent that partial formula—"

"But—"

"You always thought Nick was a great mind. He was average. You were the alchemist; he was the assistant."

I shake my head.

His finger traces down to the buttons of my blouse, and his voice becomes maniacal. "Titus thought he was being kind getting him a job at the university."

"Is that where you met him?"

"Nick was a good partner. Exploiting his students' discoveries—a very lucrative plan, indeed."

I hear a snap, and something hits the floor and bounces with a click. His fingers glide farther down, to my breastbone. Another snap and another button hits the floor. I squeeze my eyes closed more tightly.

He bends his head down and brushes his full lips against my neck and drags them lightly up to my ear. His voice is a seductive whisper. "He didn't deserve a mind like yours."

"You murdered . . ." I struggle against him, batting his tentacle-like hands away from my body.

"The imbecile didn't even see it coming. Zap!" He snaps his fingers next to my turned ear. "He was a goner." He giggles like a little girl.

By the stars, this guy has an ego! "What about What's Her Name?"

He stops and screws up his eyebrows. "Who?"

"You know . . . What's Her Name, the assistant." Every time I remove one of his hands, the other shows up in another inconvenient place.

"What do you think?" His hands seem to multiply; they're everywhere. I let out a whimper as fabric rips. "It's just you and me now; no one will get between us."

"Nickolas's assistant, why her?" I squirm against the wall, shifting my body sideways to try to move away from his control.

His grip tightens on my thigh. "She was jealous of you."

Tears full of mascara roll down, leaving streaks of black on my rouged cheeks.

"Nickolas and his assistant didn't understand. The formula wasn't the prize."

I hear my shoe drop to the floor.

"You were the prize all along." He cackles as he thrusts his weight on me.

My screams echo in the room, unable to escape my prison.

Chapter Forty-Four

Textrix grips my chin, pulling my face center and slamming his mouth on mine. I gather courage, and with speed like grabbing jacks from the floor between the bounces of the ball, I bite down on his lip. He howls as my teeth draw blood. Jumping away from me, he wipes away the deep violet-red with one hand, while the other flies up and backhands me across the face.

I fall to the floor with a thud. I'm dazed but glad to have him off me.

He starts to laugh. "No worries. We'll have plenty of time to get to know each other." He adjusts his trousers and smirks as he turns his back to me. Textrix begins moving his arms, overgesticulating here and there with his hands repeatedly. A blur begins to form in front of him.

I prop myself up on my hands and use them to pull myself a little way across the floor.

My nemesis begins straightening his suit coat and tie. "I shall look presentable when I bring you through the portal."

I look toward the door. How am I going to get that open? If I don't save myself, I'll be lost forever.

Textrix walks away from me to commence shaping the new portal. My eyes blur from the stinging mascara and tears. I shake off the nausea. I need to focus. I grab a piece of my torn skirt and wipe my eyes clean. With Textrix still busy with the portal, I heave myself up and begin limping toward the door on one shoe. Looking down and then back at my tormentor, who's still busy, I slip out of my remaining shoe and tiptoe toward the door. Putting my hand out, I tease out all the anger that wells up inside me and motion for the door handle to move. I'm not sure I can expect diddly-squat, but I'm desperate.

The handle doesn't turn—

The whizz of heavy metal hurls past me. My eyes follow the sound; I can see Textrix turning around, startled by the door handle crashing into the wall in front of him. It just missed his skull by millimeters.

I run.

I can hear him closing in behind me.

I enter the atrium. It's still silent—no search party yet, and everyone is still in lockdown.

The sudden pain in my wrist is intense. Textrix's hand clenches tightly as he spins me around. He's speaking strange words and, with one hand, is making symbolic gestures in the air. I struggle to be free. I can feel what is coming; the nausea rises in my stomach slowly. Heat rises from my belly, forcing my mouth open, and a shrill scream erupts. I can hear it echoing throughout the great hall.

He begins pulling me toward the swirling vortex of air. I pull back with all my weight. Thank the stars I'm not one of those skinny little beanpoles, otherwise I'd already be a goner. Textrix leans into me as he yanks me forward and yells, "It's too late!" He jerks me closer to the portal. I keep trying to pry his hand from my wrist, but his meaty claw is practically glued on; I can't get him to let go. I'm getting closer and closer to my impending doom.

I keep struggling. Textrix has not fully disappeared into the portal yet, so I still have time. My mouth opens to let out another howl, but the sound that follows is not my scream but another from behind me.

"Pip!" I hear Mae shriek.

A jarring howl echoes through the atrium. Textrix's eyes bug out in pain; dangling from his arm is my other nemesis, Pip the dogacorn.

I feel arms wrap around my waist and anchor me to this plane.

Out of the corner of my eye, I see my parents, stepping out of thin air.

Everything then happens so quickly—a matter of moments that seem to stretch into a long reel of celluloid.

My father shouts a few weird and eerie words—"Simagicae salapotentia prope simostium . . ." and a few more I can't comprehend—and the portal begins to close.

Someone rushes toward me and tackles me and my anchor.

I open my eyes and scream and cry. Textrix still has a cement-like grip on my wrist, and Pip hangs off his arm, growling.

"It's okay . . . it's okay . . ." I hear over my cries. My brother, who still has his arms wrapped around my waist, hugs me tighter.

"Pip! Bad doggy! Let go of that dirty arm." Mae scuttles over and begins to pry Pip's misshapen jaw from Textrix's arm.

I swing my head around wildly. Chance, who plowed us to the floor, is working on removing Textrix from my wrist. My weary, blurring eyes follow the attached infliction up the arm and to nothing. All that's left of the plague known as Textrix is what stayed attached to my flesh. The rest of the scourge was caught in and cut off by his own portal.

Couldn't have happened to a nicer guy.

"Hang tight, Doc." Chance looks at me with his calming baby blues as he works to release me from the last grasp of this nightmare.

I look over and see my mother crying. I give her a smile. Wasting no time, she runs over and hugs me. I cry like a little baby in her arms. All I can say is "Mama . . . Mama . . ." She smooths out my hair and pulls my skirt down to cover my knees. "Father knew. He knew everything," I finally blubber out.

My mother and Ephron dart their gazes to my father. "What is she talking about?" Mother asks.

"I wasn't sure," he mumbles. "I didn't know this would happen," he bumbles. "I needed to catch him," he continues, stumbling over his words as my mother's face becomes redder with anger. "I wasn't sure who else was involved." He begins making excuses and apologies. "I'm sorry. We didn't mean to get you hurt. We thought we could keep you safe."

Ephron's the first to ask, "Who is we?"

Chance reaches out to put his hand on my shoulder. I violently shrug it away. "It's you! You and my father used me as bait to draw Nickolas and crazy-pants Textrix out."

Chance moves closer to apologize. "I thought I was doing the right thing. I could protect you, your father said, and—"

"Get away from me, you—you—you . . ." I look around the room and yell, "Somebody give me a word! I need a word!"

Mae leans down, cradling my strange hero in her arms. She raises an eyebrow and whispers, "Knuckleheaded ninny-pants."

I stare at Mae for a moment and then turn to a bewildered Chance. "What she said," I say, thumbing a gesture at Mae.

"We need to get her to the infirmary," Mother interjects.

Father puts his hands to his chest. "My dear daughter, I didn't mean—"

"Hush, Titus! You and I will talk later!" my mother shout. She turns abruptly to give me a kiss on the cheek and says to my brother, "Scoot."

"Please, Doc—Zelda, please let me explain," I can hear Chance calling as Ephron carries me toward the lift.

"Not now!" Ephron shouts back at Chance as the lift doors shut with a hush.

Chapter Forty-Five

I lie on the hard, thin mattress of a bed in the infirmary, wondering how any of the past couple of strings ever happened to me. I've always kept to myself. I've always done my work. I've always tried to do the right thing. I was taught to think.

So how could I have been so naïve? I'm not just furious at Textrix or my father, or even just angry at Inspector Chance Greyson or Nickolas or anyone else. I'm miffed at myself. I was unable to defend myself; I swear that will never happen again.

Mae peeps her head in. "How are you feeling?"

"Scratchy in this paper gown," I complain.

"Yeah, not the head of fashion, I would agree," she jokes gently.

"Mae?"

"Yes, darling?"

"Get me some clothes."

"I really don't think that's a good idea."

"I'm done, Mae. I need time to process."

"Can't you do it from here?"

"Mae, get me some clothes."

I curl up in a ball and close my eyes. People continue to file in and out, checking on me. My mother comes in, cries, and then leaves again. I can hear her out in the hall, telling my father that it isn't a good idea for him to see me right now. Okay, so it's not as polite as all that, but who can blame her? She's warlike, beyond hostile toward Titus right now.

Soon, Mae returns with tinker overalls and my riding boots and skullcap. Good. She knows what I intend to do.

Mae gives me a hand changing clothes. Being my best friend, she does me a massive favor and keeps a lookout, allowing me to slip out without anyone noticing. I climb onto my Zenith, give her a good kick, and pull her out of the garage. Once outside, I sit for a moment, contemplating turning around and having one more look, but I decide against it. I take a deep breath; somehow the air seems fresher than usual. Revving up the engine, I put her in gear and head out onto the road.

I chuckle to myself as I realize that I'm starting the journey my mother read in the cards.

Don't miss out!

Visit the website below and you can sign up to receive emails whenever Lisa Hogan publishes a new book. There's no charge and no obligation.

https://books2read.com/r/B-A-LTTG-NFPU

BOOKS 2 READ

Connecting independent readers to independent writers.

About the Author

Lisa Hogan is a writer, artist, and photographer living an inspired life in Texas. She loves fast talking racy movies from the 20's and the 30's. She is a mystery addict, a Sci-fi and fantasy geek. She writes what she loves to read and watch. Lisa is a Science and History fangirl and Homeschools two of her children. When she is not creating interesting characters or has a paintbrush in her hand, Lisa volunteers at the local animal shelter photographing the dogs and cats to assist in finding them fur-ever homes. Twitter @ljh_artInstagram @lisaj.hoganE-mail ljhunlimitedart@gmail.comFacebook @lisajhoganauthor

Made in the USA
Middletown, DE
26 November 2018